Homeland Burning

Callahan Family Saga Book 2

Brinn Colenda

Southern Yellow Pine
Publishing

Published by:
Southern Yellow Pine (SYP) Publishing
4351 Natural Bridge Rd.
Tallahassee, FL 32305

www.syppublishing.com

This is a work of fiction. Names, characters, places, and events that occur either are the products of the author's imagination or are used fictitiously. Any resemblance to actual persons, places, or events is purely coincidental.

The contents and opinions expressed in this book do not necessarily reflect the views and opinions of Southern Yellow Pine Publishing, nor does the mention of brands or trade names constitute endorsement.

ISBN-13: 978-1-59616-103-0
ISBN-13: ePub 978-1-59616-104-7
ISBN-13: Adobe PDF eBook 978-1-59616-105-4
Library of Congress Control Number: 2018933664

Printed in the United States of America
First Edition
January 2018

Praise for *Homeland Burning*

In *Homeland Burning*, Brinn Colenda delivers an epic story about the conflict between good and evil. You will love his characters and find yourself on a dizzying roller coaster ride of action and suspense. Be prepared to lose sleep over this one. Highly recommended.
—**Joseph Badal,** Tony Hillerman Award Winner and Amazon #1 Best-Selling Author of *Sins of the Fathers*.

Brinn hit a Homerun with his latest! He knows pilots, politics, and weaving an intriguing story well.... *Homeland Burning* takes us on an international flying adventure that shows the impacts of international relationships—right where we live!
—**Tim Hale, Colonel, USAF (Retired)** Former Secretary, New Mexico Department of Veterans Services

Flowing with urgency, *Homeland Burning* plays out a frantic cat-and-mouse quest to stop a shadowy foe from setting America on fire. When Tom Callahan practices a touch-and-go landing near Chesapeake Bay, he stumbles onto the trail of a terrorist believed to be dead but who not only is alive, is on his own path to burn the American heartland, to kill its leaders, and to get his own revenge against Callahan. *Homeland Burning* is written with pace and detail reminiscent of Gayle Lynds' The Assassins and with the complexity of Vince Flynn's Mitch Rapp series, a page-turning thriller to read deep into the night.
—**Jack Woodville London**, Author of the Year, 2012, *French Letters Series*

The writing in Colenda's books is always nuanced and characteristic of someone, who does exquisite research on his subject matter. He brings his own experiences into many of the situations but has expanded and supported his exciting story with terrific background work.

Particularly with his pilots—both male and female—he makes the situations realistic and compelling. The man knows what he's talking about when it comes to aviation scenarios. It's been tremendously satisfying to see his connection for his female pilot-characters to The Ninety-Nines, the world's oldest and largest organization for female pilots.
—**Jacqueline B. Boyd, PhD**, Amelia Earhart Memorial Scholarship Fund, The Ninety-Nines

This book is dedicated to the men and women of the armed forces of the United States, especially the New Mexico National Guard; forest rangers, firefighters, police, the Civil Air Patrol, and all the first responders, second responders, and third responders nationwide who labor long and often dangerous hours to keep the rest of us safe and secure.

And

Rick Sprott,
Lt.Col., USAF (ret)
1946-2017
R.I.P.

This is a work of fiction. It takes place in the year 2000 before the terrorist attacks of 9/11. The naïveté of the characters and organizations in this novel reflect a national "it can't happen here" mentality that many of us felt back then. Since 9/11, many things have changed.

Many good people helped in the writing of this book. My thanks go out to:
Scott Archer Jones; Phaedra Greenwood; Jim Tritten, Cdr, USN (ret); Daniel Brown; Jacque Boyd, PhD, Ninety-Nines; Bill Scott; Stuart Ewing; Scott Kraus, Cdr, USN (ret); Walter (Buck) Buchannan, LtGen, USAF (ret); Dick Dickerson, MSgt, (ret), NM National Guard; CW4 Lonnie Colson, NM National Guard; Chief Brad McCaslin, AFPD; Officer John Matula, AFPD; Chuck Howe, LTC, U.S. Army (ret) and President, National Veterans Healing and Wellness Center; Dave Pangrac; Stephen Hundley, LtCol, CAP; Terri Gerrell; and Dave Oberg, Chief Pilot, Regal Air.

Callahan Family Saga
Brinn Colenda

Cochabamba Conspiracy

Homeland Burning

Chita Quest

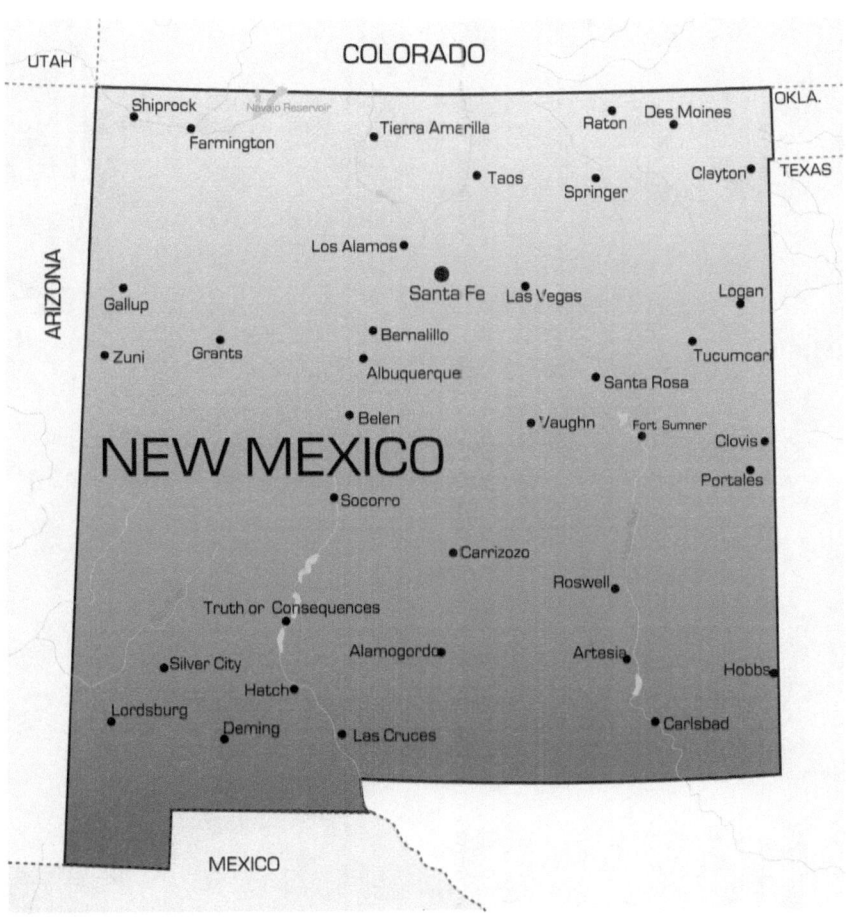

Chapter One

Chesapeake Bay Bridge
Annapolis, Maryland
May 2000

The red Piper Pawnee aircraft roared out of the rain and fog just above the water, smashed into a massive bridge abutment, and exploded. Burning wreckage cartwheeled across the water's surface for fifty yards, then sank. The pilot's body catapulted clear and splashed into the choppy waters of the bay.

Another Pawnee screamed out of the clouds and streaked under the bridge, just clearing the concrete abutment. The other pilot tried to circle back to see the flames, lost visual contact with the wreckage in the heavy rain shower, and disappeared into the murk.

The first pilot's body surfaced, swirled for a moment in the eddies around the bridge abutment, then slid into the strong tide. Nobody on the bridge saw the crash; traffic remained steady, and quiet returned to the bay.

***

Captain Peter Liebhold, fourth generation Chesapeake oysterman and fifth owner of the skipjack *Virginia Marie*, balanced himself as he stood behind the boat's wheel. He swore softly as he peered through the rain, looking for signs of other vessels as he steered the skipjack for the middle of the channel.

A crewman called out, "Hey, Cap'n, there's something in the water, starboard." A pause. "Sweet Jesus, it's a body!"

Captain Liebhold adjusted course. The crewman leaned over the side with a gaff and, expertly timing the motions of the boat, hooked the body. Two more men helped him heave the soaking mass onto the deck. The first mate, an Emergency Medical Technician instructor, knelt beside the body and checked for a pulse. "Hey, he's alive!" He turned to the crew. "Get him below and out of those clothes."

Ten minutes later, the mate re-appeared. "Capt'n, he's in real bad shape. Multiple fractures, probably internal injuries, exposure." The mate took a deep breath, "And what looks like a bullet hole in his leg."

Liebhold looked up in surprise. "Okay, Joey, radio it in. We'll be in port in an hour."

The landmass of Maryland's Eastern Shore was sometimes in sight to port through the rain and fog as they worked their way south towards Bloody Point. Liebhold swore again as he adjusted course. The *Virginia Marie's* radar indicated several vessels ahead, lights occasionally visible on the horizon. Liebhold was in the marked channel, and he trusted the other professional sailors to be where they were supposed to be. It was the amateur sailors that he worried about in weather like this.

The skies were clearing, and the sun was low on the horizon as they entered the mouth of Dogwood Harbor, Tilghman Island, the "Pearl of the Chesapeake Bay." Separated from the mainland by Knapps Narrows, this was a working waterman's village, home to the last commercial sailing fleet in North America.

Captain Liebhold brought the *Virginia Marie* into the harbor and alongside the pier where a red and white ambulance waited. Three EMTs from the Volunteer Fire department swarmed aboard. They loaded the unconscious man onto the litter, carried it topside and into the ambulance. The driver crossed the drawbridge and turned onto Maryland Highway 33 before switching on the siren for the run to the nearest hospital in Easton.

Twenty minutes later, the ambulance drove into the emergency entrance of Talbot County General Hospital, an elegant three-story brick structure. Two hospital medics wheeled the gurney down the highly polished linoleum of the corridor into the receiving area. Nurses

2

swarmed the gurney and cut off the injured man's remaining clothing. A doctor appeared.

"Doc, this is the guy the *Virginia Marie* fished out of the Bay," said the senior EMT. "He has multiple fractures, probably internal injuries, severe loss of blood. How he didn't drown is beyond me. He must be one tough S.O.B."

Doctor Tom Miller examined the unconscious patient. "Prep him for the OR, stat. We need X-rays." Nurses shuttled the patient towards the operating area.

"Somebody up there must be watching over this guy, Doc," said the EMT. "Are you going to report the gunshot wound?"

"Of course, but right now, that hole is the least of this guy's problems."

***

Thirty hours later, the patient woke up with a start in bed in a dark room. His head pounded. He tried to move and couldn't. He clawed at the constrictions on his chest. *They got me! I'm in jail!*

Slowly, his mind cleared. He could see the bandages, tubes and wires running down his arm. Stainless steel cables suspended his leg. A bank of electronic machines, LED screens hummed and blinked as they monitored his vital signs. His mouth tasted like the inside of an old shoe.

He ordered his still woozy mind to focus and take inventory: plaster around one leg; bandages around his chest and other leg. He lifted his arms slowly and painfully. It hurt to breathe, to move. The only thing that didn't hurt was his hair.

How did I get here? And where is "here"? He vaguely remembered flying through the clouds, trying to shake that American *schiesskopf,* Callahan, off his tail. The window was open a few inches and he could smell the land mixed with the antiseptic smell of what must be a hospital. He could hear speech from the next room and occasional laughter coming from a television. He listened carefully. *English.* So he was probably still in America. Wherever he was, the people did not know who he was or there would be bars on the window and guards at the door.

3

Or they would have just let him die—unless they were healing him in order to try him for his crimes.

He fought back panic at the thought of prison. *Nein*, he reminded himself, *there are no bars. No guards*.

Memories crowded his mind. His failed partnership with Fidel Castro to overthrow democratic countries in South America to create an Andean Socialist Union, his plot to bring terror to the United States, the planning, flying the Pawnee up to Maryland in order to spray death on the American people in the form of a weaponized virus. He prided himself on being emotionless; in his chosen line of work—international terrorism—one had to be cold and implacable. But, yes, he was glad to be alive and apparently anonymous. He was confident that nobody in America knew that Kurt Wallerein was helpless in a rural American hospital.

The door swung open, and an attractive young woman appeared, dressed in a hospital green uniform. She moved quietly and smoothly as she checked the readings on the machines.

Wallerein feigned sleep as she worked her way around the room. He needed a plan. He needed information.

"Where am I?" he said.

Startled, the woman said, "Oh, you're awake." She approached, produced a small flashlight, examined his eyes, then checked his pulse. "How are you feeling?" She smiled. "You are in the Talbot County Hospital in Easton, Maryland. Who are you?"

"I don't remember. How did I get here?"

"You were found floating in the Chesapeake." She smiled again. "You had us worried for a while." She pushed the intercom button. "Our patient has regained consciousness. Please call Doctor Miller."

Doctor Tom Miller looked up from his examination of his unidentified patient.

"I'm quite pleased with the healing so far. You are a lucky man, sir." He gestured to the nurse to reapply bandages. Miller gave a quick, professional summary of the injuries. Wallerein listened, dispassionate

4

as if the injuries were to somebody else. Now what he needed to know was his identity status.

"Will I get my memory back?"

The doctor smiled, "Probably. Trauma like this occasionally results in temporary amnesia." He looked back at the chart. "Forgive me. I am required to notify the authorities that you are conscious. They will come speak to you. Perhaps they can help find out your identity. With your accent, perhaps they can help trace you back to an embassy." He made a notation in the chart, then waved a cheerful good-bye.

The nurse handed Wallerein a small mirror. "Let's get you cleaned up, shall we?"

Mein Gott! He looked into the mirror again. His blond hair had turned white overnight, and the stubble on his face was flecked with gray. Only the piercing blue eyes were familiar. He looked closer. Never a handsome man, Wallerein had joined the Baader-Meinhof gang as a young man while it terrorized Germany in the 1970s. His reward for being the only member still at large was this aging body. There was never enough time for exercise, and the middle age paunch was claiming him as another victim. Still, this change was a shock.

The nurse reached for a razor.

"No, no, leave the beard," he said, thinking it would help his disguise. "But I would like a bath, please."

***

Early the next morning, Wallerein studied the local Chamber of Commerce guide to Easton and waited impatiently for the pain medicine to kick in. He was startled by a knock on the door and looked up to see a beefy man in a policeman's uniform, a pistol on his hip.

"Good morning, sir. I am Deputy Sheriff Dalton. How are you feeling today?"

Wallerein steeled himself for an interrogation. He hated cops. "Much better, *danke*."

Dalton settled into a nearby chair. "I'm here to ask you a few questions."

5

"The hospital staff has questioned me twice already, Deputy. I am afraid I wasn't much help."

Dalton smiled. "Well, first you could tell me your name," he said with a chuckle.

"I am sorry, Deputy. I do not remember."

"Well, we're going to have to find out."

"Yes, I hope you can do that for me. I would like to know why I was shot."

"No knowledge of that, either? Or how you came to be in the Bay?"

Wallerein shook his head.

"We usually call men who have lost their memory John Doe. Guess we'll just call you Johannes Doe." Dalton laughed at his own wit.

Wallerein bit back a sarcastic reply. *With imbeciles like this in their police, how can we not defeat the Americans?*

"We've checked with the German Embassy. No German national reported missing. Ditto for the Swiss and Austrian Embassies."

"Could I be a naturalized American citizen?"

"Nope. I checked with the State Department. There are no records that apply to you."

Wallerein shuddered. As the world's most wanted terrorist, the last thing he needed was a background check. He assumed they took his fingerprints while he was unconscious. What else had they done?

The deputy asked several more questions, none of which Wallerein answered truthfully. "Well, anyway, we've notified the German embassy. They say they'll have an assistant consul over here Monday morning to check you out. Maybe they'll be able to help figure out who you are."

"And today is?"

"Friday."

"Thank you, Deputy."

Dalton reached down and handed Wallerein a small cardboard box. "These are all the things you had in your pockets."

Wallerein's eyes lit up as he spotted his cell phone. It looked innocuous but to Wallerein, it was like the deputy had just handed him a Glock.

As if reading his thoughts, the deputy said, "Never seen a cell phone like that. I checked it over to see if there were any numbers I could trace. It seems to be password protected. None of our technicians could make it work. Even my teenage son couldn't figure it out." He stared at Wallerein. "Any thoughts on why you would be carrying a waterproof encrypted phone?"

Perhaps this cop was not as dumb as I thought. "I have no idea," said Wallerein. "Anyway, I do not remember any passwords." He mimed punching numbers on the phone. "If I do, I will call you first."

Deputy Sheriff Dalton stared hard at Wallerein. "Do that." He stood up and handed Wallerein his business card. "I'll see you on Monday. Let's hope you can remember more by then."

Wallerein clutched the phone as if it were a flotation device and he was back in the frigid waters of the bay. In a way it was true. This phone was a lifesaver. He examined it closely and could discern no tampering. It could have been bugged by those criminals in the National Security Agency, but he had no real alternative. If he stayed where he was, the German consul would be in Easton in three days, meaning that Wallerein would be locked up by lunchtime.

He reached for the remote for his television and turned it on. Using the prattle from a morning talk show as cover, he punched in a number from memory and waited impatiently. He paused for the chirp that told him that the encryption program was on and working. He spoke quietly but forcefully into the mouthpiece, then disconnected. He felt better after issuing the orders. In charge. Alive again. Alive and determined. Now all he had to do was play dumb for two more days.

***

An hour after midnight on Sunday, the door to Wallerein's room eased open and two masked men in dark clothing slipped in. Doctor Miller and the pretty nurse, whom Wallerein now knew as Betty, were pushed from behind by two more masked men.

Wallerein nodded to the men. "Get me ready to leave," he whispered. "Quick. Quiet." Dr. Miller hesitated. A masked man jabbed a pistol into a kidney and propelled him forward. The doctor and Betty joined forces, disconnecting the wires balancing his injured leg, then his IV tube. The Americans gently shifted Wallerein from the bed to a gurney. Pain shot through Wallerein, and he pointed back towards the bed. "There are two pain pills under my pillow. I saved them for the trip." Miller found the pills and handed them to Wallerein with a disapproving look. One masked man checked the hall and motioned the others to follow. They wheeled Wallerein down the first-floor hall, out the door of the hospital's emergency entrance, and loaded him into a waiting ambulance.

The ambulance eased down the hospital drive and out to the highway. Wallerein's attention moved to his captives. Miller, wide-eyed with fright, stared back at him. Betty's stifled sobs could be heard over the road noise in the ambulance.

Miller said, "Why are you doing this? Why are you taking us?"

"I am needed elsewhere." That was the crux of the situation. His life was necessary. Theirs were not. Wallerein paused. Still, they had saved his life. He would make it quick.

Chapter Two

Easton/Newnam Field Airport
Easton, Maryland
Six weeks later

In the left seat of the glistening blue and white USAF C-12 Beechcraft Super King sat Colonel Tom Callahan, a slender, not-quite six foot, not quite forty-year-old fighter pilot. He entered the traffic pattern for Runway 22 precisely at the prescribed angle of forty-five degrees, exactly on speed and at the required traffic pattern altitude. He checked over the instruments, glanced at the runway, and adjusted for the wind. Abeam the touchdown point, he called for the Before Landing Checklist. They rolled out on final at 120 knots, high intensity runway lights indicating right on glide path. Over the threshold, Callahan gently retarded the throttles and began the flare, holding off the touchdown as the aircraft settled into its landing attitude. The main gear tires spun as they kissed the runway surface.

"C'mon, Colonel," said Captain Ron Ford, the instructor pilot, from the right seat, "you could have bounced at least once."

As the pilots began the procedures for a touch-and-go, the aircraft abruptly veered to the left.

"Blown tire," said Tom, calmly. He quickly adjusted thrust, brakes, and propeller settings to bring the aircraft to a stop near the center of the runway.

"Pretty good job, Colonel, for—" Ford stopped.

"For a White House staff puke?" Callahan asked, smiling.

"No sir, I meant, pretty good job considering this is your first flight here."

"Well, Captain, I used to be a pretty good fighter pilot once upon a time." He looked over the instruments. "Let's shut this beauty down and see about getting a mechanic and a tow bar out here."

***

Thirty minutes later, Tom Callahan sat in the nearly deserted airport café as Ford made arrangements with the airport maintenance staff and called his squadron. A middle-aged woman who wore a smile and a nametag that said Edna approached brandishing a coffee pot. "Good morning, sir. Would you like some coffee?"

He nodded.

She poured a stream of hot, black liquid into a thick china cup. "Pretty fancy airplane, Colonel."

"It belongs to the 89th Airlift Wing over at Andrews Air Force Base."

"I know. They come here all the time for touch-and-goes but hardly anybody ever stops in to say howdy." She handed him a menu. "Most of those C-12 pilots are headed overseas. Are you?"

"No, I'm just back from a tour in Bolivia. I'll be stationed in Washington." Tom sipped his coffee and stretched his legs, annoyed that he wasn't still shooting touch-and-goes. Tom lived to fly. This checkout was a gift from a grateful president for services rendered, although it was a far cry from the command of a fighter squadron he had worked his whole career to earn. As far as he was concerned, even the below-the-zone promotion making him the youngest full colonel in the Air Force wasn't sufficient compensation. Now his finely-honed combat skills would be confined to fighting the bureaucratic Washington turf battles that he loathed.

Tom realized that Edna was still talking to him. "Excuse me?"

"I said nothing much happens around here. Our biggest news is that our local doctor ran off with one of the nurses from the hospital a few weeks back. A real looker, that one. They stole an ambulance and took off."

"Really?"

"That's what the deputy sheriff said. He thinks it had something to do with the German."

"What German?"

"The one who was fished out of the Bay by an oyster boat out of Tilghman Island. Nobody ever found out his name. He had amnesia and was pretty banged up, too. Doc Miller and the nurse took care of him." Edna leaned closer. "All three disappeared the same night, as a matter of fact. Sunday, about five-six weeks ago."

Alarm bells went off in Tom's head. "Could I have the deputy sheriff's number?" he said, trying to sound casual. "I'd like to talk to him about this."

"I'll call him, honey. He usually comes by around lunch anyhow."

Twenty minutes later, Deputy Sheriff Dalton walked into the café. Edna pointed out Callahan, and he walked over and introduced himself.

Tom motioned the deputy into a chair. "Edna tells me you had an injured German pulled out of the Bay."

Dalton nodded. "Yes, sir. He claimed he had amnesia, but I didn't believe him."

"Why not?"

"First, the foreign accent."

"Deputy, my wife has a foreign accent."

"Yeah, but she doesn't have a bullet hole in her leg, along with amnesia and multiple fractures and internal injuries. Not to mention the phone." Dalton shook his head. "That still bothers me."

"What phone?"

"He had a funny phone, a little bigger than normal, password protected and waterproof. I ask you, who has a waterproof, encrypted cell phone?"

Tom pulled a phone from his flying bag. "Like this?"

Surprised, Dalton took the phone and looked it over. "Sorta."

Tom took it back. "It's a special classified military issue cell phone, not available on the open market. What did this guy look like?"

"White male, mid to late fifties, stocky. His medical chart estimated him at around five-ten, one-ninety or so."

"Blond, blue eyes?"

"No. White hair, but the bluest eyes I've ever seen. Not friendly."

"Did you get any fingerprints? Photos?"

Dalton looked troubled. "Colonel, all this information is close hold. I'm not sure I should even be discussing it with you."

Tom handed Dalton his White House credentials. "I am a special military assistant to the President of the United States." He leaned forward across the table. "Let me tell *you* something classified, Deputy. Your information may be more important than you can imagine. Long story, but six weeks ago today, the president told me that a German terrorist named Kurt Wallerein was the most dangerous man on the planet. Later that afternoon, I was in a Piper Pawnee chasing him as he tried to escape after killing dozens of Americans and planning to kill thousands more." In his mind's eye, Tom saw Wallerein's red Pawnee silhouetted against the angry black thunderclouds as he tried to escape.

"Terrible weather. He tried to fly under the Bay Bridge to shake me, only he didn't make it, hit an abutment and exploded. I lost sight of the wreckage. Only a few pieces were found. No body. We assumed, hoped actually, that he was dead."

Tom's eyes bored into Dalton. "Now, I ask you again, did you get fingerprints or photos of this guy?"

Dalton took a deep breath as he eyed the credentials. "Yessir. We have all that information at headquarters."

"Good man. What else can you tell me about the patient?"

"I interviewed him myself the Friday afternoon before he disappeared. Gave him back his personal items, including the phone." Dalton stopped. "Damn! I told him the German consul was coming over for an interview on Monday morning. He disappeared Sunday night."

"Before the consul could identify him," Tom said, thinking out loud. "He probably used the phone to call his people. He'd need lots of help if he was as badly hurt as you say."

"The state cops found the ambulance over by Glen Burnie, Colonel. Wiped clean. No evidence of foul play, no fingerprints, nothing."

12

"Where again?"

"Glen Burnie. Anne Arundel County, over by Baltimore."

Tom reached into his flying bag and produced a map. "Show me."

Dalton searched for a moment, then pointed.

"Damn," said Tom. "Look. Here's the Baltimore-Washington International airport right next door."

Tom pulled out his phone again and punched an application. "See this address book? That's the direct number for Jacob Borenstein. Do you know who he is?"

"Yessir. He's the deputy director of the FBI." Dalton eyed Tom with respect that now bordered on the profound.

Tom motioned Edna over. "Do you have a fax machine in here?"

"Of course." She handed him a card with the café's details.

"I'm going to call a colleague about this, Deputy, an investigative journalist," said Tom, "then call the FBI while you and I visit Tilghman Island to interview the fishing captain." Dalton nodded, and Tom hit the speed dial.

"Hi Porter, this is Tom Callahan."

"How's my favorite bureaucrat today?"

Tom bristled. "Now don't start that crap with me, Nelson."

"Okay, okay, then how's the lovely wife of my favorite bureaucrat these days?"

Tom chuckled. "Colleen called just before I took off. She wants to buy what has to be the most expensive house in Georgetown."

"Ooh, that's saying something, my friend."

Tom said, "Porter, I want you to fax that FBI poster of Wallerein to this number. Then I have what might be some very bad news."

Moments later, Edna handed the fax to Dalton who looked it over. As she and Tom watched, Dalton pulled a pencil from his pocket and carefully sketched in a beard. He locked up. "I think this is the guy, Colonel. Pretty close anyhow."

"Okay, we'll go with that for the moment until we can get some better proof. Porter, I'm going to put this on speaker." He placed his cell phone face-up on the table. "I'm sitting here in Easton, Maryland with Deputy Sheriff Dalton. He tells me that a middle-aged German citizen

13

was pulled out of the Chesapeake Bay by a fishing boat north of Tilghman Island six weeks ago. The German had what Dalton describes as 'convenient amnesia' and a bullet hole in his leg."

"No way! Where's this guy now?"

"The cops thought he was just a civilian and gave him his belongings back, including his cell phone. He disappeared two days later. Also, the night shift nurse and doctor disappeared along with an ambulance which was recovered near BWI."

"Damn. He must have called in one of his teams."

"My thoughts exactly. Dalton has fingerprints for the FBI. I have a task for you."

"This is serious, buddy," said Porter. "If Wallerein is still alive—"

"Let's not jump to conclusions, Port. I'm going to call Jacob Borenstein and get him to compare the fingerprints from the hospital with the fingerprints found when Wallerein was wounded. If they match, we'll know for sure."

"Oh man, I wouldn't want to be the guy who tells the president."

Tom frowned. "That'll be my job." He took a deep breath. "In the meantime, I need you to check a few details. ID all the private jets that arrived and departed from BWI the day Wallerein disappeared and where they went. Somebody ought to remember a medical evacuation flight. I suspect our boy would head to Cuba given that his associates on his last operation were Cubans. Probably via Miami or somewhere in Mexico. Find out what you can. You're the journalist, do your stuff."

"Why not have the FBI do that?"

"You make less noise than a bunch of feds in dark suits. Work your system, pal." Tom glanced up at Dalton, then back to the phone on the table. "And, Porter, let's keep this closely held until we have some better evidence." He hung up and motioned the waitress closer.

"Edna, this is probably the most exciting thing you've heard in your life, but you can't tell anybody."

Dalton added, "Not even your best friends, Edna, until I clear it myself. I mean it."

Edna sniffed. "I'd already figured that out for myself. Don't worry." Then she grinned. "You boys want some sandwiches for the drive?"

14

Dalton made a call to his headquarters, then collected the food from Edna. "Colonel, my boss says that I'm at your service."

"How long will it take to get to Tilghman?"

"About twenty minutes with the flashers."

They got up to leave. "And Dalton?"

"Yessir?"

"I think the doctor and the nurse didn't run off together."

"Way ahead of you on that one, Colonel."

Chapter Three

Wallerein's Command Post and Headquarters
Libya

Kurt Wallerein sat at his desk in his stark concrete lair beneath the Libyan desert, mulling over his options. He had been flown from Baltimore to Mérida, Mexico, then loaded on a different plane to Cuba. After two weeks in a Cuban hospital, he was airlifted to Libya. Neither Fidel nor Raul Castro, nor any of Wallerein's contacts within the socialist brotherhood that ran Cuba had found the time to visit him.

Wallerein knew his current status as a revolutionary leader was uncertain—maybe even in peril—because his plans in Bolivia and his attack on *Amerika* had been thwarted by that bastard Callahan. He needed a success to get his reputation back—and fast! His hero, Ché Guevara, a great revolutionary writer, was a miserable failure in the field. Wallerein had a different ending in mind for his own career.

Wallerein had been the world's number one freelance terrorist for hire ever since Ilich Ramirez Sanchez, better known as Carlos the Jackal, had been kidnapped from Sudan by the French *Direction de la Surveillance du Territoire* and locked up for life in *La Santé* prison. Wallerein had been trained by the KGB in sabotage techniques as well as bomb and weapons skills. He was not shy about the use of violence though he firmly believed that it wasn't the numbers, but the symbolism of the deaths that was important. His biggest problems now stemmed from the loss of funding that had accompanied the fall of the Soviet bloc. While Wallerein had gained many former operatives from the various defunct communist intelligence services, he now had to share power and decision-making with whoever was paying his bills.

This has to be done exactly right, he thought. He was taking a gamble engaging with his war staff this soon after his return, but running an international terrorist organization was much like controlling any large international conglomerate. Wallerein was realistic enough to recognize that his "corporation" was dealing with a bad fiscal quarter. Now he had to deal with an angry—perhaps out-for-blood—board of directors.

Ali Muhammad would be the problem. A Saudi, he was a true Bedouin—intelligent, ruthless, and ambitious. He trusted no Westerner, always referring to them as infidels. Wallerein was a confirmed atheist, but he kept that to himself around Ali. Being an atheist was worse than being a Christian as far as Ali was concerned. Always dressed in traditional Saudi clothing, Ali was tall and handsome, and his connections to the Wahhabi-leaning portion of the royal family made him more dangerous. Ali also coveted Wallerein's leadership position. Wallerein knew he had to deal with that soon or end up with a knife in his back—perhaps figuratively, possibly literally.

He stood, took a deep breath and strode down the concrete corridor into the conference room. He took his place at the head of the long mahogany table where the seven others were already seated.

Ali launched his offensive immediately. "You failed."

"I brought terror to the United States," said Wallerein, keeping his voice soft.

"You failed in your mission. People died, our people."

"I didn't—"

"That's right. You didn't. You didn't accomplish any of your goals. You didn't inflict any significant damage. All you did was alert the Americans that we were coming."

Wallerein turned to the others at the table. "Comrades, what we need to do is strike the Americans again, and quickly. We don't have to kill millions. Look at what we do in Palestine; a simple attack by a freedom fighter that kills four, five, twenty can derail any peace initiatives. Americans have no moral depth, no courage. They are weak."

17

"Yes," countered Ali, "but they are intelligent. And vigilant now thanks to your failure. Even a camel learns from beatings."

This sparked a rush of fury in Wallerein. He felt his blood pound and his skin go hot. The conversation was in danger of getting out of hand. He paused for a sip of water. He had to slow things down, twist them back to his agenda, away from Ali's.

He looked at the seven men seated around the table—imams from Iran next to a Bosniak, a Muslim from Kosovo. They sat side by side with Europeans and a Cuban, an odd mixture of Western and Middle Eastern. While they were committed to destroying America, all had their own agendas. His gaze swept across their faces as he tried to read their body language and gauge their intentions. Two refused to meet his eyes. Ali had been sowing discontent.

Wallerein continued, "We don't want to attack targets like New York City. We don't want to defeat cities, we want to terrorize America. Small towns, big towns. We must go for the interior of America because in their mythology, that is the 'Homeland.'"

He reached under the lip of the table and found his computer keyboard. He tapped in a few commands and a map of the United States flashed up on the screen behind him. "We need to terrorize Wichita...." He used a red laser pen to point to the location of the city. "Sedona, Leadville, Albuquerque, places like that to really show how we can reach anywhere, any time. Comrades, we make strikes in Jerusalem and Tel Aviv at will where security is tight. Surely we could do the same in Boulder and Tucson. We need to disrupt life, create volcanoes of violence in those cities, erupting at our bidding."

He studied the seated men. "There are already those in America who oppose their government—even hate it. Let us fan those flames."

Wallerein knew his history. One of his favorite episodes was the Hundred Years War in the 14th century. After the French were defeated at the Battle of Poitiers in 1356 where their King was captured, the power structure of the nation was divided and weak. The central government could not protect the peasantry from roaming bands of raiders who plundered Northern France at will. The peasants questioned why they

18

should support a government that passed ever more oppressive laws and taxes and could not fulfill its duty to protect them.

Eventually, the combination of outrages sparked the Jacquerie Revolt, a series of rebellions starting in 1358. Even though the revolt was smashed by the nobility, it supported Wallerein's theory that a government's primary role was to provide the people with protection or face unrest and revolt.

"The key is that Americans give up much of their freedoms to their government in exchange for protection. If the government can't protect them, the government will be seen as illegitimate. The attacks don't have to destroy cities. They merely have to show that we *could* destroy cities. Terror, panic, anger, recriminations are what we're after.

"I have already dispatched several teams to the United States." Wallerein put away the pointer. "I will leave for America within a fortnight."

"Why you?" challenged Ali.

"I will lead from the battlefield."

"You are better utilized here."

Wallerein shook his head. "No," he said, steel in his voice. "I have had enough of leading from afar. I will not be like your *mujahedeen*, hiding in the mountains."

Ali's face darkened. He jumped to his feet and addressed the rest of the group. "That is for us to decide. Another leader needs to be chosen. It is time for Comrade Wallerein to admit that he is better suited for headquarters work and writing papers."

Ali looked around the table for approval. He glanced at Wallerein just in time to see the muzzle of Wallerein's Beretta 9 mm pistol before he fired. And fired again.

Ali spun around, slammed into the wall and slid down to the floor, leaving a slash of blood on the concrete wall, and an expanding red stain on the carpet. He slumped over, eyes open and a surprised look on his frozen face. Wallerein deliberately slid the weapon back under the table top as he stared down each of his remaining associates. Nobody moved.

"I am in charge. I pick the targets and the times." He paused. "Any questions?"

There were none. Wallerein continued, "One hundred days, comrades. We cannot overthrow the United States government by ourselves. It is too powerful—but we can hurt it. Only the American people themselves can topple their oppressors. We need to show them why they should rise up. These attacks will annoy the clumsy monster that is their government. It will react, and react against its own people. It will pass new, more restrictive laws. More laws, more law enforcement, more paranoia. More clashes between citizens and the police, leading to even more laws, more anger. Citizen will be set against citizen."

He paused as he tried to burn his will into each remaining man. "One hundred days, comrades, and we will introduce America to the pain and suffering it has visited upon other nations of the world. We will rip her apart from the inside out and begin the process of bringing her to her knees."

Wallerein's gaze swept around the table. Nods, tentative smiles, then the Bosniak started a slow clap. The others joined in. Two rapped their knuckles on the table, riotous behavior for such normally reserved men. Wallerein exulted for a glorious moment before forcing himself to address immediate issues.

"I had planned on leaving Ali behind to organize the next phase." He gestured towards the bloody body. "This is no longer possible." He picked another Saudi, "Omar, you shall assume the planning for phase two during my absence. We will communicate by courier as always."

***

One hour later, Wallerein was back in his spartan office. With shaky hands, he punched a few buttons in a bank of electronics behind his desk. Strains of Wagner filled the room. He sank into his chair, closed his eyes and dreamed of German warrior heroes.

Wallerein wanted a place in history, for his life not to have been wasted. Most of his comrades of the left were in jail, dead, or co-opted by the very system they had vowed to destroy. Some in his own organization viewed him as an anachronism, a dinosaur. Even the world-famous Carlos, now locked up in a Paris prison, was reduced to an occasional sound bite on the evening news, unable to dominate world events as he did decades ago.

Wallerein shook himself out of his daydreams and took a sip of mineral water, hoping to cleanse his mouth to remove the taste of the words he had had to say to his assembled "partners." Words of compromise and conciliation, words he never thought he would ever say. His plan for phase one had been dissected and revised by these holy men, academics who knew nothing of operations, of combat. A wet ops attack had been demanded by these amateurs. At least he had been able to steer it into his primary target area, the American Southwest.

After a moment, he sat up, opened a drawer and took out a picture of a man wearing the uniform of the United States Air Force and a tall, smiling woman, holding hands. They were the reason his last operation had failed. They had thwarted his plans of world terror. They had reduced him to this state of near irrelevancy.

Wallerein studied the picture, burning the image into his brain. "Callahan, I will have my revenge. I will kill you and those whom you hold dear. This is my promise."

Chapter Four

Pentagon
Conference Room 3E284

Colonel Tom Callahan looked around the crowded conference room again. It seemed like half the flag officers in the Pentagon were present. The topic was Washington's current obsession, former Soviet strategic bases, nuclear submarines, and heavy bombers. Most important for Tom in his capacity as the White House nuclear proliferation expert, the locations of all known nuclear weapons. Russia was imploding, and the prospect of loose nukes was everybody's major worry.

The briefing officer ended his delivery with an attempt at humor. "In summary, the latest *Washington Post* editorial said that compared to the security systems on most Russian nuclear storage sites, the average American liquor store looks like Fort Knox."

As the assembled officers made the expected chuckles at the dark humor, Tom sighed at the joke he had heard five times already and cast a discreet look at his watch. He despised these meetings, even though his four-year sentence in the Washington bureaucratic maelstrom had just begun. Tom again studied the charts the earnest young major from the On-Site Inspection Agency presented to the group so enthusiastically, all of which Tom had seen in various forms from different intelligence agencies.

At the end of the meeting, a stocky, gray-haired Air Force lieutenant general beckoned to Tom. "Walk with me to my office, Colonel."

The men strode down the hall, their uniform shoes clicking loudly on the Pentagon linoleum floors as they distanced themselves from the dispersing group.

"Those eagles on your shoulders look good on you, Tommy."

Tom grimaced. "I feel like a fraud, Uncle Harvey."

"In this town, son, a lieutenant colonel is nobody. The president was right. As one of his advisors, you had to be frocked as a colonel."

"I would rather be a lieutenant colonel squadron commander. Heck, I'd rather be a captain in a flying squadron."

General Walters chuckled. "So would I, but that is no longer an option, young man." He changed the topic. "How's that gorgeous wife of yours this morning?"

Tom's wife, Colleen O'Kelly Callahan, mother of a newly adopted baby boy was two months pregnant with a baby she had thought she would never be able to have. "Still pregnant, sir. Every day is a victory."

The men exchanged looks. Both knew the difficulties and heartbreaks the Callahans had experienced trying to have a baby. Harvey Walters had been wingman for Tom's father, Brigadier General Sean Callahan, when he was shot down in the last months of the Vietnam War. Walters had functioned ever since as Tom's surrogate father; there were no secrets between them. Walters held up his left hand, his fingers crossed. "Let's hope and pray that this pregnancy goes to term, kiddo."

"Thanks, Uncle Harvey."

They walked in silence for a moment. Walters said, "The Army Chief of Staff wants to have lunch with you next week."

"Why?"

"He wants to say thanks."

"What for?"

"Tom, just over a month ago, you stopped Wallerein and his spy, an Army scientist, from spreading a deadly virus stolen from an Army facility, and you don't think the Army wants to say thanks? Hell, the General wanted to give you a medal but the president said no because he wants to keep the whole mess classified."

"The president's right. But I will be delighted to eat an Army steak with the good general."

"Very gracious of you, young man," Walters said with a smile.

They were interrupted by Tom's vibrating cell phone. "It's my office, Uncle Harvey. Could I use your secure phone?"

The General's aide stood as the two men entered the office suite and went straight into Walters' private office. Behind the desk sat a silver framed picture of a much younger Harvey Walters standing in a group of smiling, sweat-stained pilots clustered around the wing of a McDonnell Douglas F-4D after a mission over Vietnam. It was one of Tom's mother's favorite pictures because, posed with his arm around Walters' shoulders stood Tom's father, with a broad grin, flourishing his trademark after-mission cigar. The same photo resided on the bedside table in her home outside Taos, New Mexico.

Tom picked up the STU III secure phone and dialed his office. "Callahan."

"Hi. Tom, it's Porter. I'm sitting at your desk. Nice office, buddy, a window and everything. And you told me that you were just a flunky."

"How'd you get in there?"

"We had an appointment, remember? Your secretary dialed you up, and presto! Here we are."

Tom grinned. "Porter, you could charm your way inside the Kremlin."

"That's right. And I have."

"Okay, what's the story?"

"You were right. There was a medevac flight out of BWI on the day in question, bound for Mérida, thence to Havana. The fixed-base folks at BWI said that an ambulance with 'Easton Hospital' painted on the side pulled up and a man on a stretcher was loaded onto the plane, a Gulfstream IV."

"Damn! I knew the Cubans would get into this mess. I'll call Jacob Borenstein and set up an appointment. Can you meet me at the FBI Building?"

"For you, the man who saved me from a slow and horrible death in Bolivia? Anything, my friend."

"That's great news, Port. You can stand next to me when I brief the president."

"No way!"

Tom laughed. "Didn't you just say, 'Anything, my friend?'"

Porter snorted. "I would probably have gotten back to La Paz safely by myself anyhow."

"Oh, how quickly they forget. See you in thirty minutes, my friend."

***

Tom and Porter arrived nearly simultaneously at the J. Edgar Hoover Building. They shook hands and exchanged a quick embrace. The diminutive Porter was one of Tom's favorite people. Very bright, curious and with an impish grin and a sense of humor to match, Porter had nearly died chasing a story in the mountainous jungle of Bolivia. Tom, newly arrived in-country, had organized a difficult helicopter rescue. Porter later became an integral part of Tom's team.

A very large agent met them in the lobby. "Good afternoon, Colonel Callahan, Mr. Nelson. The Deputy Director is waiting for you."

Startled, Tom asked "Do I know you?"

The agent chuckled. "No sir, but I had the honor of working with you and your group running Kurt Wallerein to ground and stopping the attack on Washington."

"Too bad it's all classified," said Porter.

"Yes sir. It would be a great story to tell in a bar during Happy Hour. There I was, saving democracy—"

They all laughed.

"Thank you for what you did for our country, gentlemen." He handed them visitor's passes. "It's an honor to meet you."

Tom and Porter silently rode the elevator up to the Deputy Director's office and were immediately ushered in to find Jacob Borenstein in earnest conversation with Robbie Robinson.

"Hey, Robbie," said Tom, offering his hand. "How are things over at Langley?"

"Settling in, Tom. It's good to be back at work."

Robbie Robinson was a fifty-something, stocky and gray-haired employee of the CIA who had been "medically" retired largely because

25

of his penchant for asking embarrassing questions of his superiors. He and Porter Nelson had been responsible for uncovering the terrorist attack on the United States that Tom Callahan had prevented. Robbie was now reinstated at Langley at Tom's request and newly-promoted, his reward from a grateful president and a grudging CIA.

"Tom, those eagles look good," said Jacob. "No more than you deserve."

"I was frocked," said Tom.

Borenstein nodded and smiled. "I know, I know. So you get to wear the rank but don't collect the pay until your promotion number comes up."

"And he'll need every dime," laughed Nelson. "Colleen found a house in Georgetown."

"Oooh, Tom, it'll take more than a colonel's pay to live there," warned Robbie.

Tom gave all three men the finger as he settled back into Jacob's leather couch. They had become close as brothers during the events of the past few months. All were aware that Tom's financial status did not fit the mold of the average military officer. Thanks to shrewd investments by generations of Callahans, he could pay cash for any house in Georgetown and they knew it. "What do you have for us, Jacob?"

"The worst news imaginable. The prints and blood samples from Wallerein's shot-up hide-out and the mystery man in the Easton hospital are the same. Wallerein is alive, or was six weeks ago when he escaped from the hospital."

"Damn!" said Tom. He motioned to Porter. "Give him the rest of it, Port."

Porter filled in the details of the flights out of BWI and Mexico.

"We'll confirm this if you don't mind, Porter."

"Be my guest. He's probably in Cuba."

Tom surveyed the group. "So what does this mean for us?"

"It means that the world's number one terrorist is still at large," said Porter.

"His stock can't be too high in the terrorist world," said Jacob. "As in Hollywood, you're only as a good as your last operation, and his failed."

"Perhaps, but he aimed pretty high, and that's always good for terrorist brownie points," said Tom.

"The terrorist world is extremely Darwinian, Tom. Succeed or die," said Robbie.

"We can only hope," said Tom. The others nodded.

All four men lapsed into silence as they contemplated the truths they had hoped to disprove. Tom looked off into space as he mulled over the situation.

"So, we're agreed that the evidence supports Wallerein being alive?" he asked. Hearing no dissent, he said. "Okay, I'll go brief the president. Maybe the silver lining in this will be that he'll fire me before I actually get into this new job and send me back to the Air Force, so I can just fly jets."

Borenstein chuckled. "Pretty extreme action just to get out of having to pay for a house in Georgetown."

Robbie spoke up, "Tom, I'll go with you if you want. I suspect the president will want the CIA involved in whatever he decides to do."

"Me, too," said Jacob.

"I'm in," said Porter. "I smell a great story here."

"You know he's going to muzzle you, don't you, Port?"

"Don't worry, Tom. I'll write the story anyhow, even if I have to wait to publish it posthumously. No way I'm going to miss out on this."

"Thanks, guys," said Tom, genuinely touched by the support. "I suspect that the president will form an inter-agency group to track down Wallerein, probably by sunset. He will not be subtle, he will not be diplomatic. He will be screaming. All of us will be there among way too many other people and organizations. It's going to be the number one issue in all our lives for months."

"Weren't you planning to be gone next week, Tom?" asked Robbie.

"You're right, damnit. I'm supposed to go to a wedding in California up near Napa."

"Who's getting married?" asked Porter.

"One of my best friends, Brice Adams. I flew with him in the Gulf War where he saved my butt. He's a colonel in the California Air Guard. His first wife died a couple of years ago from cancer, and he's getting remarried. I'd do pretty much anything for the guy."

"I feel the same way about you," said Porter, going slightly pink.

Tom laughed. "Does that mean when we brief the president you won't whine?"

"Tom, I owe you a big one, and you know it."

"Oh, please. Save the smoke, Porter. You don't owe anybody anything. Without you, we wouldn't have stopped Wallerein in the first place, and this city would be littered with bodies."

"Yeah, but you flew the plane that ran him into the Chesapeake Bay Bridge."

"Didn't kill him, though, did I?"

Oval Office
White House

Tom, Jacob, Robbie and Porter were ushered into the Oval Office by Mark Freiberg, the president's chief of staff. "Five minutes, Colonel," he whispered. "Not a second more." Then he turned and announced, "Mr. President, Colonel Callahan and associates."

The president looked up from a stack of papers spread on his desk. "Hello, Tom," he said, flashing one of his trademark smiles. His smile of welcome faded into a look of puzzled concern as the others came into view.

"Thank you for seeing us, Mr. President," said Tom.

"I assume this is important, Colonel."

Tom took a deep breath. "Yes sir. It's not good news. We have reason to believe that Kurt Wallerein is still alive."

The president's eyes bored holes into Tom. He gathered up his papers and set them aside. He came out from behind his desk and collapsed into a leather chair. "Please, take a seat, gentlemen," gesturing at the couch and chairs. "I assume you have proof of this?"

"Yes sir."

28

The president turned to Freiberg. "Mark, hold my calls."

"Sir, you have a meeting with the Indian ambassador—"

"I know. He'll have to wait." He turned back to Tom. "Let's have it."

Five minutes later, Tom said, "That's it, Mr. President. All we know and all we can guess."

The president slumped in his chair and stared off into space for what Tom felt was an hour but was less than a minute.

He sat up. "We need to keep this under wraps for the present. I want you four to form a small working group. And I mean small. Find Wallerein. Find out where he went, how he got there and what, if any, plans he's cooking up. Report directly to me. If I am unavailable, through Mark." Another pause. "Tom, I want you to head this up."

Tom felt his body tense. "Me, Mr. President?" he blurted.

The president said, "I don't know why you're surprised. Who is better qualified to lead this group? You've done it before, even if unofficially."

He looked at Jacob Borenstein. "Do you have a problem with that, Jacob?"

"No sir. Good choice. What shall I tell my boss, Mr. President?"

The president thought that over a moment. "I'll speak to him." He looked to Robbie. "And how about a cover for you, say, a special duty assignment as liaison to the FBI? Would that work over at Langley?"

"That would be fine, Mr. President. I head up a small group but we're not exactly busy over there."

"Mr. Nelson, you seem to be a floater. You can go places these others can't go and do things they can't do.

Porter smiled. "That's just what Tom told me yesterday."

The president looked at Tom, "See what I mean? You're already out in front. Keep it up."

He glanced at his watch. "I want you to adjourn to Tom's office and work out the details, but I don't want you to meet there anymore. Find a less conspicuous place." He stood and the group rose as one man. "I'm sorry, I have to go."

29

The president shook Tom's hand, "When you first reported in, I told you to tell me what I needed to know, not what I wanted to hear." He made an attempt at a smile. "Well, you certainly have done that, Colonel. This is the worst news I've had in weeks." He shook the hand of each member of the group. "But I needed to know it." He headed for the door. "Stay in touch."

***

Four hours later, after a tumultuous series of meetings at the White House, a weary Tom Callahan drove his red 1960 Jaguar XKE up to the rented luxury condominium complex in Georgetown where his family was staying. He dreaded telling Colleen about Wallerein. There were many things about this new job that he couldn't tell her, but she deserved to know about the German terrorist. His organization had targeted her in Bolivia and had tried to kill her twice. It was Colleen who pieced together the full scope of the threat to the United States. Tom had succeeded in stopping the terrorist's plans only because of her quick thinking.

Colleen already had so many things on her mind he hated to load her up with another one. In the past six weeks while he had been trying to learn his way around the White House, the Australian-born ex-model had flown to Arizona to defend her dissertation, had visited a baker's dozen homes for sale in Georgetown, interviewed a parade of applicants for an au pair position for their newly adopted baby boy, and accepted a position as an economist at the World Bank while caring for baby Mikey and masking her bouts of nausea with a smile. She was thriving here in Washington, a factor that made his disappointment in losing a flying command easier to bear.

As he walked into the condo, Colleen glided into the living room from Mikey's room. Standing an inch taller than her husband, the statuesque Colleen moved with the easy grace of a model. She wore a brilliant, white blouse and casual slacks, her blonde mane drawn up into a ponytail. She greeted Tom with a hug and a long drawn out kiss. "Mikey's asleep, luv."

"Damn," he said, disappointed. "I never get to see the boy anymore." Another reason to dislike the Washington rat race.

Colleen caressed his cheek. "You can peek in to say good-night while I get you a glass of wine." She chuckled. "You'll see him soon enough."

Tom slipped into the nursery. His son was asleep on his back and making sucking motions with his mouth. He gently stroked the boy's cheek and marveled at the softness of his café au lait flesh and his beautiful, lush eyelashes. Tom had been a father for less than two months and would be a father of another baby in about seven more. It was all still somewhat disorienting, but he loved it. Mikey had been a preemie and was still so small that he couldn't eat enough to last for more than a few hours. Tom insisted on doing the nighttime feedings, meaning he hadn't had a full night's sleep in weeks, but it was the only opportunity he had to spend any time with his baby. Colleen did not object to his decision.

As Tom began dinner, Colleen spread out a map of D.C. on the counter to show him the location of her preferred house, along with three separate routes to and from work. She was a demon for details, as was Tom. They talked easily and of nothing important. Tom bustled about the kitchen and slipped on a chef's long apron. He asked Colleen to choose some music from their extensive bank of CDs. Thanks to a series of Italian nannies when he was young, Tom was as at home in the kitchen as he was in a cockpit. He loved to cook. Colleen was perfectly willing to stay out of his way.

"By the way," she said, "somebody's been following me."

Startled, he asked, "What makes you think that?"

"All that counterterrorist training we had before heading to Bolivia, that's what. I noticed a man following me the last few times I walked Mikey."

"If it happens again tomorrow, let me know, and I'll have the FBI look into it."

"Oh, Tommy. It's probably Jacob Borenstein using me as a training exercise for new agents. It'll stop soon enough." She laughed, "My goodness, six weeks at the White House and already you're making the

31

FBI jump." She chuckled again. "Just let Jacob know that his agents aren't as good as they should be."

Meal finished, Tom sat on the couch and sipped his after-dinner coffee.

"I hired an au pair for your sons this afternoon," Colleen said, as she slid next to him.

"Sons, plural?" Surprised, he reached for her and stroked her tummy. "Why are you so sure this one's a boy?"

"Because, Colonel, you are all male, the poster boy so to speak for masculinity."

"If I'm such a macho stud, why do I volunteer to do stuff like change diapers and mix formula?"

"Because, Colonel, you are also a warrior. You possess an innate need to breed and care for more warriors, or the species will die out."

She straddled his thighs, then leaned away from him, reached up and let her hair loose to cascade down over her shoulders. She smiled, took his hands in hers and placed them on her breasts. "They're swelling. Can you tell?"

"I'd like to examine them more closely before I pronounce judgment."

"You'd better make me yours soon and often, matey, because pretty quickly I'm going to bloat up like a blimp."

As he watched her unbutton her blouse, Tom decided any discussion of Wallerein could wait until morning.

Chapter Five

San Francisco International Airport
International Arrivals area

Brice Adams checked his watch for the third time in two minutes as he scanned the new arrivals streaming past. The passengers from the American Airlines flight from Madrid should be through Customs momentarily. Adams' fiancée, Ruhi Talebreza, fidgeted next to him as she screened each new arrival, searching for the face of her father.

More people hurried down the crowded corridor. Adams noted the subtle change in clothing; these newer people were in the expensive clothing that tended to mark the first-class passengers. He spotted a scowling, sour little man. *This must be him,* thought Brice. Short, dark, and balding.

Adams heard a sharp intake of breath from Ruhi. She waved to the short man, who gave a slight nod. He made his way to a break in the fence and headed to them. "Good morning, daughter," he said in cold, formal Persian.

Ruhi blushed, then hesitantly kissed the man on the cheek. "*Buenos días, Padre,*" she said, in Spanish for Adams' sake. "I would like to present my fiancé, Brice Adams."

Spanish it is, thought Brice as he extended his hand. "An honor, Professor. Thank you for coming."

The large, dark eyes that stared up at Adams were the only physical resemblance between father and daughter. Except the eyes regarding Adams were lifeless and dull while Ruhi's eyes usually danced with life. His skin was mottled and wrinkled; hers was supple and delightfully smooth. His hair was gray and thinning; hers the gorgeous, thick, jet-black mass so often found in Middle Eastern women. The elder Talebreza had dropped out of the UCLA doctoral engineering program and retreated into obscurity as an adjunct professor at the *Universidad de Toledo* in Spain. Ruhi had a newly minted Stanford MBA, spoke five languages fluently, and was a rising star in the California financial markets.

Adams, trim at forty-three, carried himself like the California surfer that he still was. He knew he probably represented everything that Talebreza, former Islamic radical, thought decadent about the United States.

Adams flagged down a skycap, organized the professor's luggage, and led the group out of the terminal, weaving through the crowds, through the sliding doors and out to the taxi stand.

"Take us to the general aviation area, please," he said, handing the cabby a one-hundred-dollar bill. The cabby smiled as he looked at the bill. Adams often over-tipped people who needed the money, especially when they provided him with service above and beyond.

Ruhi hated it when he deliberately overpaid somebody. He knew it drove her crazy to see money wasted, a legacy of all those years scrimping by in tiny apartments, working all day, studying at night. The fact that she was about to marry a wealthy man simply had not yet sunk in. She was probably going to go to her grave as thrifty as she was now.

Brice opened the cab door for his young fiancée and future father-in-law, then got in the front seat. Ruhi spoke to her father in Persian, trying to jump start the communication that had dried up so long ago during her childhood years in Iran and Spain. The professor was understandably grumpy about being flown halfway around the world to meet a future son-in-law that he thought he'd never have, one that was just a few years younger than himself, even if the ticket was free and first class.

Adams was not sympathetic. He was only being civil to the man because Ruhi wanted her father's blessing on the marriage. After escaping a dismal childhood in Tehran, she had lost touch with her father and had despaired of ever finding him again. Brice decided that he would find her father for her, as sort of a living wedding present. The U.S. high tech world was not dominated yet by foreigners but there were a surprisingly large number of them in California. Adams had made a few calls, ending with a source at the UCLA engineering school. The academic engineering world just wasn't that big, and the Iranian segment was even smaller—just a matter of asking the right people.

Adams had donated millions of dollars through the Adams Foundation to young people like Ruhi, desperate immigrants, impoverished students, single parents, and just plain folks who needed a financial break to jump start their futures. He had also given millions to lawyers and groups who pushed to protect children, especially from sexual predators and/or abusive parents. Talebreza's medieval attitudes towards women certainly fit him into the latter category. Adams had promised himself that he would be on his best behavior for Ruhi's sake, and he was determined to make good on it.

The cab snaked its way through the airport interchanges and pulled under the portico of the general aviation terminal. The taxi doors were quickly opened by the attendant, "Good morning, Colonel Adams. Welcome back."

They entered the foyer, all glass and marble, with thick carpet. His co-pilot, Bill Walker, was waiting there, flight documents in hand. "Good morning, Colonel. Miss Ruhi." Adams introduced Walker to the professor.

Walker handed the papers to Adams to review because he never flew anywhere without checking every detail himself. The plane was ready to go. Flight plan filed. Weather no factor.

Brice pointed to the enormous wall map of the United States found in almost every ready room in the country, "Professor, this is where we are now, right on the Bay, just south of San Francisco. Up here is our destination airport, just north of Santa Rosa, and about ten miles from our home. We're going to take off to the north, swing out over the bay, then fly up the coast. You can ride in the cockpit if you'd like to get the best view of our small portion of the world."

Walker took the bags and they headed out to the waiting aircraft, a Challenger 350. Normally for a flight this short, Adams would have used

35

his personal Beechcraft King Air, a nimble enough seven passenger turboprop with just enough speed to make the flight interesting for him and slow enough to allow passengers to gawk at the San Francisco scenery. Not this time. Adams was determined to blow the professor's socks off. Despite his professional successes, Adams didn't consider himself much of a marital catch. He was determined to show this second-rate academic that Ruhi now had a family who would love her for the woman she was and could take care of her in a world completely beyond her father's comprehension.

The Challenger was as perfect as Adams' staff of mechanics could make it. Adams had spent thousands of hours in California Air National Guard fighters, jammed into cramped cockpits with peeling gray paint and lumpy seat packs. This particular aircraft was sexy; there was no other word for it. Sleek, shiny, and sparkling. Wicked fast and bathed in luxury. Something even a macho fighter jock would not be embarrassed to be seen flying. The capacious interior was laid out for comfort with wide, soft leather captain's chairs, thick carpets, and inlaid wood tables. A flat screen plasma television monitor was framed against the forward bulkhead to project the aircraft's route of flight. A state-of-the-art entertainment center was positioned aft, designed to keep Adam's two teenage sons busy with DVDs and video games on long flights. The table would soon be set with crystal, linen, silver and adorned with the fresh flowers and fruit so treasured by Persians. It was luxury like the professor had likely seen only in museums.

The cockpit was as richly appointed. The instrument panels wrapped around and over, dazzling with their myriad switches, knobs, lights, and screens. Totally baffling to a ground pounder like the professor.

Ruhi slid gracefully into the right seat.

"A cockpit is no place for a woman," spluttered Talebreza.

"It is in this country," shot back Adams, biting back the multiple profanities he wanted to use on this little prick. He motioned the fuming professor into the jump seat, then turned back to the business he loved most, getting ready to "slip the surly bonds of earth." He cued Ruhi to read the "Start Engine" check list.

The weather was perfect, nearly unbelievable for San Francisco this time of year. Light winds, crystal clear skies, a few puffy clouds for texture. Adams smiled to himself. This was going to be a Jonathan Livingston Seagull-like flight. After the inevitable delay for takeoff clearance, they took a sweeping turn around the bay. Sailboats were out in force this morning, white sails and colorful spinnakers on the cobalt blue of the bay. Then out over the Pacific to clear the controlled airspace around San Francisco. Up the jagged California coast, just like a television documentary. Off the left wingtip, the Pacific. Off the right wingtip, the Pacific Coast Highway snaked along, twisting through the rolling hills.

This ought to show Talebreza that we mean business, thought Adams. He was pulling out all the stops for this guy. He knew he could use his business contacts to have the man fired from his job at the University, crushed, figuratively swept under the rug where he couldn't make any more problems for Ruhi. God knew the man had done some terrible things to her. By all rights, Adams thought that she should banish the man from all future family functions. But she was the kindest, gentlest person he had ever known and would not hear of it. And Adams loved her, so that was that, as they say.

Adams found his estate, nearly six thousand acres nestled in the foothills adjacent to a national forest and with a clear view of the valley below, much of which belonged to him. The main house, guest houses, stables, tennis courts, and gardens were clearly visible. He pointed out the house to the professor who gave another curt little nod.

Okay, buddy, thought Adams. *Two can play this game.* "Ruhi, you have control. You are set up for a straight-in approach runway zero one. We are nineteen point three miles from the airport."

After a moment's hesitation, Ruhi gave him a big smile and took the controls. Adams knew she wouldn't be able to resist. Ruhi loved to fly and savored every opportunity to get some stick time, just like co-pilots the world over. She chewed her bottom lip in concentration as she began her approach to the county airport.

Adams started reading off the "Before Landing" items. He could feel the heat of the professor's anger.

After engine shutdown, Adams loaded the professor's luggage into the ranch Range Rover and drove Ruhi and her father through the vine-covered valley to the ranch. The tree-lined driveway wound its way to the main house, a fourteen-thousand-square-foot, stone-faced mansion with a red-tile roof, built in the late 1880s and completely restored.

They were met by the ranch manager, Alonzo Garcia.

"Alonzo, this is Professor Talebreza, Ruhi's father. Please have his luggage taken to his room."

"Your sons are in the game room, *señor*."

Ruhi moved with an easy grace across the massive living room to the game room, as she pointed out some of the more significant artwork to her father, who made no comments.

The game room was also immense, dominated by an ornately carved oak pool table, a ping pong table, several arcade pin ball machines, and a big-screen television where the boys were engaged playing a video game involving huge, noisy war machines.

"Will, Caleb, please turn that off and come meet my father."

The boys paused their video game, slowly stood, and dragged themselves towards the adults.

Ruhi put her hand on Will's shoulder as she introduced the boys to her father. Will shook it off as he took the professor's hand. Caleb slid by her as he offered his hand and mumbled a greeting.

Adams sighed. The boys were still resentful of Ruhi and this wedding, still missed their mother. Hell, he still missed their mother, but she was gone, and Ruhi was here. He was reminded of the old Army officer's manual he had recently purchased for his library that talked about "silent insubordination;" not quite sullen but borderline. Resentment of the wedding filled the room and was obvious to everybody, understandable in teenagers, inexcusable in the professor. Adams knew that if there were a vote within this group to approve or disapprove the wedding, he and Ruhi would be voted down three to two.

The professor looked at Adams, then shifted his still angry glare to Ruhi. "I will go to my room. Wake me for dinner."

Adams looked at Ruhi. He had never seen her look so sad.

Chapter Six

Albuquerque International Sunport
Albuquerque, New Mexico
June 10, 2000

The Mexicana Airlines Boeing 737 from Mérida made its approach from west to east, allowing the passenger in seat 7A an exquisite view of Sandia Peak and the sprawl of Albuquerque as it pushed north and west against the high-altitude desert topography of central New Mexico. The stunning green ribbon of vegetation along the banks of the Rio Grande sliced through the rocky landscape from the north, bringing life-giving water to the thirsty farms and ranches that flanked the river.

The passenger was entirely and deliberately unremarkable. Blondish hair, going gray at the temples, lean muscular body dressed as a tourist, one with a taste for the outdoors: safari shirt, cargo pants, laced boots. It was turkey season in New Mexico. If asked, he could give a convincing dissertation on the wonders of hunting wild turkeys and different methods of preparing the delicious meat.

His forged British passport listed him as Peter Hinneman from Leeds, but he was really Lukas Dietz from Dresden. "Hinneman" was a hunter of sorts: he had been a field operative and assassin for the *Hauptverwaltung Aufklärung* (HVA), the defunct foreign intelligence service of the German Democratic Republic, generally regarded as the most effective foreign intelligence service during the Cold War. Hinneman was skilled in sabotage, hand-to-hand combat, and fluent in English, French, and Spanish. He had been compromised during the post-reunification era because he, a committed socialist, had refused to take the oath of allegiance to the new Germany. With the official reunification of Germany in October 1990 came the accusations, recriminations, and trials of former communist officials, especially from the *Staatssicherheit* (Stasi) and the HVA. Hinneman had eluded all attempts to bring him to justice and had slipped away to join Kurt Wallerein's international terrorist organization, along with at least two dozen other HVA officers.

As the airliner taxied to the gate, Hinneman could see the F-16 aircraft of the New Mexico Air National Guard sitting in the early morning sunlight, as well as about a dozen Blackhawk helicopters. The Albuquerque Sunport was immediately adjacent to Kirtland Air Force Base and shared the runways with the military.

Hinneman collected his in-flight bag from the overhead bin and joined the herd of passengers shuffling towards the exit. He made his way through the terminal corridors, astonished at the casual security measures that Wallerein had insisted would be in effect. Hinneman had fought against the United States all his adult life. He had completed missions fighting capitalism all over Europe and even one foray into South America, but this was his first opportunity to experience firsthand the pernicious evil that was America.

He bypassed the baggage carousels and made his way to the rent-a-car desks where he picked up his paperwork using another set of forged documents. As he exited the terminal in the direction of the rental car parking lot, he was joined by another man from the flight, similarly dressed, and similarly a former East German agent, though from the *Stasi*.

As they arrived at their designated SUV, they surveyed the parking lot and, as a precaution against the criminals in the *gottverdammt* FBI, selected another SUV at random. Hinneman met his partner's eyes, who nodded agreement. Hinneman walked alone back to the desk and handed his envelope of papers to the surprised clerk. "I prefer black instead of the silver one you assigned me, if you don't mind." Softening his words with a smile, he said, "The black one also has a nicer CD player."

Back at the huge black car, the two men threw their bags in the back and climbed in. Hinneman took his time checking out the SUV's unfamiliar cockpit before starting the vehicle.

The day was clear, with visibility to the horizon which seemed to stretch forever. The midday sun burned overhead, the rays' intensity accentuated by the altitude. Albuquerque was much like any city, though smaller and more sprawling than most. He thought the road network was strange with all the major thoroughfares laid out in straight lines instead of the rabbit-warrens of the more familiar, older European inner cities. In their pre-mission study of the area, Hinneman and his partner had memorized the principle arteries and the main geographical features of the sparsely populated, enormous state. Germany was only slightly larger than New Mexico but contained almost forty times as many people. No surprise to Hinneman. *Who would live in such a desolate place?* He shuddered at the thought as he looked out over the landscape that appeared moon-like to his eyes, bleak and rocky, an infinity of sagebrush stretching towards the distant mountains.

As he drove through the twisting airport access roads, he noted tufts of fluff floating in the breeze, seeds cast from the abundant cottonwood trees wafting along, and strange plants erupting from the center median after the long winter, due, no doubt, to the profligate use of irrigation. He could see streams of excess water running along the pavement. The arrogance of these aggressive Americans, moving to the desert, then trying to turn it into a garden, fighting against even nature itself.

His first destination was a memorized address which they found on the map provided by the car rental company, a low-slung storage building in need of paint located off a main road. The combination padlock opened at the first try, and Hinneman lifted the heavy garage door. The advance man had done his work well. There were two bags of equipment and a briefcase that contained more instructions, United States Geological Survey (USGS) maps for New Mexico and Colorado, two hunting rifles and Beretta 9 mm pistols, ammunition, boxes of flares, two-gallon gasoline containers (empty), camping gear, and a sizable amount of U.S. dollars. Curious, Hinneman studied the USGS contour

41

maps. He'd have to get used to the sheer scale of the countryside, as well as using feet instead of meters.

The men quickly loaded the equipment into the SUV. Hinneman gave a satisfied nod, then drove out to join the inferior American autobahn system, here called Interstate 25, and headed north.

Chapter Seven

Adams Residence
Northern California

The day of the wedding dawned bright and cheery, under a cloudless azure sky. The florists arrived early, filling the grand flagstone patio at the rear of the mansion with huge bouquets of exquisite flowers. Caterers brought in enormous quantities and selections of foods. Brice Adams found himself staring at the many exotic Persian dishes, intrigued by the presentation, and trying to imagine the lists of ingredients.

The atmosphere was decidedly upbeat. A small orchestra played soft music in the background. Guests were arriving early. Many of the guests were Ruhi's Bahá'í friends, some from her graduate school days, a few from the bank where she worked in the international finance arena. Adams had met Ruhi as he was arranging financing for a major business investment overseas. He had been struck by her competence and gentle demeanor. A business lunch led to social ones as he fell under her gracious spell. Ruhi attracted people like flowers attracted bees. Some people, especially in the business world, mistook her kindness as weakness. Adams knew better.

He watched her from across the patio as she embraced each new arrival, handing them a flower and spending a few moments of her special day with them. Ruhi was lovely in a brocaded white wedding dress, flowers woven into her hair. She wore an elaborate diamond necklace and matching earrings that had once belonged to a seventeenth century Persian princess, bought in a Sotheby's auction in London, and part of his wedding present to her. She looked regal standing there, smiling her special smile and exuding grace and charm. If it were not for her father who was a world-class jerk, Adams could easily believe that a bit of royal blood flowed through her veins.

He moved to take his place next to her, trying to work the crowd as she did with a smile and kind words. He introduced his fiancée to several state senators and representatives, the state attorney general, the state adjutant general, the mayors of the three largest nearby towns, several county supervisors, and the CEOs and Chief Operating Officers of some of California's largest high-tech companies.

In between smiles and handshakes, Adams noticed some of his Air Guard flying buddies near the bar, clustered around Tom Callahan, no doubt swapping lies about flying. He saw his sons sulking over by the food tent, probably sneaking glasses of champagne. Fasheed Talebreza stood alone off to the side, a sour look on his face.

Colleen Callahan held court in a circle of admirers. He had never seen her look so happy. Pregnancy suited her well. He glanced back at Ruhi, still cheerfully greeting guests. Ruhi would never experience childbirth. Her endometriosis was so advanced that she was unable to have children. Family was important to her, probably more than to most people he knew. She had few living relatives and treasured them all.

In keeping with the requirements of the Bahá'í Faith, Ruhi needed her father's permission to marry. Adams knew that Talebreza, a former Iranian militant and fanatical Muslim, had been outraged that his daughter had converted to the Bahá'í Faith as a teenager. Technically, she was considered an apostate to all Muslims. Despite repeated United Nation condemnations, Bahá'ís were openly persecuted in Iran, home of the Bahá'í Faith. Talebreza had been difficult during the past days but had said nothing in opposition to the wedding.

As the time of the ceremony approached, the guests clustered around a white stage. The hills in the background were framed by overhanging live oaks. Massive flower displays surrounded the stage providing a subtle fragrance in the warm, early-summer breeze. Since there are no clergy in the Bahá'í faith, the Stanford roommate of Brice's late father, a Federal District Court judge, presided over the ceremony.

44

The requirements for a Bahá'í marriage are simple: consent of the couple's parents; a one sentence vow—"We will all, verily, abide by the Will of God"—and two witnesses to the ceremony. There are no other specific marriage rites, though local civil marriage requirements, if any, also had to be met. All other wedding details—complexity, further vows, music, et cetera—are left to the couple.

The judge stepped forward on the stage. "Friends, thank you for coming here on this glorious day to witness the joining of these two people in marriage." He motioned to Brice and Ruhi to step forward.

"Stop!" shouted Ruhi's father.

Everyone froze. Talebreza forced his way into the aisle. He glared at Ruhi, then Brice. He turned to address the crowd.

"I forbid this marriage."

A gasp swept the audience. Ruhi's face went pale.

"What are you doing, father?"

"It is done. You will not marry."

"Please, father, do not do this," pleaded Ruhi.

"You may not proceed. I have spoken."

A blast of anger coursed through Brice Adams. With hot blood pounding in his temples, he started towards Talebreza. He felt Ruhi's hand on his arm. Her eyes pleaded with him not to lose control. Adams took several deep breaths, and reached back for her hand before turning to face the crowd.

"Please excuse this public display of family politics. We need a private moment for a family conference. Have another drink, and we'll be right back." Adams strode over to Talebreza and propelled him towards the house, Ruhi in tow.

Inside, Adams turned on Talebreza. "What in the hell are you trying to do, Fasheed? You already gave your consent to our Local Spiritual Assembly."

Defiant, Talebreza looked up at Adams. "It is rescinded. I am her father. She cannot marry."

"Why, father? Why did you change your mind?" asked a tearful Ruhi.

45

"You are barren. Allah is punishing you for betraying Allah and your family."

"She hasn't betrayed God, you pompous little man," said Adams. "She escaped from your tyranny. That's what you're really angry about." He moved closer. "And you know, Fasheed, she left you because you treated her so badly. You didn't want a daughter, you wanted a slave. You should be proud of what she has become, what she's accomplished—without any assistance from you or any other man, I might add."

Talebreza waved his hand as if to dismiss that argument. "I could have arranged for her to marry another rich man. She would have everything she needed, courtesy of that man."

Ruhi turned and walked away, trying to conceal her face, but her emotion was betrayed by her hands.

Adams watched her as she collapsed on the couch, tears running down her cheeks. He turned to Talebreza and said in a low voice. "Ruhi's marrying me in spite of my money, in spite of my past, you moron. She is a wonderful, kind person. You don't deserve an heir. You're a petty little man. The world is a better place now that your bloodline is ending."

Talebreza's face reddened. "I have spoken," he repeated.

Adams wanted to throttle the man. Just before he lost control, he felt Ruhi by his side. He turned to face her and looked into her sad, but determined eyes. She took his hand, held it to her cheek and smiled through her tears. "I have no idea why my father has done this. But I do know that I love you." She lifted up her face and kissed him on the lips. "Brice Adams, will you do me the honor of marrying me in a civil ceremony before God and this collection of good people, permission or no permission?"

Talebreza nearly shouted. "You cannot do this. It is in violation of your Bahá'í laws."

Ruhi said, "We will be married this day in a civil ceremony in accordance with the laws of the State of California. We no longer need nor seek your approval." She looked him straight in the eyes. "I have spoken."

Adams nearly cheered. "That's my girl, Ruhi," he said as he hugged her. "Well done, my love." He kissed her again. Then he faced her father. "And when this ceremony is over, Professor, I want your ass out of here!"

Talebreza's face colored and he glared at Adams.

"No, my darling," said Ruhi. "Please let him stay."

"What, after what he just tried to do?"

"He is still my father." She turned to Talebreza. "You may stay as a guest as long as you follow the rules of common courtesy as prescribed by your Holy Book."

***

After the ceremony and the luncheon, Brice Adams stood under an oak tree, champagne glass in hand, and surveyed the scene. Knots of guests still lingered on the patio, and the orchestra played on. He couldn't be prouder of his Ruhi. He hated bullies, a trait he had managed to pass along to his boys. Even his sons seemed to have gained a modicum of grudging respect for Ruhi from the day's events. Maybe that would translate into some affection, but he wasn't hopeful.

Tom Callahan approached and put his hand on Adams' shoulder. "Nice recovery, pal."

"That little bastard was planning this all along." Brice shook his head in disbelief. "He flew all this way just to hurt her one more time."

"No doubt," said Tom. "What will you do with him now?"

Adams took a deep breath. "Ruhi has already said he can stay here as long as he wants."

"What? Even after this?"

"Yep," said Adams as he took another sip. "She's as stubborn as he is."

"Man, you've got one hell of a woman. Give her an A plus for forgiveness. Colleen would have just put him in a hospital."

Brice laughed. "I've heard that she's done that once or twice."

47

Tom nodded. "Three times and still counting. Colleen is a typical Aussie, pretty friendly and easy to get along with most times. But when she starts to get agitated, she goes straight to nuclear."

Brice touched his glass to Tom's. "You, sir, also have one hell of a woman."

They sipped their champagne. Tom asked, "So where are you going for the honeymoon?"

"All over the United States," said Adams with a grin.

"What do you mean?"

"Ruhi wants to get her multiengine commercial license. We're going to take the King Air and fly all over the country. We'll start out having breakfast in Los Angeles, lunch in Austin, dinner in Tallahassee and then see every major city and airport in the country for two weeks. Anywhere she wants to fly into. Our version of the famous "hundred dollar hamburger" that we pilots are so fond of. She'll log some serious flying time."

"You're going to instruct your wife?" Tom shook his head, "That's a recipe for disaster, my friend. Even one so willing to forgive as Ruhi."

"Hold on, Tom," protested Adams. "You taught Colleen aikido didn't you? She's a black belt, as I remember."

"I *helped* instruct her. I assisted. There's a big difference."

Brice shrugged. "I offered to take another instructor along but she said 'No way, this is our honeymoon.'"

"So, she's really into flying, eh?"

"She joined the Ninety-Nines."

"The international women's pilot's organization? No kidding! Great support group."

"Yep. Shades of Amelia Earhart and all that. Ruhi's met female pilots from all over the world already. One of the instructors from the local chapter owns a Cessna 206 and has been helping Ruhi get instrument time." He took a sip of his champagne. "Now I get to take over."

"Okay," Tom laughed and again touched his glass to Adams'. "After tomorrow, I'll be sitting at my desk back in Washington, complete with my shiny-new King Air type rating and begging for flying time. If you need me as an extra instructor—or marriage counselor—just swing by or call. Any time."

Chapter Eight

Gila National Wilderness Area
Southwestern New Mexico

"Peter Hinneman" and his partner, "Gordon Osborne" a.k.a Joachim Bosche, drove the rented SUV slowly, jolting over the winding mountain road as the almost-indistinct track led them along a ridge. It was hot down in the plains—over one hundred two degrees Fahrenheit—he had mentally translated that into Celsius where it had really meant something. Hinneman stopped the car, their third rental in two weeks, and scanned the horizon. Mountain silhouettes lay in all directions. In the distance, thunderheads swelled above the peaks; to the east, a few rain clouds trailed streaks of virga.

The men had worked their way across New Mexico, logging lots of miles, changing their vehicle twice to avoid detection. Hinneman had been to remote places in his career, but nothing had prepared him for the vastness of land like this. New Mexico was full of emptiness, pockmarked with small towns and a few cities. The big skies, wide horizons and empty landscape were not what these Europeans were used to. Every night, rolling thunder split the quiet and lightning streaked the sky. Hinneman had yet to see any precipitation. Dry—he'd never been anywhere so dry. The state bird, after all, was a roadrunner, a desert bird that fed on lizards and rattlesnakes. He had learned from early morning television that the roadrunner was apparently much more intelligent than the wily coyote.

What the New Mexicans called rivers wouldn't even qualify as streams in Germany. Creeks maybe. And the so-called Rio Grande was a joke. The first time he had driven across the river in the southern part of the state, he had been staggered. The view from the bridge showed more mudflats than river, mere thin sluices of dirty, sluggish water masquerading as a proper river. Hinneman simply did not like the state, probably, he conceded to himself, because he hated America so much that he had no room in his heart to appreciate any kind of beauty he might find there. For all his international sophistication, at heart Hinneman was a true German who still preferred the familiar cool, lush valleys surrounding his beloved Dresden in eastern Saxony.

From his pre-mission study, he knew that while some of New Mexico was desert, more than a quarter of the state was forest and woodlands. The Gila National Forest, where he was now, had the occasional small creek and a few springs and supported a surprising amount of vegetation—scattered alpine meadows, pines, piñon, ponderosa, and even aspen and sycamore groves. All were suffering the effects of the recent drought due to *La Niña*. Forest Service signs proclaimed the fire danger "extreme" which, of course, was exactly why he was here.

He drove up the tortuous narrow road into a valley. Cumulonimbus clouds lurked in the north. Menacing, towering monsters unlike anything he had seen in Europe. No lightning yet but he knew it would come, perfect cover for his set fires. He checked his GPS. They had climbed to nearly eight thousand feet above sea level with a drop of maybe a thousand feet to the barren country below. Empty land stretched as far as he could see. Off in the distance to the southwest, stood a phalanx of mountains that jutted into the plains. In the mountains, the feeling was different. He was used to mountains—he was a skier. In his mind, mountains were special, even rough, dry mountains such as these. And, after all, the mountains were where the Jew, Moses, had climbed to talk to the non-existent god—a useful myth—but it explained why Hinneman felt better in the mountains.

Closer, only a couple dirt tracks scarred the land, no other signs of humans. He looked at the map, then outside. There it was, their destination—an arroyo that snaked further up and into the tree covered mountain.

51

"This is the place," he said, pointing up the hillside while handing over the map. "And that ravine is our target."

Osborne studied the map, looked up the ravine, then back to the map. A former Stasi secret police operative, Osborne was thoroughly professional, but Hinneman thought of him as an urbanite, not comfortable in this rural setting. Wallerein had sent him on this mission because Osborne had international operational experience, unusual for an East German secret policeman. He had been part of the Stasi team that sabotaged the Sandoz chemical factory in Switzerland in November 1986. The attack had been ordered by the KGB to create a diversion from the Chernobyl disaster and to take international pressure off the Soviets. It was a major success. The chemical spill had turned the Rhine red and wiped out miles of marine life in the river. Stasi records recovered by the West Germans in 1990 fingered Osborne's participation in this action, forcing him to flee the country to join Wallerein.

Osborne shoved the map into its case. "Nice work. *Los geht's*—let's do it."

He jumped from the car and started unloading the tools of their new trade: axes, chain saws, gasoline containers, and starter flares. They shouldered their packs, grabbed chain saws, and hiked up the ravine. At just over six feet two inches tall and almost two hundred pounds, Osborne carried his burden with ease as he led them up the slope and through the rough terrain to a slit in the ravine.

"Excellent choice," said Osborne, stopping to catch his breath. "This is perfect."

It was perfect. Lots of standing dead trees ravaged by beetles. Good sources of fuel. Hinneman looked up at the sun. Also perfect. Between eleven and three o'clock was the hottest part of the day, lowest in humidity. Best of all, the location was hard to spot, remote and shielded from the eyes of the authorities so the fire would have a good start before being noticed and give them time to escape.

Hinneman smiled at the compliment. "Take the left fork."

Osborne gave a thumbs up, and the men continued upward another three hundred yards. Conditions here were even better than Hinneman had hoped. The ravine narrowed, forming a natural venturi which would funnel and speed air into the fire, feeding and forcing it into the trees. Hinneman could feel the wind eddies swirling around him. The men dropped their packs, tied bandanas over their faces and began to cut the dry brush methodically to stack around a clump of dead ponderosa pines. It was hot and dusty work. On the other hand, it was easier than pulling off an urban assassination.

Setting good fires was trickier than he had expected. Their first two had self-extinguished prematurely. The next five made the nine o'clock news. Several thousand acres were consumed by flames and twelve houses near the forest destroyed. New Mexicans were worried and demanding more support from the federal government.

That was gratifying.

Hinneman understood the emotional power of fire. His family had been incinerated during the February 1945 firebombing of Dresden by the British and American air forces. His parents, both teenaged Hitler Youth, had survived because they were in a camp outside the city. The firestorm had consumed all his relatives, their houses and possessions, as well as some fifteen square miles of the city and tens of thousands of their fellow countrymen.

He was about to unleash Hell's fury on New Mexico, which gave him much pleasure. This particular fire was placed to burn a large swath of the sixty thousand square mile watershed to the Gila River, a major tributary to the Colorado River. Not to mention incinerating the town of Reserve, the county seat of Catron County, the largest county in New Mexico. "Environmental terrorism" was what Wallerein called it. He had multiple teams like Hinneman's scattered across the western states to start this opening phase of his attack on the United States. Hinneman didn't care what it was called as long as it horrified Americans, preferably while roasting as many as possible. He wanted people dead, assets consumed, lives wrecked, and the government humiliated.

He was ready to move up north and set fire to the thicker, higher-altitude forests. His next target would be in the Cibola National Forest in western New Mexico, designed to imperil Interstate 40, one of the main east-west commercial arteries of the United States. Then he could move on to the watershed for the city of Los Alamos, located in the Santa Fe

National Forest to the west of the city, a special mission for Herr Wallerein. That would bring Hinneman great personal satisfaction. Los Alamos was the birthplace of the American atomic bomb, a city built in the wilderness with the sole purpose of creating bombs for aircraft to drop on defenseless cities. If the conditions were right, he might be able to burn down the entire *gottverdammt* city and military complex. Wallerein had been quite specific with instructions for that fire. Hinneman was determined to exceed even Wallerein's expectations for Los Alamos.

Hinneman signaled Osborne that the brush piles were large enough. The men put down their chain saws and reached for their gas cans. Working quickly, they splashed the piles with gasoline, then carefully placed some burning flares.

Boom!

The fire exploded. Blue-black smoke swirled around, choking them. The flames surged through the brush. A river of fire raced up the bone-dry dead trees.

Suddenly, the wind increased. Flames blew back into Osborne's face. Blinded, he dropped his gas can. Tripped over the chain saws.

Fire reached for him. He kicked out and rolled backwards. Flames engulfed the equipment. The gas can exploded, spraying burning fuel everywhere. Osborne screamed as he slapped at his flaming clothes. Hinneman grabbed a shovel and lashed Osborne with dirt again and again.

Flames out, Osborne collapsed and lay still. Both men were breathing hard from this near disaster. Hinneman pulled Osborne to his feet. Osborne bent over, still shaken, filthy, and pockmarked with small burns. He looked up at Hinneman and nodded his thanks.

Abandoning the still burning chain saws, the men threw tools into their packs, and jogged down the ravine, slipping and stumbling in their haste to escape. Breathless, they reached the SUV, heaved the gear inside and sped down the mountain without a backwards glance.

Chapter Nine

Callahan Residence
Georgetown, Washington, D.C.

Tom Callahan finished changing Mikey's diaper and placed him in his Snugli child carrier, facing outward the way Mikey liked it. The six-month-old baby smiled at his daddy, then cheerfully threw up on Tom's shoes. Tom sighed, wiped the baby's face, then his shoes, and went back to the business of setting up today's meeting. He swore to himself in frustration as he rooted through the kitchen drawers. The house was still in the grip of moving-in chaos, and he couldn't find the bloody wine bottle openers. Discarded boxes were neatly stacked in the back yard, art work leaned against empty walls, containers filled the garage. Slowly, the household was taking shape but not fast enough for Tom.

Colleen's decision to live in Georgetown had been exactly right for the family. Georgetown, one of the oldest cities in America, proved to be a fascinating blend of old town houses and upscale residential areas, sprinkled with fabulous restaurants and fine shopping. Neither adult had a long commute, the neighborhood was perfect for Mikey, and the house was spectacular. A white two-story colonial built about 1875 by a descendant of Thomas Jefferson, it stood on two manicured acres dotted with towering mature oak trees. Sunlight cascaded through enormous windows into large rooms with high ceilings and hardwood floors. The spacious flagstone patio was shaded and overlooked a singles tennis court.

"Great house, Colleen," said Porter, as they emerged into the kitchen after the house tour, along with Jacob Borenstein and Robbie Robinson. "It's gorgeous. Love what you've done with it."

"It's not quite furnished yet," said Tom. "There's still some money in the bank that she hasn't spent."

Colleen smiled as she gave Tom the two-fingered Australian salute, along with the missing bottle opener. "Thank you, dear, for your total support."

"I don't know, Colleen," said Porter, eying the baby carrier. "It looks to me like you've got him pretty well trained in the baby department."

"Yeah, Tom," said Robbie. "I'm no expert on kids, but don't you have Mikey on backwards? Shouldn't he be facing in instead of out?"

Tom laughed. "Mikey won't let me hold him facing the regular way. He cries unless he's facing out. I guess he spent so much time stored away indoors in the Bolivian orphanage that now he just wants to see everything."

Colleen said, "Porter, why don't you pick some wine from the wine cellar? We have some splendid Bolivian reds, plus some excellent Australians."

"Your wish is all I could hope for, O Gorgeous One," Porter said and vanished into the walk-in wine cellar.

"Jacob," said Tom, "I didn't know if you were kosher or not so we've limited ourselves to beef and lamb, no pork."

"No problem, my friend. When I was a kid we had a kosher kitchen. Then my dad went on an overnight business trip by train. He went into the dining car for breakfast and smelled something really good and asked the waiter to bring him whatever that other guy was having. He loved it, then asked what it was. 'Ham and eggs,' says the waiter. That was the end of our kosher kitchen." Jacob chuckled. "Now I can even eat a cheeseburger guilt-free."

Porter re-emerged with several bottles of wine. He and Tom went through the proper wine opening rituals. Tom poured, then ushered the group outside.

The weather was patio-perfect, low humidity—always a rarity in Washington—and a light breeze. Tom put Mikey in his portable crib.

Colleen made sure a bottle of juice was within his reach and sat next to Tom.

"Okay," Tom said, settling back in his chair, "it's time we got this meeting under way. As you know, the president originally assigned me to the White House to work nuclear, chemical, and biological weapon proliferation issues with the Russians and our NATO allies. That changed once Wallerein rose from the dead. Finding him is now my number one priority. This comes directly from the president.

"It's better for us to meet here instead of the White House, quietly and away from prying eyes. Here we can gripe and whine." He held his glass up to the light. "And wine some more, decant as it were."

He took a sip. "Please drink up. Then my jokes will seem more amusing."

"Not really, Tommy," said Colleen. Everybody laughed.

"Thank you, darlin'," he said with a chuckle. "Okay, proliferation issues are my cover in the White House, and I will work them as I can fit them in. While the general public is not aware of it, Kurt Wallerein attacked the United States so he is, at least unofficially, Public Enemy Number One. We need to work this as hard as we can. At the same time, we simply must keep the number of people in the loop to a minimum. That means the five of us, plus whomever you have to bring in for the investigations."

He looked around the group. "Any questions so far?"

There were none. He looked to Colleen. "Anything you want to add, sweetheart?"

She shook her head and smiled. "You're doing just fine, luv."

Tom turned back to the group. "We should plan on meeting here every Sunday afternoon to exchange information. Jacob, we'll need to get the house swept for bugs each week before the meeting."

Jacob nodded. "No problem."

Tom nodded to Colleen. "Sweetheart, you're up."

She put down her glass and looked around at the group. "I start next week at the World Bank, officially as a liaison with the U.S. Treasury Department, working international financial issues. I will be seeking out unusual money transfers and laundering. Terrorism floats on a sea of money—unregulated, unreported, untaxed. We know that Wallerein's organization is short on funds. The main reason he started his operation in South America was to gain funding through drug cartels. Now that he's lost that opportunity, he'll have to look for other sources.

"Alternative choice number one will be the Mid-East. We know that Wallerein has contacts there, and we know that there is a lot of money available. One of the interesting things about the oil-producing countries is that we know where every barrel of their oil goes but not their money—how much goes to terrorists, how much is squirreled away in secret bank accounts, how much is spent on weapons, none of these. That's what I hope to discover."

The men nodded as they digested her statements.

Tom said, "Robbie, anything on your radar scope over at the CIA? You and your little sub-group…, what are they called?"

"The Immaculate Degenerates," laughed Robbie. "More accurately, they're the Immaculate Degenerates, not me. I'm not so immaculate." He sipped his wine as he thought about the answer. "During your little confrontation with Kurt Wallerein in Bolivia, we discovered that the *Hauptverwaltung Aufklärung* had buried some American turncoats—traitors—what we now call 'moles,' deep inside our government. At least two of them had transferred their allegiance to Wallerein. That is indisputable.

"What we don't know is—are there any more moles in our government and, if so, who's running them now that the HVA is no more? Wallerein? The Russians?"

"That's where the FBI comes in, Tom," said Jacob. "Recruiting idealistic college students into espionage is not a new concept. The KGB was quite good at it. Probably the most famous example is the "Cambridge Five" which included Kim Philby, Donald Maclean, Guy Burgess and Anthony Blunt in the 1930s. Later, the HVA proved to be particularly adept at recruiting American students off European college campuses.

"I have agents quietly working to identify all those who attended university or graduate school overseas during the '70s and '80s, then entered government service. Because of the elapsed time from

58

recruitment to today, any moles would be fairly senior officials now so we're starting with résumés for the top levels of government, the GS-15s and the Senior Executive Service. We'll check out their careers for unusual or early promotions and plum assignments."

"Add me to that list," said Tom. "I spent a semester at the French Air Force Academy my junior year."

"I know. And you are the youngest colonel in the Air Force and quite highly-placed in the White House. You're scheduled for interrogation and a polygraph test tomorrow," dead-panned Jacob.

Tom felt his face flush as the words sank in. Damn, he'd have to rearrange his schedule. What a pain. Then Jacob smiled and Porter and Robbie laughed out loud.

"Gotcha, Tom."

"So this is an example of what passes for humor at the J. Edgar Hoover Building?" Tom turned to Colleen. "Don't send him an invitation for next Sunday."

Everybody laughed.

He looked over at Nelson. "Porter, I want you to keep digging. You are the least visible of all of us. With your knowledge of German and Russian and your journalist background, you have contacts that we cannot ever have. Work them hard. You can also function as a courier of sorts between us."

Tom looked at each of them. "Remember, our government has been penetrated. How badly, we don't know. And may never know. I cannot emphasize enough that we need to keep the number of people working this to an absolute minimum."

He took another sip of his wine. "So, after that cheerful note, anybody have anything to add, anything unusual happening around the country that you're looking at?"

"We have a bunch of wildfires in New Mexico and Colorado, even some small ones in Idaho as well," said Jacob.

"Why is the FBI interested in fires?" asked Robbie.

"They're on federal land and look like arson. In fact, there's a big one west of Albuquerque. Nasty son-of-a-bitch, too."

"I read about those," said Tom. "When I was flying F-15s in Arizona, we'd often head up to Nevada and even Idaho to different bombing ranges. If we saw a fire in the national forests, we'd radio it in with the coordinates. The Forest Service guys always took those reports seriously."

"These fires are starting to tax our resources, and it's still pretty early in the fire season, too," said Jacob. "Could be a long hot summer in the West."

"Anything else?" Tom asked the group.

"To summarize," said Jacob, "there is nothing to make us think that Wallerein is on the march right now or that we have anything to worry about, is that what I'm hearing?"

"We always have something to worry about, buddy," said Tom.

"Maybe he's hiding in a hole someplace," said Porter.

"Yeah," said Tom, "an unmarked grave in the Libyan desert would be nice."

Chapter Ten

Mayor's Office, Town Hall
Montero, New Mexico

"You're killing the real estate market!" said J. David Hunt II.

"No, I'm recognizing that our forest is unhealthy," replied Javier Hernandez, the muscular, twenty-nine-year-old mayor of Montero, a small town located just off I-40 in the western part of the state between Grants and Gallup. "If we don't thin it, Mother Nature will—either by disease or fire. It's as simple as that. We have to act now to prevent a disaster."

"Your ordinance to require thinning of our town forests, Hernandez, is unneeded and unwanted."

"Oh, it's unwanted all right—thanks to you stirring up opposition with your business cronies. But unneeded? Not true."

Javi knew that this debate represented a clash of cultures as well as a clash of interests. He was a sixth generation New Mexican with jet black hair, olive colored skin, and a square jaw that marked him as a blend of Hispanic and Native American. He was the youngest mayor in the state and took his job seriously. J. David Hunt II was a fifty-ish architect and land developer Texas transplant with offices in Dallas and Albuquerque, trying to cash in on the recent real estate boom.

Javi tried to reason with the angry man facing him. "David, we've been dealing with difficult issues ever since I've been mayor. We fixed up Main Street. Attracted new businesses. Montero is a New Mexican success story. That's why you moved here, what attracted you. Opportunities.

"Look outside, David," Javi said, and gestured towards his office window. "Most of those trees surrounding Montero are in the national forest. The Forest Service hasn't thinned them for decades and has suppressed fires as well. Now forests all over the state are choked with standing dead trees and undergrowth. To top it off, New Mexico is locked in a multi-year drought cycle. All those things are bad by themselves. Together they could lead to disaster."

"Listen to Mr. Doom-and-Gloom! Do you know what talk like that does to property values?"

"Do you know what forest fires do to peoples' lives?" Javi shot back.

"You pass that damned ordinance, and I'll sue your ass!"

Javi locked eyes with Hunt. "Give it your best shot, Davey-boy! Public safety and welfare take precedence over your making more money."

Javi sat back in his beat-up leather chair and listened to Hunt's hand-tooled cowboy boots stomp down the corridor. He shifted his eyes out the window towards the nearby mountains looming over his town and despaired. Rain. We need rain. This drought was of epic proportions, the driest spring season on record. The spring rains had not come, and the early summer sun had brought mind-melting heat. Then the winds rose up and extracted whatever remaining moisture there was. The landscape withered, the forest became almost Mojave-dry and brittle. The streams that normally flowed down the slopes were mere trickles in some places, non-existent in others. The town reservoir, Lake Montero, normally brimming with fish and surrounded by happy tourists in RVs and tents, was half empty and surrounded by slopes of scruffy dried mud. His town was barely hanging on.

Just months after returning from a two-year hitch with the active duty National Guard, Javi had been elected to the Town Council in a wild and raucous campaign. When the previous mayor and the other three councilors were impeached and sent to jail for extortion, bribery, and election fraud, Javi found himself the last man standing and stepped into the mayor's office. He loved the challenge of re-invigorating his town. He even loved being teased by his cousins and life-long friends, of whom there were many in Montero. They often called him *Señor Alcalde*,

Spanish for Mr. Mayor. Older Latinos sometimes called him Don Javier, a term of respect he savored. Fortunately, his wife, Juanita, and their two young sons kept him grounded and his hat size stable. Dealing with greedy carpetbaggers like J. David Hunt II was one of the few drawbacks to the job.

The emergency radio sitting behind his desk squawked. "Fire chief to mayor. Over."

"This is the mayor. Go ahead, Willy."

"Javi, we have a smoke plume. I need you out by the lake."

Damn! The very thought of fire terrified Javi. Given the current conditions, the smallest of fires could explode into a monumental catastrophe in mere hours. Guillermo "Willy" Lujan was one of Javi's oldest friends. He wouldn't call if it weren't serious.

"Javi, do you copy?"

"On my way, amigo."

He raced down the hallway, burst out the front doors and leapt into his battered Ford F-150. Tires spinning, spewing gravel on the winding, rutted dirt roads, Javi worked his way towards Lake Montero, the main source of drinking water for his town. As he crested the first ridge, he could see the eighteen-wheelers on I-40 off to the north.

He turned to the southwest and caught sight of the smoke plume carried by the wind, flowing across the mountains like a malignant cancer. Sweet Jesus! Where had that come from? Upwind from his precious town in the worst possible location. It was still distant but a fire anywhere in New Mexico was too close for Javi. There hadn't been any lightning storms for days. Probably started by a careless hunter or camper. *Damn city dwellers!*

He turned his truck and aimed at the western edge of Lake Montero, tucked in the rolling hills studded with piñon and juniper, and soon spotted his chief's truck next to a green pickup with U.S. Forestry Service markings. Good for Willy, thought Javi. We're going to need all the help we can get.

Javi climbed out of his truck, embraced his friend and shook hands with the forester. "Looks bad, Javi," said Willy. "It's just so goddamn dry and hot." He gestured towards the plume. "The fire is moving this way pretty fast. You know that country as well as I do. We can't get in there any time soon."

Javi nodded. In his mind's eye, he could see the tortuous canyons, boulder fields, rocky outcroppings and the vegetation, sometimes packed so dense that a man on horseback couldn't push through. This was going to be a bitch.

The forester said, "We're going to have to assume the worst here, Mayor. I've already sent word up my chain of command. They'll set up an operations center and get us an incident commander."

Javi studied the plume in despair, then turned back to the men. "Activate our emergency plan, Willy. I'll get the county manager on the horn. He'll get the bureaucrats hopping in Santa Fe."

Albuquerque, New Mexico

Azim Muhammad was lost. Sprawling, decentralized Albuquerque was normally easy to negotiate. Tonight, construction workers had re-routed rush hour traffic, and Azim had to deviate from his planned route. He maneuvered the battered Nissan pizza delivery pickup through the evening traffic and tried to quiet his nerves. Azim was a well-educated, upper middle-class Saudi from a medium-sized city and completely disoriented by the overwhelming complexity of this western city. So fast, so different, so foreign. His training had failed to prepare him for this assault on his senses. The call for the mission had been too sudden. Not enough time to calculate options and plan for contingencies.

Today was meant to be the beginning of the end. To advance the Cause. To bring fear and despair to the people of the Great Satan. To show them Allah's fury and His reach through His chosen ones, His enlightened ones. Today, he, Azim Muhammad, chosen, educated and trained by the great imam, Bashir, would complete his appointed task and bring death and fear to America. *Allahu Akbar*.

Azim means "Defender." What could be more right than this mission, defending the Faith? Azim had come of age as the genocide against Bosnian Muslims had unfolded in Eastern Europe, which had led to his becoming disconnected from mainstream Saudi society. He was recruited by a pan-Islamic group whose ideology sought the creation of an Islamic caliphate ruled by Sharia law. The message of the group was sophisticated, subtle, and seductive. Recruits were led to believe that, by joining, they could achieve something great with their lives and were promised a piece of Utopia on earth. For young men like Azim, there were also those seventy-two virgins awaiting him in Paradise.

Right now, there were so many cars, so many lights, so many enormous billboards that blocked Azim's vision and distracted his thoughts. Everything going so fast! And all those police. This area was more complex than his planned route. His progress towards the target was painfully slow. Tail lights erupted in the twilight as impatient drivers rode their brakes. Horns blared. All around him were bars and strip joints, the distractions and temptations of the corrupt western lifestyle. He tried to concentrate on the mission, to block out the noise. He was God's instrument and must stay focused on the exalted task with which he had been entrusted. Azim had spent a year in Córdoba studying Spanish, waiting and training before being assigned to this mission. Nothing must be allowed to stop him.

Córdoba, the home of some of the world's most glorious Moorish architecture. The accursed Spanish infidels desecrated the *Mezquita*, the Great Mosque of Córdoba, by inserting a Gothic Church into the very heart of the mosque after the *Reconquista* in 1236. The Holy Muslim building had been renamed the *Catedral de Nuestra Señora de la Asunción*, where unbelievers had trampled the sacred stones for almost eight hundred years. Imam Bashir promised this year would be the last.

Azim inched the truck forward with the traffic, trying to get through the last few orange cones and across the intersection. He glanced down into the cab. Next to the pizza box he was supposed to be delivering, lay the satchel that held his Glock pistol and the bomb that he was to use to complete his mission. He suppressed his nervous excitement. Only a few more minutes.

There! An opening in the traffic flow. Azim gunned the engine, and the battered truck sped through the intersection. Tires squealed as Azim wrenched the pickup around the turn and rolled out on a direct path toward the Kirtland Air Force Base gate. The traffic was suddenly light.

Adrenaline shot through his system, and he wiped his sweaty hands on his jeans.

A siren behind him shattered his inner calm. Flashing red lights erupted in his rear-view mirror.

Azim bit back a curse and pulled over. He had violated the first rule for a Soldier of God: Do not attract attention. He breathed a prayer. Surely Allah would not bring him so close only to have him stopped by a mere policeman. He slowed his breathing and forced himself to review his cover story. Spaniard, complete with false passport to cover his dark features. And a false Spanish accent to cover his Saudi accent. The imam had said that Americans were so provincial they wouldn't even know the difference.

He watched in his mirror as the policeman approached the pickup. The officer had skin darker than Azim's. His nametag said Montoya.

"May I see some identification, please?"

Azim answered in broken English, and stressed his Spanish accent. "*Por favor, señor*, I no unnerstand."

Officer Montoya smiled and switched to Spanish, "*Señor, sus papeles, por favor.*"

Azim's heart sank as he fumbled with his wallet. He briefly considered shooting the policeman, but he could be seen by the Kirtland gate guard. He would have to brazen this out and ask for Allah's help. He handed over his driver's license and the truck papers.

"*De dónde es usted, Señor de la Mancha?*"

Azim played dumb using mixed English and Spanish. He had been coached to act like an immigrant struggling with the new language. He was suddenly not confident enough in his Spanish to try to fool a native speaker.

Montoya leaned closer and continued in Spanish. "I stopped you because you were speeding through the intersection. I don't know the laws in Spain, *señor*, but in America, it is forbidden."

"*Por favor, señor*," Azim pointed to the sign attached to his roof. "I have delivery and *mi jefe* angry if I late."

"Where is your delivery?"

Azim blurted an address on Kirtland.

"They don't allow deliveries from off-base vendors."

Azim pointed to a sticker on the windscreen. Montoya shone his flashlight on it and shrugged.

"I am not going to ask where you got a base sticker. I'm going to let you have that discussion with the gate guard. He can decide." He handed back the papers. "Keep your speed down."

Azim drove to the Kirtland gate, checking over his shoulder at the police car back on the side of the road. He turned into the gate. The guard took one look at the base decal and waved him through. Azim's confidence soared. He knew the road layout perfectly from his study. Kirtland Air Force Base was massive, sprawling over almost 53,000 acres. It hosted the Air Force Weapons Laboratory, Phillips Lab, various nuclear sites, and a long list of classified programs. More important to Azim, it was home to the 150th Fighter Wing, the infamous "Tacos" who were deployed overseas with their F-16s at this moment. Azim was deeply offended that the American military had once again blighted the soil of Saudi Arabia and still had its people occupying The Prophet's chosen homeland.

Killing the family of the Tacos' commander was his mission.

Officer Montoya watched the rusty Nissan drive through the gate unchallenged. He mentally reviewed the conversation. Something just didn't fit…, the accent just wasn't right…. *Shouldn't have let that one go*, he thought.

Annoyed with himself, he pulled out his cell phone and called a bowling buddy, a master sergeant, a "Skycop" in the Kirtland Air Force Base Security Police. "Hey, Garcia, how they hangin'?"

"Hiya, Montoya. Listen, man, I'm on the duty desk. Make it quick."

"I just stopped a dude who said he was delivering a pizza to Base Housing."

"So?"

"Just a hunch, Garcia…, beat-up 1988 Nissan pickup with New Mexico plates… driver had an international driver's license and a Spanish passport…. It seemed so…, I don't know, maybe 'orchestrated' is the word. And as for this kid's Spanish, well, let's just say it wasn't *Castellano*. You know, proper Spanish."

"Did you run the plates?"

"Yeah. Nothing out of the ordinary, but still feels strange."

"Okay, I'll have my guys check it out… an old Nissan truck, you said?" A pause. "Hold on, Montoya. Let me call the house. I'll put it on speakerphone for you."

Another pause. "Mrs. Johnston, this is Master Sergeant Garcia of the security police. Sorry to bother you, ma'am, but did you order an off-base pizza delivery?"

"No, we didn't."

"No?"

A pause. "Is there a problem, Sergeant?"

"Tell me, ma'am, is your husband the commander of the Tacos?"

"Yes, he's deployed to Saudi Arabia."

"Mrs. Johnston, not to alarm you, but we have a suspicious vehicle heading to your house right now. I need you to get out of your house! Grab your kids and go out the back door…. NOW! My men are on the way…. GO!"

"All units, all units…"

Montoya sped through the gate, lights flashing. He slowed in the passing lane, window down. "Lock it down!" he shouted at the surprised gate guard. "Lock the base down!"

He hit the siren and accelerated down the main street, searching for any security police vehicle. Spotting one, he rolled in behind and tried to keep up.

Azim followed the programmed route to the target. He guided the car slowly, determined not to attract any more attention. His world narrowed to the precise turns he was to make. First left, then right, right again. He had memorized turns without reading the signs. Houses and trees passed by almost unnoticed. His breathing slowed. He could feel his heart thumping, blood pulsing. Soon he would be in Paradise alongside the other martyrs of the Cause. His senses were all focused towards carrying out his glorious mission.

A short burst of acceleration brought him to his last turn. He slowed as he spotted the target's home. He brought the car to a halt directly in front of the park that faced the house.

Azim stared at the home, a one-story brick building, separated from the neighbor's house by a brick wall that ran along the driveway. The hated American flag floated on a pole protruding from the covered front porch. That same flag was now being flown over Azim's homeland by the man whose family Azim intended to kill. It filled him with anger and strengthened his resolve. He twisted in the seat, and reached for his satchel. He armed the bomb, then carefully slung the satchel over his shoulder. He stepped out of the car, picked up the pizza, and turned towards the house.

The shrieking of many sirens broke through his concentration. Several white and blue cars accelerated towards him. Another car, lights flashing, crashed across the park directly at him.

Azim drew his pistol. He took aim at the nearest car and fired three quick shots. He missed. All the cars slid to a stop. Men jumped out, screaming for him to halt.

He covered the distance to the house in five quick strides. He shot the lock and smashed through the door, staggering into the living room. He ran through the house, searching for victims. Empty. He was too late.

Despairing, Azim reached into the satchel and pressed the detonator button.

***

Officer Montoya walked across the front lawn. The Skycops had brought in portable light units to illuminate the crime scene. The neighborhood looked like a battlefield. Devastation was everywhere. Spears of furniture stuck up from the wreckage. Pictures, clothing, children's toys were strewn across three yards. A veil of dust smothered the remains of a family's entire history. Armed base security police staked out the yard and kept the neighbors at bay.

One of the sky cops spotted Montoya. He turned and shouted, "Captain, here he is." He motioned Montoya towards a large man issuing orders to the other cops.

Montoya waited until the captain finished speaking.

The captain turned and gave Montoya the once over. "You called this in?"

Montoya nodded. "Yes, sir."

The Captain offered his hand. "Good work, Montoya. Really good police work."

"Thank you, Captain… permission to ask a question, sir?"

The Captain nodded.

"What the hell was he trying to do?"

Chapter Eleven

White House
10:00 AM

Tom Callahan sat at his desk and sighed as he reached into his in-box for yet another official report. The White House was the pinnacle of American government with a paperwork mountain to match. Not for the first time, he blessed the unnamed instructor at the Academy who had mandated a speed reading class doolie year. His thought process was interrupted by the chirp of the phone. He answered: "Callahan."

"Colonel Callahan, the Chief of Staff would like to see you, now."

"On the way."

When Tom entered the newly refurbished office, he found Mark Freiberg seated on one of the two cream-colored couches, deep in conversation with Isabella Orsini, one of the president's plethora of Special Assistants. Orsini was dressed in what Tom had come to think of as the Washington power suit for women on the rise: a severe dark suit, white blouse, and red paisley power scarf. Her autocratic manner—and hair style—had inspired the staff to refer to her as "Cruella de Vil."

"Have a seat, Tom," said Freiberg, motioning to a chair. "I thought this would be a good time for you to update me about the Wallerein situation."

Tom glanced at Orsini. "With respect, Mr. Freiberg, shouldn't we be alone? Didn't the president decide to keep the number of people involved in this to an absolute minimum for security reasons?"

"It's been undecided, Colonel," snapped Orsini. "Are you questioning the Chief of Staff?"

Tom looked at her, decided not to say the words that popped into his mind, then back to Freiberg. "Is this really what you want, sir?"

"Doctor Orsini has been around Washington for years in different capacities, Tom," said Freiberg. "She knows how to get things done. You, quite frankly, are a neophyte. Quite capable, of course, but politically naïve."

Tom had to agree with the "politically naïve" part, though Freiberg made it sound like a character flaw. But to assume that letting more and more people in on what had to be the biggest secret in this administration would somehow not compromise security, now that was naïve. Politicians talk for a living. Nothing is too secret for them to reserve comment. The bigger the secret, the juicier it was, not to mention more newsworthy. That also applied to their staffs.

Now in her mid-forties, Isabella Orsini had been a professor of international affairs at a small West Coast college, a political organizer, a Senate staffer, and a researcher at the left-leaning Center for Policy Studies in Washington. In Tom's limited exposure to Washington politics, he had noticed that some staffers wore the rank of their boss and were ruthless in using it to promote their own agendas. Isabella was one of those.

Nevertheless, he proceeded to give a concise summary of how the team was proceeding.

"What do you think is the connection between the bombing in Albuquerque and Wallerein?" asked Freiberg.

"We don't know. We are merely suspicious. Jacob Borenstein has a team en route to go through the remains of the building and to try to identify the now very dead terrorist. The only possible link so far is that we've never had any suicide bombings like this in the United States. Wallerein is not bound by the past; he strives for originality. And he loves killing."

"Pretty thin, Colonel," said Orsini.

He matched her stare. "Yes, it is, Isabella." That earned him another frosty look.

"You're right, Tom," said Freiberg. "The president wants you to go to Albuquerque. Today. Look around for yourself. If there is any—and I mean any, possibility of Wallerein's involvement, I want to know."

"Yes, sir. On the way."

***

As Tom entered his office area, he spoke to Ellen Mora, his office manager. "Ellen, please book me on the next flight to Albuquerque. Leave the return date open."

"I'm on it, boss," she said, "And you have messages from Jacob Borenstein and a Colonel Adams."

Tom settled in at his desk. He put off the requisite call to Colleen, reached for the phone, and hit the speed dial. "Jacob, what's up?"

"Background checks are moving along, albeit slowly, since I'm limited in the number of agents I can use."

"We have another name for the list. Isabella Orsini."

"Orsini? Just great. I've never liked that woman. She seems genetically incapable of humility and has an extremely pliant moral compass. Not even sure how she fits in this administration. Appointed as a favor to somebody, no doubt." Borenstein paused. "I thought it had been decided that we were keeping personnel to a minimum."

"It has been 'undecided' then, as Isabella so eloquently stated to me a few minutes ago."

"Damn!" Tom could almost hear Borenstein shaking his head in disgust. "I assume you protested?"

"Of course. And the net result of my heart-felt plea is that we have another person on board. See how influential I am?"

"Don't underestimate your influence, Tom. You are an advisor to the president, one that he trusts. That is a very big deal in this town. It gives you as much clout as you can handle no matter what your official rank might be. That you are in charge of this is probably unprecedented. Hang in there, buddy."

"I'm not convinced, but will listen to your sage advice. Anyhow, the president wants me to go to Albuquerque this afternoon to look into the bombing."

"Okay, I'll let my people know to expect you. You'll see a lot of smoke out there, by the way."

"More forest fires?"

"There's a new one west of Albuquerque, a real bastard. Apparently another arson." He paused. "That's not for public consumption. Until we get a better handle on this, we want to keep the word 'arson' out of the papers."

"Maybe I'll look into that fire as well."

Tom hung up and dialed Brice Adams.

"Adams."

"Brice, it's Tom Callahan."

"Tom, old buddy, old pal. When are you going to unstrap yourself from that desk of yours and go flying with us?"

Tom laughed. "Be careful what you ask for, Brice. Where are you now?"

"Chicago. Ruhi's still logging instrument approaches all over the country."

"How about meeting me in Albuquerque tonight?"

"Deal. We can get in some mountain flying tomorrow. Where will you be staying?"

"At the Airport Sheraton. Dinner's on me."

"Okay. I'll have my assistant book us into the most expensive restaurant in the city."

That task out of the way, Tom took a deep breath and dialed his wife's direct number at the World Bank. To be truthful, he had grown used to the family scene. He liked being daddy. He liked staying home. For the first time in his life, he wasn't looking forward to a business trip. He shook his head, disgusted. "Thomas, my boy, you have finally been domesticated," he murmured.

Colleen answered on the first ring. "Dr. Callahan."

"Hi, Sweetheart. This is your loving husband."

"Who never calls me during business hours unless something is amiss."

Jeez. Am I that predictable? Another deep breath. "I have to go to Albuquerque."

A pause. "When?"

Surprised at the mild response, Tom said, "Today. This afternoon." Another pause. No explosion. This was going better than expected. "I'm sorry," he blurted, surprising himself, and no doubt Colleen as well.

He had a thought. "Where's Mikey?"

"The au pair took him to Rock Creek Park."

"How about I swing by there to see him, then dash home to pack? Could you meet me at the airport? We can have a late lunch before my flight."

***

As Tom drove into his garage an hour later, he was surprised to see Colleen's car already there. Sandalwood incense burned on a side table as he entered the living room. He plopped his briefcase on a chair and stretched. Turning, he watched Colleen glide out of the bedroom dressed in a mid-thigh, exquisite, embroidered silk robe. Purchased in Hong Kong, it was possibly the most expensive single article of clothing that she owned, which was saying something. She paused, her silhouette posed against the living room windows. She was starkers underneath. This was nice.

She smiled as she swayed closer to give him a soft, welcoming kiss on the lips.

Tom glanced up at the antique grandfather clock, a gift from his mother. "I can't believe that I'm saying this, but now is not a good time, Colleen."

"I've packed your suitcase, Tommy. And you're already checked in. Your ticket and boarding passes are on the kitchen counter, courtesy of the White House courier." She slid her arms around his neck. "I decided that you could stay here a bit longer and eat lunch by yourself on the plane." She kissed him again, softly. "It's been a long time, lover."

"What are you talking about? As I remember, and I always remember, it's only been three days."

"Like I said, a long time," she grinned. "And you're heading off on a business trip without me. Who knows how long you'll be gone."

Tom smiled as he ran his hands over her silky backside. "I remember another business trip, a very long flight to Sydney, where we spent some time together in the first-class lavatory."

She giggled. "If I keep swelling up like this, pretty soon I won't be able to fit into a lavatory by myself, much less with you."

"Colleen, your body hasn't changed one centimeter in any direction."

"Oh, yes it has. Your eyesight is faulty, sir. However," she said as she tugged on his tie to lead him towards their bedroom, "you are very gallant to say so. Let me show you my appreciation."

Chapter Twelve

Montero, New Mexico

Javi trudged down Main Street towards his office. Sunlight filtering through the smoke-filled eastern sky turned the landscape an eerie yellowish tinge. He was amazed at the amount of air activity this morning, a mere three days after the start of the fire. Helicopters churned through the haze delivering supplies, people, and water drops. He saw small, fixed-wing aircraft flying in lazy orbits to the east and west. Javi hoped that they were positioning to lead in the aerial tanker support he had been pushing for. He reckoned that there were now more aircraft over his little town than in the traffic pattern at the Albuquerque International Sunport.

From behind the western ridge, a massive plume of smoke boiled up to the heavens, marking the location of the main fire. The sky was dark with ash that fell on the town and covered the streets like the champagne powder New Mexico ski resorts loved to advertise. Here and there burning embers smoldered. Town firefighters patrolled the almost-deserted streets to spray fires in the town proper. During his deployments with the National Guard, Javi had seen huge tropical thunderstorms that towered over the landscape. This smoke plume cloud was bigger and worse. It reminded him of pictures of the volcanic ash plume at Mount St. Helens years ago.

One of Javi's first acts as mayor had been to drag the New Mexico Secretary of Tourism to the town to show off the area. Decades of demolition-by-neglect had reduced the town's main street to a strip of dilapidated building skeletons. All the charms of an old fashioned western town had faded to non-existence. With the Secretary's enthusiastic help, Javi negotiated with the byzantine New Mexico bureaucracy in Santa Fe to obtain state funding, which led to federal tax credits and a jumble of assorted other grants designed to reinvigorate the downtown area.

Javi overcame the inertia and no-change mind-set of the locals and organized "Paint the Town Days," declared the downtown area as a historic arts and cultural center to qualify for additional grants, forced passage of a purchase of a right-of-way along the river, and created a river walk along the downtown area. Now, Montero had a main street where streams of tourists flowed through lively businesses, municipal parks, and more than the normal complement of Mexican restaurants. Just when the fruits of all that labor were about to kick in, all the color and sparks of life in his town were being drowned by that goddamned ash.

He turned to look west towards the two narrow canyons that would dump the fire from the national forest into the small Montero Valley if it weren't stopped. To his left, he could see the steep overlook where the local charter high school kids had proudly etched the letters MVHS for Montero Valley High School.

His muscles tensed and anger surged through him. He shook his fist at the smoke plume. "We'll beat you yet, you son-of-a-bitch!"

His radio came to life. "Town Manager to Mayor."

"This is the Mayor. Go ahead."

"Javi, we need you—we need you now! At the command center for the morning briefing."

"Roger that. On my way." His manager sounded rattled. He'd have to have a chat and calm him down. The townspeople were already on edge. Panic in a radio call could be contagious to anyone with a scanner. Javi glared again at the plume before heading to the Command Center located a mile north of town.

The mood in the Center was all business, no time for fear, anger, or doubt. The Incident Commander, a large man from Clovis surrounded by his command staff, appeared calm and confident. Reports poured in from all directions. All of them bad news. NASA satellite photos tacked to the walls showed the extent of the scorched earth. A colossal gray smoke and ash trail stretched across the state right over Santa Fe and into Oklahoma.

Decisions had to be made. Javi found himself involved in commanding from the rear rather than leading in the field, something he didn't like very much. It was better to be with his troops with a weapon than sitting in the background telling people what to do by radio—even if his weapon was only a shovel.

The IC planted himself by the conference table and waved his audience of decision makers closer. The meeting began with a weather briefing and a summary by the intelligence officer. Questions answered, the IC took over. "Good morning," he said in a steady voice. "Thanks for all your efforts so far. It's going to get tougher from here on in, guys. You already know that the fire refused to lay down last night." He pointed to the table map. "It grew over here. Then the wind direction changed again, effectively doubling the size of the front. The fire is now moving aggressively towards the lake and the town. If the winds pick up, it'll be coming fast, right down our throat here in Montero. I've directed fire lines be cut here and here." Everyone leaned in to check the locations. Most made notes on their own maps. "Make no mistake about it, people. This thing could turn into a monster in a flash. Be careful, and use your brains."

The IC motioned towards the Air Ops guy. "The good news right now is that weather has improved enough for aerial tanker support. The planes are flying out of Albuquerque and Winslow, so we should have some quick turn-arounds. Stay close to your radios for coordination in your areas." He paused and took the time to make eye contact with everyone around the table. "The bad news is that the whole country has moved up from a Level Two condition to a Level Three. Meaning that the U.S. has serious fires all over. We are now competing with other states for national resources."

"Boss, we need more people here," said the sector chief from Silver City. "Right now!"

The IC nodded. "In the last week, there has been a rash of fires in Southern California, surprising for this time of year. I have a buddy in

79

San Bernardino County I could usually depend on for help. Not this year–he's staying local, and his priority with the Feds is higher than ours simply because he has more people and structures in danger than we have.

"However, we have more crews coming in from other parts of New Mexico. Two from Questa, two from Peñasco, one of the Snowball teams from Taos. Should be rolling in around noon." The IC cleared his throat. "One more thing. Early this morning, a bulldozer driver, Jorge Medina, got himself stuck in an arroyo. The fire turned on him. He didn't make it out."

That got everybody's attention. Most knew Medina, a long-time firefighter from Questa. He was one of them, and safety was something they all lived by, depended on. Fires were relentless and unpredictable. Tired people made mistakes, and stress was the ultimate fatigue generator, no matter how tough, fit, smart, or experienced a person was. The image of Medina flashed in Javi's mind, a man in agony, screaming as the flames reached for him, roasting his body until his skin split, his blood boiled, and his organs burst. Javi shuddered. Maybe being burned to death wasn't the worst way to die, but in his opinion, it ranked up in the top two or three. The cadre around the table, all veterans of multiple fires, became subdued and angry at the same time, a hush punctuated with quiet curses.

The IC turned to Javi. "Mayor, the incident happened in the sector where your guys have their pumper trucks. How about if I put you on a helicopter? You can get out in the field and reassure your people. Let them know that you—and the rest of us—care about them. Don't let them think it was their fault."

Javi took a deep breath. "I've had to do this kind of thing before. I lost one of my guys last summer."

"I know." The big man touched Javi's shoulder. "Get out there with your troops. Then hustle back here and help us beat this bastard."

***

Javi made his way towards the parking lot that functioned as a temporary helipad. Around him were mounds of equipment, boxes of water and food, bundles of axes, pulaskis and shovels, spare trucks, bulldozers, four wheelers, and all the logistical requirements for this massive effort. He had to jump aside twice for speeding forklifts loading trucks for delivery to fire crews. The sights and sounds made him feel like he was on yet another overseas deployment with the Guard. This was a war of sorts, fighting for the survival of his town, and the logistical effort could make or break the campaign.

At the parking lot waited the sturdy Bell 205, blade turning. The crew chief escorted Javi into the aircraft. Over the roar of the turbine, he shouted, "Have you ever been on a helicopter before, sir?"

"Are you kidding? In the Guard, I was Air Assault qualified. We used Blackhawks like taxicabs."

"Excellent, sir. Here's your flight vest. Put that on, and I'll get you into the monkey harness before we lift off."

Javi grabbed the vest and snugged it tight. He stood with his hands on his head while the crew chief wrapped the harness on him, which would allow him to move about the cabin, even stand in the door for a better view. He sat, fastened his seatbelt, and put on the headset.

The crew chief took his seat, strapped in and adjusted his headset. He keyed the intercom. "Testing, testing, you with us, Mayor? How do you read?"

"Five by five," Javi said and gave the chief a thumbs up.

The crew chief said, "All strapped in and ready to go, pilot."

"Roger that. Pull pitch."

Javi felt the chopper go light in the skids and rise to a three-foot hover. With a touch of the cyclic, the pilot dipped the nose, pulled the collective, and they were flying. The pilot flew an orbit over the town as a courtesy to his VIP passenger. The view dropped his heart straight into his gut. Main Street was deserted, and the entire downtown area coated with ash, devoid of almost all color. The river was clogged with debris, and sluggish gray water spilled out into the town soccer fields. He pounded his knee. "Shit, shit, shit!"

The pilot rolled out on a heading along the face of the main fire. The helicopter bounced and wallowed in the hot, gusty air. Javi tugged on his safety strap to check it and leaned out of the sliding door for a better view through the haze. The desecrated earth slipped beneath them. In the distance behind the fire, the ravaged landscape was dead, covered with that goddamned gray ash, littered with debris.

The forest was a snarl of smoke, hundreds of small blazes devouring a prime piece of New Mexico. He spotted a charred fire truck, burnt down to the rims. He prayed that the crew had escaped with their lives. He could see fire crews humping chain saws and backpack pumps, trying to mop up spot fires along his route. Flames burned their way down the flanks of the mountains, lapping at tourist cabins in the foothills. Blackened trunks resembling gigantic matchsticks that yesterday were living, breathing ponderosas leaned drunkenly in the mid-morning air, now sulfur-colored through the ash and smoke. Along the fire line, waves of flames raced through the forest. The smoke plume writhed and roiled across the landscape. Death and destruction joined hands to roar inexorably towards his town, home to the Hernandez family since before the Civil War. He could barely breathe at the sight and extent of the damage. The NASA photos couldn't compare with what he saw with his own eyes. The fire was closer to Montero than he had allowed himself to believe. The acrid smoke filled his lungs and burned his eyes as the aircraft fought its way through the fire-fanned turbulent currents. He swore as only a soldier can, using words dredged from all three languages he could speak.

The helicopter circled the small meadow that was designated Landing Zone Loon by virtue of a wind sock stuck in the ground off to one side. Willy Lujan stood next to his truck, waiting to take him to the crew.

As the skids touched ground, Javi jumped out of the chopper. He ducked under the blade as the pilot powered away. Willy, sweat stained and filthy, looked like he'd been up all night.

The men embraced. Willy handed Javi a wet bandana. "Here, put this on over your face. Otherwise, you'll be useless in minutes." They trotted to Willy's truck. "Let me give you a quick rundown on our sector before we meet with the guys," said Lujan. He laid a map out on the hood. "It's turning into a monster, big and growing fast, *amigo*." He pointed to an area outlined in red. "Here's where we think it started. It blew down this draw and spread out. It's in the ponderosas now. The stuff we had scheduled to thin next year." He looked up at Javi and shrugged. "There won't be anything left to thin."

Javi produced his own map and laid it over Willy's. "This is where the IC cut some fire breaks last night, amigo. The flames jumped this line not ten minutes ago."

Willy studied the creased document and nodded. "Yeah, I heard it on the radio. The wind's picked up, gathered speed and created its own firestorm. It's crowned in the ponderosas. We've got flames almost a hundred feet high in some of these areas, bro. If the fire pops over this ridge here," he pointed, "it'll take out our watershed. Then we'll be well and truly screwed." He paused, pain etched on his grimy face. "It's just happening so goddamn fast. Thank God for the aircraft water drops. They might save our town."

Javi winced as a pang of despair lanced through him. "Willy, I hate to tell you this. Just as I left, the IC got a phone call from the National Interagency Fire Center. The nation is upped to a Level Three. More fires in Colorado and California. They may have to shift the aircraft to those sites."

"Goddamn it!" Willy slammed his helmet on the ground. "They're going to sacrifice Montero? We can't win here without those planes!"

Javi clamped his hand on his friend's shoulder. "You know the rules, bro. You taught them to me! Assets get shifted according to population centers."

"Those bastards! Just because we're a fly-over state! Not enough voters! Not worthy!" Willy stormed off, screaming like a wounded animal. "Goddamned bureaucrats!

Javi ran after him, grabbed his arm and yanked him around. "Where the hell are you going!"

"Let me go!" Willy lashed out. He threw a punch at Javi's head.

Javi ducked the blow. And another, which infuriated Willy.

Willy feinted a left, then swung again.

Javi let the punch slide off his shoulder, then shot a hammer-fist into Willy's nose. He crashed straight back and down, arms flailing.

Javi stood over his fallen friend, breathing hard. "Listen to me, Chief Lujan. You have your orders. You have a job to do. If you can't or won't get your shit together and rally your men, I'll find a lieutenant who will."

Willy stared up, bleary eyes defiant. He shook his head, and took several deep breaths. He clenched and unclenched his fists, then wiped a trickle of blood off his face.

"You know, *Señor Alcalde*, you can be one tough son-of-a-bitch."

Javi reached down to pull Willy to his feet. "I had to grow up tough, *amigo*. You used to beat me up twice a week in fifth grade."

"That was before you grew so much in seventh."

The men looked at each other, then embraced.

Willy murmured, "Sorry, Javi. I nearly lost it there."

'Don't worry about it, bro. Never happened."

They separated, embarrassed.

Willy clicked his chest-mounted radio and called in his crew. In minutes, two more trucks pulled up and eight grimy and exhausted men piled out. Javi knew each and every one. He had gone to school with several. One had joined the Guard with him. Another was a cousin. He embraced and said a few words to each man.

Out of the corner of his eye he caught movement. A herd of cattle burst out of the trees heading right for them. Wild-eyed and terrified, the cattle stampeded across the small meadow, bellowing and throwing up dust clouds.

"Look out!" shouted Javi. The men jumped behind their trucks and let the fear-crazed animals flow around the vehicles. Three steers crashed into Willy's truck, rocking it up on two wheels. Then the herd vanished into the forest, bellowing in fear as they crashed through the undergrowth.

"Jesus Christ!" breathed Javi.

Willy laughed. "That's the second time. Last year we were almost trampled by a band of wild horses in Arizona."

Javi chuckled in relief. "I don't suppose you saw the brands on those cows?"

"Not a chance. I was too busy trying to crawl under my truck just like you, Oh Fearless Leader."

They laughed again, still shaken.

Javier called out, "Gather 'round, *chicos*." He cleared his throat. "The Incident Commander—and I—are going to order a mandatory evacuation of the town and the surrounding areas."

Willy objected. "Javi, you know our people out there are not going to want to leave their homes."

"We've been through this, bro. Most people have left already. All the rest have to do is stand in their front yards to see what's happening. They'll leave. They're smart."

"Yeah, but they're stubborn, too. Can you imagine old man Molina ever leaving his place? Or Patricio Torres? Their families have been here for two hundred years. They won't leave even if you put a gun to their head."

"Well, do everything you can short of that. The sheriff's deputies and state cops'll be helping. You need to convince the people to at least be ready to go to the evacuation points." He dug into his backpack and produced a sheaf of papers. "These are release forms stating they refused to evacuate. Give the stubborn bastards one of these. Tell them to list their next-of-kin and phone numbers so we know who to contact to come get their bodies after the fire. That'll get their attention."

Willy flashed a smile. "I say again, *amigo*, you are one tough s.o.b." His radio erupted with his call sign. "Montero Two, this is Command. Do you know the twenty for Montero One?"

Willy unclipped his mic and handed it to Javi.

"Command, this is Montero One."

"Javi, I need you back here *muy pronto, amigo!*"

"Roger that. Where's the chopper?"

"The chopper crashed. Crew's dead. Get a truck and get out of there, now!"

"Wilco. On my way." Javi cursed the fire again and again.

He handed the mic back to Willy. "You heard him. I'm outta here. I need your truck."

85

Willy nodded. "Okay, but be careful, amigo. The fire's building." He pulled out his map again. The two men studied it for the best route back. Javi watched his friend scribe the safest—and slowest—way through the national forest back to town.

"Go this way, Javi. Here and here. This area is a mess. Do *not* go there."

Javi knew the terrain, the trails, the arroyos, the creek beds. He had camped and hunted these mountains almost all his life. He was going to have to take shortcuts, ones that both he and Willy knew were treacherous. This run would not be easy. Even with the anticipated short cuts it would be well over an hour before he was in Montero, if he didn't get lost in the smoke—a big if. But he had to do it. His town was in danger. More importantly, his people were in danger, most of whom he had known all his life. He was responsible for their safety, whether they liked it or not.

"Do you want me to go with you?"

Javi stared into his friend's concerned face and shook his head. "Your place is here with your troops."

"Okay, *jefe*. But only if you take a fire shelter kit, a chain saw, and emergency water. There's a radio and a spare battery in the cab." Willy motioned to one of the firefighters who climbed into the truck bed, lifted out a chainsaw and gas can and handed it down to another firefighter. They refueled the saw, started it, then shut it down and put it into the Chief's truck. Two other men tossed in a fire kit and another man put two-liter bottles of water on the front seat.

Javi embraced each of the men, climbed into the truck, jammed the map under his leg, and set off on a trail that corkscrewed its way down the mountainside. He reached a fork at the bottom and stopped to consult the map. Willy had marked the right fork. Javi shook his head. Too slow. He gunned the engine and turned left, back towards the leading edge of the fire—and Montero.

Chapter Thirteen

Albuquerque International Airport
9:00 AM

As the hotel limo drove across the general aviation parking ramp, Tom Callahan sat in the front seat and stared down the Kirtland AFB flight line. Air National Guard F-16s, HH-53 Pave Low combat search and rescue helicopters, even a couple T-37s from Sheppard AFB. He sighed.

"What's the matter, Tom?" said Brice Adams with a laugh. "Miss the smell of jet fuel? Rather be back in the Air Force instead of flying a desk in Washington?"

"Yes and yes." Tom turned to face Brice and Ruhi. "You know that from the White House, you can't see any smokestacks or evidence of any industry in the entire city. The only thing produced in that city is politics."

"No, the only thing produced in Washington is bullshit, pure and simple," said Brice. "Politicians spend their time selling bullshit to each other and to the American people."

Tom laughed. "Oh my, and I thought that I was the cynical one."

As the limo slid under the general aviation terminal porte-cochere, a slender man wearing a dark suit, white shirt, and an aura of self-confidence stepped out of the building and opened the limo door.

"Morning, Colonel Callahan," he said with a smile.

"Good morning, Jerry," said Tom as he offered his hand. Tom turned to his companions. "This is Special Agent Jerry Bennett of the

FBI's Albuquerque Field Office. Yesterday, he took me through the bombing at Kirtland and showed me the wreckage.

"Any words of wisdom from Jacob this morning?" asked Tom as the group made its way to the Flight Planning area.

"Deputy Director Borenstein says to cooperate with you in any way I can."

"Great. So tell Brice and Ruhi what we're going to look over today."

Bennett escorted the group into the flight planning room. He gestured to the ubiquitous giant wall map. "Here we are in Albuquerque." He pointed to the central dot on the map. "The state of New Mexico is big, fifth largest in fact, but with less than two million people. Very agricultural, very rural." He slid his finger down the center of the map. "The Rio Grande bisects the state north to south and leaves a swath of green, mostly irrigated farmland. There's lots of wide open space. Down south and west of here is open desert with forests at the higher elevations. To the east are the plains and some big cattle ranches, plus extensive oil and gas fields. Up north are the Sangre de Cristo Mountains covered by two or three large national forests. Much of the north-central part of the state looks and feels like Colorado."

Bennett turned back to his audience. "Other than the unexplained bombing at Kirtland, the issue right now is that the fire season has only just started and we've already exceeded our normal annual number of forest fires. And they're spread all over the map. For example, here, here, here, and here. Some, if not most, were probably the result of arson."

"Any proof?" asked Brice.

Bennett shook his head, then turned back to the map. "The fire down here in the Gila took out the town of Reserve and killed ten people. It was certainly arson. We found burned chain saws and accelerants nearby in the national forest. We have two witnesses who saw a black SUV in the area just before the fire was reported. The recent Montero fire was almost certainly arson. Earlier in the week, someone set a fire out east. Two more reports of a black SUV nearby."

"But why?" asked Ruhi.

"We don't know, ma'am. These fires appear to be well orchestrated and executed here in New Mexico. Whether there is a connection between these fires and those in California and the rest of the country remains to be seen."

He pointed to the map again. "Here's Las Vegas, New Mexico out to the northeast of Albuquerque about seventy-five air miles. This area's where the grass fire raged. It forced the evacuation of several small towns and parts of Las Vegas."

"Montero is over here, almost due west of Albuquerque out near the western border of the state, on the other side of the Sangre de Cristo Mountains."

Tom said, "There should be a 'Notice To Airmen' from the FAA restricting the area." He knew the air over and around Montero would be swarming with firefighting aircraft and media helicopters. Mid-air collisions did not fit into his plans that day.

Bennett handed Tom a computer printout. "Here's a copy of the NOTAM, Colonel. We have overfly permission and I have a list of frequencies to monitor. We just need to let the air traffic control center know our plans. Right now, much of the aerial tanker support in the western part of the country is committed to this fire and one in Idaho, so this airspace is pretty active."

Brice Adams studied the map. "Pretty lumpy terrain around Montero," he mused. "Must be a hard fire to fight."

"Interestingly, all these fires have begun in remote places, not randomly as in past years," said Bennett. "This one in Montero is particularly bad. Have a look at these satellite photos taken eight hours apart."

"Looks like the fire is heading towards the watershed around the town reservoir," said Brice, handing the pictures to Tom. "That's really bad news."

"Why is that a factor, sir?" asked Bennett.

"Healthy watersheds are absolutely crucial, Jerry. Basically, a watershed is the beginnings of a river. My family's farms and my vineyard are totally dependent on a reliable water supply. So is every city on the planet. If a watershed is destroyed—in this case, burned—you have no vegetation to help capture the water runoff from rains and melting snow. So the next rainy season after a fire, instead of a slow filtering of the rain, you have flash floods and soil erosion. Toxic ash and fire debris fills reservoirs and lakes, rivers die, the whole enchilada. It's a major catastrophe, both for the nearby towns and lots of folks downstream."

Tom handed the photos back to Bennett. "This fire is worse than bad. Those smoke trails go all the way to Kansas." He turned back to the map and pointed north. "After Montero, I thought we'd take a look up around Taos where my mother lives. We'll need to land and get some gas by then, so I'll show you the town and even take you to my favorite Taos restaurant and spring for the finest green chile cheeseburgers in New Mexico."

"I thought you grew up overseas," said Ruhi.

"I did. After my father was shot down in Vietnam, we lived in Spain and Italy for a time. My mother moved to Taos when I was at the Academy. My siblings graduated from Taos High School. I spent most of my leave time in New Mexico."

After the pilots completed their flight planning, Ruhi disappeared in the direction of the bathrooms.

"What's up with Ruhi?" asked Tom. "She seems quiet this morning. Did you tell her this was not supposed to be a check ride?"

"She's broken-hearted," said Brice. "I called the boys last night and had a nice chat. When I tried to pass the phone to Ruhi, Will hung up." Brice's jaw tightened. "He and I will have a 'Come to Jesus' meeting when I get home."

"I don't know much about raising teenagers, but I do know they're pretty volatile, even on their good days."

"It's one thing to not want to accept Ruhi as a stepmother. It's quite another to be flagrantly hostile and rude. He's seventeen years old and he knows better."

Brice put his hand on Tom's shoulder. "And since we're voicing our opinions about family, let me say what I wanted to say last night but didn't since Ruhi was there. In my far from humble opinion, the reason Colleen is so concerned about her body changes is that she was a professional model. When I was attending the Stanford Business School, I met and dated two supermodels. They could tell me their measurements

90

down to the micron level and their weight to the gram. It was astonishing."

"So you're saying that because Colleen was a model, she would fall into that category?"

Brice nodded. "Not just a model, she probably would have blossomed into a world class model if she hadn't stumbled across you."

"Thanks, buddy."

"Any time, Tom."

"I guess this little quirk of hers fits into the pickles and ice cream aspect of pregnancy."

"Yep. Always remember that crashing hormones make pregnant women the third gender of the human species."

As they made their way across the tarmac, Tom could see that Brice's aircraft was not the USAF C12 D that he was used to flying. This was a rich man's airplane—same basic Beechcraft airframe all right, but the deep carpet, burnished woods, and plush leather seats screamed money. The cockpit layout was familiar, but in typical Brice Adams style, it had all the latest electronic updates. Even the C-12s Tom flew with the Presidential Wing at Andrews Air Force Base were not fitted out as well. Tom looked out the cockpit windows and took solace in the fact that at least the Pratt and Whitney PT6A engines were exactly the same as he was used to flying.

"Well," he said," it doesn't look like much, but maybe we can wrestle this crate into the sky."

Tom reached into his flying case and found his pair of thin beige leather flying gloves. Standard issue in the Royal Air Force and Royal Australian Air Force, Tom preferred them to the USAF issue leather/Nomex blend because the leather was thinner and more sensitive. He settled into his seat and strapped in. Ruhi slid into the copilot's seat and did the same. She handed him his headset, then held up the checklist.

He nodded. Ruhi read the items, her delicate hands traveling around the cockpit touching all the right switches and knobs in the correct order. The airplane came to life. Soft classical music wafted through the air from a hidden MP-3 player. She marched them through the "Engine

Start" and "Before Taxi" checklists before checking in with ground control and obtaining taxi clearance.

Receiving takeoff clearance, Tom looked over his shoulder at Brice, then to Ruhi. Both gave him a 'thumbs up" and a smile, the secret smile of aviators about to aviate. All three loved airplanes, all three shared a common bond—the sky belonged to them, and they belonged in the sky.

Chapter Fourteen

Near Montero, New Mexico

Javier Hernandez drove his truck up to the next ridge and paused. Through the haze, he could see airplanes making run after run against the fire. His spirits rocketed up as he watched multiple passes of aircraft bombing the inferno with streamers of red retardant. It was airpower against the might of Mother Nature at her most ferocious. The only way this monster could be stopped was if they kept up a relentless assault from the air.

Javi drove along the ridge watching the fire gallop through the treetops, flames thrusting high into the sky. He spotted a faint jeep trail that led down into a canyon. He knew it connected to a larger trail if he could only manage to traverse the steep mountainside. It was impossible to judge his chances through the smoke and haze. He drank some water and soaked the bandana. Then down he went, ever closer to the fire's track, crossing over behind the flames, hot spots smoldering all around.

Animal carcasses littered the forest. In a secluded meadow, he saw a small herd of dead deer, cooked where they were dropped by the fire's super-heated air as the inferno raced by. Even through the smoke he caught the pungent smell of charred flesh and burnt hair.

As he drove the twisting, rutted trail, he gasped for breath in the hot air. His eyes stung from the smoke. The wind-whipped fire suddenly erupted to his left and showered him with embers and burning fragments.

A massive downed ponderosa pine tree blocked the trail. He slammed to a stop, grabbed the chain saw, and ripped through the smoldering hulk. Sweat dripping and nearly exhausted, he threw the chainsaw in the truck bed, then grabbed the cable from his bumper winch and wrestled it around the tree. He backed his truck to drag the trunk away enough to squeeze by, unhooked the cable and slalomed down the trail.

He was driving into a crucible. The furnace-like heat sucked his energy. The truck cab sweltered. He was soaked in perspiration. His hands were scorched from the smoldering tree. His skin glowed red from the heat. The intensity and violence of the wildfire threatened to overwhelm him. It hurt too much. He screamed and cursed, "Goddamn it, Javi! Don't give in, you weak dick! People need you!"

He grabbed his water bottle and sucked it dry, then doused the bandana, his head and shoulders with the second.

The thick smoke eddied around him. Flames raced to cut him off. Smoke enveloped him. Where was the road? He crashed through a copse of small aspens and bulldozed down a gauntlet of juniper saplings.

There! Nearly concealed in the haze was a logging road. He punched the accelerator and willed the truck through a mass of orange flames. Sparks flew past the truck and bounced off his windshield. He shot through another narrow curve, desperate to outpace the voracious inferno. More embers rained down on the truck, clattering on the roof like shrapnel.

He raced ahead to a familiar logging road that now looked like a superhighway. Javi spun the wheel left and climbed the twisting high road through the forest's unforgiving terrain.

The smoke was thinner now. He glanced at his watch. Nearly two hours had passed since he started. The last ridge blocked his view towards Montero, but he could see the fire as it raced eastward. He searched the sky. Nothing. Where were the planes? Where were the goddamned planes!

Despairing, he plunged down the mountainside into the canyon and climbed the final slope. He crested the ridge and skidded to a halt at the town overlook. He grabbed the binoculars, leapt from the truck and stood between the letters of the high school sign.

To the west and northwest, a massive, towering plume of smoke. At its base the flames raced towards Montero. The monster fire was ready to pounce on the town.

The hills west of town were also a mass of flames. The narrow canyons leading into the business district sluiced flames, ember showers and super-heated air into the heart of Montero. The town center was a death trap. He watched buildings light up in a flash. Flames leapt from building to building, accelerating down Main Street. The roof of the old school collapsed, then the stone walls.

His beautiful town was being consumed right before his eyes, the lifeblood of dozens of families. A solid wall of fire moved inexorably towards the structures, then enveloped and devoured them like some giant organism sucking the life from its victims and moving on, leaving a series of shattered carcasses behind as it searched out more helpless prey.

Two figures burst out of the hardware store, and sprinted towards the distant highway. The second person tried to leap over some burning debris but stumbled. His clothes burst into flames.

"Drop and roll," screamed Javi into the wind. "Drop and roll!"

The victim lurched forward and collapsed, then rolled over, thrashing in agony. His torture continued for what seemed an eternity. Then it stopped abruptly.

Nothing was left alive in Montero.

Javi's heart shattered in agony. He dropped the binoculars, fell to his knees, then all fours and retched. He spit out the sour bile. His stomach contorted and knotted again and again until his abdomen was sore. Exhausted, he rolled over on his back, panting and tried to gather himself.

He struggled to his feet. No human being could be this tired, he thought. He stumbled to his truck, slid behind the wheel and tried his radio. Nothing. He swore. Of course it doesn't work. He found the spare battery under the seat, then tried again.

"Command, this is Montero One. Come in."

A pause, then an excited voice barked, "Montero One, this is Command. What's your twenty?"

"I'm on the overlook south of town. I just watched the town burn down."

"Montero One, looks like downtown is totaled, four dead so far, a couple dozen missing."

"Make that five dead. I just watched a citizen die on Main Street about ten minutes ago."

Another pause, then the voice came back, softer now. "Copy that, Montero One. Javi, we need you at the command center to help sort things out. Can you make it on your own?"

"Roger that, Command. On my way. Montero One out."

Javi slumped forward, head on the steering wheel.

He sat, breathing deeply as he searched for a handle on the moment. He sat up and grasped the wheel with both hands. "We rebuilt Montero once, damn it. We can do it again.' He slammed a fist on the wheel. "Better this time!"

He started the engine, took another look at the smoldering remains of his town, then drove slowly down the hill.

Albuquerque Airport

Tom Callahan brought the power up and began the takeoff roll. Because of Albuquerque's high altitude, the Beechcraft accelerated slower than Tom was used to from his East Coast flying, but considerably faster than in the thinner air of La Paz. Ruhi handled the co-pilot duties well, smoothly and efficiently cleaning up the aircraft and talking with Control.

They turned west towards Montero and climbed higher to avoid the aircraft congestion as well as the colossal smoke plume. Ruhi entered the required frequencies and checked in with the Southwest Coordination Center, which was responsible for the airspace around Montero. Tom felt like a voyeur, watching the activity below as the aerial tankers crisscrossed the enormous fire zone. The radio chatter, though disciplined, was nearly constant, and sometimes excited. It felt and sounded to Tom like the air war waged over Baghdad. In a sense, it was a combat zone. Fire fighters scattered in groups around the difficult terrain, the "boots on the ground" arrayed against the enemy. Sometimes fighting the fire, sometimes fighting for their lives. Instead of man against man, it was man against nature.

It was a subdued group that made a sweeping turn north towards Taos.

The flight took them over the vast semi-desert Chaco Mesa and over the green forests of the Jemez Mountains. The Valle Caldera, massive remains of a collapsed volcano, was off the right wing. The city of Los Alamos slid past. They could see where the ribbon of the Rio Grande was squeezed through narrow canyons, small farming villages scattered along its banks.

"We'll belly out to the east over Angel Fire and loop up towards the town of Red River then fly west back over Wheeler Peak to the Taos airport," said Tom. "We have to avoid the Taos Pueblo. That's a no-no. It's a World Heritage site."

He pointed out Hwy 64, the major highway crossing northern New Mexico and Hwy 38 that rounds out the northern part of the Enchanted Circle, a roughly one-hundred-mile drive through national forest connecting the towns of Taos, Questa, Red River, Eagle Nest and Angel Fire. The Red River sliced through the Sangre de Cristo Mountains where it had carved a deep canyon with steep walls. The river flowed west, side by side with Hwy 38 through the town of Red River towards Questa. They could see the shallow, rushing water glistening on the rocks as it cascaded towards the junction with the Rio Grande.

"I've fished that river hundreds of times. Nice cutthroat trout in there," said Tom.

"Is that smoke in the forest?" asked Ruhi, pointing off to the left. "It just erupted from the trees."

Tom dipped the left wing for a better look.

"Jerry, get the binoculars," Tom ordered. "That black dot down there could be the missing SUV."

Bennett scrambled forward clutching the binoculars. Ruhi pointed out the smoke.

"Got 'em, Colonel." He adjusted the focus. "Looks like two men. They're loading up to leave." He paused as he braced himself against the back of Ruhi's seat. "Son-of-a-bitch. They've got chainsaws, just like in the Gila." He paused again. "Fire's catching on, building pretty fast."

"If the wind catches that fire, it could flash up the canyon and incinerate Red River."

"Jesus, they see us!" said Bennett. "They're jumping into their car. No question, they set that fire."

"The arsonists!" said Brice.

"Same style of operation," Tom said. "Jerry, use your cell phone. Alert the FBI. And Brice, get on the second VHF radio and call this into Center. Have them alert the Forest Service and the Marshall in Red."

"Tom, we haven't much fuel," said Ruhi.

Callahan looked at the gauges and did the math. Damn. She was right.

"If we leave, those guys can get away before the cavalry gets here," said Brice.

The dust trail thrown up by the big SUV was approaching the highway. Time was running out.

"If we can stop them, Colonel, we should," said Bennett.

"I'll take that as authorization from the FBI. Everybody sit down and strap in," Tom ordered. "We only have gas for one, maybe two passes, so let's get this right the first time."

Tom pointed at the highway. "See where the dirt road comes to a T-junction, Ruhi? To their left is Red River, their right is the canyon. I'm going to roll in on these guys and try to force them towards Red. If they go through the canyon, they'll be able to lose us in that maze of logging roads in the national forest. That's a lot of space to disappear into." He rolled into a turn. "Watch my airspeed, Ruhi. I'm going to drop behind the ridge so they can't see us."

The airspeed built up rapidly and the aircraft sliced down towards the mountains. *Damn. We're too high.* "I'm going to side slip this beauty to kill some altitude. Hold on, everyone."

Tom turned the yoke to the right and kicked in left rudder. The aircraft plummeted towards the mountains. "I'm going to get as low as I can. We'll pop up right in front of them and take them head on. I'm going to try to scare the bejeezus out of these guys."

98

"It's working on me," said Bennett on the intercom.

"This would be a lot easier if only I had some guns on this crate."

"You, Colonel, are a dangerous man."

The aircraft knifed through the air as Tom drove the airplane lower still. Turbulence increased, bouncing them against their straps.

Over the ridgeline, he could still see the trail of dust thrown up by the SUV. Tom only knew where the road went; the driver of the vehicle knew where he was going, yet surely he was making a run for it, afraid to hide, afraid that the "eye in the sky" would vector in the forest service or the state cops.

The ridgeline flashed underneath. Tom rolled the aircraft up on its left wing and kicked in left rudder. The nose sliced downwards. The aircraft arced into the valley directly at the oncoming SUV.

Tom could see the vehicle as it bounced along the narrow, dusty road, hurtling towards the junction. He rolled out and kept the nose pointed at the junction and accelerated, skimming the treetops.

A figure leaned out of the passenger window. He leveled a pistol at the plane. Tom had been shot at by experts; this guy had no chance of hitting a moving plane from an automobile on a bumpy road.

The two machines raced at each other. The SUV streaked underneath.

Tom soared the aircraft, turning back towards the canyon as he clawed for altitude. "Which way did they go?"

"Into the canyon," said Brice.

Damn! He swiveled his head, searching. There! "Okay, I've got a visual."

He rolled out of the turn and paralleled the highway towards the canyon. Tom watched as the SUV entered the depths of the canyon and was promptly swallowed by the granite walls.

"Well, that didn't work, damn it," he said. "But they shot at us. We know they're the bad guys."

Tom checked the fuel. Enough for one more pass. "It's going to be harder the second time. Anybody want to bail on this?"

A chorus of no's echoed on intercom.

"Okay, we're going in lower." Tom made an adjustment to course. "Ruhi, do you see the horseshoe turn up ahead?"

"Yes."

"We are going past it. Then we'll double back and drop down into the canyon to meet him head-on right there, as low as we can get. Just as he comes around the turn, boom! We'll be there in his face, gear down and landing lights on. We're going to scare him enough that he either turns around or goes off the road into the river. You're going to put down the gear and lights on my command. Got that?"

She took a deep breath. "Yes."

"Anybody see any traffic on the road?"

"Negative, Tom," said Brice. "Clear as far as I can see."

"If you do see anybody, let me know. I don't want to roll out of the turn in front of a beer truck."

Tom used the ridgeline to mask the plane from the arsonists as he raced to cut off the SUV. The dust trail of the vehicle gradually slipped behind as the sturdy Beechcraft accelerated.

Two miles past the horseshoe turn, Tom rolled up on his wing and pulled the nose around and down. The aircraft sliced into the canyon and leveled off twenty-five feet above the black, water-polished boulders littering the riverbed.

He had run this river in Cessnas during his Academy summers, one of the many dumb and dangerous things he had done in his youth when mortality and danger were mere theoretical concepts. This time was different. He had to stop these guys.

The narrow valley floor was a tight fit for the Beech. The river twisted and turned as it wound its way through the rugged canyon and between vertical granite cliffs. Tom struggled to straddle the space between the road and the river. He had to maintain maximum distance from the trees and rocky outcropping that reached up at random intervals.

He powered the plane through the choppy turbulence. A quick glance at Ruhi. Her face was pale. He was sure she was about to blow breakfast, though she appeared calm. He was used to this nap of the earth stuff. She wasn't. Too rough now to risk her swapping seats with Brice. No time.

They swept through the canyon, hurtling over the rocky river bed. Up ahead, the river disappeared around the corner. Tom gauged the rate of closure as he slid to the outside of the turn. He honked the nose around in a steep turn, standing the plane on its inside wing and rolled in on the road, wings level at less than twenty feet above the surface. The SUV was a bit further back than he had estimated, but close enough.

Tom aimed the aircraft like an arrow at the SUV.

"Ruhi, gear down! Landing lights on!"

The SUV hurtled towards them, cliff face right, river left.

Tom edged the aircraft lower still. The SUV grew in large in the windscreen. He could see the faces. The big vehicle wavered, hunting for an escape route. No chance. The driver hit the brakes. The car slewed sideways as it flashed under the plane.

"Gear up, lights off!" called Tom.

"They're in the river!" shouted Brice. "The car's on its side."

"Call it in. Maybe the marshall in Red can pick them up. Make sure you warn him that they're armed."

Tom smoothly advanced the power and climbed to a safe altitude. He reached and put his hand on Ruhi's shoulder. "You were great—"

Ruhi held up her left hand to silence him as she reached for her airsickness bag. In the rear, Tom could hear Jerry Bennett using his.

Grinning, Tom re-set throttles for max range cruise and set a course for the Taos airport.

Chapter Fifteen

Cancun International Airport,
Quintana Roo, Mexico

Kurt Wallerein's return to the New World was pleasantly uneventful. Commercial flying was always dangerous for people in his profession; even the most loutish immigration official occasionally got lucky. Transiting the Madrid airport had proven to be a simple task, and the security in Mexico was still as lax as it was on his first trip nearly a year before.

One of the busiest airports in the Caribbean, the Cancun airport served millions of tourists every year as a gateway to the *Mundo Maya*—Mayan World. Quintana Roo, located on the Yucatan peninsula, was one of a federation of thirty-one states that made up the *Estados Unidos Mexicanos* or the United States of Mexico, the official name of Mexico. Cancun airport was connected to nearly every major city in the world, important and helpful to an international terrorist who needed to lose himself in a flood of humanity. An additional advantage was avoiding the monstrosity of the Mexico City airport, jammed into the cesspool that was *El Distrito Federal*.

Wallerein loathed large cities, and there were few larger than Mexico's capital. The advantage of an urban population to disappear into was offset by a city's big, relatively well-informed police department. Wallerein preferred smaller towns. The *policía* on the Mexican Riviera had the more laid-back attitude familiar to the Caribbean lifestyle, which suited him just fine.

He was met by a battered van driven by one of his men, a Bosniak from Kosovo. The driver, nicknamed Avdo—short for Abdullah—Kulenović, was a stocky man of thirty years, and a battle-tested veteran of the Bosnia-Herzegovina and Kosovo wars. He was competent and dedicated without the ambition to challenge leadership—nearly the perfect "employee" in Wallerein's mind. Kulenović threaded their way through the mass of vehicles milling around in front of the airport arrivals area and blended in with the dozens of other battered vans driving up and down the highway between Cancun and the Belize border.

In silence, they drove south forty miles as the highway made its way down the coast. Wallerein felt the tension of the flight gradually dissipate. His leg ached from the confinement of multiple flights, though he would rather die than admit physical weakness. These operations were high risk for Wallerein, and he knew it—both to his reputation, and possibly, his life.

He breathed in the warm moist air, reveling in the humidity, one of the few positive memories from his childhood in Hamburg. He watched as they passed through numerous small villages with dogs and children playing in the highway, almost daring the tourists to hit them. Massive vacation resorts appeared at random on the beach side of the highway, surrounded by high cement fences and gated entrances.

The small city of Playa del Carmen was the perfect cover for his headquarters. Within sight of the more famous tourist island location of Cozumel, it was laid back, cosmopolitan, and full of international tourists. Playa del Carmen boasted a bustling pedestrian-friendly shopping area, Avenida Quinta or Fifth Avenue, famous for its restaurants, shops and bars.

The safe house was located in a white, three-story concrete condo complex within walking distance to the beach and the Avenida. Wallerein looked up to see several antennae on the roof. He nodded. His men had selected well. What could be more ordinary in a resort than a condo near the beach with antennae to pirate international television stations? They were hidden in plain sight, just as he had instructed.

Kulenović pulled Wallerein's bag out of the van and led him through the gardens and up the stairs. The condo occupied the entire top floor of

103

the complex. Inside, six men rose to greet them. Four were members of his extended organization, inherited from the Stasi or Abu Nidal's group. He had hand-picked them all, veterans of other operations. Good help was hard to find, and he trusted nobody except men who had shown courage in action. He looked to the senior man, Joachim Richter, and raised an eyebrow and made a circling movement with his index finger.

"The condo is swept for listening devices every day, comrade," said Richter, a tall, muscular ex-Stasi lieutenant colonel.

Wallerein nodded his approval. "Languages?"

Richter pointed to the four. "We speak Arabic, German and English." He indicated the other two, shorter and darker than his own men. "They are Mexican nationals and speak only Spanish and some English."

"We will speak English then." Wallerein addressed the men. "I am pleased to be here," he said. "And part of that good feeling comes from being with my comrades, back in the field."

A smile appeared on each man's face, as he knew it would. Wallerein glanced around the condo, full of wood and wicker furniture, bright colors, and splashy art work. Not to his taste, but he supposed that was the décor in upscale Caribbean resorts.

Richter pointed to a table loaded with refreshments. "Would you like something to eat while I brief you on our current operations in the United States?" Wallerein chose a plate of tropical fruits, several of which he had never seen before, and settled back into a chair facing the group.

Richter spent the next twenty minutes detailing the many recent successes of the organization. Then he hesitated. Wallerein sensed that something was amiss. Keeping his voice neutral, he said. "Go ahead, comrade. I am always interested when there is something that no one wants to tell me."

"The operation in Albuquerque wasn't entirely successful, sir. The bomber arrived to the house and blew it up but the family had been alerted and escaped."

Wallerein thought for moment. "It was on the television?"

Richter nodded. "We have a recording from the Albuquerque television station, comrade. The bombing at the air force base was the major story yesterday." He glanced at the wall clock. "We could watch the video now. Albuquerque news comes on live in two hours. Perhaps there will be some fresh information."

He motioned to one of the Mexicans who arranged the television and started the recording. The announcers gave a detailed summary of the carnage at the air force base. Police and eyewitnesses were interviewed and dismissed, the wreckage of the house was shown in satisfying detail. The talking heads speculated about the identity of the bomber and his motives. It was clear the authorities were clueless.

Wallerein sat a moment, knowing the men were expecting an angry explosion. He cut another piece of a papaya and chewed it slowly. He was untroubled by this apparent misfire. The bombing had not been part of his plan to attack America. It was a useful concession, a sop, to the radical Saudis in his organization who were either uncomfortable or angry with Wallerein for shooting Ali Muhammad.

"It seems that our man did not quite accomplish what we had planned." He took another bite, then gestured at the television. "Yet, here is the hysterical reaction of the Americans for all the world to see. If it is on the news in Albuquerque, it is on the news in New York and Washington as well. All over America, people know that we can reach them." He paused for effect. "Karl von Clausewitz, the great Prussian strategist, said that if we have a good plan, we need to pursue it with audacity. We have to accept that some of our efforts will fall short of our ambitions."

He stood. "Now, I will take a walk on the beach with Richter. We will watch the Albuquerque news together in two hours." He looked around for nods from each of the men. On impulse, Wallerein motioned for Kulenović to join the walk.

***

Two hours later, Wallerein and his men gathered in the great room to watch the live feed from the United States. The opening credits of the local Albuquerque station flashed on the screen. After what Wallerein thought was an interminable amount of time devoted to commercials, the lead broadcaster, a silver-haired Hispanic man with a silky voice said, "Tonight's main story is the bombing on Kirtland Air Force Base. But first, the big breaking story is a mysterious car crash near Red River. We take you there to our KOB roving reporter, Rick Tafoya. Rick, go ahead."

Wallerein frowned, crossed his arms and muttered under his breath as the image changed to a younger man framed against rocky canyon walls, a river in the background.

"This is your KOB roving reporter, Rick Tafoya, speaking to you live from the Red River canyon, just west of the town of Red River." He gestured to the river. A black SUV was being winched from the riverbed by emergency crews. The roof was caved in, metal along the visible side mangled. Water cascaded from the broken windows. "This vehicle is all that is left in what witnesses say appears to be a bizarre game of chicken between an SUV and a low flying airplane. Was the plane responsible for this SUV ending up in the river?

"One of the witnesses, Mr. Mark Cowan, from Tulia, Texas, was fishing downstream." He thrust the microphone into the face of a middle-aged man, wearing hip waders, an equipment vest, and a floppy hat adorned with hand-tied flies. "Mr. Cowan, would you describe for us what it was that you saw?"

Cowan pointed downriver. "I was around that bend, casting for trout. There's some nice browns in this river. I seen a big plane come zooming up the canyon. Real low. Real fast. I heard a crash and ran upstream. I seen the truck in the river and ran to help. Me and this other feller pulled them boys out of the wreck. They was in pretty bad shape. The driver was unconscious. The Mexican-looking one was babblin'. He weren't speakin' Mexican, though. I think it was probably A-rab."

"What did the plane look like?"

"It was white, real big, and had a funny back end."

"You mean the empennage was different."

"Now don't you go puttin' fancy words in my mouth, sonny. I said the back end of the plane was funny. It had the flat part up on top."

"How low was the plane flying?"

106

"It was lower than them treetops, I can tell you that!"

Tafoya faced the camera. "Both passengers of the SUV have been taken to Taos Holy Cross Hospital, accompanied by state police as requested by the Red River Marshall. This is Rick Tafoya, your KOB roving reporter."

The news anchor's face appeared on the screen. "Thank you, Rick. And for more on this strange incident, we send you live to our affiliate station in Taos."

The image changed to a somber looking Hispanic man standing on the airport parking area in front of a large white aircraft, roped off from the public. In the background across a wide expanse of sagebrush, loomed the Sangre de Cristo Mountains.

"This is Eric Garcia of Channel Twenty-two, Taos local television. I am standing on the tarmac at the Taos airport. The aircraft behind me is allegedly the one that was reported flying in the Red River canyon." The camera focused on a large aircraft behind the reporter. "It is a Beechcraft Super King 300, and according to the FAA, is registered to a Brice Adams of Summit, California. Adams filed a flight plan this morning from the Albuquerque Sunport. Police kept this reporter from interviewing any of the passengers of the aircraft. Meanwhile, the occupants of the SUV that was driven into the Red River are still in intensive care at Holy Cross Hospital in Taos. Both are listed in critical condition…"

The camera caught movement on the tarmac. It zoomed in on a man and an attractive long-haired woman holding hands as they emerged from the airport offices. Another man stuck his head out of the aircraft and bounded down the aircraft stairs. Wallerein leaned forward in his seat and focused on his face. It seemed familiar somehow.

Verdammte Hüerenshon! Damn son-of-a-bitch! He jumped to his feet and kicked over the coffee table, scattering plates and food. He stood, fists clenched, breathing hard, staring at the screen. "Callahan!" he roared.

He watched as the woman smiled and kissed Callahan on the cheek. Callahan clapped the other man on the shoulder and all three laughed.

Then Callahan started an exterior inspection of the aircraft as the couple climbed up the stairs and disappeared inside.

"Richter, find out who this Adams is and where he lives in California. We are going to step up our offensive."

Chapter Sixteen

Motel 8
Truckee, California
5:00 AM

Helmut Kriege heard his laptop computer chirp. He rolled out of bed and checked his e-mail account. There it was, another order from Kurt Wallerein. Kriege had worked missions for Comrade Wallerein before, mostly kidnappings mixed with a few killings. This current mission had him masquerading as a wildlife photographer while setting forest fires. Boring. Kriege wanted some action.

Kriege wasn't his real name of course, nor was he a photographer, though he carried a case full of top-of-the-line Nikons. He had been born Joachim Hartmann in Gosen, East Germany, recruited as a teenager by the *Hauptverwaltung Aufklärung*, and trained in languages and clandestine operations.

His partner, "Emilio Vasquez," asleep on the next bed, had been born Asim Guzelbey in Turkey. Wallerein often mixed nationalities on his teams. Because he had spent so much time in Libya and working in the Middle East, his organization included many Arabs. He tried to have a European paired with an Arab to help lower the team profile in European, and now American, operations. Kriege wanted a South American partner for his next mission. Any country other than Cuba. He had worked with a Cuban on his last mission, the ill-fated foray into the United States. Their food was too pungent, and they did not bathe often enough for Kriege's taste.

During this mission, Kriege had let his blond hair grow and was cultivating a three-week growth of beard. He wore outdoors attire that fit with his new persona of hiking enthusiast. Always punctilious about his appearance, he looked like a walking Cabela's catalogue, right down to his leather hiking boots which he cleaned every night.

In contrast, his Turkish partner had cut his hair and trimmed his beard in order to look less Middle Eastern and more Hispanic. As long as he refrained from speaking too much, he could pass for a Latino, unremarkable in California.

Vasquez sat up, startled by the glare of the laptop. "What does it say?"

Kriege was only a little irritated at this interruption. The good news contained in the email made his partner's presence bearable. Kreige would need a capable man for this hit. The German was tired of stopping five times a day, no matter where they were, so Vasquez could pray. He was especially tired of listening to him rant about the Great Satan and how satisfying it was to cause death and destruction to Americans.

Why Wallerein had entered into an alliance with religion-crazed fanatics was curious. Kriege assumed he was forced by political expediency and economics. Life for Kriege was pretty basic. He was a professional assassin, long past any idealism. He killed whomever and wherever Kurt Wallerein dictated. Simple enough. His HVA masters had provided him with the skills, and his current master now provided him with job opportunities. Vasquez was younger and still idealistic. *The British have a pejorative for people like him. "Wog." Three letters, one syllable. Wog. He's just a bloody wog.*

"This should be a simple ambush," said Kriege. "I've done it many times. The target is some rich American aristocrat. Something of a cowboy. Lives in northern California. He has somehow annoyed our comrade Wallerein. We are to eliminate him and anyone close to him."

"When?" asked Vasquez, eyes lighting up.

"Two, three days. That will give us time to check him out. I don't like hurry up assassinations—too many things can go wrong. *Scheisse,* too many things go wrong when operations are planned in excruciating detail." Kriege stood up. "I'll take a shower while you pray. We'll have breakfast on the road."

***

The two drove into the village of Summit at mid-afternoon. The village was typical of Northern California, prosperous stone buildings along a short tree-lined main street, crowded with cars and pedestrians bustling about. Shops, restaurants, and hotels were doing a brisk business. The importance of tourism was evident in this area of Mendocino County.

They paid cash for a room at a cheap, inconspicuous motel, then drove twenty minutes out to the Adams hacienda through the verdant, gently rolling hills of the Northern California countryside. Well-tended farms stretched in all directions as they approached the Mendocino National Forest in the mountains to the east of Summit. The two-lane road snaked through the hills, and the weather was nearly perfect. It would have been a lovely drive on a different day.

As he drove along, Kriege noticed several state police cars parked in odd positions along the way. When they approached the enormous stone arch that marked the entrance to the Adams hacienda, he was startled by a sheriff's vehicle parked in front of the locked gate. Kriege did not slow, but gave a friendly wave to the deputy in the vehicle

Moments later, he cursed and slammed his fist on the steering wheel. "I've seen enough. We can't do it the way I planned. There are too many *verdammt* police around." Kriege thought a moment. "This target is a more prominent man than our good comrade realized."

It was clear that they couldn't take the house from the front without an elaborate ruse, a project that would take several days and more people to handle it properly. They needed a new plan in a hurry.

They passed a sign pointing towards a trailhead into the national forest. That gave Kreige an idea.

He spun the wheel and headed back to town, waving again at the deputy. Kriege stopped at the local fly fishing and outdoors store just outside the main shopping area.

He found what he wanted—a large rack of maps. He picked up three or four and shook his head. To a man who had grown up in a society where maps were classified, it was incredible how casually Americans regarded them. Here, the government printed maps and made them available to anyone for a nominal charge. Fascinating. Kriege found a map of the Mendocino National Forest. He was searching the U.S. Geological Survey maps when the owner approached. "May I help you fellas?"

"Yes, thank you," said Kriege. "We're looking for some good places to hike. We were just out past this enormous ranch and saw a sign that pointed to a trailhead in the national forest. It looked interesting."

"Oh, that was probably the Adams Ranch. Big stone arch?"

Kriege nodded. "Very pretty area."

"That belongs to our local rich guy, Brice Adams. In fact, his plane flew over town less than an hour ago. He'll probably be out there with those kids of his at first light tomorrow. He always rides in the morning with his kids when he's home. They spend more time in the national forest than the rangers."

He glanced through the stack of maps and pulled one out. "Here's our local area. And here's the Adams place. It abuts the national forest."

Kriege nodded. "So they can just hike out the back of their ranch?"

"They can but usually they go on horseback. Adams rides a big black stallion." He traced along a trail. "Up to the mesa here. It's gorgeous there."

"So we can park our car at the trailhead and hike into the forest?"

"Sure. It's a national forest. The trails are marked pretty well. See, here's the one from the trailhead. Takes you up to the mesa."

Kriege nodded. This was exactly what he was hoping for. He loved the forest. This one was different from the oak forests of his youth in East Germany, but he felt at home in the woods. He could set an ambush along the trail in the morning. If that didn't work, he could set it again the next morning. According to the store owner, Adams was nearly certain to ride his horse up there sooner or later. If his sons were along, too bad for them.

They drove the short distance to their hotel. Kriege spread the maps on the small motel table. The men pored over the trails, visualizing the topography and detailing the operation. This should be an easy operation—killing unarmed targets. After two hours of discussion, Kriege fired up his computer and wrote a short message. Will deliver package tomorrow.

Operational security dictated maintaining a low profile so Kriege used the motel phone to call out for delivery pizza and Pepsi. Kriege promised himself that after this hit was over, he was going to treat himself to a beer. Better yet, a good German beer—maybe a St. Pauli Girl lager, served ice cold—and a juicy sausage. He smiled. Alcohol and pork, two things guaranteed to drive his partner into a frenzy.

Adams Hacienda
7:30 AM

Ruhi followed her stepsons into the enormous stable. Stalls lined the capacious building, and the rich aroma of horses and leather tack wafted through the early morning air. "Will, I don't think this is wise. Your father specifically said for you to keep your head down. That means stay inside."

"The horses need exercise. And so do I."

"Please, don't you think your father knows that? Your safety is more important than exercising the horses. The grooms can do that for you, and you boys can play basketball in the gym. Your father will be back this afternoon."

Will turned to face her, his face contorted with barely-controlled contempt. "Look, Ruhi, you may have seduced my father, but I don't have to like you. And I don't have to do what you say."

She watched as he saddled Brice's magnificent ebony stallion. Will was as stubborn as his father.

She reached for a bridle. "Then I must go with you."

Will slid a rifle into its saddle scabbard and handed another to his younger brother. "Hurry up, Caleb," he ordered. "Ruhi, if you're coming, you'll need a rifle. And stay close. Dad says there's another mountain lion out there." Without another word, he led his horse outside, mounted, and rode off.

With a sigh, Ruhi threw a blanket over her mare's back, then the saddle. Caleb silently moved in to help her cinch it tight. He slid a rifle into her scabbard. "He'll come around, Ruhi. He's just afraid that he'll forget our mom."

"I'm not trying to replace your mother, Caleb. I honor her memory."

"I know." He cupped his hands and gave her a boost up. "Like I said, he'll come around."

"God willing." Ruhi sighed, then set her horse on a course through the back pastures into the trees.

Will rode hard, heading through the forest up over a ridge and down through a small meadow flanked by a ravine. They rode single file as they followed the narrow trail through the trees and back out into the knee-deep grass. Ruhi brought up the rear. Both of the teenagers were superb horsemen. She marveled at their expertise. They rode as if they melded into the saddle, while she could barely stay on. She was only able to keep up through a combination of sheer determination and some intensive riding lessons she had taken after her engagement to Brice. She gradually fell behind, then spurred her horse forward to close the gap.

She glanced around to appreciate the early morning sunlight streaking across the boulder fields and the meadow, the fresh smell of the pine forest.

In the distance, she glimpsed two armed men crouched in the shadows, watching the boys. They raised their weapons.

"Will, look out!" she shouted.

Will yanked on his reins. His horse reared and spun around.

Shots rang out.

Caleb's horse screamed and went down. Will's head snapped around. He wheeled his stallion and galloped to his brother. Ignoring the shots, he grabbed Caleb's arm and pulled him up behind.

Ruhi spurred her mare and charged towards Will, placing herself between the boys and the shooters.

"Go, go!" she shouted, as she rode towards the safety of a ravine. More shots cracked overhead. The trio hurtled down the incline. Ruhi's horse stumbled. She tumbled over the mare's head and crashed down the slope. Will rode towards her. Both boys slid to the ground. Will yanked the frantic stallion down on its side. He pulled his rifle from its scabbard and threw it to Caleb, then scrambled through the brush to Ruhi's to get the other rifle. Caleb yanked Ruhi down behind her horse.

"Two men. With rifles," she said. "Why are they shooting at us?"

"They must be after our dad."

Everyone was breathing hard; Ruhi could feel her heart slamming against her ribs, and there was an ugly taste in her mouth. This was insane!

"We can't stay here," said Will. "No cover." He glanced back at the shooters. "Caleb, go that way to the trees," he ordered. "Ruhi, follow Caleb. Stay low. I'll bring up the rear."

The boys had grown up hunting this land. They moved quickly, with the deliberate movements of skilled hunters. Only now they were the hunted. Ruhi's lungs were bursting as they scrambled, slipped, and slid down the ravine, dodging downed trees and rocks. Her breath was ragged as she tried to keep her footing.

The group crouched behind a downed tree. "They don't know that we're armed. I'm going behind that rock," said Will. "Count to twenty. If they show themselves, shoot to kill."

"Are you sure?" asked Caleb, as he gasped for breath.

"Dude, they're trying to massacre us!"

"Shit!" Caleb's face was ashen and his eyes wide with fear. His hands shook as he chambered a round.

Will ducked behind a large boulder.

Ruhi glanced back. The men were running out of the trees, weapons at the ready.

Will's rifle barked once, then again. Then Caleb opened fire. One of the attackers went down, arms flung wide, rifle tumbling away. The other hesitated, then sprinted for safety behind Caleb's dead horse. Will's gun barked again. The man fell to his knees and toppled over.

Will fired twice more, one shot into each body. Then he slowly stood, rifle trained on the attackers, watching for signs of movement. He approached the bodies and nudged each with his boot, looking for life. "All clear. This one's still alive—I don't know how."

He kicked the wounded man. "Get up, you son-of-a-bitch."

"No, Will!" shouted Ruhi. "He's wounded."

"That bastard shot our horses! And tried to kill us."

Ruhi knelt beside the wounded man. Blood spattered the grass, his shirt, and his hands as he clutched his stomach and writhed in agony. He looked Middle Eastern. She spoke to him in Farsi, then Arabic. He moaned.

"Tell that son-of-a-bitch that if he tries anything, I'll shoot him right in the head," said Will. Without taking his eyes off the wounded man, he said, "Caleb, ride back to the ridge. Call the house. Tell Alonzo where we are and what happened. Tell him to call the state cops–and the rangers. I'll stay here with Ruhi."

Caleb sprinted for the remaining horse. It shied away. "Whoa, boy…, easy, boy," he said as he lunged for the reins. The horse reared and bolted towards a clump of trees, then skittered to a stop about forty yards away. Caleb trotted after it, paused at a safe distance and stalked the animal, speaking in a soft voice. He caught the reins and swung himself into the saddle.

Will shouted, "Tell Alonzo to alert the staff and arm anyone who wants a weapon. There may be more of these guys out there."

Ruhi watched as Caleb rode off.

"This is the first man I've ever killed," Will said, voice trembling. He gulped air and swallowed hard. "But I had to. Caleb is my brother. He's all I have."

"No, you're wrong. You have a wonderful father who loves you both."

After a long moment, Will met her eyes. "He loves you, too."

She smiled. "Your father loves life."

Will let out a shaky laugh. "Yeah, he does. He's a hell of a guy, isn't he?"

"And you are very much like him."

"Why did you come back for me?"

"Because you are now my son. That's what mothers do."

"You really believe that don't you?" He focused on her face, as if seeing her for the first time. "But you could have been killed, Ruhi. They almost got you."

"I could never have faced your father again if I left you behind." She touched his cheek. "Couldn't you please think of me as your new mother? Call me Mother"

He shook his head. "I already have a mother. She just happens to be dead." He met her eyes again and grinned, "But what's the Farsi word for Mom?"

***

Two hours later, mounted on a Sheriff's Department ATV, Will and Ruhi arrived at the hacienda. Professor Talebreza came running from the house, his pudgy face livid.

"Where have you been?" he shouted at his daughter in Farsi. "Whatever were you thinking, woman? You could have been killed."

"They tried to kill my sons. Will saved us all."

"He is not your child!" Talebreza snarled.

She faced her father, hands on hips, chin out. "He is the child of my husband. He is my child." She reached over and took Will's hand. "Everyone is somebody's child, Father. All those innocents who are slaughtered by suicide bombers are somebody's children—even the bombers. The killing needs to stop."

"You are a stupid woman. You know nothing of the world."

Will moved closer to Ruhi. "Is he giving you trouble again, Ruhi?"

Talebreza shook his fist and shouted in English. "Don't you interrupt me, you young whelp!"

Will stepped forward into Talebreza's personal space and backed him up a step. He looked down on the shorter man and said through clenched teeth, "Listen, Professor, I don't understand why you're such an asshole, and I don't care. You're a guest in our house, at Ruhi's request, and I'll accept that. But if you ever talk like that to her again and my father isn't here, I'll kick your ass myself."

117

Chapter Seventeen

Summit Valley Hospital,
Summit, California

Fasheed Talebreza drove his daughter's Maserati sedan into the hospital parking lot. He saw two Summit County sheriff's vehicles parked in front. A quick look showed one in back as well. Talebreza was impressed at the sheriff's efficiency, though not surprised. His son-in-law was a prominent American capitalist, and America certainly knew how to protect its wealthy citizens.

He parked the car and walked towards the main entrance. Once inside, he studied the directory and hospital map to ensure that nothing had changed from the information he had memorized from the Internet, then slipped down a corridor to the doctors' locker room. He glanced around to ensure he was alone, then searched the names on the lockers. Finding the name, he was looking for, he reached into his gym bag and produced a bolt cutter. He snapped off the combination lock and removed the plastic identification badge from inside, closed the locker, and clicked a new lock in place.

Talebreza adjourned to a toilet stall. He put on latex gloves, then used a scalpel to slit the edges of the ID tag. He removed the photo and name, and inserted his own photo along with the name "Antonio Ramirez, MD." He sealed the edges and took a moment to inspect his work. The job was crude, he thought, not up to the normal exacting standards he had used in the Iranian Revolutionary Guards, but adequate.

He slipped into a fishing vest that he had stolen from Brice and transferred several items from the gym bag to its many pockets. Then he put on his own lab coat, attached the fake ID tag, and hung a stethoscope around his neck. He wiped down the gym bag and its contents and placed it in the trash can for later retrieval.

Talebreza walked past the nurses' station and turned down the west corridor where a sheriff's deputy sat reading a book.

The deputy eyed the identification badge pinned to Talebreza's lab coat. "Excuse me, Doctor Ramirez, I need to check your identification against my access list."

"Certainly, deputy," Talebreza said, handing over his ID. "I understand the need for security. Thank you for your efforts." The deputy checked the ID card, nodded and waved him through, just as Talebreza expected. Americans really had no idea of security.

Talebreza paused at a bulletin board and pretended to read the announcements until the deputy returned to his book. Then he slipped into the hospital room where the wounded terrorist slept, heavily bandaged and handcuffed to the bed to prevent him from escaping. One leg was in a cast and tethered to the overhead bed frame. Talebreza took the lone chair in the room and placed it against the door, carefully secured the man's other leg, wrapped a towel around the handcuffs to muffle sound, then slapped duct tape over his mouth.

The terrorist woke with a start. Talebreza pulled out the drip attached to the surprised man's left arm. "This has an anesthetic in it," he said in Arabic. "You don't need that any more, you Sunni bastard. There are other things to worry about now."

The terrorist tried to scream and thrash in the bed. Talebreza thrust a scalpel under the man's chin. The sharp blade sliced through the skin. Blood ran down the man's neck onto the sheets.

"You need to be quiet," he said. "I will quite happily slit your throat if you make another sound." The man's body went rigid, and the thrashing stopped.

"Excellent decision. Let me explain why I am here." He began to take surgical tools from his vest. One at a time, he showed them to the terrorist and placed them on the side table. "I am an engineer. To me a doctor is just a mechanic with nicer tools, as you can see. These tools are quite lovely, sharp, and potentially deadly." He paused and held a scalpel

119

close to the man's face. The frightened eyes followed the glistening instrument.

"Deadly."

Talebreza pulled down the bed sheet and exposed multiple bandages. He ripped the bandage off the man's abdomen. The terrorist tried to scream as he writhed in agony.

"Oh, did I hurt you?" Talebreza's scalpel sliced the chin and more blood flowed. "I told you to be quiet. Your next sound will cost you an ear. Understood?"

The terrorist nodded, then closed his eyes as if to shut out this nightmare.

Talebreza said, "I have not always been an engineer. I used to be a soldier. I have killed men like you before." He examined the multiple wounds. "Your injuries must be painful." He cut through the stitches, then jerked out the thread. At each tug, the man moaned in pain.

"The people you attacked are part of my family. Did you know that? The woman you tried to kill is my daughter." He picked up his scalpel. "Last night, I had an epiphany. Do you know what an epiphany is, you worthless dog?"

He waited for an answer. The terrorist did not move. Talebreza placed the scalpel under his chin. "I asked if you knew what an epiphany was." The terrorist moaned and shook his head.

"I thought not," Talebreza said in a conversational voice. "I will tell you. My daughter is a kind person, a very loving young woman who just wants to live with her new family. And you tried to kill her. I was surprised at how that affected me. I found that I really loved my daughter. Admired her, as well. That is an epiphany."

He sliced through the remaining stitches. "I, on the other hand, am not such a kind, loving person. In fact, I am an unpleasant person. And I am not happy with you, young man."

Talebreza ripped apart the edges of the incision. The man thrashed around the bed, silent in his agony, tears in his eyes.

"You profess to be a devout Muslim. I do not agree. I think you have perverted Islam in order to push your own personal prejudices and the agenda of the men who sent you here to kill my daughter. This is heresy,

120

not religion, not what Muhammad preached. The Prophet was a great man, a godly man. You are neither."

Talebreza put on a pair of latex gloves, then reached into his coat to a vest pocket. He withdrew a plastic bag. "I have something for you. This is the foot of a pig. I am going to put it in your abdomen. You will have a hard time reaching heaven with a pig inside you, you filthy peasant.

"This is a tape recorder. You will tell me all you know or I will insert the pig meat into your stomach cavity and sew it back up. Then I will slit your throat. I am able to cleanse myself; you will not be so fortunate."

He turned the recorder on. "Remember my promise. Answer my questions, and all will be fine. Scream, and I will stuff the pig inside you and slit your throat. Your decision."

He reached into his coat pocket and withdrew a sheet of paper. "We will do this in English. I have a list of questions that you will answer. First, what is your name?"

Adams Mansion
California

Talebreza drove up the half mile driveway of the palatial Adams mansion. He spotted two workers tending to the elaborate gardens, pruning and trimming. He parked in front of the impressive entry. He sat for a moment to gather himself. What he was about to do would not be easy. In fact, Talebreza was afraid it would probably alienate his daughter and her new family for all time, a family that, to his own astonishment, he had come to admire.

He looked up at the enormous house. His son-in-law lived like a prince. He was a prince of sorts in this capitalist society, entry bought by enormous wealth. In fact, Adams was richer than most present-day princes. And yet, he lived an honorable life. Talebreza shook his head. Facts, ideas, and ideals that he had been so sure of in his youth were just not proving correct. His world was upside down. But his recent act had been the correct thing to do. Of that, he was sure.

His thoughts were interrupted by the appearance of a member of the staff, ready to park the car.

121

He walked up the steps through the huge, oak-paneled front door and through the enormous living room. He heard murmurs coming from Brice's office. He knocked.

"Come in."

Talebreza pushed open the door. Brice sat behind a polished black walnut desk, Ruhi in a chair covered in the richest tan leather imaginable, Will and Caleb on a matching couch. The office was every bit the lair of a rich man. Bookshelves lined two walls dotted with surfing and golf trophies, another wall featured an enormous flat-screen television; the remaining wall was nearly all glass with a splendid view of the vineyards sloping down towards the river. Sterling silver models of Air Force fighter jets sat on the desk; the only other decoration was a framed family photo taken the day of the wedding. Talebreza had refused to pose. He studied the picture for a moment—another opportunity for joining the family lost. He forced himself to look Brice in the eyes.

"Am I interrupting?"

Ruhi stood and kissed him. "Father, this is our weekly family meeting. You are welcome."

He had not been invited. It was natural, he thought. He didn't deserve to be a member of this family. "May I speak? I am sorry to interrupt, but it is important."

Brice eyed him, as if wary of another wedding day tirade.

Talebreza motioned towards Will and Caleb. "The young men should hear this as well."

He took a deep breath. "I have been to the hospital."

"What—?" said Brice.

Talebreza held up his hand. "It was necessary, Brice. I spoke to the terrorist who attempted to kill my daughter. And my only grandsons."

"Fasheed, you didn't do anything stupid, did you?"

"I did what was necessary." He produced the recorder and placed it on the desk. "I have his confession on tape. You need to listen." He glanced at Ruhi. "I am sorry that you have to hear this, daughter, but it is important that this information get to your authorities quickly."

"Are you sure the boys should be here?" she asked.

Talebreza looked at Will and Caleb and nodded. "This concerns them also." He paused. "The situation is quite serious. Kurt Wallerein, a German terrorist, ordered the attackers to exterminate this family. And many more." Talebreza punched the recorder button. A muffled moan of a man in great pain was the first sound. Talebreza watched his step-grandsons, curious—and afraid—to see their reactions. They would be the litmus. They peeked up at him as they heard his voice ask the first question: "What is your name?"

The name "Wallerein" was something they must have recognized. Both boys were scowling—they clearly didn't like the idea of their father and their stepmother being targets, oblivious to the fact that they themselves had also nearly been killed. Boys and their sense of immortality. Talebreza heard Will mutter a curse, then he turned and gave Talebreza a gesture he recognized as a "thumbs-up."

Five minutes later, Talebreza turned it off. Not a sound came from any of the Adams family. Ruhi's eyes were wide and her face drawn and pale.

Talebreza said, "This man does not know all of Wallerein's plans. He is just a peon, a lowly foot soldier who was told just enough to induce him to join Wallerein's army and to make him useful in the field. I brought it to you, Brice. You can get this information to where it will be used. Perhaps your friend who works in the White House?"

"Tom Callahan? Yeah, that would be a good place to start. He can get it where it needs to go." Brice drummed his fingers on his desk. "I have to ask this, Fasheed. How did you induce this guy to talk?"

Talebreza related his actions, sparing no details. Ruhi was horrified; the boys seemed fascinated. Brice looked thoughtful. "Speaking as an officer, I am appalled." He paused. "But speaking as a husband and father, I wish you had left that pig's foot in his goddamn stomach." He shifted his gaze to his family. "Sorry, sweetheart. And you boys forget what I said as a parent… no, better that you don't. But remember my first reaction was that of an officer."

Talebreza forced himself to finish his confession. "I am ashamed of my past behavior. Ruhi has taught me much in the few weeks I have been a guest in this house. I see her and the world through new eyes. I have

123

not been a good man in my family life. But when those men attacked I thought I had lost Ruhi—and you boys—forever. I realized how much of life I had missed. Many things that I used to believe have been proven false. I hope that obtaining this information in some way will make up for the way I behaved." He looked at Will. "I think the American word you used to describe me was 'asshole.'"

He faced his daughter. "What these men are doing is wrong. I am learning from you, daughter—what I did was not a kind thing, but it needed to be done."

Ruhi stood and hugged her father. He held on to her like a life ring. The unexpected embrace ended too soon for him.

Brice said, "I need to call this in to Washington. Will you all please excuse me? Ruhi, you should stay, sweetheart."

Will stood, hesitated, then gave a light tug on Talebreza's sleeve. "Come with us, sir. We're going to watch a Major League Soccer game—Los Angeles versus San Jose. We know you love soccer."

Talebreza looked at the eager young faces. Being called "sir" by these boys was not as good as "grandfather" but it would do. It was certainly a big step up from "asshole."

He said, "Thank you, Will. That would be delightful." He shifted his gaze back to Brice. "I assume that you will call the police?"

Brice nodded. "Sorry. But first I have to call Callahan." He came out from behind his desk and offered his hand to his father-in-law.

Talebreza studied the hand, then slowly clasped it with both of his. "Thank you, my son."

Brice Adams studied the receding backs for a moment before shutting the door.

"Ruhi, I never thought that I would ever say this, but your father is a better man than I expected."

"But, Brice, what he did to that poor man!"

"That 'poor man' was here to murder me and was perfectly happy to slaughter you and the boys to get to me. Sorry, honey, I can't work up much sympathy for him." He held up his hand to silence her protest. "Yes, yes, what Fasheed did was a crime. I understand that and he will have to face the consequences. But, by God, I am glad he did it."

Brice sat at his desk and opened a panel to reveal a safe. He worked the combination and produced a classified telephone, provided him by the California Air National Guard. He dialed the White House switchboard.

"White House."

"This is Colonel Brice Adams. I need to speak to Colonel Tom Callahan, please. It's important."

"Stand by, please, Colonel."

"Callahan."

"Tom, Brice Adams. Let's go secure."

"Roger that."

Both men listened as the phones matched codes and went secure.

"Tom, you're not going to believe this…"

***

"You know, of course, Brice, that because of the torture this confession could never be used in a court of law? That it may even set the terrorist loose?"

"Way ahead of you on that, Tom. I suggest that we inform this terrorist that we plan to provide copies of his conversation with Fasheed to several Middle Eastern intelligence services. We know they're riddled with terrorist sympathizers who will pass along his confession to 'Terrorist Incorporated' headquarters. He might not be so enthusiastic about pressing charges or even returning to the land of his birth."

Tom chuckled. "It should give him something to think about." A pause. "I will need you out here to brief the Wallerein working group and possibly the president."

"No problem. But first I have to get my father-in-law the best lawyer in history. He's going to need it."

"So the rabid 'I-hate-the-United-States-and-all-it-stands-for' Fasheed Talebreza is turning out better than expected?"

"Yeah. Who woulda thunk?"

Chapter Eighteen

Wallerein's headquarters
Playa del Carmen

Kurt Wallerein sat at his desk to consider his next step. Finances and security were any organization's two biggest headaches; but as the son, grandson and great-grandson of international bankers, armed with a degree in economics from the prestigious Philipps Universität Marburg, Wallerein had a firm grasp on finances.

Right now his major problem was communications security. His organization was stretched, the span of control was tenuous, and he knew it. He had been burned in Bolivia by the Americans and their sophisticated systems, and he was determined not to let it happen again. Those systems had destroyed his Bolivian operations and his reputation as the world's most dangerous terrorist. Humiliation aside, more importantly the Americans had nearly killed him. Him. Kurt Wallerein! Even here in Mexico, who knew who could be listening, watching? Those criminals in the American National Security Agency could be monitoring his heartbeat for all he knew.

And Callahan! That son-of-a-bitch! Wallerein threw his carefully arranged notes at the wall. The packet exploded, individual sheets drifted to the floor like feathers from a dove blasted by a shotgun at close range. Breathing hard, he muttered, "I will have to kill him before he kills me."

He shook his head. "*Scheisse*," he whispered. "I'm getting paranoid, jumpy like an old woman." He corrected himself. "Not paranoid, cautious. I still don't trust electronic communications. Maybe I am too suspicious of this new Internet. Perhaps I'm old-fashioned, but I am still alive. I will continue to send crucial communications by courier. It's simply good tradecraft. Just get back to basics, Kurt. Stick with what you know works."

Wallerein stood, gathered up his papers, arranged them in order and put the neat stack precisely in the middle of his desk surface. He walked to the door. "Richter, Kulenović. Come in here."

He motioned them towards his conference table. "Sit."

Wallerein unrolled a map of the United States on the table. "I have made some changes to our timetable as well as the target list." He paused. "Fire and floods."

Richter said, "Fire and floods, comrade? I don't understand."

"You will."

An hour later, Wallerein settled back, pleased with the questions and suggestions from his two lieutenants. Kulenović sounded like one competent bastard, exactly what Wallerein needed. He studied the face across the table. Short, dark hair framed broad cheekbones, brown eyes, chiseled chin. It was a face with many possible origins, a perfect face for a terrorist.

Another decision confirmed. "Avdo, I need to send someone to a meeting. I have people based in Paraguay, Ciudad del Este to be precise. We need to accelerate their training and get ready to deploy sooner than I had anticipated."

Kulenović nodded. "When?"

"Right away. Tomorrow morning. The first flight out of Cancun Airport for Mexico City leaves at ten minutes to five. Paraguay is not easy to get to. I'll have your documents and final instructions ready by dinner."

He pulled out a second map. "Here's Paraguay. Over here is Guaraní airport, about twenty-five kilometers outside of Cuidad del Este. The city itself is right on the border between Brazil, Argentina and Paraguay. An interesting place, at once the foulest example of capitalism gone berserk and at the same time, full of progressives—or at least allies. Many Muslims live there. Many freedom fighters hide there waiting for a call. This is such a call. Because the city is full of sympathizers—many rich sympathizers by the way—there is a great deal of money passing through this city. You might meet someone you know. Ours is a small world. That's why Richter and I cannot go. We're too well known. And anyway, I have something else for Richter to do. If you do stumble across a former colleague, shake him, kill him, whatever, but do not talk to anyone you don't expect. They could be plants, or agents, of the Americans or the Israelis."

Kulenović said nothing.

A man of few words, thought Wallerein. Kulenović was as cold blooded as he was. *Exzellent.*

TAM Airlines Flight 2121
Near Ciudad del Este, Paraguay

Abdullah (Avdo) Kulenović watched out his window as the Boeing 737 sliced through the moon-lit clouds on its descent into Guarani International Airport. He was bone weary and bored, both dangerous conditions to the life of a mercenary. His long journey had started with an early morning take-off from Cancun to Mexico City. His second flight was late into São Paulo, Brazil's busiest airport. The airport exceeded its reputation as a place where travel plans went to die as he sat many hours waiting for another plane. Because of his late arrival and departure, he had missed his connection in Asunción. He glanced at his watch again. No time for his meetings tonight.

His luck changed in Guarani; he breezed through immigration and customs as expected. His fake passport was perfect—Wallerein's organization contained some of the world's best forgers, courtesy of the former East German Stasi. He stopped at the kiosk advertising local hotels, memorized two names and addresses, then exited the modern terminal into the hot, humid night air. He held back at the taxi stand to let other passengers jostle for the white taxis, then stepped in front of the line to select one at random.

Kulenović gave the driver the address of one of the hotels, then settled back for the ride. The air rushing through the vehicle was warm, sticky, and scented with tropical flowers. Traffic began to back up as they approached the city; soon they were enveloped in a massive traffic

128

jam. His highly trained senses were assaulted by noise, movement, and the smells of the city. People from all races and nations swarmed the streets—Asians, Indians, Middle Easterners, blacks, Indians, and their mélange of languages assailed his ears from loudspeakers and his eyes from neon signs and billboards. Ciudad del Este, Paraguay's second largest city, was living up to its reputation as an ungovernable mess.

At the hotel, Kulenović paid the cabbie, watched him drive away, then walked several blocks to a different hotel, paid for a room with cash, and went to bed.

He woke early, muscles stiff from his travels. He was restless and had hours to kill before his backup meeting time; sitting in a hotel room was not his style. He decided to break the monotony and to clear his head with a long walk around the city before meeting his contacts. In the daylight, the area around the hotel was surprisingly run-down—cheap buildings, tiny stores, and bars, lots of bars.

The walk was informative and at times fascinating. A country boy, Kulenović could not understand why people chose to live jammed together in cities, especially urban disasters like this one. The sidewalks were packed to overflowing with sweaty bodies, the streets chaotic—if anything, more so than at night—people everywhere selling everything imaginable. He was stunned, then amused by the sight of so many bodies wandering the streets and even shopping wearing nothing but bathing suits and sandals. Wherever did they keep their money? Through the buildings, he caught a glimpse of the *Puente de Amistad*—Friendship Bridge—over the Parana River into Brazil, surrounded by the only green space he had yet discovered in this jam-packed city.

He felt a hand in his back pocket, spun around and came up with the attached arm.

"Ow, let me go!" screamed the pickpocket.

Kulenović tightened his grip, torqued the arm tighter and slammed the thief against a wall, left forearm pressed hard against his throat. The terrified boy looked all of fourteen years old.

"Bah!" said Kulenović and snapped the boy's arm, then pushed him away. "You bad thief," he said in broken Spanish. "Find other job. Save your life."

The sobbing boy clutched his ruined arm to his side and disappeared into the crowd. Kulenović watched until the boy was out of sight, then shook his head. He hated bullies yet he had just bullied that boy, possibly into a crime-free life.

He had been just about that boy's age when stories of Serbian atrocities in Bosnia-Herzegovina had filtered down to his village. The idea of the stronger Serbia forcing Bosniaks out of their own country was too much for his then-idealistic self. In 1994, he joined the Army of the Republic of Bosnia-Herzegovina and was assigned to the 7th Muslim Brigade. Trained in explosives, he had been a good soldier. At the end of the war, he was sent to Saudi Arabia and Afghanistan for more training. Now he was a mercenary, useful to Wallerein for his skills. That he was also a Muslim had some advantages but Kulenović, like most Bosniaks, took a moderate approach to his religion.

He wandered the crowded sidewalks, taking in the sights of this city that had been created less than fifty years earlier in an effort to move some of Paraguay's population from the teeming ghettos of Asunción. Gradually, he saw more evidence of Middle Eastern influence. He observed mosque after mosque, from traditional domed ones to modern, multi-storied ones.

Hungry now, Kulenović found a Lebanese falafel restaurant. The smells floating out of the front door made his mouth water. He took a seat with his back against a wall, studied the menu and ordered a traditional *meze* or platter of small dishes. While he waited for his food, he surveyed the tiny, crowded restaurant. A set of eyes met his and his heart nearly stopped.

Leka! His comrade-in-arms for so many years.

"Avdo!" The men embraced like the brothers they had become while killing Serbs in the Bosnian mountains. They huddled at Avdo's table to renew old ties. Both men stopped talking out of habit while the meal arrived. Avdo took a bite of the first decent food he had tasted since his departure from Europe, closing his eyes as he chewed in order to savor the taste and texture of the falafels with tahini, prosciutto, pickled vegetables, cheeses, and olives.

"What are you doing here, my friend?" Avdo asked.

"I'm here to help raise money to rebuild our country's mosques."

Both men paused, remembering the senseless destruction as the Serbs had deliberately razed dozens of mosques throughout Kosovo as part of their genocidal onslaught. "There's a lot of money generated in the Muslim part of this city," said Leka. "My job is to direct some away from Hezbollah into constructive, positive uses." He took a sip of his coffee. "Why are you here, Avdo?"

Kulenović was quiet for a long moment, hoping he appeared to be lost in thought, instead of surprised—and wary. "Leka, you must not tell anyone that you saw me here. It is important."

Leka looked puzzled. "If you say so, Avdo. I know whatever you are here to do is important. I won't ask anything more." He brightened. "So, how is that gorgeous sister of yours?"

Avdo's throat tightened and his temper flashed. "Don't talk about my sister!"

Leka winced and fell back into his chair. "Why not? She's wonderful."

"She was murdered by the goddamned Serbs!"

Leka shook his head. "No! When?"

"Two years ago. Taken out and shot."

"No, No, Avdo!" Leka blurted. "They are alive. Your sister and mother are alive!"

"You lie!" Avdo shouted and slammed his fist on the table.

People in the restaurant stared in alarm at the outburst. Several moved away. Leka grabbed for Avdo's hand and said in a hushed voice, "Please, please, Avdo. Listen. I saw them last month. They are living in the capital, in Pristina. Katarina works at a hotel. They think that you are dead. So did I, until five minutes ago. Oh, Allah is great!"

Dazed, Avdo said, "I searched days for their bodies—"

"I know, Avdo. I was there. I saw many mass graves. Believe me, my friend. I saw your sister. She hugged my neck. I held her hand. It was warm flesh and blood, I promise you." He paused, his face lit up. "You must contact them, they will be so happy!

"How? Where?"

"There is an Internet café not far from here. Go there and look up The Swiss Diamond Hotel, probably the best in the capital. Then go to one of the little stores with phone boxes where you make international calls and call Katarina from there."

How could this be possible? Confused and scared, Kulenović looked down at his plate. The food held no interest for him now. What to do? "Leka, if anybody but you had told me this I would cut his throat for lying." Kulenović glanced at the wall clock. Paraguay was Greenwich Mean Time minus four hours; Pristina GMT plus one, a five-hour time difference.

Leka laughed. "Go, my friend. I would lead you, but I need to meet a very rich man who has promised much money to my cause. Go with Allah!"

Kulenović threw money on the table and stumbled out the door, Leka's cheers echoing in his ears. He found the cyber café, paid for an hour and settled in front of the screen. It was a simple matter to find The Swiss Diamond Hotel. Pictures of the opulent reception area popped up along with the phone number that he needed. He rushed out of the café in search of a store with telephone booths. The closest one had too many lights. Three blocks away, he found another. Passed it by. Too many people. He slowed his walk. "Avdo, you coward," he muttered. "Just do it—now!"

He stopped outside the third store but couldn't force himself inside. His head swirled. What would he say? What if Leka was wrong? Why would Leka be wrong? Leka knew Kat. He said that he had held Katarina's hand. But how could it be possible? Kulenović had found the mass grave outside his village. He had endured the pain of loss once. If this turned out to be a mistake, he wondered if he could handle it.

Cursing himself for a weakling, he forced his legs forward across the sidewalk, through the door and paid the owner for a booth. Breathing ragged and with pulse racing, he punched in the digits. His finger paused over the last button, then reluctantly, he finished. After the third ring, he heard a voice, "The Swiss Diamond Hotel. How may I direct your call?"

His mouth went dry, his heart pounded.

"How may I direct your call, please?"

He blurted, "Katarina Kulenović, please."

"Thank you." A click.

"Group Sales section. Katarina speaking. May I help you?"

Avdo's heart seemed to stop. He would know that voice anywhere. It was the voice that he had grown up with, that had always charmed him, charmed everybody. The voice of his sister. Instantly, he was transported back to their village in Kosovo. Memories flooded back, threatened to overwhelm him. Digging in the snow, hands bloody with the cold, frantic to find his sister's body, his mother's body. Arrested by the authorities for "desecrating a grave." As if he would foul the graves of his family! His knees gave way and he slumped against the wall of the tiny booth. His baby sister was alive! Allah is truly great!

"May I help you?" she repeated.

He managed to stammer, "Kat, is that really you?"

A silence. A hesitant "Avdo?"

"Yes, baby girl," he sobbed. "It is Avdo, your brother."

A scream. "Avdo, my darling! Is it possible? Is it true?"

They stumbled through their conversation, talking over each other.

"How could this be? I searched for you and mother. Everyone said you had been shot."

"The whole village was murdered, Avdo. We were marched out through the snow. I heard the shots behind us when they started shooting."

Her voice cracked. "It was horrible."

"What happened...? How did you...?"

"How did we survive? Avdo, the United Nations forces arrived...; they were American Marines. They saved us."

"Americans?" he croaked.

"Yes, my brother. Just in time. Like in the American movies. They arrived in their enormous metal machines and drove the Serbs away."

Twenty minutes later, they reluctantly hung up. Katarina had extracted a promise from her brother to call again as soon as he could. Dazed, Kulenović meandered his way through the crowded city streets while he thought about how the world had suddenly changed. The skies

133

were more beautiful, lights seemed brighter, people seemed happier. His sister and mother were alive! Amazing.

***

An hour later, Kulenović headed to the park in the plaza behind the city's main cathedral. He thought it ironic that an atheist like Wallerein would schedule the rendezvous near a church. It had to be irony, since the German had no discernable sense of humor. As he neared the plaza, his situational awareness kicked in and he made two slow circuits of the plaza, eyes reflexively moving left and right as he walked. He found a bench where he could survey the entire park, made one last sweep of the terrain, then sat and tried to appear relaxed.

After fifteen minutes, a black Land Cruiser slowed and stopped next to the sidewalk. Three men got out. Kulenović immediately made the older one as his contact because he looked like Wallerein's cousin, a bit younger and more densely muscled, but German for certain and probably ex-Stasi. He was accompanied by two bodyguards whose eyes never stopped searching the sparse midday crowd. All three men were dressed in slacks and the ubiquitous *guayabera* shirts so typical of the tropics. Bulges under the shirts indicated weapons. No surprise there. Kulenović gave a slight nod to the German and picked up his small travel bag. Without a word he accompanied them to the Land Cruiser.

They drove in silence for several hours. Once outside the city environs, the land changed rapidly to scattered farms and small villages then into ranchland with fields dotted with cattle stretching to the horizon in all directions. The population numbers dropped off sharply; Paraguay was seriously underpopulated. Kulenović knew that Paraguay had suffered heavily in the War of the Triple Alliance in the 1860s which cost the country dearly—nearly half its territory to Brazil and Argentina, and over sixty per cent of its people killed in what is considered by many historians as the most devastating war of modern times.

And it was hot. Sweltering hot. Secure in the air-conditioned Toyota, Kulenović could see the heat shimmer off the coarse grasslands.

As he sat, Kulenović pondered his sister's story. He had fought in Bosnia to defend his faith and innocent villagers from the horrible acts of the Serbs. He fought in Kosovo to defend his country against the Serbs. After hearing of his family's "massacre," he had joined Ali Muhammad and Kurt Wallerein for revenge. They fanned his hatred for the Serbs. During the war in Kosovo, he had used his skill with explosives to blow up a dozen Serbian Orthodox Churches, savoring the destruction. Later, Wallerein had redirected Kulenović's hatred towards powerful countries like the United States.

Kulenović knew Wallerein well enough now to understand that he was a committed socialist whose view of the world was filtered by his heroes, Marx and Engels. He was stuck in a time warp of his own making. He hadn't changed his politics to reflect the changes that had swept the planet in the past decade. It was like his brain was put in backwards. Nobody in the world was a Marxist these days, not even the Chinese. Maybe those nut jobs in the *Sendero Luminoso* in Peru were still Marxists, but they were now mostly dead, hunted down by their own government like the prehistoric political dinosaurs that they were.

Wallerein said he wanted world change, but Kulenović suspected that what he really wanted was a new government where he was the boss. To gain that position, he was quite willing to kill as many innocent people as it took.

***

Two days later, having delivered his message and conducted two training seminars in explosives, Kulenović strode back into Guarani airport. He checked in and slipped into a telephone booth across from his departure gate to call his sister one more time.

"Avdo," she said in a hesitant voice. "I am pregnant."

He sucked in his breath. A brief pause. "Who is the father?"

"He is American. A sergeant of their Marines. We met in the refugee camp. He protected us."

"Where is he now?"

"In America. Somewhere in California."

135

"He abandoned you? That bastard!"

"No, no, Avdo. When his time with the United Nations was up, he was sent home. He came back to visit, and we fell in love. He wants me to join him, to marry him."

"You would leave Kosovo?"

"To be with the man I love, the father of my baby? Yes, tomorrow if I could. But there is a problem with getting a visa and Mama is sick, very sick. I cannot leave now."

Kulenović glanced at his gate. His flight was boarding. Only minutes more. "I have to go, Kat."

"Avdo, don't go," she pleaded. "I don't know what you are doing but come home to me, my brother. Promise that you'll come back to me!"

***

Kulenović sat back in his seat as the airplane leveled off. He sipped his ice water, then his shook his head. All that anger, all the hatred that had poisoned his life was based on a lie. His sister and mother were alive, saved by United States Marines, agents of the very country he was now plotting to attack. An American wanted to marry his sister. That would make this Marine his own brother-in-law! A Marine! Allah surely had a bizarre sense of humor. And here he sat, about to unleash terror on unsuspecting innocents in the United States, precisely what he had gone to war to stop in his own country.

Images of death and destruction lacerated his mind. Anguish lanced through him. The intensity of his reaction shocked him.

What have I done? No, wrong question. I did what I thought was right at the time. The real question is what am I doing now? And why am I doing it?

Chapter Nineteen

Mexico City
Noon

Avdo Kulenović could not remember being this nervous. If this plan didn't work, he was a dead man. Probably, he confessed to himself, he was a dead man anyhow. He watched as his target, dressed in workout shorts, a sweatshirt and running shoes, left the United States Embassy, checked for pedestrian traffic, turned right and began to jog down the *Avenida Paseo de la Reforma* towards the massive *Bosque de Chapultepec*, Latin America's largest city park.

Kulenović, similarly attired, slipped in behind the man, and followed at a safe distance. If his information was correct, the man, Major Michael Turri, United States Marine Corps, would stop at the edge of the park for a few warm up exercises before he ran a ten-mile course.

Kulenović made his way along the crowded sidewalk, keeping several pedestrians between him and Turri as he stalked the target, a tall, muscular man with short hair and an easy stride. Turri paused for his warm up exercises. Kulenović did some of his own. The confrontation was coming; he used the warm up time to get his emotions under control. Turri turned and began his run along the marked trail. Kulenović loped along behind, through the trees until Turri disappeared into an underpass.

"Shit," he thought as he accelerated. He sprinted into the tunnel. And skidded to a halt. There stood the Marine, holding what Kulenović recognized as a Glock 19 pistol. He pointed the pistol at the ground between Kulenović's feet.

The American said in flawless Spanish, *"Señor, quiere algo de mi?"* Do you want something from me?

Avdo raised his hands and smiled at the turn of events. This guy was good. Impressive.

"*Necesitamos hablar, señor,*" he said—we need to talk.

"*Por qué?*"

"I have information," said Kulenović, switching to accented English.

The Marine must have noted the accent. "Would you prefer Spanish or English?"

"My Spanish not good, too. You Marine officer?"

The man nodded. "Major Michael Turri, United States Marine Corps, assistant Naval Attaché to Mexico. I must warn you, señor, that I have diplomatic immunity in Mexico so if I have to shoot you, the worst that can happen to me is to be returned to the United States. I will shoot you if I need to. Consider yourself warned."

"I need talk. Where?"

Turri thought for a moment and pointed to a clump of trees. "There are benches over there and it's private." He motioned Kulenović to move. As they walked, Turri scanned the area. Apparently satisfied that Kulenović was alone, he slid the pistol into a holster tucked in the small of his back. The men sat facing each other. Turri waited.

Kulenović pointed to his pocket. "I have tape recorder. Is okay?"

Turri nodded. Kulenović produced a small voice activated recorder the size of a pack of cigarettes and placed it on the bench between them. He punched a button and a red light lit up.

"I not have much time. Have much to say. Name is Abdullah Kulenović. I am Kosovar. I work with Kurt Wallerein. You know name?"

The Marine took a deep breath in surprise. "Every intelligence officer in the world knows that name."

Kulenović paused to steady his nerves. This recording would probably cost him his life. He plunged ahead. "Wallerein responsible for attacks and fires in your country. He has many teams setting fires. We have two man teams. Usually European and non-European, ex-Stasi or KGB. Many Cubans and many Mid East. Now he wants move from fires to other things. New groups arrive in America soon. Will have explosives. I help train. Wallerein wants kill many Americans, most ordinary peoples."

"Why?"

"He hate America. And there is man, colonel in your Air Force. Callahan." Kulenović smiled for the first time. "'Thomas Patrick Callahan, that dirty Irish bastard' is what Wallerein say many times in day. He hate Callahan for stopping him in Bolivia. He is mad. You say crazy?"

Turri nodded. "Yes. Crazy. What are the new targets?"

Kulenović spoke for three minutes, reciting from memory every detail of Wallerein's plans he could recall. "That is all I know.... Wallerein very careful... I know only few things... others know only what Wallerein thinks they need know... You understand?"

Turri nodded again. "He is compartmentalizing."

Kulenović shook his head. "No understand word."

"He tells each man or each small group only what they need to know to do their job, but they do not know the whole operation. That is compartmentalizing, keeping people in compartments, small boxes."

"Yes. Compartmentalizing. Is good word." He paused. "I need go. Plane leave in three hours."

Turri looked thoughtful. "First, Abdullah, why me? Why here?"

"My sister, she tell me that she rescued by American Marines in Kosovo. She beautiful girl, work at fancy hotel in Pristina." He choked up and put his hand over his eyes. His vocabulary limited his ability to convey his thinking to this American. This was important. Someone else needed to understand what Kulenović himself was just beginning to grasp. He wanted to atone for his sins, make things right. "I love my country. I proud Kosovar. What Wallerein is planning is what happened to many of my peoples and almost to my own family... I cannot do this more."

Then he chuckled. "Sister..." he paused and made a big stomach with his hands, "with baby."

"She's pregnant? With the Marine?"

Kulenović nodded. "They want marry. I just find out. Problem with visa for sister. Marine in America. Now Katarina need stay Kosovo because mother sick."

"What is the Marine's name. Where is he?"

Kulenović searched his memory. "In Kaliff... Kaliff something."

"California?"

"Yes. Kalifornia."

Turri thought some more. "Come with me, Abdullah. I can get you protection. If you go back, I cannot help you."

"No. I need go back. Get more information. How I call you?"

Turri recited a phone number. "This is unlisted. Call any time. And I mean any time." Kulenovic recited it three times to burn the numbers into his memory.

"You're pretty damned heroic, Abdullah."

"I not hero. I do many bad things. Want do good things now."

"You are a hero to me, pal. You are to me. Thank you for trusting me."

Kulenović looked him in the eyes. "Marines saved my family. I have nobody else to trust." He offered his hand. "Take care of my sister."

"You have my word."

Ambassador's office
U.S. Embassy, Mexico City

"Jesus, Mary and Joseph!" said the stunned Ambassador as he turned off the tape recorder. He cast a worried glance around his conference table at his Deputy Chief of Mission (DCM), the CIA Station Chief, the Defense Attaché, and back to Major Michael Turri. "How in the world did you manage this, Major? Is this for real?"

Turri felt his face flush. Already acutely uncomfortable sitting in the ambassador's ornate office still sweaty and dressed in his running shorts, now he had to confess his errors. "Sir, Kulenović told me that it was easy to track me down," he said. "He found my information on the Embassy web site and spread some money around town to get a photo. Apparently, I have been too predictable about my lunchtime runs."

The Station Chief, a thin man with gray-streaked hair and an angular face, gave a small smile. "That's good to know. If Kulenović really found you so quickly, it was with some local help, probably bad boys. I'll pass the word around my shop to tighten up our security and change our habits. Thanks for having the *cojones* to enlighten us, Michael. This just might save the life of one of my guys."

The Defense Attaché, an Army brigadier general nodded. "Mr. Ambassador, we've done the same thing in our office. What needs to be done now is to get this information to Washington ASAP, right the hell now, sir."

"Agreed," said the Ambassador. He drummed his manicured fingers on his desk as he thought. "General, you write the Intelligence Report. I'll draft a cable to State."

The Station Chief said, "I'd like to make a copy of the tape and send it up through my channels, sir." He thought for a second. "Might as well make two copies and pass one to the FBI. Once this information hits D.C., it'll belong to the FBI anyway."

"Agreed again," said the Ambassador. "Get your guys out in the field to verify this information as soon as we can. The bureaucrats in Washington probably won't do anything until it's been vetted and re-vetted. But if it's true, it should cause a titanic shift in attitudes." He turned to Turri. "We'll take it from here, Major. You go home and pack."

"Sir?"

"You're on the next plane to Washington." He glanced at his diamond-encrusted watch. "You have time to catch the 1733 Aeromexico flight. I'll put the tape recorder in the diplomatic pouch and have an Embassy driver meet you at the ticket counter. Somebody will meet you at Dulles Airport. The cables will beat you there. Maybe by then there will be some confirmation on this—CIA might have some information tying this Kulenović to Wallerein." He sat back in his leather chair. "Be ready to brief the entire intelligence world, young man."

"Aye, aye, sir." Turri stood and turned to leave.

"And Michael…"

"Sir?"

"Take a shower."

Wallerein headquarters
Playa del Carmen

Avdo Kulenović couldn't help it; he was nervous again. Despite the condo's air conditioning, he was sweating, his heart racing. He dropped his bag on the condo's tile floor and stretched. It had been another long day, and now he was back in Wallerein's lair.

He watched a ski boat race along the beach towing a pasty-white and unsteady tourist. An irregular wave caught the skier and down he went, sheets of water exploding and skis flying.

"Where have you been?" Wallerein asked in Arabic.

Kulenović jumped and spun around.

"You startled me, comrade. I didn't hear you come in."

Wallerein glared. "Can you hear me now? Where have you been?"

"Missed my connection in Mexico City."

Wallerein stepped closer, face close to Kulenović. "I checked. Your flight was not that late. You had fifteen minutes. You could have made it."

"I didn't, though."

"Did you run?"

He shook his head. "I was tired and frankly, pissed-off for being late again. I walked and I missed the flight. So I got a cheap hotel and slept the clock around. I caught the first afternoon flight to Cancun, and here I am."

Wallerein's ice-blue eyes bored into him. Kulenović stared back with what he hoped was the proper mixture of defiance and respect.

Finally, Wallerein laughed. "After our revolution is completed, I will put you in charge of fixing the Mexican airlines." He gestured towards the beach. "Come, have a walk with me and tell me of your meetings. The teams in Paraguay were impressed with your instruction. And I have another mission for you."

Chapter Twenty

Georgetown

The limousine wove its way through the Sunday afternoon traffic in one of the more upscale sections of Georgetown. The car, a black Ford Crown Victoria, was assigned to the White House motor pool. Dr. Isabella Orsini sat in the back and watched as some of the most gorgeous houses she had seen in Washington slid by. She was convinced that the idiot driver was lost. Certainly Callahan, a mere colonel, couldn't live here. "Are you sure you know where the hell you're going, driver?"

"Yes, ma'am."

They maneuvered through tree-lined streets and pulled to the curb in front of a large, colonial style brick home. "This is the address, Dr. Orsini."

As the driver rushed to open her car door, she studied the house, which she guessed as pre-Civil War. A five-foot brick fence enclosed spacious grounds dominated by massive maple, cherry, and several large dogwoods.

As she exited the car, Orsini said, "Don't leave. I won't be here long."

Convinced she was at the wrong house, Orsini mashed a button on the gate.

"Yes?"

"Dr. Isabella Orsini to see Colonel Callahan."

A buzz and the gate swung open. Still skeptical, Orsini walked along the cobblestone path that curved through lush gardens boasting azaleas heavy with pink, purple, and red flowers, razor sharp hedges, climbing ivies and a billiard table lawn.

The door opened to reveal an olive-skinned woman dressed in a two-tone abaya dress that looked as if it were made from silk, a thought Orsini dismissed. Hired help did not wear silk dresses to work. The woman made a slight bow and asked, "May I help you?" in an accent Orsini could not recognize.

"I am Dr. Orsini. Are you Mrs. Callahan?"

The woman smiled and said, "I am Ruhi Adams, a friend. Won't you come in? I will call Colleen."

The interior was an eclectic mixture of new and old. Exposed beams and built-in floor-to-ceiling cherry cabinets attested to the epoch of the colonial house. Furniture was placed perfectly over antique oak floors. Expensive furniture, too. Orsini had strained her own budget to the breaking point to achieve a look like this and not done as well. Clearly professional work. Nothing she had seen from Callahan had hinted at any personal refinement.

The walls gleamed with art, expertly placed. Mostly Southwestern scenes, some that looked like early Georgia O'Keefe, not Orsini's style. Placed over the oak mantelpiece was a large framed work that Orsini thought might be a Chagall reproduction. She had no time for Chagall. Much too Jewish. Not to mention too dreamy, colors much too bright. She preferred more muted, more refined works.

Orsini looked up to find a tall blonde woman striding toward her. She wore a sleeveless top, colorful running shorts and a pair of spotless white running shoes. Her hair was pulled back and loosely gathered at the nape of her neck. She smiled as she offered her hand. "G'day, Isabella, I'm Colleen Callahan. Welcome to our house. Thank you for coming."

Orsini managed a fleeting smile as she returned the handshake. "The chief of staff asked me to attend."

Colleen gestured to the French doors leading out to the patio. As they made their way to the patio, Orsini remarked on the display of artwork.

144

"Oh, it's mostly Tommy's collection. His mother is an artist. He and his brother buy art like I buy shoes."

"I see that you're Chagall fans."

Colleen chuckled. "Yes, it is rather massive, isn't it?"

"Yes. I've never been a fan of Chagall. But it's an interesting reproduction."

"Oh, Tommy would never buy a reproduction."

***

Outside the weather was patio perfect. Tom Callahan, dressed in a Hawaiian shirt, shorts and flip-flops, finished setting up the bar with some of his special sangria. His guests settled themselves into wrought iron chairs around a large circular table overflowing with Spanish-style tapas. Ruhi Adams cuddled the six-month old Michael Anthony Callahan until the au pair materialized and carried the baby back into the house.

"Ruhi," said Tom, "between you and Colleen, the au pair is in danger of being out of work. That kid hasn't touched the ground once today."

After the expected chuckles, Tom began. "Before we get started on this, the second meeting of the 'Let's Catch that Son-of-a-Bitch Kurt Wallerein Working Group,' I want to introduce our newest member, nominated by the chief of staff himself, Doctor Isabella Orsini, Deputy Assistant National Security Advisor and former Congressional staffer." Tom bowed and swept his arm to indicate Isabella. There was a smattering of applause and waving from the assembled group. "Isabella, you've already met my wife, the World Bank economist. The other beautiful lady is Ruhi Adams, international finance wizard and recent bride of that ugly guy over there, Brice Adams, who likes to masquerade as a colonel but he's really a captain of industry, the only true capitalist in the group. You know Porter Nelson, journalist extraordinaire, Jacob Borenstein, Deputy Director of the FBI, and Robbie Robinson, cloak and dagger man at the CIA."

Tom took a sip of his wine. "Okay, everybody settle back and listen up. Brice and Ruhi are here for a reason. Wallerein has been heard from in a most emphatic way. But we'll save that for last. Let's take it around the circle, remembering that while each of us is an expert in something, none of us are experts in everything. Pass on whatever you have uncovered since our last meeting. Everyone gets to know everything. Questions on that?" He looked around the table. There were no objections. Tom nodded. "This week we go after Wallerein's money. That's a good lead-in for you, Colleen."

Colleen gracefully tucked a wisp of her long hair behind her ear, a movement that Tom always thought particularly sexy. "One of the things that we learned in Bolivia," she said, "is if we attack the money and money handlers, we can 'strangle the dragon,' or at least limit terrorist operations.

"As I mentioned at our last meeting, terrorism floats on a sea of money, most of it illegal. A few years ago—in 1996 to be precise—the International Monetary Fund estimated that between two to five per cent of the worldwide economy involved laundered money."

"That much?" asked Brice.

"Actually, some estimates put it higher."

He looked to Ruhi who nodded.

Colleen continued, "Obviously, not all of that is funding terrorism, but even a small percentage of a huge number is pretty significant. I will continue to attempt to identify worldwide illegal money transfers."

"Yes, but how does that tie in with terrorism and Wallerein?" asked Porter.

"In 1989, the G7 countries created the Financial Action Task Force on Money Laundering, or FATF, to address money laundering in general. Originally, the emphasis was on drug money. That's now shifting towards money laundering for terrorist activities. Thirty-four countries have joined FATF so far."

Brice asked, "Five bucks says not one Middle Eastern country signed."

Colleen nodded. "You are correct."

"Brice, are you being cynical again?" laughed Porter.

146

"Not really. Or, at least, I don't think so. Since the fall of the Soviet Empire, funding for international terrorists has come mainly from the Middle East—Iraq, Iran, Saudi, and their friends."

"Any more questions?" Tom asked. There were none. "Thanks, Colleen. You're up, Ruhi."

She handed a stack of copies to her husband who stood and passed them around. "The U.S. Treasury and INTERPOL published a study last year on the Hawala remittance system. Here are copies for each of you." She was interrupted by the sound of a low-flying jet. She glanced up and stopped talking as she watched the plane making graceful turns over the Potomac.

"Ruhi, they're making a River Visual Approach into Reagan National Airport," explained Tom.

"She knows, Tom," said Brice with a chuckle. "She flew the approach this morning. In the Challenger, no less."

Tom groaned and put his head down on the table. "You're killin' me, Ruhi."

Colleen patted him on the back, then looked up at the group. "Sometimes I find him sitting out here at night, watching the airplanes land and whining to himself about lack of flying time." She leaned over and gave him a kiss. "Poor baby."

Ruhi said, "I'm happy watching the airplanes shoot approaches, Tom. Or do you insist on working?"

Tom lurched back in his chair and motioned for her to continue.

She chuckled as the group hooted and laughed at Tom's expense, then began. "*Hawala* is an Arabic word meaning transfer. In practice, *Hawala* is an informal remittance system used throughout Asia and the Islamic world. It is a cost effective, efficient and reliable method of transferring money around the world. No paper trail, either."

"Ideal for terrorists as well as taxi drivers in New York City," added Tom.

"Exactly. Let me give you a simple example: I have $10,000 that I want to transfer from my home in California to someone in Karachi. I go to a hawaler in California and give her $10,000 cash. She uses her connections and contacts a hawaler in Karachi who arranges to deliver the $10,000 to my associate."

"Holy cow, is this legal?" asked Porter. "Who thought of it?"

"It's been around for centuries. Genghis Khan used something like this; the Knights Templar set up a similar system for the Crusaders, and today it's growing all over the world, following the flow of immigration. If things continue, the hawala trend will become a torrent."

The group paused to reflect for a moment while Tom passed around a pitcher of sangria. "Okay, Jacob, how about you?"

"The background investigations are moving along. And, Tom, yours came back clean. Squeaky clean, in fact."

Tom grimaced.

"What's the matter? You knew we were going to do this. Do me first, you said."

Tom nodded. "Yeah, I know, but I don't like having someone getting into my knickers."

"Well, nasty or not, you came out like Mr. Clean."

He turned towards Porter. "So did you, my friend, much to my surprise, you being a confirmed iconoclast and all. But we eventually found a few people who were willing to speak up on your behalf. How much did you pay them anyway?"

"I thought you said you did a thorough background check? If you had, you would know about the time I—Ooh, never mind."

Orsini spoke for the first time. "What is this all about?"

"Everybody here is undergoing an extensive background check."

"I already had one when I joined the Administration."

"Yes, done by a civilian contract firm. This one will be done by the FBI."

"Who authorized that? I've never heard of such a thing!"

"Isabella, it is pro forma. And directed by the president himself. We know that the Soviets and East Germans planted moles in our government. Fact. We have uncovered several already. Fact. We are searching for more. Fact. This search party has to be squeaky clean."

Orsini sat back in her chair red faced, arms crossed.

"Okay," said Tom. "Let's move to the big news. Last week, I was in New Mexico to fly with Ruhi and Brice. First we overflew the fire damage out by Las Vegas, then turned back to watch the massive fire near Montero." He gestured to Robinson who handed Tom a stack of photographs to distribute. "Here are some aerial photos I had the gang back at Langley print up for us," he said as the group passed around the photos. "You can see how extensive the fires were. Notice anything?"

"They look like the bomb assessment photos we had after our missions in Iraq," said Brice. "What a mess. Massive destruction."

"True, but there's something else."

Ruhi spoke up. "The time stamps." She shuffled several photos. "Look," she pointed with a manicured finger. "The earlier photos are in more remote areas. These last two fires are near cities."

"Exactly." Robinson produced another set of photos. "Here are shots of the near total destruction of the town of Montero. The date is the most recent of past fires. This last set is of the current monster burning in the Lincoln National Forest. It's about to leap on the watershed for the reservoir of the city of Alamogordo."

"That leads us into what happened later on our flight in New Mexico," said Tom as he glanced through his notes. "Up near Taos and Red River, we ran into some opposition." He spent the next five minutes detailing the confrontation with the arsonists. "The surviving bad guy is under guard at the Taos hospital. As soon as he had his rights explained to him—in German, interestingly enough—he clammed up and hasn't said a word to anybody."

"You're proud of that?" Orsini challenged.

"What?" asked Tom.

"That little stunt of yours."

"You mean when we captured the arsonists?"

"You know precisely what I mean. When you ran that vehicle off the road. Those men could have been killed."

"Because they might have drowned under the weight of their guns and the chain saws they used to kill people?"

"You had no proof."

"They shot at us."

149

"Of course they did, you were trying to kill them. They were defending themselves."

Tom bit back the hot words he almost spit out and forced himself to take a sip of sangria before answering. "Let me paint a picture for you, Isabella. They had just set a fire in the national forest. They wanted to kill people. They shot at us. We stopped them. Proud, no. Satisfied, yes. For one, we caught them early so they couldn't make a bigger, more involved fire; and two, we eliminated them as an attacking force."

Orsini shook her head in disgust. "So you are judge, jury, and executioner?"

Tom met her gaze, "We defended ourselves, Isabella. I have no problem with that." He shifted to Borenstein. "Jacob, do you have anything to add?"

"One of my guys was on-board during the flight." He turned to Orsini, "Tom, Ruhi and Brice went after those men after being authorized by my agent. They stopped a crime in progress. It made sense then and even more now. From this incident, for the first time, we know that at least some of the fires in the Southwest were arson. Now it's much more than that—it is terrorism."

Brice spoke up. "This is a good time for us to let everybody know the latest breaking news."

He looked to his wife. "Ruhi, feel free to jump in any time, sweetheart." He looked directly at Orsini. "Two days ago, two terrorists were ordered by Kurt Wallerein to assassinate me because of my involvement in stopping those other Wallerein terrorists in New Mexico. By mistake, they attacked my teenage boys and my wife. That would be that lovely lady sitting right next to you, Isabella. Ruhi. Targets to slaughter." He paused. "Let me walk you through this...."

After Brice had finished, Orsini shook her head. "I find this hard to believe, something like that happening here in the United States."

"I can understand you not wanting to believe it, but it happened just as I said."

"And your source?"

"Ruhi's father, Professor Fasheed Talebreza."

"And how did he induce the alleged terrorist to talk."

Brice hesitated. "Among other things, he held a knife to the man's throat."

"Just as I thought," Isabella said. "He tortured that man! This can't be used in court."

"We understand and agree, Isabella," said Brice. "But this group can use the intelligence he produced. We can spread the word now that we know where to look and what to look for."

She shook her head. "The information—I would never call this intelligence—isn't reliable. A person being tortured will say anything."

Brice took a deep breath. "In general terms, Isabella, this guy was a low-level drone—a true believer. He worked for Wallerein. His mission was to start fires in the Southwest. He was in Nevada and Arizona. He was sent to California to kill me."

Isabella's face reddened. She slapped her hand on the table. "But in this country, these men have rights. We have a Constitution to protect the people."

"Yes, we do," said Tom. "And we are not sitting here advocating torture. How these terrorists—and there will be more in the future—are treated will have to be decided by people higher up the food chain than we are. It's a difficult problem and will be debated forever, probably."

Orsini slid her wine glass towards the middle of the table. "Thank you for today's invitation. It has been most enlightening. I have another appointment now." She stood. "I'll see myself out."

The group watched her disappear through the French doors, high heels clicking on the wooden floor.

"I don't think that your good friend Isabella had a very good time here today, Tom," said Porter. "In fact, I don't think she likes us."

"She certainly didn't like the fact that I am going to investigate her background," said Jacob.

Orsini Residence,
R Street NW
Near DuPont Circle
Washington, DC

The Ford Crown Victoria limousine stopped in front of the covered entry to Dr. Isabella Orsini's apartment complex. The sight of the imposing building normally served as a physical testament to her rising position in the Washington political maelstrom. Betting on her continued ascension, she had paid much more than she could afford for the two-bedroom apartment located near Capitol Hill and the White House. Today she had a sour taste in her month as she contrasted her status symbol with Tom Callahan's expansive—and very expensive—Georgetown home. The faux-heraldry emblazoned over the entry mocked her as she considered Callahan's nearly two centuries old manor house.

She exited the limousine and stalked away from her car without even a thank you for the driver. Ignoring the doorman's smiling, "Good afternoon, Dr. Orsini," she strode through the marble foyer and stabbed at the elevator UP button. She entered her apartment and looked around the comfortable, albeit small-ish, apartment with its bay window overlooking a park. The contrast of her abode with Callahan's enormous, vibrant living room and huge back garden that resembled its own park was intolerable. She slammed her purse on the granite kitchen countertop.

"Whoa, who is that tornado crashing in here?"

Startled, she whirled around to see Edward Harrison the Third, her boyfriend of three months emerging from the bedroom. Harrison, sported a full head of curly, sandy hair, was lithe and athletic and dressed in his weekend attire of wrinkled khakis, a ragged V-neck sweater, and a tweed jacket with leather elbow patches. His casual attire contrasted with his position as an up-and-coming Congressional staffer. Six years her junior, he possessed one of the sharpest minds she had ever encountered. Armed with a modest amount of family money and an Ivy League education, the handsome young lawyer had penetrated the Congressional bureaucracy

152

like a streak of lightning. His influence on the Hill was profound and growing.

Embarrassed, she blurted, "I'm so angry I could spit!"

He chuckled as he gave her a brief hug. "Ooh, where is my cold-blooded killer? I've never seen you like this before in committee."

Orsini thought that over. She was a natural schemer, and proud of it. She had begun her professional development in the internecine fighting within the halls of academia, then onto Oregon state politics as a staffer. By the time she hit the Washington big-time, she prided herself in being an expert in subterfuge, intrigue, and back-stabbing.

"That bastard Callahan!" she said, scowling.

"Is that the same military cretin in the White House that you've bumped up against before?"

She nodded. "We had a meeting with his oh-so-elite group at his house. He was very condescending. He talked down to me in front of his friends, and they thought it was funny."

"Don't you think you're overreacting just a tad? This guy's star will fade. He's a fighter pilot, for God's sakes. He's probably never even visited Washington before. What did you say about how the chief of staff described him? Naïve?"

"Yes. And he is, too."

"Well, just be vigilant and seize the moment when it comes. And it will most certainly come. Then do him in. You've done it before. I've seen you."

He opened the fridge and produced a bottle of her favorite Seebass Grand Reserve Chardonnay. "This is what you need." He pointed to the couch. "I'll meet you there."

Orsini settled back and stroked the smooth surface of the aniline leather as she watched Edward conduct his bottle opening ritual. Satisfied with the results, he crossed the room, handed her a glass and sat. As they clinked glasses, she slipped off her Italian leather shoes and smiled for the first time that afternoon. "You're right as always. This—and you—are what I needed."

"What's this new group all about?" he asked.

"You know I'm not supposed to tell you."

He pulled away and eyed her. "Isabella, this game of 'I know something you don't know' is getting a bit tiresome."

She hated that cold tone of voice. As a senior staffer, he possessed security clearances that rivaled her own. He was also the first man she had let into her life in a very long while. Too long.

She stroked his arm. "I'm sorry, honey. It's just that Callahan is distracting the president from the important things that I was put into the White House to accomplish." She sipped her wine. "The president thinks Tom Callahan is some kind of macho genius."

"Why?"

"That's all very hush-hush. Even my boss doesn't know much." She related the details of the afternoon meeting. "Those paranoid bastards actually think the United States is under attack by some shadowy group! They actually believe they can go running around torturing people and get away with it."

"Didn't you say that it was the woman's father who did the torturing, not one of the group?"

"Yes, but what's the difference? They plan on using the confession that was wrung out of that poor man through torture." She gulped her wine in frustration. "And to top it off, they announced a plan to do another background investigation on all of us. Imagine!"

He touched her shoulder. "Why are you so upset about a background investigation? You've already had one. It's no big deal."

She paused, slowly swirled her wine glass then looked up at him. "The point is I just don't think it's appropriate. Or as Callahan put it so eloquently, 'Nobody likes someone getting in their knickers.'"

Edward pulled her to him and nuzzled her neck. "You didn't mind me doing that last weekend."

With a smile, she conceded the point and put down her glass. "Maybe you're right… Maybe you should try again… you know, just for a frame of reference…."

Chapter Twenty-One

Rock Creek Park
Washington, D.C.

Dr. Simon O'Donnell, PhD, rode his bike hard, slicing through the twisting roads of Rock Creek Park. He had to pay attention since a surprising percentage of American drivers either could not or did not see bicycles. He assumed that it was because so few Americans knew the joy of racing through the countryside, something the Brit in O'Donnell simply could not understand.

He squeezed this last ride into his hectic schedule before his trip to San Antonio. He was to give a speech on his specialty, applied econometrics and international development. As the World Bank in-house expert on the subject, he was in high demand. With all his business travel, it was bloody difficult to get a consistent training regimen established.

He and his wife had scheduled a ride down the Mississippi River Trail, which follows the second longest river in America for some two thousand miles and crosses ten states. The ride was already set for September. He knew he needed to get in lots of miles before then. Since his recent promotion, his workload at the Bank had grown exponentially; Sheila's workload was not even close to his. If she was ready in September and he wasn't, he'd never hear the end of it. He grimaced as he charged down the road. When he returned from Texas, he and Sheila were committed to the combined C&O Canal and Towpath plus the great Allegheny Passage ride that totaled some 330 miles over one weekend. That would give him a better feel for how his training was coming along.

Somehow he would have to arrange a bike rental in San Antonio so he could ride during his stay there.

O'Donnell turned onto his favorite stretch of the ride, a narrow two-lane asphalt strip that more resembled a country lane in his native Yorkshire, no guardrails coupled with some tight turns, which he loved. He rocketed down the road, reveling in the feeling of freedom. O'Donnell always felt invincible when he rode, sensing the air press against his skin, the variation of temperatures as he shot through patches of sunlight, patches of shadow.

He surveyed the road ahead as far as he could see through the curves and plotted his track. He felt, rather than heard, a car behind him as the terrain flashed by: a dirt embankment as high as his head to his left, trees and a deep ditch to his right. Cranking another high-speed turn, white striping whipped by so fast that the dashes almost blurred into a solid line. Wind whistled through the slits in his helmet. Then he slid as far as he could to the right and motioned the car to pass.

The black car inched its way into his peripheral vision and then seemed to freeze into position. O'Donnell saw the next turn coming and gauged the diminishing space between his bike and the car.

"Move over, you bugger!" he shouted. The man in the passenger seat stared. Then smiled. O'Donnell braked so the stupid bastard would pass. Inexplicably, the car slowed. It slid towards him, pushing him towards the ditch.

O'Donnell hit a hole. Lost his balance. Flew sideways. His world exploded. He slammed into the ground and bounced into the air. A tree flashed by. Another. He crashed into a thicket of oaks. Fiery pain. Blackness.

Ronald Reagan Washington National Airport

Colleen Callahan's taxi pulled up under the porte-cochere for Tritten Aviation's private terminal. An attendant was at the taxi door before the vehicle was completely stopped. Colleen was ushered through the imposing foyer, replete with leather and glass furniture and plush carpeting. Thick windows kept outside aircraft engine noise to a whisper.

An attractive young woman approached. "Good afternoon, Dr. Callahan," she said. She pointed to a door marked Flight Planning. "Your pilots are mission planning."

Flight Planning was almost as plush as the foyer. Colleen's first thought was how much Tommy would love to be here. Ruhi leaned over the flight planning table, engrossed in their flight details. "Hello, Ruhi," Colleen said with a smile. "Or should I call you 'Captain'?" The women embraced.

"Colleen, this is Bill Walker. He's going to be instructing me during the flight."

Walker was youngish, maybe thirty, with a military haircut and an engaging smile. "Good morning, Dr. Callahan," he said, offering his hand.

"Please, it's Colleen." Walker nodded and smiled.

"Ruhi, this is so wonderful of you. *Domo arigato*," she said with an exaggerated bow.

"No, no, *mijita*, don't thank me. This is a great opportunity. I get to fly. Bill gets to fly. A real mission, not just drilling holes in the sky. And I get to attend the symposium and listen to your first-ever speech as a World Bank big shot."

"Oh, yeah, a real World Bank Big shot I am. The only reason I'm here is because Simon O'Donnell was injured, and I was the only one in the office available to take his place."

"Well, your office is lucky to have you as a back-up."

"Colleen," said Walker, "if you'll excuse me, I'll take your bags out to the aircraft and finish the walk around inspection while Miss Ruhi gives you the quick and dirty flight brief."

Five minutes later, Colleen and Ruhi walked briskly across the tarmac towards where the glistening Challenger 350 crouched, ready to fly.

The aircraft was as gorgeous inside as it was outside. Colleen was an experienced traveler who had flown hundreds of times with her husband—but never in a private aircraft like this. She watched as Ruhi slid gracefully into the pilot's seat and tried to get a good visual picture of the cockpit, sure that Tommy would ask her question upon question

157

about the layout. The roomy cabin was appointed with four leather captain's chairs and even a couch! A flat screen television, walnut table, and accents lent an air of luxury to the cabin, Ruhi's touch no doubt. Colleen walked down the aisle without a need to duck her head–a delighted grin broke out on her face. This was class!

She settled herself at the cabin table and stowed her briefcase and purse for takeoff. Soft music wafted through the cabin as the aircraft taxied. She saw the Washington Monument and the Capitol building slide by as Ruhi negotiated her way to the active runway. After takeoff, Colleen watched the sprawl of the Washington metroplex disappear below her.

She could feel her muscles loosening as she started to relax. Finally she felt secure, surrounded only by friends. She was sure she had been followed for the past several weeks at least. Despite her husband's promise to end it, she knew someone was still watching her. She'd detected them a couple of times. They were good, but her training courses in the Special Forces Counterterrorism School at Fort Bragg had prepared her for this. She had played along with the FBI enough. She was tired of being a training exercise. Fine, she thought, since Tommy's obviously forgotten, I'll write Jacob myself. She opened her laptop and composed a short but direct email and placed it in her outbox to be sent from her hotel in San Antonio.

Satisfied, Colleen settled back into the luxurious leather seat. She had to admit that she was excited by this unprecedented opportunity to address such a prestigious group. In fact, she could hardly contain herself. Her newly minted doctorate was not even out of the box, yet here she was, off to her first professional symposium. A pang of guilt shot through her—she was leaving her family behind at point eight mach. Well, she smiled and patted her tummy, part of her family. This part was still with her. She laughed out loud. At long last, she was facing the dilemma faced by so many professional women—how to balance family life and children with a career, something she had believed she would never be able to address. She and Tommy would work this out. She had no doubt. Life was good and getting better.

Back to work. She opened her briefcase and pored over financial intelligence reports from all over the world, attempting to penetrate the opaque finances of Wallerein's operations. Because of her unique perspective gained from working in Bolivia, she was looking for connections between terrorist organizations and organized crime. Wallerein had already done that once, with *narcotraficantes* in Bolivia, Peru, and Colombia. The information provided by Major Turri's informant in Mexico confirmed at least one criminal contact in Punta del Este and one in Mexico. Were they an aberration or a trend?

After level off, Ruhi came back and sat down across from her.

"Working hard?" Ruhi teased.

"This is a big deal, and I don't want to blow it. I'm glad you came; it means a lot to know there will be at least one friendly face in the audience. Just hope the symposium is not too boring for you."

"Surely you jest, *mijita*. I majored in economics. After Stanford, I was consumed by the finance of international development. It is my passion. It's how I met Brice, at an international finance conference in London."

"I met my Tommy in a bar in Sydney," said Colleen. They both laughed.

"By the way, Ruhi, I booked us in adjacent rooms. We're right on the Riverwalk so we can do the town in style. Lots of restaurants. Tommy was envious. He could eat Mexican three times a day."

"Brice, too," laughed Ruhi. "Well, back to work for me. Bill is a nice guy but the very devil about flying procedures. Thunderstorms up ahead as we cross the Red River, so we may have to make a few course adjustments."

Colleen nodded. "It's thunderstorm season in the Southwest. I know it well. You do what you have to do. Don't worry about me."

She studied the countryside as it slid past. Lush forests and rivers gradually gave way to the forested mountains of western Virginia, then West Virginia itself, followed by larger farms, then flat flat flat. Colleen had lived in the United States for less than half of her married life. She was used to big countries—she was Australian, after all—but at nearly four million square miles, the U.S. was large even by Australian standards.

She loved flying with Tommy over the gorgeous countryside, watching the colors and textures change from region to region, state by state.

She forced herself back to her notes. Immersed in research, the flight passed so quickly she was surprised when she felt the thud of the landing gear being extended. Colleen watched the Texas countryside slip underneath as she tried hard not to grade Ruhi's approach as Tommy would have.

After landing, the women said goodbye to Walker and took a taxi to the Grand Alamo Riverwalk Hotel. Perched alongside the San Antonio River and its famous Riverwalk, the beautiful thirty-eight story resort lived up to its advertising hype with a gorgeous lobby and front desk area. They strolled through the terrace landscaped with gorgeous flowers in limestone planters sheltered by long-limbed live oak trees. The area was calming, a bit too hot, but both women came from hot climates and were used to the heat. The view from their adjoining deluxe suites was fascinating—a few tall buildings, the famous Tower of the Americas and lots of Texas stretching out to the horizon.

After quick showers and brief phone calls to their respective husbands, the women went for a stroll on the Riverwalk, a sinuous walking strip of greenery, elaborate landscaping, restaurants and shops that winds through the city core. They paused in the boutiques sited amongst the lush, elaborate landscaping. Colleen, fashionista that she was, delighted in a find of exquisite Jimmy Choo knee high suede cowgirl boots. They accumulated several more purchases, then settled down at a Mexican restaurant where Colleen limited herself to a single— she felt an obligatory—'virgin'margarita. Even though it lacked alcohol, she felt less guilty by limiting herself to one. She insisted that they speak Spanish to keep herself current in the language. Pleasantly stuffed, they chatted and strolled arm in arm along the concrete path back to the hotel.

Inside her spacious suite, Colleen slipped on her new boots and was admiring them in her full-length mirror when she heard a knock on the door between the rooms. She opened it. There was Ruhi, eyes open wide. A large man with a stone-cold stare had an arm across her throat as he pressed the muzzle of a gun to her temple.

"Good evening, Frau Doktor," he said. "No noise, or she dies."

160

Something moved behind her. Someone in her suite? Then a blow to the head sent her to her knees. A second blow knocked her out.

***

Colleen Callahan fought her way back through a brain-numbing fog. Something rough against her cheek—a hood. Her hands and feet were bound. She felt, then heard twin propeller engine noise—an airplane. Cold. Kidnapped. Somewhere… She slipped back into unconsciousness.

Chapter Twenty-Two

Washington, D.C.

Tom Callahan emerged into the morning overcast from the bowels of the Metro Center hub. He glanced up at the gloomy sky and hustled through the crowds of late morning commuters. He was already behind his usual schedule. Instead of receiving a good-bye kiss from baby Mikey, the youngster had chosen that precious moment to puke his breakfast all over his daddy's shoulder. That required both a change of clothes and a shower. It had been a big breakfast.

He passed through White House security with a few casual words, then a salute and a "Good Morning, Corporal" to the Marine guard and strode through the hallways of the building and into his office. He plopped down at his polished walnut desk, stared out the window, and sighed. Ever more papers crowded the in-box. He was behind already. Good thing he had read the European papers on the Metro. As was his habit, the first document he read at his desk was *The Early Bird*, a DoD clipping service compilation of current news events, almost required reading in Washington government circles. Tucked away on the next-to-last page was an unexpected item about an explosion at a wellhead for the water supply of the town of Hildago, New Mexico. Tom had passed through or flown over the small town many times. Located just off I-25 south of Las Vegas, Hildago had a population of around a thousand. Why the local water well would blow up was a mystery and under investigation. In the meantime, water for the residents would have to be trucked in from Las Vegas.

He reached for his copy of the *Washington Post*. The intercom buzzed. "Colonel, the chief of staff would like to see you."

"On my way."

Tom grabbed his leather notebook, sniffed his shoulder to make sure the sour smell of baby vomit was really gone, and headed towards the West Wing.

Mark Freiberg, the chief of staff, sat behind his massive desk in his shirtsleeves. Freiberg was a long-time Washington politico, a former Congressman who resigned in order to run the reelection campaign for the current occupant of the Oval Office. When he spoke, he spoke for the president. Right now, Freiberg was plowing his way through an enormous stack of correspondence. His in-basket was even more overflowing than the one on Tom's own desk. The man must be a machine to handle all that work. Isabella Orsini was seated on one of the cream-colored couches that flanked the desk, wearing what Tom had come to consider her usual uniform—dark suit, white blouse buttoned all the way to her neck, and a red power scarf. She glared at Tom, a tight-lipped smile frozen on her face.

"Good morning, Mr. Freiberg," Tom said, then nodded to Orsini.

Freiberg motioned Tom to the couch opposite her.

"Your reaction, Tom?"

"To what, sir?"

"If you would get to work on time you would know what he is talking about," snapped Orsini.

Tom fixed her with a cold stare. Orsini sat back in her chair, arms crossed.

Freiberg came out from behind his desk and seated himself in a chair. He handed Tom a folded copy of the *Washington Post*. "Page eight."

Tom zeroed in on a short article circled in red.

"Mr. Freiberg," said Orsini, "I told Callahan that his home was an inappropriate place to hold meetings—"

Freiberg silenced her with a wave of his hand. "Let him finish reading and collect his thoughts."

Tom skimmed the three-paragraph article, then again more slowly.

163

"I don't see that there is a problem with this, sir."

Freiberg sat back in his chair and steepled his fingers. "Really? The story alludes to a secret group of high-level administration officials meeting in secret in a private home in Georgetown. It also hints at a conspiracy of arson in the Southwest with more details to come."

"Sir, the purpose of our meeting was to address Wallerein issues at my house to keep a low profile—"

"Didn't work, did it?" snarled Orsini.

Tom ignored her. "Sir, has anybody actually called in on this?"

"Not yet but they probably will."

"Maybe not. It's pretty obscure." Tom could see that his answer surprised him.

"That's how these things start," said Freiberg.

"Okay, but the important issue alluded to in the article is the problem in the Southwest." Tom produced a two-page report. "We now have two sources of intelligence that indicate that Wallerein is directing operations in our country. I've sketched out a brief for you and the president—"

"Isabella informs me that the sources for this information are unverified and thus unreliable. And torture, Tom? In this country? In this day and age?"

"Sir, both the FBI and the California authorities are dealing with the torture issue. But the information from one of Wallerein's soldiers in California meshes with what was reported through the U.S. Embassy in Mexico City. I met with the officer who turned up the intelligence." He gestured to the papers in Freiberg's hands. "It's in my report. We need to do something about it. Right now."

"Does the CIA stand behind this information?

Tom said, "Robbie Robinson left for Mexico City last night. He will work with the CIA Station Chief and the Defense Attaché Office."

"That's not what I asked. Does the CIA stand behind this information?"

Orsini said, "My sources say that Robinson has no stature in the CIA. He was rogue, forcibly retired, and only got reinstated because of some HR quirk."

Tom bit back an angry reply. "Mr. Freiberg, the information is new. We—our group that is, which includes both FBI and CIA assets—are working to verify the stories."

"And in the meantime, there are security leaks in your so-called group," snapped Orsini.

Freiberg leaned forward. "Right now, Tom, from where I sit, the big issue is where did this Post story come from? Somebody leaked this. The president loathes leakers. This needs to be fixed. Right now."

"No problem, sir. I will speak to Jacob Borenstein. The leak could have come from anywhere, although why or how is beyond me."

"No," said Orsini, contempt in her voice. "It could only have come from someone at that meeting and there was only one journalist present."

"If you're accusing Porter Nelson of writing this, you are way off base."

"We're supposed to take your word on that? If not him, who then?" She looked to Freiberg. "Now that this is out in the open, sir, you need damage control. I know how to work the press. Callahan has shown he cannot."

Freiberg said, "Tom, I know I approved these meetings at your house, but it seems your security arrangements were less than satisfactory."

"Sir, the house was swept for electronic bugs before and after the meetings. Only those present knew of the meeting."

"Obviously not, Callahan," said Orsini.

Freiberg said, "Tom, I am not going to the president with this report until we have a consensus in the intelligence community of a terrorist orchestrating a wave of attacks within our borders. No way."

The intercom buzzed, and Freiberg paused to take a call from the Secretary of State. Tom had time to regroup. What had gone wrong? Why was Freiberg more concerned with a silly gossip column article rather than following up on Wallerein and the wildfires? And all Orsini wanted was to burn him. He rubbed the back of his neck and grimaced at his choice of words.

"Just a second, Mr. Secretary. I have a few people in my office. Let me end the meeting." Freiberg covered the mouthpiece with his hand and said to Tom and Orsini, "I'll see you this afternoon. My secretary will call you about the time. Make yourselves available."

White House

Tom Callahan sat at his desk, stared out the window and smoldered. Life in the Washington was turning out to be just what he had envisioned. Nasty, brutish, and he sincerely hoped, short. The issue was how to deal with this latest episode, a leak which, in the real world, would be no big deal; here in Washington it was monumental, tumultuous and potentially career-ending. None of which bothered Tom, except in this case, he had to stay locked-on the larger issue of Wallerein. The intel generated by the Embassy in Mexico City was red-hot and needed to be addressed ASAP. Tom's conduit to the president through the chief of staff was throttled shut as effectively as a tourniquet on a ruptured artery, thanks to Orsini.

So far, Wallerein's name had not come up in the papers. The high number of wildfires was put down to the drought affecting the Southwest, more than the usual number of lightning strikes, careless campers and a few individuals acting on their own for unknown reasons. There had been no mention of a concerted, coordinated series of arson-set fires. Most of the discussions in Washington focused on how much of the Forest Service budget was being consumed by fighting fires; most of the media output concerned people's homes and individual family tragedies. Nobody had yet put together the strategic implications of a concerted wave of fires focused on watersheds and water sources. That would change soon. Tom needed to get decision makers focused on what was about to happen, or Americans would start dying.

This current leak was a problem with a newspaper. Porter Nelson knew all about newspapers. Calling Porter was the obvious next step. Tom reached for the phone and was startled when his intercom buzzed.

"Colonel," said Marge. "There's a call for you from Dr. Khozein at the World Bank. He's quite insistent that he speak with you."

"Callahan."

"Colonel, sorry to burst in like this but do you know where your wife is?"

Odd question, thought Tom. "Why?"

"She didn't show up for her speech this morning."

Tom's heart skipped a beat. He spoke as carefully as he could. "Are you sure?"

"We have a driver and an escort at the hotel. They knocked on her door and had no response."

Alarms went off in Tom's head. Blood pounded in his temples. He took a deep breath. "Dr. Khozein, I will call the hotel and have security check it out. Thank you for alerting me. I'll get back to you."

"Please do, sir. We are quite concerned."

Tom mashed the intercom button. "Marge, please get me either the manager of the Grand Alamo Riverwalk Hotel in San Antonio or the head of security. Quickly, please!"

What was going on?

The intercom again. "Sir, I have the head of the hotel security on the line. A Mr. Sprott."

"Mr. Sprott, this is Tom Callahan in Washington."

"Colonel, I went to the rooms with the World Bank escort. There is nobody in either room. The connecting door is open. All their stuff is here. Beds not slept in." A pause. "And Colonel, there appears to be signs of a struggle."

"Are you sure?"

"Colonel, I'm standing in the rooms right now."

Tom covered his eyes with his hand. *Oh God!* He took a deep breath. "Of course. Thank you, Mr. Sprott. Please secure the room. I'll contact the FBI."

The light on his phone lit up. "Colonel," said the White House operator, "we have a Major Turri calling from the Embassy in Mexico City on the classified line."

"Put him through, please."

"Sir, this is Major Turri. Do you know where your wife is? Have you heard from her today?"

"Not today. Colleen called yesterday after they hit the hotel in San Antonio. Why?"

A pause. "Sir, my contact says your wife is in danger."

Oh no! "Are you sure?"

"He said that Kurt Wallerein had a team watching you and your wife for a couple weeks." Another pause, this one longer. "Sir, my contact thinks Wallerein sent a team to kidnap your wife."

Tom's hand hurt from squeezing the handset. *Sweet Jesus!* "How confident are you about this, Major? Did you record the conversation?"

"Colonel, everything he's told us so far has been right on the money. And no, I could not record it. The call came in on my cell phone."

"Tell me all you know," he said, breathing hard and desperate for information.

"My contact is privy to Wallerein's plans—at least some of his plans, to be precise. This was his first opportunity to call me about your wife."

"Where are you now, Major?"

"In the Embassy. I just spoke with my guy. He was very insistent."

"I'll try to track down Colleen." He choked out the words, still unable to grasp the concept of Colleen's possible disappearance. "In the meantime, find a man named Robbie Robinson. He's around your embassy somewhere, probably with the station chief. Then call Jacob Borenstein at FBI Headquarters. Let him know everything. Every little tiny detail. Every nuance of that call. I'll call you as soon as I can."

He hung up. Then placed his elbows on his desk and his face in his hands. *What to do first? Hell, what should I do, period?* Only his iron will and two decades of military training kept him from screaming. But it was close. Teetering on the edge of panic. *Colleen! Oh my God, Colleen!*

He was sweating profusely, breathing hard as if he had sprinted a quarter mile. He was desperate to do something, but he didn't know what. He jumped to his feet and paced the small office. He leaned on his desk and squeezed his eyes closed. A moan escaped from down deep. Colleen! Kidnapped! He was to blame. She told him that she thought she was being followed, and he had done nothing. Even forgotten about it. He'd been a fool to leave her unprotected.

Tom dropped to his knees and grabbed for his trashcan. His stomach erupted. Again and again until his sides ached. He put his head on his desk and tried to swallow, breathe.

Gradually, the fighter pilot in him re-asserted itself. He was dealing with an emergency—not a simple in-flight emergency like an engine explosion or a surface-to-air missile, something designed to kill him. This was an emergency that threatened what was most precious to him— his wife and unborn child.

Finally, he opened his eyes. His breathing and heart rate were back to near normal.

What was Wallerein's intent? To punish Tom? To incite some rash action? If Wallerein had done any study of Tom at all, he would know Tom's temper and propensity for rash and impetuous actions.

Colleen's kidnapping was a challenge. Wallerein wanted to make this struggle personal. He wanted Tom to come charging forth, breathing fire right into a confrontation that Tom would surely lose. Wallerein might be a son-of-a-bitch, but he was a smart son-of-a-bitch. Of that, Tom was certain.

Action. He needed to take some action. What should he do first?

He picked up the phone. The FBI, Porter Nelson. Then Brice Adams

***

Colleen awoke with a start. She was in a small, low ceilinged room with dirty concrete walls. No windows. The only furniture was the pallet on the floor, stuffed with straw. A single light bulb dangled from the ceiling. Light scalded her brain. Waves of nausea swept over her. *Where am I?* She struggled to drag herself out of her mental fog. *Where is Ruhi?*

She could only guess how long she had been there. Her feet were cold. Her boots were missing. She looked at her hands. Her watch, her phone, her diamond engagement ring and wedding band were gone. She moaned as she rolled to her side. Her head ached, and waves of nausea and vertigo pulsed through her body. Eventually, she heaved herself upright, leaned against the wall and gathered herself. She stumbled to her feet and pounded on the metal door. "Let me out, you bloody bastards!" she screamed.

Nothing. No response. Exhausted and nauseated, she slid to the floor. When the nausea subsided, she forced herself to begin some slow stretches, ignoring the pain in her head and neck. Finally, she sat on her pallet and tried to collect her thoughts. How long she sat there, she had no idea.

She heard muffled sounds of boots on concrete. A lock scraped; a dead bolt slid back. Three guards burst into her cell. Muscular men, scruffy and armed. One yanked her to her feet. Two men searched her while the third held a submachine gun. The guards' fetid breath was in her face as their hands wandered roughly over her body, laughing as they pulled open her blouse to look at her "weapons." She knew better than to resist, though she wanted to break a few arms.

They cuffed her hands behind her back, then dragged and pushed her down a corridor into a large well-lit room and slammed her into an uncomfortable, straight-backed chair next to a pale wooden table. After what seemed an eternity, a steel door opened and a stocky, white-haired middle-aged man strode in. He placed a dossier on the table.

He motioned to the guards to uncuff her. As the cuffs fell away, Colleen massaged her chafed wrists, pulled her blouse together.

The man spoke in accented English, "And how are you this fine morning, Frau Doktor Callahan?"

"I'm fine, considering that I've been kidnapped and beaten by your thugs."

He leafed through the file of papers, then looked up. "I am Kurt Wallerein. Perhaps you have heard of me?"

"Kurt Wallerein…Kurt Wallerein," she mused. "Sorry can't place it…. Oh, could you be the nephew of Augustus Wallerein, the famous German banker who was murdered by the Baader-Meinhof gang some time ago?"

Wallerein's face broke into a smile. "*Ja,* I am surprised you know that, Frau Doktor. My uncle was a capitalist pig who had exploited the people long enough. I pulled the trigger myself."

"Yes, I supposed that's what people like you do so well, shoot unarmed prisoners and kidnap women. Hardly something to be proud of."

He stiffened and spit out a string of what had to be profane German, then back to English. "It's a pity that you are ignorant of German, a beautiful language. Perhaps then we could have a decent conversation."

"For foreign languages, I prefer Japanese," and she recited a haiku about Devil's spawn that seemed appropriate. "Or Spanish perhaps? After all, your last operations were in Latin America." She spoke softly, almost melodiously reciting every Spanish curse word she could recall to direct at this murderous wanker. "Oh, I'm sorry. Perhaps you don't want to be reminded how all those plans were disasters. Perhaps we should try English again," and smiled sweetly.

Wallerein glowered, then broke into a barking laugh. "Well, I see that you have a sense of humor, Frau Doktor."

"Not as much as you do if you think your communist economic model will work. That's a world class joke. Every thinking person on the planet knows that."

"*Ja, Ja,* you are now an economist. And at the World Bank. Very impressive, Frau Doktor. I have wanted to meet you for a long time."

"As I remember, you tried to have me kidnapped in Bolivia. And failed."

"*Nein.* That was not my idea."

"You expect me to believe that?"

"If I had made the order, it would have succeeded. This time I did give the order, and, *voila,* here you are. It was not an easy thing to arrange the accident for Doktor O'Donnell and the request for your presence at the conference on such short notice."

"Am I supposed to congratulate you?"

He stood, walked around the table, and stopped in front of her.

She forced herself to look at him. "So, why am I here, Kurt? Why did you kidnap me?"

"Your husband has caused me much trouble in the past year."

"Not as much as he's going to unless you release me."

Wallerein laughed. "Release you?" He laughed again.

171

"Where's Ruhi?" she demanded, determined to keep this madman talking. "What have you done with her?"

"Your companion, Frau Doktor?" He smiled. "I think I will pass her along to my men. They do not like Iranians. Especially Baha'i Iranians. They are considered apostates, as I recall. I fear for her safety. Perhaps you would like me to intercede for her? Cooperation has many benefits."

"Your type are always the same, Kurt. Lots of lofty talk, rhetoric really. But flowery speech stripped away leaves nothing but lies and thuggery."

"Perhaps in time you will begin to see things my way."

"Not a chance, Kurt."

His face went pale with anger. Her throat tightened. The man was insane. She realized that this murderous crazy man who delighted in killing his own family members would not hesitate to kill her and her baby—perhaps even enjoy it.

He meant to hurt her.

Another guard entered the room. Colleen glanced over at him.

She didn't see Wallerein's punch coming. The impact was hard enough to send her crashing to the floor.

He grabbed her by the front of her blouse and yanked her upright. His fist smashed into her face. Her nose gushed blood. Off balance, she tried to knee him in the groin but he blocked the blow with his leg. He punched her again and again. The thin material of her blouse ripped and she crashed to the floor. She saw flashes of light in front of her eyes and shock waves of pain swept through her body. A savage kick to her kidneys made her scream in agony. And another. She blacked out.

Chapter Twenty-Three

FBI Headquarters
Washington D.C.

Tom Callahan sat, lost in morose thought as the White House SUV made its way through the chaos of Washington late morning traffic towards the J. Edgar Hoover Building. His nerves had been stretched and abused, and he was far from recovered from the shock of Colleen's disappearance.

The SUV stopped in front. Tom was met by two agents, handed a visitor's badge, and whisked up to Jacob Borenstein's office. The sight of his friends did little to brighten his mood. Both Borenstein and Porter Nelson embraced him and murmured sympathies.

"Any word of Colleen, Jacob?"

"Nothing yet, Tom. My guys are on the way to the hotel."

"The security guy said there was evidence of a struggle."

Borenstein nodded.

Tom crumpled into a chair. "My first reaction was to jump into a plane and go to San Antonio," he confessed. "But that wouldn't help anything."

"Sit tight, Tom. Let us do our job. We'll figure this out. I have a team of agents with your son. Your house is secure."

"Thank you." Tom was trying to appear calm, but it was increasingly difficult as the enormity of the situation percolated through him.

Borenstein sat down next to Tom and placed a hand on his knee. "Major Turri called. He said his contact says Colleen and Ruhi are being held somewhere in Mexico at a narcotraficante base. Apparently

Wallerein has bought some friends in the narco community. The narcos are providing him with a secure location and access to weapons and explosives."

Porter said, "I caught Robbie on his way out of the Embassy in Mexico City. He says he still has good contacts in the country. He's on his way to work them."

Tom held up both hands, fingers crossed. *"Ojalá"*– God willing.

"Hang in there, Tom," said Porter. "If anyone can pull it off, Robbie can. I saw him in action in Europe. He's one of the best."

"If Wallerein had men tailing me as well as Colleen, why didn't he just take me out instead of kidnapping her?"

"Tom! Use your brain!" exploded Porter. "He's playing with you. He wants to hurt you as much as he can. Colleen isn't the main course, you are. To him, she's the appetizer. And the good people of New Mexico are the dessert."

Borenstein said, "She's alive, Tom. Hold on to that thought. Wallerein could have had her killed on the street—he's trying to make a point here."

"Actually, Jacob," said Porter. "He has made his point. He can strike anywhere, anytime."

The three men sat quietly, lost in their own thoughts. Finally Tom said, "On top of the kidnapping, I just had an unpleasant time in the barrel with the chief of staff and our good friend Isabella Orsini." He gave a thumbnail sketch of the conversation and handed Porter a copy of the newspaper.

"You know, guys, that geopolitically this could be extremely dangerous," said Tom. "If the United States is seen on the world stage as weakened from domestic problems like these attacks, any serious international issue could blow up—diplomatically, economically, even militarily. That would be catastrophic. We have to convince the president this internal threat is serious."

"How will you do that?" asked Jacob.

"I don't know yet. Orsini keeps getting in the way."

"Isabella was unhappy with us from the start," said Jacob. "She'll be doing her best to pin the blame on you."

Porter nodded. "She wanted to be either in control of the group or out of it. Now that this leak has surfaced, she'll try to shellac you, then get you booted out of the White House in disgrace."

"I don't know why she's concerned with me, I don't want her job."

"It's not just that she's a mean person," said Porter, "It's that she's so good at it."

Tom smiled for the first time. "It's like she rehearses or something."

Borenstein piped up, "She sees enemies everywhere, Tom. It's a professional affliction in Washington."

"This little article is not yet a big story, but if people notice and it catches on, the city will soon be bristling with rumors, lies, and innuendos," said Porter.

"Yep," said Tom. "Well, I can't do anything about that. What we need to do is build a solid case against Wallerein, one that we can beat the chief of staff over the head with to get his attention. He has me on a short leash now. Wants Orsini and me available to meet this afternoon."

Porter said, "The president is in Asia working on the trade deal, the biggest issue of his administration. That's what everybody—the Administration, the Congress, the press are focused on right now, Tom."

"Not me." Tom stood. "I need to work on this. I need to keep busy. But first, I need to go home and hold my son."

"I'll whistle you up a car," said Jacob. "And I'll call Freiberg, tell him about Colleen and attend the meeting for you. The intel from Mexico about Wallerein is crucial, and I'll make Freiberg listen. You stay home. Play with Mikey. Porter and I are on it. I'll stop by after the meeting."

"I'll go with you now, Tom," said Porter.

"No, Jacob's right. You stay here with him and figure out how to catch this son-of-a-bitch."

Mexico

Her eyes did not seem to respond. Colleen opened the one that obeyed her command. She was lying on the floor of a different concrete box, a cold concrete pen with cheap, crumbling concrete that stank of damp and rat urine. She shivered. She hated rats. She could not remember how she got there, only a vague memory of being carried by one of the guards, one who had been gentle. In her dream, he had spoken only once. *"Coraje, señora"*—courage.

Colleen shivered again. Pain shot through her body. Every movement sent shocks racing to her brain. Her right shoulder was not responding, and crusted blood stopped up her nose. She forced her left hand to probe her abdomen. "Please, God, not the baby." She moaned and clutched her midsection. She fought back a surge of nausea, tasted bile.

Colleen found a relatively clean spot and carefully moved to it. She sat with her arms wrapped around her knees and placed her forehead on her arms. She tried to calm her herself, to block out all the pain and fear. She was well and truly frightened, more frightened than she had ever been, not for herself but for her baby. And for her Tommy. Wallerein was determined to kill him. And she was the bait.

Chapter Twenty-Four

J. Edgar Hoover Building,
Washington

Porter Nelson exited the FBI Headquarters, turned left, and walked several blocks in the direction of his car, a red classic 1967 Ferrari 330 GT, stopping only at a newsstand where he bought a copy of the Post. He drove to his Georgetown townhome, made himself an espresso and paused for a moment to inhale the fragrance. Smiling, he wandered into his office, settled into his chair, opened the paper to the offending article, and scrutinized the text.

He made several phone calls, left one voicemail, set the alarm on his phone for four thirty, and spent the next several hours scouring the Internet.

After a short walk, he arrived a few minutes before six at his favorite Georgetown restaurant, was greeted by the maître d' himself, and escorted to his requested isolated table near the back of the outdoor patio. Porter sat facing the front entrance, and stood when the maitre d' guided his guest to the table.

Michelle Duregger was slender, taller than he had anticipated. She carried a full head of dark auburn hair, had green eyes and an unexpected regal air. Early thirties. Still young enough to have a spark of enthusiasm, but old enough for cynicism to begin to devour her fresh-out-of-journalism-school idealism. Dressed in a casual yet fashionable suit, she bore her situation well, a journalism major trapped in a backroom cranking out anonymous filler, hoping for a break.

"Thanks for meeting me," Porter said.

A lovely smile. "An invitation for dinner and drinks from a Pulitzer Prize winner. How could I refuse?"

Porter made some small talk to put her at ease while the waiter fussed over them. The sommelier made his appearance, and he and Porter discussed the pairing of wine with the evening's specials. They settled on an Australian cabernet and the sommelier made an elaborate show of opening the bottle and pouring a sample. Porter studied the color, holding his glass up to the light, gently swirled the wine, and inhaled the fragrance. This was his favorite time, his day's first glass of wine. He knew this particular vintage would be exquisite, and he wasn't disappointed.

Porter raised his glass. Michelle gently touched hers to his and sipped. "This is a wonderful wine," she said.

Porter smiled. "I have two particularly bad habits. I love expensive wine and very fast sports cars."

"Only two bad habits? Then you're way out in front of most men I know."

Porter laughed. "I said two 'particularly' bad habits. I may hold the world's record for my collection of bad ones."

They sat still for a moment, savoring the silence and the aromas wafting gently from the nearby kitchen on the pleasant evening air.

"Mr. Nelson, why am I here?"

Porter suppressed a smile. He loved direct, no-nonsense people. He reached for his briefcase, produced a folded copy of the Post, and placed it on the table. A red circle surrounded a short, three paragraph section. "The blurb in today's paper about the secret meetings at a private home in Georgetown."

Surprised, she blurted, "You read that?"

Porter nodded.

She sat back in her chair, visibly pleased. "Oh, that was just for openers. There's quite a story here. Two more installments to follow, next Monday and Friday."

And a move up in the news world, get a byline, thought Porter. "Good source?"

A glimpse of suppressed excitement. "Rock solid."

178

"What I'd really like to do is ask where you got the information—"

"You know I can't divulge my sources!"

"Relax, Michelle. Please notice that I did not ask." He put the newspaper back in his briefcase. "I presume that you know the names involved and dates of these alleged meetings."

She did not respond.

"The Callahans are friends of mine, probably the best friends I have ever had. Tom saved my life once."

"Really?"

"In Bolivia. I even wrote an article about it for the *Post*." He took a note card from his jacket pocket. "This is the paper's issue date and page numbers. It'll be in the *Post* archives or on the Internet. Look it up. Good solid piece, if I do say so. Not fluff."

Her smile faded. "My piece wasn't fluff. Got your attention, didn't it?"

"Yes, it did." He hesitated, then said. "It's causing Colonel Callahan problems. It needs to stop."

"Are you threatening me, Nelson?"

"No, no. You're a journalist, I'm a journalist. Let's simply have a journalist-type discussion." Porter regarded the younger woman in silence for a moment. "Some years ago, I was like you are now, sitting in the newsroom, a general assignment reporter writing anonymous stuff, bored out of my mind. Hoping, praying for a break. Then I got one."

"What was it?"

"It was here at the *Post*, as a matter of fact. Largely because I speak pretty good French, I was sent to Beirut in 1983, along with your city editor, by the way. I've known him for years." He took a sip of his wine, again savoring the rich texture. "Anyhow, I was there when the Marine barracks were bombed. Got the first story out. Front page stuff. That led to an assignment overseas as the only Western journalist embedded with the Soviet Army in Afghanistan and my first Pulitzer. All because some editor pulled me out and gave me a break."

Porter paused again and studied the eager face across from him. Decision made, he said, "I know your background, where you went to school, the papers you've worked for. That you took a couple years off after college to race sailboats in the Caribbean and the Mediterranean. And you now live on a boat named the *Ruby Slipper* near Annapolis." He smiled again. "I made a few calls. I even read some of your stuff. Not bad."

She sat up a bit straighter. "Thanks, but so?"

"Word is that you're a person of integrity—depressingly rare these days in our profession—so I'm going to go with my gut and make you an offer." He took another sip of his wine. "There is a story here, Michelle. A big story. Bigger than you can imagine."

"Oh, I can imagine pretty big, Mr. Nelson."

Porter smiled. *Now we're back to Mister Nelson.* "Then this will intrigue you. It's juicier than anything you've ever written with the added benefit of having some *gravitas.* Real significance. Massive. It will burnish your rep as a journalist."

She hesitated. "What do you want from me?"

"Sit on the Callahan story."

Duregger sat back in her chair, crossed her arms and said nothing.

"A week, maybe two. Then we'll write the piece the public wants to read, no, has to read. We will be quoted all over the world."

"You know, Mr. Nelson, if it was anybody other than you making this proposition, a proposition bordering on blackmail, I would have tossed this wine, wonderful even though it is, right in your face."

Amused, he asked, "What have I done right to prevent taking a wine shower?"

She smiled. "I, too, have done my homework. I know your background, where you went to school, the papers you've worked for. I, too, made a few calls and even read some of your stuff. Not bad." She raised her glass, took a hearty pull and settled more comfortably into her chair. "You're a charter member of the International Consortium of Investigative Journalists. Word is that you are man of integrity. There has to be a good reason that you're asking me to do this. And I'm glad I don't have to waste this cabernet."

Porter raised his glass. "*Touché.*"

"So, we would be in this together?"

"Yes."

"It'll get published with your byline," she mused.

"And yours. I'll see to that."

She said nothing.

"Take your time, Michelle. I'm offering you a major step up in your—our—profession."

She said, "One question. Why me? I could name twenty journalists in Washington alone who are better qualified to help you than I am."

Porter laughed. "Probably more like fifty, Michelle." He shrugged. "In my far from humble opinion, the Callahans are two of the finest people on the planet. It pisses me off that someone is using you to stick a knife in them, Washington style. I think it would be a bit poetic, elegant even, to have you part of our happy band when we chase down the bad guys and prove Callahan was right all along.

"By the way, Michelle, how did you land this assignment?"

"I was hanging around the bull pen, hoping something hot would pop up." She chuckled. "And sure enough, got a call from the city editor to come to his office."

"Did he say where he got the information for you to check out?"

"He didn't tell me, and I didn't ask. And," she said, "I wouldn't tell you if I did know." She paused, "Actually, he seemed distracted. More interested in talking with some guy about setting up a squash tournament. It was like I interrupted them."

"No kidding?" he said. "I play squash with him. Have for years. Did this other guy have a name?"

"Not that I remember..., they both mostly ignored me as I read the info sheet. Wrapped up in squash stuff."

Porter took a stab. "The visitor had curly hair? Sort of preppy?"

Surprised, she said, "Yes, as a matter of fact. Very tweedy. Herringbone jacket and a college tie. Do you know him?"

"You have a good eye for detail, Michelle. I suspect it's a frat brother of your editor—different schools but same frat—and a member of the same squash club. I've played him in tournaments several times."

"You don't like him," she said.

"Is it that obvious? Sorry. This guy thinks quite a lot of himself. He's not as important as he thinks he is. And he's not that good at squash, either."

After a moment, he added, "There's one little problem." In fact, there were several problems but Porter decided it would be better to bring them up later.

"What's that?"

"Thinking out loud, it might be harder to sit on your stories than you may think."

"Why?"

Porter toyed with his glass. "Colleen Callahan's been kidnapped."

"No shit?" She blushed, "I mean, I'm sorry to hear that."

Porter nodded. "Believe me, I would not joke about this."

"Who did it? Any leads?" She leaned forward, eyes riveted on his face. "And why?"

Porter checked his watch. "This is a new development. The president doesn't even know yet, though I suspect that he's being briefed right about now."

"The president? Of the United States? You have access to the president?" she asked, now on the edge of her chair.

"Yep. This has to be kept quiet or Colleen and her friend Ruhi Adams could die." He gave her another long look. "So, are you in or not?"

"Oh, yeah!" There was a bounce in her voice as she extended her hand. They shook. "How can I explain this to my boss?"

He paused, then said, "Thinking out loud again, I'll get the editor-in-chief, who I also know, to assign you to me for a feature. She will agree because I'll offer her a much bigger story than the meetings in Georgetown. You have two jobs now. Go back and beaver away for her during the day and after hours do background work for me. Shouldn't be long." He reached into his briefcase and produced a folder. "Since you're in, here's a list of background materials you need to read to get started. Lots to do. Players, motives, locations. More will come, faster and faster, my young friend."

She skimmed the list. Her eyes widened as she looked up.

"This is serious stuff, Duregger. You're in the major leagues now. Don't blow it."

Chapter Twenty-Five

Near San Miguel de Allende, Guanajuato, Mexico

Robbie Robinson drove his rental car through the cobblestone streets of San Miguel de Allende, one of his favorite places in the world. He loved to walk the narrow alleys and browse in the hundreds of little shops that were scattered throughout the colonial city. Oh, and the food! He could smell the spices as he passed. He had a long list of restaurants that he wanted to visit. But not this trip. This was all business. Yet he still found time to pause on a bit of high ground tucked in between fruit orchards and alfalfa fields where he enjoyed a splendid panorama. The two towers of the seventeenth century, neo-gothic *La Parroquila de San Miguel Arcángel* dominated the historic city center. The city's tile-roofed stucco buildings and vibrant vegetation and flowers spread across the valley floor in a gorgeous display.

He continued on the winding country road and stopped in front of an ornate iron gate. An eight-foot fence surrounded the plush grounds of a private hacienda. Three armed guards stepped out of a guard shack that was as large as a small barn. Robinson got out of the car, holding his hands clear.

"My name is Robinson. Señor Estrada is expecting me." One guard approached him as the other two spread out, Uzis at the ready. Robinson slowly opened his suit jacket to expose his shoulder holster. The guard motioned to him to hand over his weapon, then patted him down. Satisfied, the guard motioned him through the gate and into a black SUV for the drive to the main residence.

Robinson had never actually visited the hacienda before, but knew it sat on about thirty lush acres of rolling hills. The main house of twenty-three rooms dwarfed two additional guest houses, a pool, a tennis court, and a massive patio with two *parrillas* for grilling local meats and entertaining neighbors and business associates. The driver sped up the sinuous driveway and stopped in front of the enormous residence.

Standing in front of the main entrance was Francisco Estrada, a stocky, well-built, middle-aged man, flanked by a large, muscular young man whom he introduced simply as Antonio, his *ayudante*–assistant. Robinson suspected that Antonio was ex-*Fuerzas Especiales*–Mexican special forces—and also his body guard.

The two men embraced with smiles and jokes about expanding waistlines and receding hairlines.

"You have done well, Francisco," said Robinson, sweeping his arm toward the estate. "The years have been good to you."

Estrada chuckled. "Yes, thank you, Roberto. It has been a long and exciting journey since those months we spent killing Sandinista bastards in the Nicaraguan jungle." He led them through the capacious main room that was easily larger than Robinson's Georgetown townhouse. The furnishings were elaborate, enough to cause Robinson to pause. A huge Diego Rivera original featuring Mexican peasants working with flowers covered one wall. Once in his cavernous office, Estrada proved to be a gracious host, pouring the requisite coffees himself. They spent time leisurely catching up on more than two decades of memories. The two men had been close once, joined by ideology and near-death combat experiences.

Estrada said, "Your Spanish is a bit rusty, my friend. What happened?"

Robinson had been expecting this. "After the Iran-Contra fiasco, the CIA yanked me out of South America for good. I was assigned to Europe. German and Russian was all I spoke for years." He chuckled, "But just wait. In a week, people will think I was born in Guadalajara!"

After his second coffee, Estrada seemed ready to get down to business. "I am sure this is not simply a social call to catch up on old times. What can I do for you, *amigo*?"

"I need information. Quickly." He handed over several photos of Colleen.

Estrada nodded in appreciation. "Very beautiful. Who is she?"

"Her name is Dr. Colleen Callahan. She is an economist for the World Bank."

"If all economists are this lovely, I will encourage my son to attend business school in the United States."

Robinson swallowed a smile. Latinos never stopped with the Don Juan stuff. "She's Australian originally but what is more germane here is that she is missing."

Estrada raised an eyebrow.

"Our contacts say she is in Mexico somewhere, probably close to the border of Texas. She was kidnapped yesterday, probably last night between eight and ten o'clock from her hotel in San Antonio."

Estrada studied the picture. "She is important to you?"

"On a personal level, Francisco, she is the wife of one of my closest friends, a man I admire immensely. But this is bigger than just the woman. The man who kidnapped her is Kurt Wallerein."

Estrada's face reddened and he slammed his fist on his desk. "Wallerein! *Dios mío!* That *pendejo!* Here in Mexico?"

Robinson nodded. The reaction was just what he expected. Estrada was a proud Mexican and loathed Communists. "At least one of your business associates is providing him with weapons, explosives, and more importantly now, a logistics base somewhere in the desert where he is holding Colleen." Robinson related an abbreviated summary of Kulenović's information. "We need to find him before he launches more attacks on the United States."

"What are you asking me to do?"

"Find out where this woman is, where Wallerein is. Or at least the location of his base. We need to take out that base. And, we hope—I hope—we recover the woman alive."

"And Wallerein?"

"We need him, too."

"But not necessarily alive?"

Robinson didn't answer the question. "The husband, Colonel Thomas Callahan, is an advisor to the President of the United States. Callahan asked the president to let me talk to you before the president talks with the FBI or the DEA. If we don't locate her quickly, my president will call the President of Mexico for help. With Wallerein in the equation, your president will be unable to resist. My president will turn the attack dogs in the DEA and FBI loose in your country. Your president will send out the army and the *federales* to find whoever aided this madman."

"And how does this concern me?"

"You know everyone worth knowing in northern Mexico. Your network is discrete and efficient. You know how the DEA works—it will bust in and start kicking over anthills, arresting everyone in sight. If the DEA starts looking, the whole world will know instantaneously."

Estrada thought for a moment. "Wallerein will disappear back to wherever he came from."

Robinson nodded. "Both the American and Mexican agents will be ruthless. Collateral damage will be the issue here."

"It will be bad for business." Estrada paused to consider Robinson's words. "I rather like the status quo, my friend. Nice and quiet. Predictable."

"We want Wallerein, Francisco. We want him now." He handed Estrada a dossier. "Here is our file on Wallerein. There's a CD with pictures, maps, the address of Wallerein's headquarters in Playa del Carmen, everything we have so far. His number two is an ex-East German Stasi assassin named Joachim Richter. Several of Wallerein's men are ex-Stasi, by the way. Nasty buggers."

Estrada moved to an exquisite painting that covered a wall safe. He produced a cell phone and closed the safe. "Take this. It's untraceable and already programmed to call me direct. Use it only if you have more information." Then he turned to Antonio. "I hear Playa del Carmen is lovely this time of year. Are you ready for a trip to the beach?"

Somewhere in Mexico

Colleen snapped out of her daze. A key turned in the lock. The door swung open slowly as if expecting her to attack. A man stepped in, a stocky man with a grizzled beard. She recognized him as the guard who had carried her back to her cell. He held a tray of food. He put it at her feet. "*Por favor, señora, cómalo*—please eat this, ma'am."

She hesitated. As hungry as she was, she did not trust Wallerein. There might be drugs in the food, and she had to protect her baby. She shook her head. The man pushed the tray closer. "*Que usted lo coma, señora.*"

She shook her head again.

He gave a brief smile as if he understood her hesitation. He reached for one of the tortillas, tore a piece and ate it. He poured some coffee into a cup and sipped. He smiled and pushed the tray even closer.

Footsteps in the hallway. The guard leaned closer and whispered, "*Coraje, señora,*" then left. The door clanged shut.

Colleen paused only briefly, then devoured the food. Even stale tortillas and cold *café con leche* tasted miraculous now.

***

Ruhi huddled in a corner of her concrete cell, an icy feeling in her stomach. She had no idea of why she was here, wherever here was. But she knew precisely what her captors were like. She had known men like them all her life in Iran, pitiless men who had no scruples about killing or torturing women. She had escaped once and knew that if she did not escape again, she would die. It would be agonizing—and only after she had endured an avalanche of pain.

Where was Colleen?

***

Some time later, Colleen heard footsteps coming down the hall and the key in the lock. The "friendly" guard slipped in with another tray of food and shut the door behind him.

Colleen attacked the food with only a brief smile of thanks to the guard who stood watching her.

"My name Abdullah Kulenović."

Colleen swallowed the last bite and gave him one of her best smiles. "Colleen Callahan. But I suppose you know that already." She offered her hand. "Thank you for the food."

He took her hand but would not meet her eyes. "I sorry."

"Sorry for what?"

"You here."

"You mean the kidnapping?"

He nodded. In his broken Spanish he stumbled through the story of his sister and mother. "My country Kosovo. When I boy, part of Yugoslavia. You know it?"

Colleen nodded.

"I listen radio. Tito, he say communism good, Soviets good."

She nodded again.

"Wallerein still talk like that. I work for Wallerein many years. I not like what I do any longer. This wrong. Wallerein wrong. America not enemy." He paused. "I think Wallerein crazy."

Colleen smiled. "You are what Americans would call a 'white hat.'"

He looked at her, a puzzled look on his face.

"Bad guys wear black hats, good guys wear white hats."

"White hat," he said softly, then smiled. "I like."

"Where are we?"

"Coahuila state, Mexico. Near border with America."

"Abdullah, I will fight to get out of here. Will you help me?"

He nodded. "Not yet. Many men here now. No like womans. Want hurt you and friend. I protect. After dark we try. I have plan."

They heard boots pounding down the hallway. Kulenović stood, gestured for her to remain seated, then started speaking to her in a simulated angry voice.

189

Two men burst into the room, the same men who had helped beat her. They seemed angry that he was in the cell. One shouted at Kulenović. He shouted back. Another man pushed his way into the tiny room.

Colleen cringed at the angry shouts and squeezed into the corner.

The leader screamed at her. He tried to push past Kulenović, who blocked him, then slammed him into the wall. The man pulled his pistol, snarling in a language Colleen couldn't make out. The leader yelled and one of his men ran out of the room. The leader thrust his pistol towards Kulenović's abdomen and said something ugly. The small room reverberated with angry men shouting. Kulenović knocked the pistol away and punched him in the face.

The other guard pointed his pistol at Colleen. The opening in the barrel looked like a cannon. She lunged forward, seized the man's arm with both hands and bent it backwards. Locked in a struggle with his own assailant, Kulenović lashed out at Colleen's man and kicked his legs out from under.

The man twisted as he fell. His arm slipped out of Colleen's desperate grasp. The pistol went off. The pain was instantaneous and incredible.

Colleen screamed and collapsed.

Chapter Twenty-Six

Wallerein's Forward Base

Ruhi heard boots running in her direction. Her heart pounded. She murmured a short prayer and stood to face whatever was coming. The door slammed open, and a guard burst in. He pushed her into the corner and clubbed her with his pistol, knocking her to the floor. She nearly blacked out. Hot blood crawled down her forehead.

He jerked her to a sitting position. He punched her. The blow knocked her over again. A blaze of agony tore through her. She fought to stay conscious. He jerked her back up. "You will die, woman!" he snarled in Arabic.

Ruhi looked into the face of the man who was about to kill her. "You do not have to do this," she managed to whisper.

She could hear shouts. Then a gunshot reverberated down the hall. She flinched. So did the guard. Another gunshot. And another.

The guard slammed her head against the wall. She gasped as more pain lanced through her body. He jumped up, ran out the door, and turned towards the shouts. Two more shots. He clutched his chest and staggered against the doorway. He turned and raised his pistol toward her. Another shot. He collapsed on the floor.

A guard staggered in, blood on his shirt and pants, gun in hand. His eyes had the wild look of pain and anger. She knew she would die now.

Instead, the man kneeled in front of her. "I Avdo Kulenović. I friend."

Ruhi sobbed. "Thank you." She reached for his bloody face. "You're hurt. Let me look."

He shook his head and pushed her hand away. "No time. Please, help woman friend. Hurt bad."

"Colleen?"

He nodded. Ruhi struggled to her feet but staggered, fell backwards and slid down the wall. Despite his own wound, her new friend hoisted her to her feet.

"Hurry! More guards maybe come."

Still dizzy, Ruhi followed him to Colleen's cell. It was a slaughterhouse. Two guards lay in pools of blood; one leaned drunkenly against the blood splattered wall, dead eyes staring straight ahead, another lay dead in the hallway. Colleen sprawled unconscious and bleeding. Ruhi gasped at the ugly wound and stepped over the bodies to kneel beside the still form of her friend. She felt for a pulse. It was faint.

Her own pains forgotten, she ripped the shirt from a dead guard and tore it into strips. She had to stop the bleeding.

Avdo stood by the door watching down the corridor. "You are pilot, no?" he asked as Ruhi tied the last bandage. She nodded. He handed her his pistol, slung a submachine gun over his shoulder, and picked up the inert Colleen. "Go!"

They moved as quickly as their wounds allowed. She knew this escape attempt was doomed, but anything was better than sitting waiting to be slaughtered. She forced her tired legs forward, a stumbling hopeless run. She rounded a corner and skidded to a stop. Two men were in the hall. She leapt back. They must not see her! Avdo crashed into her from behind. Colleen moaned in pain. The men, distracted by shouts from another direction, turned and ran off.

After several turns, the corridor ended at a steel door. Avdo gestured for her to open it. She stepped into a darkened, closed up aircraft maintenance hangar. Probably used by *narcotraficantes*, she thought. Two aircraft sat inside, a Piper Aztec and a Cessna 206. Her eyes lit up. *Thank you, God!*

Something was strange about the Aztec. The right wing was held up by jacks and the right landing gear was missing. Ruhi's heart sank. She looked at the Cessna. It was dirty and dilapidated and looked as if it were overdue for every inspection mandated by the manufacturer. No surprise that it was in a maintenance hangar.

Colleen's moans caught Ruhi's attention. *She'll die if we don't get out of here.* Avdo looked as if he would collapse at any moment. Outside she could hear the loud wind gusts of an approaching thunderstorm. No time to waste. She looked back at the Cessna. It simply had to be good enough. Ruhi circled the plane, looking for any missing panels or obvious problems. She tried to open the cabin door. Locked! She had to get inside. She pounded on the door in frustration.

She glanced around the hangar, searching for a good idea—or even a marginal one. There! Against the wall, a workbench! The key might be there. She started to run to the bench but had to stop and kneel as waves of dizziness and nausea swept over her again. She took deep breaths. She had to be strong, or they would all die. Ruhi stood and staggered to the bench. Two sets of keys hung from a nail. She grabbed them both, then limped back to the plane. Ruhi tried the key in the pilot's door lock and cried out with relief as the door swung open.

She scrambled into the cockpit, slid into the left seat, and flipped the battery switch. She held her breath as the instruments wound up. Both fuel tanks read just more than half full. She breathed a prayer of thanks. If she could get this plane started, they would have a chance. The manifold pressure dial read 3600—a turbo! Wonderful! More speed to get Colleen to safety!

Ignoring the pain, Ruhi clambered back out the cargo door and motioned Avdo to load Colleen in the plane. Now for the hangar doors.

She limped as fast as she could to the massive sliding doors at the front of the building. Rain outside pounded the heavy metal. She pulled the door locking bar up and out of the way, forced her fingers into the center opening between the two doors and pulled. The door didn't budge. She gathered her strength and pulled again. Still no movement. The tracks were rusty and full of sand from the wind. *I have to get these doors open!* She took a deep breath and pulled, straining at the heavy panel. It moved two feet and ground to a halt, almost jerking her off her feet. She tried pushing. Slight movement. Desperate now, she slammed her shoulder into the stubborn door again. She had to fight the pain and nausea. Finally, the door broke free and moved a little. She pushed again, grunting with agony. It moved again, then slid a foot, two feet. She pushed harder. The door kept moving, shuddering as it met the other panel in the accordion-like door.

Wind blew rain and debris into the hangar through the widening gap. Outside, tumbleweeds bounced and stacked themselves against the rusty fuel tanks next to the building. A flash of lightning on the eastern horizon, too far to hear the thunder. The dark clouds, swirling, promised more violent weather. Sheeting rain pounded the taxiway, clouds scudded across the sky, thunder now rumbled in the distance. The storm was closing fast. Only a desperate fool would fly on a day like this. Ruhi was both. She would take her chances in the air. She'd rather die in a fireball off the end of the runway than stay here another minute.

Ruhi moved to the other side of the hangar. This door panel stuttered along the track, slowly but steadily until there was room to taxi the Cessna through. Rain dripped from her hair. She wiped the water from her eyes. In her mind she could only envision the taxi, takeoff, and the flight away from this, this awful place of death and fear. She was determined to save her friend and bring these murderers to justice. This she swore.

She pulled the chocks from underneath both wings and climbed in. The door from the building burst open and two men charged in, weapons raised, screaming. Avdo fired two quick bursts. Both men crashed to the floor, thrashing about as they died. He turned towards the plane. His eyes met Ruhi's. "Tell my sister Avdo good man."

He slammed the cargo door closed, then motioned for her to start the engine and go. She pleaded, "Avdo, come here! Get in!"

He waved again. He turned, pointed northeast and shouted "America! Go now!" then limped towards the door, submachine gun at the ready to meet further attackers inside.

Ruhi watched as he disappeared into the building. Tears ran down her face. She took a deep breath. She had to do this. Master switch on again, mixture rich, aux pump low, then she hit the ignition switch. She shouted, "You must start!"

The engine turned over and over, then caught, noisy and rough before finally smoothing out. Joyous, she released the ignition switch and turned off the aux pump.

More shots from inside the building. Ruhi brought power up and taxied through the doors. Clear of the building, she scanned the horizon to gauge the winds and taxied across the tarmac. The winds pushed and tugged at the aircraft, rain hammered the metal skin. The cockpit noise was tremendous. As she turned onto the narrow taxiway, two running men emerged from the building, firing their weapons. She goosed the power and taxied as rapidly as she dared, careful with her controls while straining to ensure her instruments were up and running.

She had no idea where to go but anywhere was better than this. Avdo had pointed to the northeast. She checked the whiskey compass. "Northeast it is." She glanced back towards the hangar almost expecting to see more gunmen coming after them. At the end of the taxiway, she slowed almost to a stop before turning onto the runway and pointed the nose right into the teeth of the storm. She gave a glance back at the inert form of her friend, then pushed up the power. The plane lurched and trembled, bouncing a bit over the rough runway. Liftoff, gear up. Turbulence slammed into the aircraft, almost driving it back into the ground. As they climbed, Ruhi fought the savage winds and the bucking aircraft. She banked to the left, set a course to imitate Avdo's pointing arm and climbed away from the weather.

Northern Mexico

Kurt Wallerein fidgeted in the leather seat of the lead vehicle in a convoy of four black SUVs as they sped across the desert road towards his temporary headquarters, a hangar and warehouse complex he rented from a Mexican *narcotraficante*. The weather was bad and getting worse. In the distance, he could see the sky growing darker; cumulonimbus clouds towered and lightning flashed. It felt so unlike his childhood home in Germany, but very much like the home he had recently left in the Libyan desert, complete with blowing sand and gigantic thunderstorms.

He shifted his weight to make himself more comfortable. Riding over long distances and crude roads hacked into the desert floor exacerbated the pain in his legs, pain inflicted by that *Hüerenshon* Callahan.

The Callahans intruded into his thoughts yet again. He was delighted that Colleen had fallen into his hands. He savored the memory of her writhing on the concrete floor, bleeding and in pain. He smiled to himself thinking about the agony Tom Callahan was experiencing, knowing that Colleen was at his mercy. Or lack thereof.

As he moved towards the building complex, the thunderstorm was nearly upon them, winds lashed the area, and a wall of rain was hurtling towards the field. The bad weather was inconvenient but he could deal with it. Wallerein forced himself to focus on his upcoming operation.

As the convoy rolled up to the parking area, he heard popping sounds. Wallerein instantly identified it as gunfire. He saw men running along the exterior walls, shooting as they ran. A firefight at his headquarters?

His eye caught more movement out on the taxiway. The Cessna 206. In this weather? Without his permission? Who ordered that aircraft to leave?

It must be the prisoners!

"Stop the plane!" he shouted at his driver. He pointed at the mid-point of the runway. "Go! Get in front of it!"

The SUV surged as the driver stomped the accelerator. The big car raced towards the runway. "Call the other cars. Have them secure the buildings!"

The aircraft turned into the howling wind and started its takeoff roll. Wallerein judged the closure rate. It would be close.

"Faster!" he commanded as he watched the airplane lift off. It staggered into the air, nose high as it cork-screwed and floundered in the swirling winds. A wing dropped and the aircraft half-rolled. Wallerein held his breath, hoping for the plane to stall. He willed it to smash down into the runway and burst into flames.

196

The pilot fought the wings level and Wallerein watched the aircraft slowly rise higher, wings flexing, buffeted all the while. Wallerein slammed his fist on the SUV dashboard. *Scheisse*!

As the aircraft was swallowed up into the churning clouds, he took a deep breath and turned his attention to the buildings. He drew his pistol and walked among the dead. Even in death, he recognized everyone. His own men, highly skilled, all had been ready to undertake his last mission, a massive attack on Amerika. He stood over them, rain running down his face. Soaked to the skin, he took a mental inventory. All this damage, all this unnecessary waste. Why? He raised his hands over his head and screamed. He fired his pistol until it was empty.

Then he screamed again.

Chapter Twenty-Seven

Over Mexico

The rain ended, and the turbulence lessened as Ruhi Adams outran the storm. She checked the instruments of the aircraft, then checked them again. They were making good time but to where? She had no idea where she was. There must be a map somewhere.

She engaged the autopilot and started a methodical search of the cockpit. Tucked under the seat she found a folded aeronautical chart of the state of Coahuila in northern Mexico. A small runway was drawn in pencil near the center of a desolate area of the state presumably by the *narcotraficante* pilots to mark the location of the airfield. According to the chart, Texas was supposed to be only about a hundred miles to the northeast.

Below her, desert transitioned to low mountains, which blended into flat rolling hills of prairie covered with low-lying scrub. The cloud cover was breaking up, and blue skies beckoned her on towards the border. She studied the chart to find a city with an airport and a hospital. Ciudad Acuña was somewhere off to the northeast, now basically dead ahead. Just across the Rio Grande was the city of Del Rio...and Laughlin Air Force Base! Surely she could land there! She checked the chart again, dialed in the navigation aid, and identified the station. The nav aid needles showed her to be roughly where she thought she should be. She breathed a short prayer and adjusted course.

Ruhi cast an anxious eye on the moaning Colleen. "Hang in there, *mijita*. I will get you home, I promise." In the distance, she could see smoky haze, possibly a city. Gradually, the hills led to a large metroplex with an airport but she refused to land in Mexico. There was a huge lake off to the northwest. She could pick out a dam, a bridge, then a river emerged. The Rio Grande? In the distance on the other side, she saw a smaller built up area, right where Laughlin should be. On course! She flew over the larger city, then the river.

She turned on her transponder and dialed in 7700. "Laughlin Approach, this is—" she searched for the aircraft identification numbers, "Cessna November Seven Two Bravo Charlie on 121.5. Request a frequency, please."

"Aircraft calling Laughlin Approach on guard, try frequency 119.6."

Ruhi set the new frequency. "Laughlin Approach, this is Cessna November Seven Two Bravo Charlie. I am declaring a medical emergency. I have a passenger who has been shot. Say landing runway and altimeter setting, please."

"Negative, Bravo Charlie. Laughlin is a military facility. You must use Del Rio Airport. I say again, you must use Del Rio Airport. Contact Del Rio approach."

"Negative, Laughlin. My husband is United States Air Force Colonel Brice Adams. My passenger is the wife of Air Force Colonel Thomas Callahan. We were abducted by terrorists and escaped. I *will* land at your base. Please have a medical team ready."

Wallerein Headquarters
Northern Mexico

Not normally a demonstrative man, Kurt Wallerein was instantly furious with himself for displaying his emotions. He reloaded, then went inside the building. Bullet holes were all along the corridors. The cell where the Callahan woman was kept was full of blood smears and dead bodies. He followed the route the prisoners took to the hangar, evidently the hangar area itself had been the scene of a major shoot-out. Spent cartridges, blood smears, shot-up equipment and more bodies. The Piper looked like a carnival shooting range target.

What the hell happened?

Damn. It was clear that the Callahan woman must have been on that plane. He shook his head. *I should have killed her when I had the chance. That's a mistake I won't make again.* He thought a moment. *I'll just kill Callahan himself and let her suffer instead of the other way around, that arrogant Schlep.*

Wallerein looked around and did some quick calculations. He still had his necessary equipment, the remaining explosives and most importantly, a knot of hard-core operatives from the convoy. All ex-Stasi, all competent, all experienced. They could do anything he ordered. Fortunately, he had already dispatched the bulk of his organization and the precious explosives. Coupled with the teams already over the border and moving into position, he had enough. Not as many as he had scheduled, but this would work. He just had to get these men out of here and into Amerika.

He assembled his remaining operatives and pointed to his two Stasi leaders. "You get the explosives loaded on the trucks. The rest of you men, get ready to move out. We need to leave quickly." Both groups trotted off to obey.

There was comfort in orders as both Wallerein and his men struggled to cope with this setback. An hour later, they were ready.

He assembled the teams around his collection of maps and French SPOT satellite imagery. "Here are the points of crossing. We will go as planned, one day early." He pointed at a map. "You men in the trucks drive these roads to New Mexico. The border is porous, you can cross almost anywhere at night." He pulled out another map. "The rest of you men, head for the Texas border. Mix with the other illegals and get over the river. Infiltrate, then fan out and make your way to your target areas. I'll go with the trucks. Any questions?"

There were none. As expected.

Conference Room
Headquarters, 47th Flying Training Wing (FTW)
Laughlin AFB, Texas

Captain Lysa Gimbel, 47th FTW executive officer, slipped into the conference room and stood beside her commanding officer, Colonel Lee Hopson.

"Sorry to interrupt your briefing, sir. We have an emergency." Hopson motioned for her to continue. "A civilian aircraft wants to land here. Pilot says she has a wounded passenger aboard."

"Wounded?"

"That's what she said, sir. Shot. She also says they were abducted by terrorists."

"Terrorists? In Texas?"

"The aircraft is coming in from Mexico, sir. The pilot refuses to land at Del Rio International."

The Deputy Commander for Operations (DO) Colonel Bill Hughes leaned in. "Colonel, this just doesn't seem possible. How do we know they are who they say they are? I don't like this, sir."

"Bill, if these women have been abducted, they won't be carrying ID cards." He turned back to Gimbel. "Any names?"

"They're in a turbo Cessna, sir. The pilot says she's the wife of an Air Force colonel." She searched her notes. "A Colonel Brice Adams. And the wounded woman is the wife of a Colonel Thomas Callahan."

"I know a Lieutenant Colonel Tom Callahan. If it's the same guy, last I heard he was down in Bolivia doing some pretty hairy operations. An abduction could be true."

Hopson looked up at his exec. "Lysa, get on the horn to the tower. Have them give permission to land. Alert the emergency crews, and an ambulance. Let the flight surgeon know we may have a gunshot victim."

"Security, sir?"

"You bet. Everybody you can find. Armed, locked, cocked, and ready for anything." He stood. "Let's go, Bill."

***

Colonel Hopson wheeled his staff car out to the flight line and parked on a cross taxiway. He nodded in satisfaction as emergency and security vehicles sped into position. The car radios crackled with the traffic between the base and the aircraft as arrival control gave vectors for a straight-in approach to the center runway.

Hopson grabbed a set of binoculars and both men got out of the car, leaving doors open so they could hear the radio chatter. Instinctively both pilots checked the wind sock as the hot wind gusted across the runway. Hopson leaned against the hood and took a long look through the binoculars before handing them to Hughes.

Hughes studied the plane. "Looks like a 206."

"That's what I thought." The radio crackled with a command. A female voice responded with a crisp acknowledgment.

"The pilot sounds like she has everything under control," Hopson said, approval in his voice.

"Yep, right on glide path. Pretty gusty, though. She's going to have to stick it on."

They watched as the plane was flown right down to the runway and planted firmly. A security police Humvee followed the aircraft as it slowed then stopped near Hopson's position. Fire trucks moved in and security police surrounded the aircraft, weapons ready. The engine shut down and the cargo door opened. Colonel Hopson could see a dark-haired female, face covered with dirty smudges which could have been blood. On the aircraft floor was another body, long blonde hair swirling in the wind.

The flight surgeon pushed his way through security, climbed aboard and squatted at the side of the wounded woman. He spoke with the pilot, then waved over the waiting ambulance attendants who carefully loaded the woman onto the stretcher and gently moved out to the ambulance.

Hopson made his way through the crowd to the ambulance and approached the doctor. "How is the patient?"

"Alive, sir. But just barely."

"Take good care of her, Doc. Do your magic."

"Always, Colonel." He climbed in the ambulance, and it accelerated away, lights on, siren wailing.

Chapter Twenty-Eight

Laughlin Air Force Base, Texas

Ruhi Adams sat in the Wing conference room. Dressed in a flight suit and boots provided by Captain Gimbel, she was wrapped in exhaustion, and her head ached. Colleen was now in good hands, being readied for a medevac flight to Fort Sam Houston in San Antonio. Ruhi sipped a cup of tea she had laced with extra sugar. She would need the energy to meet her next challenge.

The door opened and Colonel Hopson appeared leading another man, stocky and muscular, dressed all in black. He wore wrap-around sunglasses, a flak vest with a radio clipped to the chest and a pistol belt. His baseball cap had stitched in large gold letters the letters FBI. He stopped in front of her and removed his glasses and cap, revealing short-cropped salt-and-pepper hair.

"Good afternoon, Mrs. Adams. I am Special Agent Jay Mitchell. I'm glad to see you looking so well."

She gave him a tired smile. "I have not slept or eaten for three days. And I desperately need a bath. I assure you, sir, that I have seen better times."

Both men sat. Mitchell produced a police sketch. "Is this the man you met in Mexico?"

She took the paper. The face that stared back at her was a cleaner version of the man who had burst into her life that morning and wrenched her from a certain death by torture. None of the fear and pain in his eyes that she had seen so clearly was evident in the sketch. But it was the same man. Her throat tightened as she nodded. "I only know his name as Avdo."

"His name is Abdullah Kulenović. He is a Bosniak from a small village in Kosovo."

"He is much more than that, Mr. Mitchell. He is a live action figure, a hero. He saved my life as well as Colleen's."

"Yes, ma'am. He took an enormous risk. That's part of the reason I'm here."

Ruhi sat back in her chair, arms crossed. "You're after Kurt Wallerein."

"I have two Blackhawk helicopters full of agents parked outside on the tarmac and permission to enter Mexican airspace. With your help, we will capture Wallerein and bring both men back."

He showed her a map of northern Mexico and smoothed it down on the conference table. "You flew here in one of Wallerein's aircraft. Where exactly is the airstrip?"

She shook her head. "I am not going to tell you."

Surprised, Mitchell blurted, "We want to rescue Kulenović, Mrs. Adams. He deserves our help. We need to move fast."

She nodded. "Agreed."

"Great. Then please tell me."

"Mr. Mitchell, I am going with you. I will tell you the target location when we are airborne."

"No, ma'am, you are not going. We can't take a civilian into what might become a firefight."

She knew that it would come to this. She repeated, "Yes, Mr. Mitchell, I am going. Again, I will tell you the location once we penetrate Mexican airspace. Not before."

"Absolutely not. I cannot do that."

"How do you propose to find the airstrip? Head west and wander around until every *narcotraficante* and farmer in northern Mexico knows that the gringo *federales* are on the prowl? In Mexican skies?"

"We had hoped that you would be more cooperative."

"I will help you. Just take me."

"I told you, I can't."

"Sure you can. Just load me on the aircraft and off we'll go." She watched his poker face for clues to his thinking. "How do you plan on communicating with Avdo when—if—you find him? He speaks broken Spanish and even less English, but good Arabic. You need me."

Mitchell paused. "Mrs. Adams, this mission comes directly from the president. If I took you along, he would have my head."

She smiled. "But if you failed to even start the mission, it is likely that the president would—my husband uses this phrase quite a lot—cut your nuts off."

Mitchell laughed. "True that, Mrs. Adams." Like most men, Mitchell probably valued his nuts more than his head. He sat for a moment, as if considering his options. "Excuse me for a moment," and slipped out the door.

Ruhi sipped her now-cool tea as she waited. Two minutes later, Mitchell re-appeared. "It seems I have no choice." He stuck out his hand. "Deal."

She took his hand and smiled her most gracious smile. "I will give you the coordinates once we are in Mexican skies."

***

Twenty minutes later, Ruhi sat in the lead Blackhawk, wearing a flak vest and headphones, sandwiched between two burly FBI agents. She watched as they passed over the thin trickle of the Rio Grande, Lake Amistad off to the right. Special Agent Mitchell turned around in his jump seat and pointed down at the river.

"Mexico, Mrs. Adams," he said on the intercom.

She handed him her map with the location marked with an X. Next to the X she had neatly written in ink the lat and long coordinates. "I had some time to work this out for you."

Mitchell studied the markings, then handed the map to the co-pilot. "Put these in the GPS."

The aircraft heeled over as the pilots changed direction. As they flew, Ruhi let her exhaustion gradually overcome her, and she slept.

205

She awoke to rapid radio chatter and caught sight of the airstrip and buildings. Two vehicles sat in the parking area, a Black Suburban and a black dune buggy. The hangar doors gaped open, and several bodies lay scattered in front. Mitchell barked out his orders as he organized the attack, speaking rapid Spanish as he coordinated with two UH-60 Blackhawks belonging to the Mexican *Fuerzas Especiales* that had come up from the south.

The helicopters split up and streaked towards the airfield. Mitchell wheeled around and motioned for Ruhi to stay behind. As the aircraft touched down, the men, bristling with guns and equipment, leapt to the tarmac and ran towards the buildings. The pilot pulled up on the collective and the Blackhawk soared upwards away from the buildings to provide visual cover.

Ruhi listened as the FBI agents and Mexican soldiers searched the complex. No resistance. No enemies to kill or capture. The operation lasted less than three minutes, though to Ruhi it seemed like a decade. Mitchell gave the all clear and the Blackhawks settled back on the tarmac. The crew chief unstrapped Ruhi and helped her out of the aircraft. She trotted over to the hangar. Bodies and weapons were strewn inside and outside.

While she searched, she listened as Mitchell called in his report on his cell phone. "No sir, we got here too late. There must have been a massive firefight, though. Looks like Davey Crockett at the Alamo, sir. Dead bodies everywhere, including Davey. But he put up a hell of a fight. I count ten dead... Yes sir, including our boy. No sign of Wallerein."

Then Ruhi spotted what she was looking for. He was sprawled on his back, still clenching his weapon. She walked to him and slowly sank to her knees. She paused, and regarded his face as she remembered how he saved their lives. She reached out, stroked his cheek, gently closed his eyes and arranged his body so he lay straight, his arms crossed on his chest.

"You were a good man, Abdullah Kulenović. Colleen and I owe you our lives. Thank you." She kissed his forehead. "Forgive me, Avdo. I do not remember any Muslim prayers, so I will pray for you from my own faith."

In a soft voice she repeated the Bahá'í Prayer for the Departed. Then hot tears came, and sobs wracked her body.

Estrada Hacienda
Near San Miguel de Allende

"Good morning, Señor Richter," said a smiling Francisco Estrada as he seated himself behind his walnut desk across from the Wallerein organization second-in-command. "Would you care for *café con leche?*"

Richter said nothing.

Estrada gestured to Antonio who poured steaming liquid into an exquisite cup, then added hot milk from another pitcher. Estrada stirred in a spoon of sugar and studied the face of his captive for a long moment while he sipped his drink. "I realize that you may be a bit disoriented after being so abruptly snatched from your condominium in Playa del Carmen. And I know that you are not interested in conversation right now, señor, but I have some information that you need to hear." Estrada leaned back in his chair. "First, I congratulate you on your kidnapping of the two American women from San Antonio. That was a clever plan, especially on such short notice."

Richter's face remained stoic.

"Please, Herr Richter, do not be so modest. We know that you organized and led that operation." No reaction from Richter. "You will be surprised, and no doubt disappointed, to learn that the women escaped and are back in the United States, bruised and battered but very much alive."

"Not a chance!" blurted Richter.

"I offer you proof, photos supplied to me this very morning by my friend in the Yanqui CIA." Estrada opened a file on his desk and produced several photos. Buildings stood out against the sand of the desert, a runway carved into the soil. "Please note the clarity of these photos of your base. They were taken from outer space. Amazing, aren't they? The Yanquis have their faults but they certainly know their technology, no?"

Richter slid his chair closer. After a moment, he sat back, a smirk on his face.

Estrada was not the least bit perturbed. "I see that those space photos do not convince you. Here are others taken from the ground by a joint FBI-*Fuerzas Especiales* operation to liberate the base. Please note that all your men were killed. Again, when the Yanquis get serious, they are capable of amazing things." He handed the sheaf of pictures to Richter. "Here are the close-ups. Recognize any of these men? Regrettably, none of them is Kurt Wallerein. He is the one they want."

Richter unleashed a string of gutter Spanish obscenities at Estrada.

Antonio, his face tight with anger, jumped forward and smashed Richter in the head. He crashed to the floor. "Nobody talks to *mi jefe* like that! I should kill you now!"

Estrada held up a hand to stop Antonio, then motioned for him to pick the German up. Antonio jerked Richter upright and slammed him into the chair, muttering under his breath.

Estrada said, "You have an interesting vocabulary, Señor Richter. I see you have paid attention to the colorful words of my countrymen who used to work for you. It is unfortunate for you that they are now dead." He paused. "But please, we are both professionals. You know the rules. I know the rules. You can cooperate or not."

Richter shook his head.

Estrada sighed. "You are being foolish, señor. As the Yanquis say, I hold all the cards. You will talk."

Richter repeated his Spanish obscenities, then added, pride in his voice. "*Ich bin Hauptverwaltung Aufklärung.*"

These damned Germans, thought Estrada. Always so–he searched for the English word—obdurate. Arrogant. Teutonic. "Come, come, señor. Everyone can be made to talk."

Richter glowered at him, arms crossed, body tense.

Estrada sat back and made a steeple of his fingers as he pondered the situation. "You have learned some of our language, señor. Permit me to introduce you to one of our business customs." He fixed Richter with a stare. "*Plata o plomo*. Do you know what that means?"

Richter shook his head.

"Plata, of course, means silver. *Plomo* means lead. Simply stated, it means you have a choice—you can cooperate and be rewarded with silver or not cooperate and get the lead."

"A bullet," Richter spit out in a contemptuous voice.

Estrada smiled. "You catch on quickly, señor. Due no doubt to your excellent HVA training. So, I ask you again, where is Kurt Wallerein?"

"I am not afraid of a bullet," he said, still defiant.

"No, no, señor, you misunderstand." He beckoned to Antonio who handed him yet another folder. He laid the pictures out, face up on the desk. "There is your father, this is your mother. Here is your brother and his lovely wife. And your nephews on their way to school. Oh, and your niece, lovely like her mother, playing in the park."

Richter's face went white. He reached for the pictures and went through them one by one. "Where did you get these?"

"My men took them this morning. In Germany." He smiled, pleased with himself. "Note the date and time stamp on the pictures. They arrived two hours ago via e-mail. Amazing technology, emails."

Estrada sipped of his now-cold *café con leche* as Richter fingered the photos, dumbfounded. "You see, Señor Richter, the *plomo* is not for you. It is for your family. And anyone else we can find whom you hold dear. Please believe me when I say we are quite serious about this." He paused. His voice hardened. "Now, I ask you again, where is Kurt Wallerein?"

Chapter Twenty-Nine

Columbus, New Mexico

The early morning sun glinted over the Florida Mountain range as Kurt Wallerein cruised into the sleepy high-desert town of Columbus. The truck slipped into town without being subjected to the inconveniences of the official Port of Entry procedures. Penetrating the porous US-Mexican border had been tense but simple, using unmarked crossings maintained by the *narcotraficantes*.

Wallerein was not impressed with the geography or the town itself. The landscape was *altiplano*—flat and dry—stretching off to mountains in all quadrants. Tangled shrubs, thorny bushes, and what seemed to be an infinite number of cactus species made up the scruffy vegetation cover. In typical capitalist fashion, the town's main street was a collection of brightly painted buildings, crying out for the almighty tourist dollar.

He stopped at a roadside historical marker, got out of the truck, stretched, and massaged his aching leg. The marker proclaimed the city's claim to fame in bold letters: "Pancho Villa invaded the United States here in 1916, the only invasion since the War of 1812."

Wallerein chuckled. *Until now,* he thought, then laughed out loud. His laughter woke his companions who had driven most of the way. Wallerein pointed to the marker and waited for the expected reaction from his men.

His immediate problem was communications. He now recognized the major weakness in a decentralized organization—it was decentralized. By definition, or design, that made it hard to get everybody on the same page. His communication system had been shattered during the shootout—three of his trusted couriers and his communications expert lay dead in Mexico. He had to regain the initiative and control. He had people scattered all over the Southwest and a shortage of couriers.

Each of his teams had a laptop computer, but because of his distrust of computers he had only the vaguest idea of how to re-establish his network. He knew the FBI was in love with its computer network—the Americans certainly liked their toys. The *gottverdammt* FBI probably had a basement full of pimple-face teenage computer experts combing through this new Internet searching out freedom fighters like him.

He mused this over. What to do? After all, he couldn't just walk into a store and buy a computer network… or could he? Wallerein had never bothered to learn much about computers. He had people for that…. But why not? This was capitalist America, where everything—and everybody—was for sale. He pulled out his map. Las Cruces was close, a university town. Surely there would be opportunities to buy computers there. He could act like a visiting professor. He smiled to himself— another revolutionary maxim obeyed—live off the land.

Wallerein's truck headed north on NM Highway 11 to the desert city of Deming, whose only reason for being as far as Wallerein could tell was that it sat at the confluence of four highways and a railroad. After a brief reconnoiter, they turned east on I-10. Entering the outskirts of Las Cruces, Wallerein found what he was looking for, a tired wooden building with peeling paint and a hand-lettered sign advertising new and used computers. He turned to his driver, "Park the truck. If I am not back in ten minutes, come after me." He got out, limped across the parking lot and went inside.

It took a few seconds for his eyes to adjust to the dim atmosphere in the cramped little store. Computers and electronic devices of all sorts were stacked in disorderly piles along both side walls all the way to the rear. Wallerein's sense of order was offended even though what he saw was precisely what he expected.

A thin young man with long stringy hair sat hunched over the messy entrails of a computer, highlighted in an arc of light. He looked up. "Can I help you, dude?"

Wallerein regarded the young man. Another stereotype confirmed. "Perhaps. I just arrived in the United States, and my computer was lost by the airlines."

The young man nodded. "Been there, dude. Shoulda packed it in your carry-on. But I guess you already know that."

"Just so. I am a visiting professor and have teams doing environmental research scattered around your state. I need to set up a secure network communications system with my colleagues. Can you do that?"

"Piece of cake."

"Really?"

"I'm almost through with a Masters in Information Technology. This'll be easy." He rubbed his hands together. "Most people who stop here only want to buy a cheap computer or have something fixed. I'm gonna enjoy this!"

"Can we do it now?"

The young man glanced at the wall clock. "I have a class in an hour."

"And I am in a hurry." Wallerein laid five one-hundred-dollar bills on the desk. "There will be another five hundred if you succeed. Is this enough for your time?"

The young man's eyes grew wide as he handled the bills. "Dude, you have me all day!" He stuck out his hand. "Name's Jeff."

***

Two hours later, Jeff sat back in his rickety chair. "Okay, Professor, do you remember how to send a link to your network where they all can download the encryption software I've installed in your machines?"

Wallerein nodded. He now had two rebuilt computers loaded with the proper software and tested. The network was alive and well, password protected. Not as secure as his previous network but adequate for the next few days. "You are a wonderful technician, Jeff. I am so pleased with your work." He indicated his companion. "My associate will pay you. Oh, and the warranty?"

"Ninety days. Call me from anywhere, and I'll fix your problem," Jeff said. "Guaranteed and no charge."

"Thank you. I respect your business sense." Wallerein placed his hand on Jeff's shoulder and smiled. "Do you speak any foreign languages?"

Jeff shook his head. "Just computer languages."

Too bad, thought Wallerein. "I find that to be the case with most Americans, my friend."

He turned to his companion and switched to German. "Take him in the back and kill him. Quietly. Make it look like a robbery. Wipe down all surfaces we may have touched. There are five hundred dollars in his pocket. Get that."

USAF C-21A Learjet over Texas

Tom Callahan stared out the aircraft window, lost in thought. Normally he would be in the cockpit, hanging out with the aircrew but not this time. He just sat and brooded, fingers drumming on the table.

A USAF Master Sergeant knelt beside him and spoke softly as he pointed to the telephone mounted on the sidewall. "Excuse me, sir, the White House is on the line."

Tom picked up the receiver. "Callahan."

"Colonel," said the White House operator. "Stand by for the president." Tom mentally reviewed the president's itinerary. He was in Tokyo, halfway into his twelve-day swing through Asia.

"Tom, this is the President. Where are you now?"

"We're letting down into Lackland Air Force Base in San Antonio, sir. On the ground in about thirty minutes."

"What's the latest on Colleen?"

Tom's stomach flipped, and he squeezed his eyes shut for a moment. "I just spoke with the commanding general of Wilford Hall Medical Center. Colleen's still in surgery for a bullet wound in the abdomen. She hasn't regained consciousness."

"I can't tell you how concerned both Lyn and I are. Would you mind if Lyn spoke with the general?" The First Lady, a practicing physician, had diagnosed the pregnancy for an ecstatic Colleen and a surprised Tom just weeks earlier.

"Sir, I—we—would be honored. Thank you."

"I'm concerned with your group's findings on Kurt Wallerein," said the president. "Your evidence has not convinced the intelligence community that he's organizing attacks within our country. Skeptical doesn't even begin to describe it."

"Nobody wants to believe this, Mr. President. Small towns in Homeland America are under siege. The Southwest is just the beginning. The intel community is inherently conservative and normally that's a good thing. But…"

"But what, Colonel? But the CIA and the rest of the intelligence community are dragging their feet on this? But they are not taking a possible attack on the United States seriously, despite what almost happened a few months ago?"

Tom didn't know what to say. He thought for a moment. "Sir, the evidence about Wallerein is accumulating. Maybe that will help change their minds. That's another reason for this trip to San Antonio. First, I'm going to check on Colleen and speak with her medical team; then I have meetings at Lackland. Robbie Robinson is flying up from Mexico City."

"The CIA agent in your group?" asked the president.

"Yes sir. He has some late-breaking intel direct from Wallerein's brain trust that indicates Wallerein is in New Mexico. And FBI Special Agent Jay Mitchell is being flown up from Laughlin Air Force Base. He led the raid into Wallerein's camp in northern Mexico. Both of these men are convinced that their new evidence supports the premise that Wallerein is systematically attacking the western United States. We'll go over what they have, then I'll head to Santa Fe."

"I want to know what happens after that meeting."

"Yes sir." Tom glanced out the window at the Texas prairie stretching to the horizon. "Mr. President, remember when you sent me to investigate the bombing at Kirtland Air Force base?"

"Yes. Why?"

"The intel from our embassy in Mexico said the reason for the attack was a reaction to the United States having troops deployed to the Middle East. Our people deploy knowing that their families are safe and secure back home. Wallerein's message to our troops is simple: deploy to our countries, and we will kill your families in your country. Obviously, that would discourage our people from wanting to leave home. Or, if deployed, their fear and anger from being away from their loved ones would induce them to take it out on the locals, driving a wedge deeper between them and us. Either way, Wallerein and his people win."

"This came from Mexico?"

"Yes sir."

"Why haven't I heard of this before?"

"Sir, it took a while to filter down to us. Once I had it, I gave the report to Mr. Freiberg. He gave it to Dr. Orsini."

A pause. "Interesting." Another, longer pause before the president spoke again. "Okay, Tom, I put you in charge, and I'll let you run with it. But know this, if it were anybody other than you and your group, I would probably agree with the intelligence people. You have those meetings at Lackland and send me a report ASAP. I want it when I wake up tomorrow. Copy to Mark Freiberg. We'll go from there. In the meantime, after I hang up, I'll call the governor of New Mexico, give him a heads-up and ask him to provide you with what you need. I would rather tell him now and have it fizzle out than not tell him anything and have it blow up next week."

"Yes, sir. Thank you."

"Until I read that report, keep Wallerein's name out of this. Just talk about arsonists. And, Tom, send me the report Orsini has."

"Yes, sir. But keeping Wallerein's name out of our discussions won't be easy."

"Easy or not, do it," said the president. "My trip through Asia was laid on eighteen months ago. I need to finish it. If I jump back to Washington early, what is a regional problem now, as tragic as it is, will become front-page news. People all over the country will panic. We can't have that."

"Panic is what Wallerein is hoping for, Mr. President."

215

"I get that. You stay in touch. Call me anytime."

"Thank you, sir."

"Stay in touch, Colonel. I mean it."

The line went dead.

Intensive Care Unit
Wilford Hall Medical Center

Tom Callahan listened to the doctors as they took him through a litany of Colleen's injuries. They warned him that the extent of her facial bruises would shock him, but those were the least of her problems. The abdominal bullet wound topped the list. The surgeon briefed Tom that while the bullet had passed through Colleen without hitting any major organs, she had suffered a massive loss of blood. Internal injuries from the beating were suspected as was a possible mandibular fracture. Colleen was concussed, groggy, and in and out of consciousness. And the baby was clearly distressed, the fetal heartbeat weak and irregular.

Tom's chest tightened as the list of injuries grew longer and longer. He wanted to scream for the doctors to stop, but he just sat, clenching and unclenching his jaw, staring hard at one doctor, then the other as they took turns explaining in doctor-speak how badly Colleen was hurt.

After what seemed like hours, Tom, now gowned and masked, was allowed to walk down the short corridor. His pace slowed as he neared her door. Emotionally drained, he leaned against the wall to gather himself. He wiped his eyes, then eased himself into the private room, anxious not to disturb her.

He stood quietly for some moments and just watched her, surrounded as she was by machines monitoring her every heartbeat, every breath. He moved closer, took her hand and pulled a chair over without letting go of her hand. He smoothed her hair and lightly caressed her cheek. He traced the ugly bruises and swelling that stained and disfigured her face like mold on a beautiful painting.

Tom had seen death. He'd actually killed two men in air-to-air combat, one with a missile, the other with his internal gun. He had seen death up close and personal in Bolivia, innocent people and guilty people, all dead courtesy of Kurt Wallerein. Life was fragile, especially when it involved someone you loved, someone you adored.

He sat for an hour and watched her breathe, knowing that she needed rest, needed the unconsciousness that enveloped and protected her from the overwhelming pain.

***

Two hours later, Tom paced across the Lackland Air Force Base Operations VIP lounge as his emotions roller-coastered from anger to anguish. His stomach was churning, and he felt the sweat running down his spine. He longed for something nice and heavy that he could smash against the wall. He glanced in the direction of the lounge's well-stocked bar. No, he told himself. There will be time for that later. Right now, he needed every brain cell that he could muster.

He heard the sounds of an approaching helicopter taxiing in. Probably Mitchell arriving from Laughlin. Nearly simultaneously, an Air Force staff car drove into his line of sight. He glanced at his watch. Should be Robbie Robinson arriving from his flight into San Antonio International. Good.

Robinson emerged from the vehicle clutching a briefcase and marched towards the door escorted by two, armed Air Force Security Police.

Tom greeted Robbie as he entered the room. The men embraced.

"Tom, I am just as sorry as hell about Colleen."

Tom nodded and pointed out the window towards the ramp. "That Blackhawk is delivering FBI Special Agent Jay Mitchell. Let's wait until he gets here so we only have to do this once."

The two men watched as Mitchell's helicopter taxied into position outside and shut down. A stocky man dressed in black utilities jumped down and strode across the tarmac, followed by three similarly dressed men carrying large cardboard boxes.

"You must be Mitchell. I'm Tom Callahan. Thank you for getting here so quickly."

"Sir, I have several boxes of papers that we captured in Mexico. Deputy Director Borenstein told me to get copies of them to you as fast as possible."

"Where's Ruhi Adams?"

"Sir, Mrs. Adams wouldn't leave Kulenović's body. She is determined that he be given a proper burial somewhere. She was working on that when I left."

"I suppose we owe Colleen's life to Ruhi and this Kulenović chap."

"Mrs. Adams says all the credit goes to Kulenović," said Mitchell.

"She would say that. Don't you believe it."

"Colonel, I heard several good stories about your wife from Mrs. Adams."

Images of a bandaged and beat-up Colleen flashed through Tom's mind. He took a deep breath and changed the subject. "Have you had a chance to go through the documents?"

Mitchell nodded. "Just a quick overview, sir."

With a movement of his hand, Tom invited the men to sit. He sat facing the picture window with its view of the transient ramp, flanked by the two men. "You're the newbie here, Jay. I need an info dump to pass along to the president. You go first. I don't want you influenced by what Robbie has to say. What were your initial impressions?"

Mitchell paused. "My first reaction is that Wallerein's organization is made up of a small number of hard-core revolutionaries, maybe as many as a couple hundred. Some true believers, some mercenaries like the ex-Stasi types who really have no place else to go these days. They are rent-a-terrorists, capable, amoral, and lethal. I don't know the relative proportions of the two groups. The second thing that strikes me is that communications are really primitive, unsophisticated even. I think it's because Wallerein is paranoid, among other anti-social tendencies."

"Do you agree with that assessment, Robbie?"

Robinson ran a hand through his graying hair as he nodded. "I think that it's right on the money. And so will you when you see what I have."

Tom made a "give it to me" gesture.

Robbie made no reply, then finally said, "What I have is white hot, Tom. Straight from my contact in Mexico."

"Whose name is?"

Robinson glanced at Mitchell. "For my man's protection, I think it best to refer to him as Paco. He got the information from Wallerein's Number Two, Joachim Richter."

"How reliable is this Paco?"

"He and I go way back, Tom. We fought the Sandinistas in Nicaragua. We were tight—he saved my life once; I saved his twice."

Tom grinned for the first time that day. "Sounds like those were exciting days abroad, my friend."

Robbie nodded. "Paco is well connected in what I would prefer to call Mexico's underground economy."

"You mean he's a *narcotraficante*."

"Among other business interests, yes. He's ruthless, efficient and loyal. He hates international terrorists, loathes communists. Old-school terrorists like Wallerein happen to fall into both categories. You can take this information to the bank."

He opened his briefcase and extracted a one-inch thick sheaf of papers bound with a metal clip. "I have a DVD and this," he said as he waved the documents. "This is a transcription of what you are about to see. Paco interrogated this guy Richter who is, or was, Wallerein's number two man. I wrote it for you myself because he keeps shifting from English to German to Spanish." He hesitated. "Tom, you're not going to like this."

"Why?"

Robbie paused, as he seemed to gather his thoughts. "Wallerein hates you, Tom, and Colleen, too, for what the two of you did to his plans in Latin America. Get used to that. He wants to kill you for almost killing him. Richter says that Wallerein is still in pain. Especially in his legs. Takes lots of pain medicine. Can't sleep very well."

"Please forgive me for not being sympathetic."

Robbie leaned forward and put the DVD into the lounge player. The men settled back to watch.

Richter sat in a leather chair with his hands unbound. Behind the chair was a clear view of a large room, obviously an office, with a magnificent desk, chairs, a large tapestry, and several ornate vases.

219

Given the sumptuousness of the furnishings, Tom was certain that the painting in the background was a Veronica Ruiz de Velasco original, one of his mother's favorite Mexican artists.

Before Richter started talking, Tom raised his hand to stop the show. "What was this guy's inducement to talk?"

"Plata o plomo."

"Was he drugged?"

Robinson did not answer.

"Robbie!"

"I think they slipped him some alprazolam to help his nervousness."

Tom nodded, not happy but at least there were no signs of physical torture. Another forced confession would not sit well with the White House staff. He gestured for Robbie to re-start the video.

A Spanish-accented off camera voice told Richter to identify himself.

"My name is Joachim Richter." Pride was evident in his voice. "I was a Stasi lieutenant colonel until the collapse of the State in 1990." He scowled. "By 1991, it was obvious that being a Stasi officer was not a good thing in the newly united 'paradise' so I left to join Kurt Wallerein. I had met him in the '70s when he was with the *Rote Armee Fraktion.* Now I am his Chief of Operations." He paused.

The voice spoke again. "Go on, Señor Richter."

Richter glanced in the direction of the owner of the voice, then told him what he wanted to hear—an overview of what Wallerein was attempting to accomplish. "The genius of the original plan is its simplicity—first the wildfires, the destruction of watersheds and water distribution systems." Wallerein planned to return with hard-core trained saboteurs to surgically smash critical nodes in America's communications, pipelines, and transportation networks. Tom listened in disbelief, both at the enormity of Wallerein's delusions and the magnitude of his hatred of American citizens.

"Security? There is no security in Amerika. The country is one massive collection of soft targets. So undefended and easy that a troop of *Deutsche Pfadfinderschaft Sankt Georg*—Catholic Girl Scouts—

could take them out." Then he stopped speaking, defiance creeping back into his expression.

The off-camera voice spoke again. "Keep talking, Richter. And don't even think of lying." A hand appeared holding a photo of a young girl in front of Richter's face.

Tom raised his hand again. Robinson stopped the video. "Robbie, who is in the picture, and was it really necessary?"

"Tom, you know what *plata o plomo* means to a narco. Richter would never talk to save his own life. The photo is of his niece back in Germany."

"Two things, Robbie... no, three. First, the president is not going to like this. Again. Second, Mark Freiberg is going to go ballistic and cause us all sorts of problems; third, it would really be nice to get some information that we could use publicly."

"I warned you that you wouldn't like this." He leaned forward close to Tom. "I suggest, my young friend, that you watch the rest of the bloody video and then pass judgment if it was necessary or not."

Tom's muscles tensed and he glared at Robinson. After a moment, he forced himself to relax. "Okay, Robbie. You're right. Sorry. Let's go with it."

Robinson punched the play button. There was a pause before the voice said, "Paraguay, tell us about Paraguay."

"Wallerein has a training facility in Paraguay."

"Where?"

"I don't know. Never been there."

"Where?" A rising menace in the voice.

Richter sighed. "West of Cuidad del Este."

"What is it for?"

"Training. Wallerein changed his plan and brought in some extra teams to train on explosives, then to deploy to Amerika this year."

"Why did Wallerein change his plan?"

"Callahan. Once Callahan got involved, Wallerein lost his mind. He changed everything, timelines, targets, training. He insisted on making more strikes, bloodier and more newsworthy. Plus at least one massive strike."

"How did you react?"

"I advised against the changes." Another pause. "But only once."

"Why?"

Richter managed a weak smile. "People who argue with Kurt Wallerein tend to disappear."

"Speaking of disappearing, tell us about kidnapping Colleen Callahan and Ruhi Adams."

Surprised by the abrupt question, Tom felt a jolt as his pulse sped up and his muscles tensed involuntarily.

"Herr Wallerein ordered it for payback for Callahan's stunt in New Mexico, killing his team members." His description of Colleen's beating was deadpan and expressionless, like he was describing filleting a trout. Tom wanted to reach into the television, grab Richter by the throat, and smash his fist into his face again and again. Instead, he sat with his hands gripping the arms of his chair.

"Where is Wallerein now?"

Richter shrugged. "I don't know. Before the women escaped from our forward base, he sent me back to the coast to arrange for more teams. He stayed behind to get men and explosives across the border."

"Why? What's the target?"

Richter shook his head. "I do not know."

"Richter!" the voice nearly shouted.

The German shrugged. "Dams, probably. I saw maps of northern New Mexico with dams marked. Earthen dams. Water systems. And more fires."

"When?"

"Again, I don't know for certain, but Wallerein told me to expect him back in Playa del Carmen in seven days."

"Sweet Jesus," breathed Tom. "Back in Playa del Carmen in seven days?" Dismayed, he lurched back into his chair. "And New Mexico is the target?"

"Tom, Wallerein is planning a massive strike before heading back to his headquarters in Libya. It looks like we have five or six days, *no mas*, my friend."

"Where is this Richter now?"

"Paco has him on ice, ready to turn over to whomever we want… like Jay's people at the border."

"No shit?" blurted Mitchell. "I can have my guys pick up Richter anywhere Paco wants."

Tom was skeptical. "Do you have any German-speaking agents in San Antonio?"

Mitchell laughed. "Texas is a wonderland of talented people, *Herr Oberst*. Fredericksburg, Gruene, New Braunfels, and some other communities in the hill country were founded by German immigrants. Lots of folks still speak German. Heck, the daily newspaper in New Braunfels is called the *Herald-Zeitung*. My guys will drain Richter like a wine skin on a ski trip."

Robinson looked at Tom, who nodded. "Make it happen, Robbie. The spooks in D.C. will want to take a crack at him, too, if for no other reason than to make sure he wasn't tortured like our other sources."

Chapter Thirty

Santa Fe Municipal Airport, New Mexico

Tom Callahan disembarked from the C-21A and spotted Porter Nelson and a woman standing near the terminal. As he walked across the tarmac, he took a quick glance around the airport he had flown into many times. He should have enjoyed the view of his beloved mountains. Instead, his heart ached.

The men embraced. After a moment, they straightened up, wiping their eyes. Porter was the first to speak. "How is she?"

"Not good. Critical in fact. The docs say she should improve, but nobody knows when."

Porter nodded and changed the subject. "Tom, this is Michelle Duregger."

Tom turned to Michelle and offered his hand. "Nice to meet you, Michelle. Porter speaks highly of you—and he doesn't do that for many people. I should warn you that this is a dangerous assignment."

"I'm ready for it, Colonel."

"If you're going to be a member of our team, you have to call me Tom."

Michelle was dressed in a sweater, Levi's and knee-high boots, long hair wafting in the gentle breeze. She smiled at the compliment. Tom thought her smile was almost as lovely as Colleen's. He felt another stab of pain. He struggled to stay focused. "I spoke with the governor. He's tied up tonight but wants to meet with everybody in the morning, about eight." He glanced at his watch. "That gives us about fourteen hours to come up with some sort of plan. Michelle, I want you to come with me to the meeting I set up with the New Mexico National Guard staff."

He handed Porter a thumb drive. "This has many of the documents that the FBI recovered from Wallerein's headquarters. They're mostly in German, some in Russian. Good for a few hours of light reading." Tom tried to smile and failed. "Seriously, Porter, you probably have a better feel for Wallerein's personality and the Stasi mentality of his assassins than does the FBI. I need your take on this, ASAP, buddy."

"Just like old times, eh, Tom?"

Tom nodded and turned back to Michelle. "You probably already know this, but under that ultra-cool exterior that Porter presents to the world, he is a serious investigative reporter. Porter'll fill you in on the details. Listen closely. He's been up to his eyeballs in Wallerein-related activities for months."

"It seems our friend Wallerein doesn't lack for ambition, does he?"

"Right," said Tom. "And it's one of the most closely guarded secrets of this administration."

"Everything's under control, sweetheart," said Porter, affecting a strange accent as he looked at Michelle. "We got the bad guys in our sights, see."

Her eyes flashed. "Call me sweetheart again, and I will strike you in an area of your body that is soft, spongy, and sensitive."

Tom laughed. He laughed again, then laughed so hard he bent over. "Sorry buddy," he choked out, "but you should see your face...."

Porter said, "Michelle, I'm sorry. I was trying out my Jimmy Cagney accent. At least, I thought I was."

She chuckled. "I know you were. A Cagney you are not. And don't do it again. Your own voice is fine with me."

Tom wiped his eyes. "Thanks for the show, Port. Just what I needed."

"Glad to be of service, Tom," said Porter, with a slight bow. "What you really need is about eight hours of sleep. You look like hell."

Tom waved him off. "There'll be time for sleep after we get Wallerein."

***

Twenty minutes later they were ushered into the immense foyer of the headquarters of the New Mexico National Guard and led down a corridor that opened into a conference room. Colonel Brice Adams met them at the door. Their handshake turned into a prolonged hug. Again Tom's emotions were scrambled.

"Sorry, Brice. I didn't get to see Ruhi in San Antonio."

"I know. She's determined to get Kulenović's body to his family. Kulenović told Ruhi that Colleen tried to protect Ruhi by being defiant and aggressive. For this she was beaten so severely that Wallerein postponed Ruhi's interrogation. If Ruhi had been beaten, she wouldn't have been able to fly them out. Colleen saved them both."

"Colleen would dispute that—if she could speak."

"She'll pull out, buddy. With the possible exception of Ruhi, Colleen's the toughest woman I've ever met."

Tom nodded. "I think we need to acknowledge that we struck oil with these women."

Everyone rose when the group entered the conference room. Tom's heart sank. Way too many people. About twenty soldiers stood around an immense wooden table, and the walls of the room were lined with soldiers in battle dress standing at attention beside their chairs. *There goes operational security.*

"Let me introduce you, Tom," said Brice. "This is The Adjutant General (TAG), Brigadier General Antonio Garcia." Garcia, a man of medium height with wide shoulders and muscles even his uniform jacket could not hide, smiled as he shook hands.

"*Bienvenido a Nuevo Mexico, Coronel.* I wish we could have met under better circumstances. I met your mother at an art festival in Santa Fe two years ago. Quite a lady."

"I hope you bought a very expensive painting, General." Both men chuckled.

The TAG introduced the ranking members of his staff, augmented by FBI Agent Jerry Bennett and two State Police captains, then motioned Tom into the chair next to him and addressed the assemblage. "I just

226

spoke to the governor. He will meet us here tomorrow morning at zero eight hundred hours. He's been in contact with the president, who," he glanced at Tom, "cleared us to know that Kurt Wallerein and his team are probably here in the state." There were murmurs from the staff as Wallerein's name sunk in. "For you younger troops who might not know this, as a member of the Baader-Meinhof Gang during the 1970s, Wallerein killed more than a few American soldiers in Germany." More murmurs, angrier now.

The General nodded. "Yeah, people, this is the guy we have to deal with. A psychopath. So listen up. What I intend to do is summarize what the president and what the governor said. Then Colonel Callahan can fill in the details and give us an operational update."

General Garcia spoke for about five minutes. The stunned silence was broken only by occasional growls from some of the Guardsmen as the origin of the wildfires that had plagued their state was labeled as deliberate arson—and murder. The New Mexico National Guard has roots going back to Spanish days before Pilgrims landed at Plymouth Rock. Most of the Guard members present in the conference room had New Mexico family roots going back generations. The rest were transplants who had lived in the state for decades.

Tom felt the weight of depression pressing down on his shoulders as the TAG enumerated each of the suspected attacks. Weak from lack of sleep and unrelenting guilt, his mind wandered. All over New Mexico, people he did not even know had died because Wallerein had targeted his home state. His own speech lasted just over six minutes. "This is a multi-pronged attack campaign. Fires are just the immediate terror part. The destruction of watersheds is the longer lasting, expensive part. Most cities don't have a plan to restore watersheds or have adequate alternative sources of water. People can move but that means mass disruptions, social instability and a massive economic impact. People will be frightened and furious. Who knows where that will lead." Tom looked around the room. The atmosphere was tense; all eyes were on him. "In summary, this is effectively a guerilla war waged right here in our own country—in our own state—armed men willing to use violence to make our government agencies look incompetent, ineffective, and uncaring about our citizens. It's up to us to prove them wrong." He turned to the TAG. "And that, General, is about all we know at this point."

General Garcia said, "I have two more things to say. First, my father used to tell me stories of his days as a sailor in the U.S. Navy during World War Two. He served in an anti-submarine task force commanded by Rear Admiral Daniel Gallery. In June 1944, they captured the German submarine U-505, the first capture of a foreign warship on the high seas by the Navy since the War of 1812. The Navy now had an Enigma coding machine and current code books which would enable the Navy to read German messages in real time."

The General paused, took a sip of his coffee and waited to let his words sink in. "Now you can imagine what the thousands of sailors in the task force were thinking. This was the best sea story ever, one that they could use to impress their girlfriends, their families, all the other sailors they were destined to meet in the bars of their next liberty port. A super stud-factor. But Admiral Gallery knew that the secret had to be kept in order to exploit the Enigma machine. He also knew that a simple order, no matter how well worded or threatening, would not stop the stampede of sailors eager to spread the tale. So he spoke by radio to the entire task force and explained to his men just how crucial keeping this secret was to the Navy and the country."

He paused again. "And, believe it or not, every man in that task force kept his mouth shut. Not a peep. The Germans never did find out. As a result, countless American lives were saved." He looked around the room, his gaze resting on individual soldiers to emphasize his message. "Now, I'm no Admiral Gallery. But the point is the same—we need to keep this mission secret until we have a good handle on it. If word gets out that we have a madman and his compadres running amuck in New Mexico, it will cause mass panic and who knows what else. Fear, especially fear of the unknown, leads to violence. And violence is the last thing we want. We need to keep a lid on this, people. When it's time, we will tell the public what they need to know. Not until then. Any questions?"

There were murmurs of assent and nodding heads. Nobody spoke. General Garcia then turned to Tom. "The second thing, Colonel, is for you to get some rest. You are nearly out on your feet." He raised his hand to stop Tom's protests before they began. "If I have to, I will make that an order. Give my staff time to work this. Colonel Adams and Mr. Nelson can stand in for you quite nicely, I think."

Tom realized the futility of an argument. He stood. "Yes, sir."

"Breakfast here at zero six hundred," said the general. "See you then."

Chapter Thirty-One

San Simon, New Mexico

José Arellano glanced to the west to catch a glimpse of the sun as it sank into the San Pedro Mountains. He never tired of watching the multi-colored play of the sun's rays reflected off the high clouds that streaked the evening sky. His grandfather's favorite *dicho*—saying— was "Only in New Mexico do the sunsets look like they are painted by God himself." Grandfather Arellano knew that from personal experience. He had been in the Army and had actually gone overseas during World War II when the New Mexico National Guard had been called up and sent to the Philippines. They arrived just in time to be captured and brutalized by the Japanese during the Bataan Death March. Jose had listened to his grandfather tell him over and over that dreaming about Grandmother's tamales and life under New Mexican skies at sunset were what gave him the strength to stay alive in that hell-hole of a prison camp.

Darkness rose from the valley floor. Arellano could still see light reflected off the ridge as he turned back to the task at hand, fixing the head gate on the *acequia madre*—mother ditch. Arellano was the *mayordomo*—ditch boss—for his local *acequia* association in San Simon, a farming community that, like so many rural communities in the American Southwest, owed its life to irrigation. Arellano wasn't sure when the San Simon *acequia* was dug but he knew that *acequia* irrigation, Arabic irrigation technology adopted by the Spanish, had been imported by the conquistadores in the seventeenth and eighteenth centuries.

A country boy at heart, Arellano was content with his life farming the land along the Rio Chama that had been in his family for generations. He had only left the United States once, a trip to Valencia, Spain along with several members of the New Mexico Acequia Association as a guest of the Spanish government celebrating the connection between Spanish and New Mexican *acequia* communities.

Dressed in his regular attire of work clothes, a heavy flannel shirt, jeans, cowboy hat, and hip waders, Arellano also wore a Model 1917 .45 revolver that had been passed to him from his father and grandfather as protection from coyotes and snakes. A life-time of hunting and working in the grassy areas near water sources had trained him to be armed at all times.

The slender Arellano, with his dark hair and shiny black eyes was nicknamed *"La Nutria"*—The Otter—because of his ready smile and ability to turn work into play. The ditches always needed repair. This head gate issue was critical. It controlled the amount of water from the Rio Chama into the *acequia madre* and thence into the network of smaller lateral ditches that bathed the fields of San Simon.

Arellano's fifteen-year-old son, Joshua, was with him tonight. Arellano knew that Joshua's primary reason to be with him was to get out of doing his homework, but he didn't mind. He was grooming Joshua to be the next *mayordomo*, just as his own father had chosen him to carry on the work.

"Hey, Dad! I think I found the problem," shouted Joshua from up on the embankment. Arellano could barely make out his silhouette against the rapidly darkening sky. "I can see it from up here. Looks like there's a small log stuck on the other side. I'll get it out."

"Wait, *mijito*, let me do it. You're not dressed properly. You'll get all muddy."

"Come on, Dad," laughed Joshua. "Gettin' muddy and making noise is what teenage boys are all about." He started to jog towards the head gate.

Arellano heard the unmistakable crack of a rifle. His son spun around, crashed down on the embankment, and slid head first into the ditch.

"Joshua!" he screamed. He ran as fast as his rubber waders would allow along the ditch towards the boy. Something punched him in the shoulder and he went down hard on his back. Another shot. Arellano groped for his pistol. He began to slide down the embankment towards the water. He tried to call out his son's name but made only a croaking sound. A silhouette appeared at the top of the embankment. Arellano fired his pistol over and over. The figure dropped. Another appeared.

The last thing Jose Arellano saw in this life before another bullet smashed into his chest was an orange flash.

Wallerein safe house
Izoro, New Mexico

Wallerein's head bounced off the passenger window of the SUV for the third time during this trip to the mountains. Despite the throbbing in his leg, sleep had ambushed him again. Stay awake, he commanded himself cursing his weakness. His aging body was letting him down.

The SUV continued along NM Highway 4 through the steep mountain sides as they navigated through the Santa Fe National Forest. Two of his teams were burrowed into a short-term rental in Izoro, a small village sandwiched between the Jemez Pueblo and near the famed Jemez Springs, within striking distance of Los Alamos. He smiled to himself about the phrase "striking distance" because what he had in mind for Los Alamos did indeed involve a major strike. As they passed through the village, most of the homes that lined the main street looked empty, probably vacation properties owned by rich residents of Los Alamos, the third wealthiest county in America.

The safe house was a large cabin nestled in a mountain canyon, sheltered by twisted, ancient cottonwoods with a river and rugged cliffs protecting it from a rear approach. One of his men stood guard on the large redwood wraparound deck that featured a spectacular view down the Jemez River Valley.

His team chief, Eric Stasser, an East German ex-Stasi major, paced the deck. Forty-ish, with graying hair and a distinguished air, he was dressed in beige trousers, plaid shirt, and vest. He looked like an advertisement for a fly fishing company.

Wallerein got out of the vehicle and stretched in a futile attempt to raise his energy level. Stasser approached and offered his hand. "*Wilkommen*, comrade," he said as they went inside. Wallerein took in the decoration—rustic, heavy wood furniture, Indian rugs, large Western-themed framed prints, a fully equipped kitchen, a wood burning fireplace, and four bedrooms. The dining table was covered with maps and papers. His men had been at work.

Wallerein brushed aside Stasser's offer of a drink. "What do you have to show me?"

"At your orders, *mein Herr*, we have come up with two additional targets. We looked at several options: electric substations, bridges, even dams. Of course we chose two outside those obvious targets. Both selections are quick, easy, and certain of success. That, coupled with low risk and maximum impact, led us to our decision." He paused.

"Proceed," barked Wallerein. "I don't have all day."

"*Entschuldigen Sie, bitte, mein Herr*—excuse me, sir. The first target should be a portion of the state's fiber optic system." He produced a map and used a pencil to trace out several lines. "The main fiber optic cables run here, here, and here. 'Head ends' are where many lines merge. They are located here, here, and here. Head ends are protected to some extent. They are also redundant, meaning there are back-ups if one fails for some reason."

"Why are you telling me about head ends if they're redundant?" Wallerein interrupted. "Are you proposing that we show the Americans how lovely their engineering is, how brilliant they are by building redundant systems? Our purpose is to disgrace the Americans, not boost their reputation."

"No, comrade. Please excuse me. The weakness of the system is in the fiber optic electronic reprocessing huts scattered along railroad lines and around the state that boost the transmissions. They take the place of microwave towers that have to be placed every fifteen or twenty miles to boost wireless communications. The huts are easily identified, pretty common, and completely unsecure. Easy targets."

Stasser produced yet another map. "I've scouted their system. It was easy to find. Here are the railroads. Straight, obvious and unsecure. Along the track right-of-way are these huts. I've marked a series of them." He pointed to dots of red marker along the railroad tracks. "We've planned simultaneous explosions throughout this section of the system. Each hut we blow up will take out a chunk of their communications and data transmissions systems. Yes, they will figure out patchwork fixes. Yes, they will be able to re-build. But that will take time. And money. Lots of money. In the meantime, thousands of people and businesses will find their lives complicated, disrupted, and maddening. They will be furious." He straightened up and met Wallerein's eyes with just a hint of a self-congratulatory smile. "*Mein Herr*, this is a low-risk, high-reward operation."

Wallerein considered the second proposed operation through a haze. He felt his strength begin to ebb. His head snapped back. He sat up, shaking his head.

He felt Stasser's hand on his shoulder. "Comrade, you are tired. You need to rest."

"Don't preach to me!"

"*Mein Herr*, this is a resort town. The hot springs are a wonderful tonic for exhaustion. I tried them myself. The experience is almost magical. Please, sir, leave us to plan these strikes. Come back refreshed and critique them."

Wallerein erupted from his chair, furious with this presumptuous pup. He stopped himself. Maybe Stasser was right. He was tired. And, he had to concede, he was in the way here. These boys could function without him, as difficult as that was for a highly involved person like himself to accept. Maybe just this once.

***

Wallerein drove himself to the springs despite Stasser's protest about security. A bodyguard was sure to attract attention in a small American town. He found the building in the center of town that had been used by Indians and settlers alike since the 1860s. Signs in the office

234

offered private concrete tubs for twenty-five-minute soaks. The attendant, a smiling middle-aged woman with a too bright smile, offered Wallerein the senior discount, took his cash, then led him into the soaking room while delivering a short safety lecture about the high temperature of the water. He stripped in the privacy of his small enclosure, adjusted the water temperature to prevent scalding himself, carefully limiting the level of water in case—or when—he fell asleep and settled in. The hot water began to soothe the dull ache in his leg.

Stasser was right. The mineral-laden waters did seem almost magical. His mind loosened along with his muscles. Sometime later, he opened his eyes. *Diversify*. He had said that months ago back in his Libyan bunker. *Why merely do the same things over and over, attacking the same targets? Eventually the Americans will either figure things out or get lucky. If we diversify—change our methods—we keep them off balance. Stasser is right; he is acting on my ideas.*

Wallerein added more hot water from the spigot and settled back. He knew Callahan would eventually travel to Los Alamos. He would have to assign one of his teams to make sure Callahan died—and died soon. While Wallerein would delight in killing the American himself, the important thing was to have him die—and Wallerein was too busy with preparations for the big event. What his teams needed to do is make one last push here in this wasteland. *Stick with the overall plan*, he told himself—pick a few more visible soft targets, hit them and get out of the country. He chuckled. While his men did this, he would keep in mind the ultimate target. That target he reserved for himself and another team known only to him. *Stasser's attacks will be the perfect distraction.* He chuckled again. *As good as Stasser is, he isn't as smart as he thinks.*

Rio Tercero Dam
Oñate State Park
Near Rio Tercero, NM

The panel van crawled through the pre-dawn mist, lights blacked out, along the narrow maintenance track that sliced through the forest. It turned into the tiny parking lot, backed near the dam access door, and shut down.

Helmut Schneider and the other members of his team, dressed in black, slipped out silently, and quickly went to work. One man crowbarred open the lock on the door. Schneider stood watch while, moving with caution, the others unloaded the van and began to move barrels containing high explosives into the maintenance tunnel within the structure of the dam itself.

Schneider, a stocky fifty-ish former East German, was an engineer by education and an experienced Stasi saboteur by training. This was his first venture abroad in the employ of Kurt Wallerein, and he was determined to exceed even Wallerein's inflexible demands for excellence. Schneider had spent the previous week searching for the right dam to blow. He was aided in his search by the National Inventory of Dams, available to anybody via the Internet. Still shocked, but gratified, by the openness of the American nation, he shook his head at the idea that the United States government would make his information search so easy. The Directory listed all 84,000 dams in the country by size, age, and type of construction. More important, it even listed the 14,000 dams nationally that were categorized as "posing a high or significant hazard to life and property," along with 2,000 dams classified simply as "unsafe." The Rio Tercero Dam was one of those.

The rock and concrete dam was built in 1880 by hand and horse, repaired in 1913, and enlarged in the 1940s. Built to control the Rio Tercero, which had shown a predilection to generate raging flash floods during the summer monsoons, the modest-sized dam now impounded a lake covering an area the size of a small city. The steady flow of water released contributed to two nearby *acequia* communities downstream with a combined total of some eight hundred acres of irrigated land. As a recreational area, the lake attracted fishermen and boaters, along with millions of dollars of tourist revenue, while the downstream farming community of Rio Tercero, had expanded to service the visitors to the state park.

It was a perfect target. Schneider grinned as he looked across the lake shimmering in the fading moonlight. This was going to be a pleasure! As a German, Schneider considered this attack revenge of sorts. It may have been on a night much like this during WWII when the Möhne and the Edersee dams were breached by Allied bombers, resulting in the drowning deaths of hundreds of Germans and massive destruction of property. He bristled at the thought, then turned to look downstream. The lights of the targeted town gleamed in the darkness. Schneider could imagine the unsuspecting victims assuming they were safe in their beds or mindlessly watching the banal capitalist television.

Pity the town was so small. Dallas and Sacramento also had unsafe dams upstream. But Comrade Wallerein had insisted that this was the point—small town America must be shown that there was no place Wallerein couldn't reach. Schneider smiled again. Dallas would have to wait. He glanced back downstream. In a few short hours, the peaceful town of Rio Tercero would cease to exist.

Chapter Thirty-Two

NM National Guard Headquarters
0600 the next morning

Tom Callahan watched as the TAG opened the early morning operations briefing with a brief announcement. "There was a double murder last night near San Simon that may or may not be connected with Wallerein." He gestured to a uniformed State Police officer. "Captain Gonzales will give us the details."

The Captain cleared his throat and stood. "The *mayordomo* of San Simon, one Jose Arellano, and his son were shot around dusk last night. When they were late for dinner, Señora Arellano went out to the *acequia*, found them and called us. There is no apparent motive for the shooting. No robbery, no explanation." The Captain swept his gaze around the room. "Before he was killed, it looks like the *mayordomo* got off a few shots and hit one of the perps. Two sets of footprints led from a vehicle, probably an SUV, to the *acequia madre*. Drag marks and a blood trail back to the vehicle indicate one guy pulled the other back. We recovered a weapon, a Heckler and Koch MP5, at the site, which is one reason we're here this morning. An HK MP5 is a very unusual weapon in New Mexico."

Porter Nelson spoke up. "I have lots of experience with the *MaschinenPistole Funf*." He went to the white board behind the TAG, drew a big red star and superimposed a crude drawing of a submachine gun. Over that he wrote in large letters, "RAF." He turned to the group. "Anybody other than Colonel Callahan recognize this?"

"The Red Army Faction!" blurted two sergeants and a major simultaneously.

"Right. In German, *Rote Armee Fraktion*. Also known as the Baader-Meinhof Gang." He put down the marker. "The RAF loved the MaschinenPistole Funf." He pointed to his drawing. "That's why they put the HK MP5 in their logo. They used it often while their 'anti-imperialist struggle' raised money through bank robberies and kidnappings. Then they attacked U.S. military facilities, German police stations and press outlets. Coincidently, the MP5 was also a favorite of the East German police and border guards. Not to mention the Stasi."

Tom leaned towards the TAG. "General, Wallerein is well known to allow his people to choose their own weapons. Many of his guys are ex-Stasi so this could be evidence that his people are here in New Mexico. At the same time, there are dozens of variants of the weapon. Our own special ops guys use MP5s."

"Yeah, but not to murder New Mexicans," growled the TAG.

Special Agent Jerry Bennett spoke up. "Captain, you give me the serial number, and I can probably find out what the FBI knows about that weapon with one phone call." The Captain slid a copy of his report over to Bennett who left the room.

A baby-faced lieutenant asked, "Colonel Callahan, why an *acequia*? What about the forest fires?"

"Good question. Don't think for a minute that Wallerein's forgotten the fires. He's made quite a bit of headway to his goals with them. He just wants to keep up the pressure, spread us out to maintain the initiative. He is trying to terrorize and polarize the people. As for *acequias*, I suspect you know a lot more about how *acequias* work than I do, right?"

"Sir, I started working on our Pueblo *acequia* when I was five years old. My cousin is the *mayordomo*."

"Then you understand the history of the *acequia*, the culture and how it influences the Southwest. An *acequia* complex is a community binder. Destroy an *acequia*, destroy the economy and the cohesion that smaller communities have, accelerate the destruction of rural New Mexico."

"Yes, sir, but why would a big-time German terrorist attack them? How would he even know about them?"

"To prove that anyone, anywhere can be hit at any time. Environmental terrorism is, or will soon be, in vogue. Especially as populations grow and concentrate. For example, our beloved Southwest grew faster in the past ten years than most of America, and is now, surprisingly, one of the most urbanized areas of the country in terms of percentage of population. We are vulnerable.

"The attack on the *acequia* was a prelude to attacking our water infrastructure. There are more than fifty thousand community water systems in the country, and all are unguarded. Shutting down water systems, even just a few, would be more than inconvenient, it would cause immediate panic."

"Tom," said Porter. "Remember that wellhead explosion a couple days ago near Las Vegas? Could there be a link to Wallerein?"

Tom's blood froze. *Of course!* He turned to the state police captain. "Sir, the explosion at Hildago…"

The captain slapped the table. "Damnit! We thought it was suspicious. I'll have our guys look at it again."

Before the captain could leave, the door opened, and Jerry Bennett entered. He addressed the group. "The FBI confirmed that the weapon recovered in San Simon was of East German manufacture. We can run ballistics on it to see if it's been used in any previous attacks."

The door opened again, and one of the TAG's sergeant aides slipped in and whispered in the TAG's ear. "Excuse me, people," the general said over his shoulder as he abruptly left the room. Three minutes later he returned, face red from suppressed rage. "That was the governor. He won't be coming here any time soon. And for a good reason." The TAG looked directly at Tom. "There's another fire in the mountains. This one simply erupted upwind from Ruidoso. It burned nearly two thousand acres overnight." He started to gather his notes. "The governor's taking a Blackhawk down to assess the situation. I'm going with him."

He gestured to the chief of staff and started barking orders. "I've laid on another Blackhawk for Colonel Callahan. Make sure he has transport to the aviation facility. Colonel Callahan, once you've been read in on our plan and are satisfied, go wherever you need to." He turned to the state police captains. "The Secretary of Public Safety just told me that the state police will issue a "Be On the Look Out" notice for Wallerein. Check with Colonel Callahan for more names.

"Let's get to it, people."

Joshua Foretich Middle School
Albuquerque, New Mexico

The roads to the school through the aging neighborhood were narrow, just wide enough to accommodate two cars at once. Stop signs and school warning signs combined to calm traffic. The early morning delivery of students and the 3:30 afternoon pickup were maddening affairs of dense traffic and overwrought parents. The rest of the day was slow with just enough action to keep Jesus Medina occupied.

Medina, the school's crossing guard, watched with satisfaction as the last of the early morning minivan mashup dissipated. Another rush hour and another safe morning delivery of "his kids" to the safety of their classrooms. He took a moment to look up at the sky—it was another beautiful New Mexico morning. Sandia Peak towered to the north; a few scattered cumulous clouds textured the azure horizon. He could smell flowers in the late summer breeze. Glorious!

As usual, he felt the warm glow of satisfaction of a job done well start to fade. He clenched his right hand over and over. Imagining how a bottle of beer would feel, nestled into his grip. Perfect right now.

Not now, not today, Jesus. One day at a time, one day at a time. He repeated his mantra over and over.

This was his first job in five years, and he was determined to keep it. The commander of the local Veterans of Foreign Wars chapter had fixed it with the principal. If Jesus could handle the crossing duties until semester break, the principal would hire him to replace the janitor who was scheduled to retire. Every morning Jesus got up at six, showered, shaved, and dressed in what he considered his new uniform: yellow vest with fluorescent stripes, button down collar shirt, and neatly pressed, faded khaki Dockers trousers that he had scrounged from a Salvation Army store.

A Latino of average height, café au lait complexion, dark hair pulled back in a ponytail, Jesus was becoming a fixture around the school. Satisfied that he could safely leave his crosswalk, he began to make his customary lap around the entire schoolyard perimeter, just to make sure of things.

The second time Medina watched the black Toyota SUV make a slow pass by the school triggered some long-buried instincts. Something was wrong. He tracked the big SUV with his eyes as it swung around and parked, engine running and partially up on the sidewalk, like some sinister beast preparing to pounce on the school. The hairs on the back of his neck stood up, and his skin prickled. The hyper-vigilance drilled into him during multiple deployments to the Middle East came roaring back.

Jesus scanned for more bad guys. Negative results, but one vehicle was bad enough. This wasn't the best of neighborhoods. He had seen some drug deals going down and reported them to the cops. Nothing had come of it. Right now, right in front of him was an ambush in the making. He was about to bet his life on it.

He pulled out his second-hand cell phone and called 911. "My name is Jesus Medina. I work at the Joshua Foretich Middle School. There are three men in a black Toyota SUV casing out the school."

"Could you spell your name, please?" asked a flat voice.

"Medina. I spell Mike Echo Delta India November Alpha."

"And your first name, Mr. Medina?"

"Jesus as in *Jesus Cristo!* We need the cops now!"

"Would you please describe the vehicle, Mr. Medina?"

"Toyota, Black, SUV. I told you. Three men preparing to attack the school."

"What is your position with the school, and what makes you think they want to attack it?"

"Dude, I know what I'm talking about! I've been in ambushes! We need cops—lots of cops. Now! If you won't help, I've gotta do it myself!"

He pocketed the phone. Broke into a run towards the school. Up the front steps. Down the corridors to the offices. He spotted the principal, Greg Johnson, in his office.

Medina leapt over the counter and dashed past the astonished secretaries. He burst into Johnson's office and slammed the door behind him. "Mr. J, I need to talk to you right now."

He leaned over Johnson's desk. "There are three hoods outside scoping out the school. Looks bad. They ain't here on a social call. Could be a drive-by. I called 9-1-1."

"How do you know this, Jesus?"

"Infantry. I know an ambush when I see one."

Johnson nodded. "I remember." He fixed Medina with a stare. "Jesus, take a moment to think about this. Are you certain?"

"Mr. J, I know what this means for me if I'm wrong. But this is about the kids."

"What do you suggest?

"Lock the school down, sir. Shelter in place. Now."

Johnson glanced at the school daily schedule of activities. "Mrs. Monroe's class is practicing a play in the auditorium right now."

"I'll go there and help her secure the room and the students."

"Go!" Johnson ordered. "I'll start getting things moving here. And, Jesus, I hope you're wrong."

"Me, too. But I ain't."

***

Officer Inigo Montoya heard the call on his radio. "Bravo 243 Charlie, suspicious activity reported near Joshua Foretich Middle School. Three men in a black Toyota SUV may be planning to attack the school."

Montoya checked his unit's GPS. He was pretty close. He keyed his mic, "Copy. Bravo 243 Charlie en route."

He hit the siren and lights and wove through the chaotic city traffic, cursing the scofflaws who were slow to move out of his way. He crossed from the seedy eateries and bars that lined the city street into rows of small, neat houses with small neat yards. Then back into the neighborhood surrounding the school.

Montoya went silent and dark as he approached the school area. He flashed past a school crossing warning sign into the parking lot apron, skidded to a stop, and jumped out of his car. All appeared normal at the school. Except it seemed quiet, too quiet. No kids in the playground. No people entering or leaving the building.

Out of the corner of his eye he spotted a black Toyota SUV as it suddenly roared into life. Tires squealing, the SUV roared towards the school like a panther on amphetamines. It skidded to a halt ten yards from the doors. Two men, dressed in black, wearing small backpacks and carrying submachine guns, vaulted out of the vehicle. Tugged on the school's door. Locked down! The first man aimed his weapon at the door and blew the lock off. They charged inside.

Submachine guns in Albuquerque! Montoya's SWAT training kicked in. *Go to the gunfire, Inigo!* He popped the trunk, slipped his tactical vest over his head, grabbed his AR-15 and started across the parking lot. Squeezing his shoulder microphone, he shouted. "Two armed subjects dressed in black at Foretich Middle School. Gunfire. Need backup. ASAP!" Montoya heard sirens in the distance. He couldn't wait for reinforcements. Only he could stop a slaughter.

He darted through the parking lot, crouched low, using the cars as cover, eyes focused on the escape vehicle. He could see the driver's head. He slid in behind the vehicle, weapon up. Cringed as an explosion and gunfire erupted inside the school. He crept forward toward the vehicle's open doors. Another explosion. Screams.

He could see a pistol on the dashboard, the man's hands rested on the steering wheel. Montoya took a deep breath, stood and shouted, "APD. Let me see your hands!" The driver lunged for the pistol. Montoya shot him twice in the back of the head. Brains and blood spattered over the dash and windscreen.

Montoya pivoted, jerked the school door open, and slid into the corridor. The two terrorists had finished their sweep of the first hall, shooting the locks, kicking open the doors, then firing randomly into each classroom. One terrorist pounded down the hallway and ducked

244

around the corner. The closer one pulled something from a pocket. *Grenade!*

Montoya fired three times. The terrorist spun around, dropped the grenade, and collapsed. Montoya dove into a door opening. The blast was terrifying. Shrapnel and shards of glass flew up and down the hall, ripping into the walls and ceiling.

There was a brief moment of quiet. Then more screams.

Cautious, Montoya moved down the corridor. Desperate to keep his focus on the remaining shooter, he forced his eyes away from the carnage in the classrooms. The terrorist poked his weapon into the hall and fired several quick shots. Bullet holes stitched up the wall behind Montoya. He dove for cover, then fired back twice. The terrorist slammed through double doors marked "Auditorium." More shots, now from inside the auditorium. More screams.

Montoya reloaded, then sprinted down the hall. Slammed into the doors and burst into the room, weapon ready. The terrorist had his submachine gun pointed at the huddled and screaming children. Montoya fired two bursts. The bullets caught the man in the right shoulder and twice in the head. Sent him sprawling across the linoleum floor.

Montoya turned back to the kids. Towards the carnage. To the horror.

A man in a yellow vest covered a boy. Blood was everywhere, the body inert. Montoya rolled him over and knew immediately he was dead. The boy beneath him screamed, wild eyed and crazed. Montoya snatched him up and cradled him as the boy sobbed. He glanced around the room. A teacher gory and unrecognizable. Children sprawled in corners, under seats. Some dead, some bloody, the rest hysterical.

Who the hell would do this?

Chapter Thirty-Three

National Guard Aviation Facility
Santa Fe Municipal Airport

Tom Callahan strode into the Guard mission planning room escorted by a major from the operations staff. Introductions were brief: Chief Warrant Officer (CW2) Beth Tafoya, pilot-in-command; her co-pilot; her crew chief. All were native New Mexicans. Tafoya, all five foot five of her, was from Carrizozo; the co-pilot sported a crew cut and was from Silver City, and the lanky crew chief, Albuquerque.

As they clustered around the conference table, Tafoya began, "My orders are to take you wherever you want, Colonel. Would you like to go check out the Ruidoso fire? It's turning into a monster. Three thousand acres burned already. Massive destruction."

Tom shook his head. "No, I've seen fires. Wallerein isn't there anymore—if he was even there when it was started. No, I want to go where he's lurking now. The question is where to start looking, and we have probably two days, maybe three, tops, to find him."

Tafoya went to the mission planning map on the wall. She had a trim athlete's figure and walked like a jock, confident, just shy of a swagger. Tom thought she would fit into any fighter ready room in the world—from him, a major compliment. Centered on the board was an enormous map of New Mexico. Around the edges of the state were swaths of the adjoining states: Arizona, Utah, Colorado, Texas and a bit of Oklahoma. She pointed north. "If I was a bad ass—"

"You are a bad ass, Tafoya," said the major.

"Thank you, sir. You say the nicest things. As I was saying, Colonel, if I wanted to really hurt New Mexico, I'd burn the watersheds up north. Either the headwaters of the Colorado River or the Rio Grande. They're the two principal rivers of the Southwest. Different headwaters, different sides of the continental divide." She traced the continental divide as it snaked across Colorado and down into New Mexico. "Between them, they bring in about half the water for the state. Take out those watersheds, and you cause immeasurable damage to our state as well as Colorado, Arizona, Texas, and even Mexico."

"But the Colorado isn't in New Mexico," protested Tom. Then he understood. "Ah, yes, the San Juan River is a tributary."

Tafoya nodded. "A major tributary, sir, along with the Chaco." She produced a set of mission planning papers. "I've taken the liberty of working out some details." She handed Tom a copy of a map with a proposed route of flight.

He looked it over. "Good choice. I've spent a lot of time up north in the Chaco Wilderness Area. It's gorgeous. Great fishing."

'Yes, sir. And easy access for visitors…. even visitors with evil on their mind."

Tom gave her a thumbs up. "Let's go with this."

Tafoya said, "Okay, sir. We'll structure this sortie like a search and rescue mission. Instead of looking for stranded people, we'll be looking for vehicles or small groups where they should not be and smoke from recently ignited fires in remote areas. On this mission, Colonel, we'll be working with the Civil Air Patrol."

Tom smiled. "I flew with the CAP when I was in high school."

"So did I, sir. We use them a lot. on Search and Rescue missions especially. They're great. Dedicated and competent. Best kept secret in the government, if I do say so. They'll have two aircraft up with us. One conducting its own SAR flight plan like us which will effectively double our search area. Typically we also use the CAP as radio relay birds. They orbit at around 10,000 feet while we're down in the weeds. Radios don't always work well in the mountains and during SAR missions, most times we fly at about 1000 feet above the ground." She wagged her right hand and said, "*Mas o menos*."

The door opened, and Special Agent Jerry Bennett entered. Dressed in the standard FBI SWAT team ninja black, he brought a more sinister air to the upcoming operation.

"Good, now we're set," said Tafoya as she shook Bennett's hand. She turned back to Tom. "We need a law enforcement guy to ride with us to make this flight legal. Jerry volunteered."

"*Posse Comitatus*?" asked Tom.

"Yes sir. A legacy of the Civil War. The Insurrection Act of 1807 also applies. Both those laws prohibit the use of military assets to enforce domestic policies. So we often fly with law enforcement personnel aboard to make the flight legal." Tom filed that away as an item to bring up with the president. Laws were going to have to be changed, or at least updated, to deal with potential future terrorist events.

Bennett handed Tom a holster and pistol. "A present from Colonel Adams. He hopes that you'll get to use it."

Out on the tarmac, Tafoya did her walk-around inspection of the big twin engine UH-60L Blackhawk helicopter while the co-pilot started the interior checks. Tom climbed aboard and strapped himself into the left side observer position. He was essentially flying side saddle but had a clean window in front of him and, by turning his head, he had a clear view of the pilot's position.

Dressed in his Air Force fight suit and boots, Tom was nearly indistinguishable from the crew. He had flown SAR missions in the much smaller Bolivian Air Force UH-1 Hueys deep into the Andes—the rescue of Porter Nelson had been the purpose for those flights—but he knew he was way out of his element doing this SAR type of mountain low flying, except as a passenger. He listened to the crew as they went about getting the aircraft ready for takeoff. Tafoya's hands danced around the cockpit, turning knobs and flipping switches. Cockpit lights and dials came alive. Engines started and systems checked, they lifted off, cleared the airport traffic area and pointed northeast.

The intercom crackled in his ears, and Tafoya's voice said, "Colonel, we're heading into the Santa Fe Mountains and the watershed for the city. It's closed to the public, which may help protect it from arson. The CAP is overflying it this morning so we can head north."

Tom watched as Santa Fe slid underneath the belly of the helicopter. Founded by the Spanish in 1607, the same year as Jamestown, it became a capital in 1610, making it the oldest capital city in the country. Santa Fe was one of his favorite places in the world. Besides being the seat of the state government, it was a flourishing center for gourmet restaurants and upscale art galleries, some of which held paintings by Tom's mother. He could pick out the Basilica of St. Francis of Assisi near the center of the city, one of only eighty-two basilicas in the United States. Tom had attended many masses and lit many candles there for his father's safety. The National Cemetery was a splash of green among the mostly adobe colored buildings.

As they approached the ridgeline of the nearby mountains, Chief Tafoya swung the aircraft around to the north into some choppy air and edged out a bit to keep from overflying the string of pueblos that ran along the highway towards Española. Tom watched as the terrain flattened out. It was nearly a perfect day for flying, a "blue bird" day, with bright sunshine, blue skies, and light winds. In pilot's terms, CAVU—clear and visibility unlimited. Mountains decorated the horizons; striated rock formations reached up to him. He was struck again by the raw beauty of this part of New Mexico. Under different circumstances, Tom would have enjoyed the flight.

Tafoya and her copilot kept a running dialogue with the CAP aircraft, passing along radio calls and position reports. Her steady hands made the helicopter come to life as they roller coastered along the ridge lines, sometimes ducking into forested valleys and narrow fingers of tree-filled arroyos. Tafoya was a natural at nap-of-the-earth flying. The one thousand feet of altitude *"mas o menos"* she had promised proved to be mostly *"menos"*—she flew bloody low, even for him. Tom knew what fast-moving low level looked like—he had become an expert as an exchange pilot flying Mirages with the Royal Australian Air Force. Australia, where he had met and married Colleen. When he first saw her across a fancy bar in Sydney, her smile had enchanted him and drawn him irresistibly to her side. The memory of his wife caused pain to lance

249

out of nowhere and roil his gut again. He swore softly, clenched his jaw, and forced his thoughts back to the flying.

They intercepted the Rio Grande just north of Española and turned northwest up the Chama River, then across the Santa Fe National Forest towards Abiquiu and San Simon. Tom thought this could easily be a potential target for Wallerein. The Chama Wilderness Area was some 50,000 acres along the Chama River with a major highway sometimes less than a hundred yards away from the Area. A series of tunnels was being built to bring water from the San Juan into the Chama. After the Chama empties into the Rio Grande, a thirsty downstream Albuquerque would pull the water to augment the aquifer straining to supply the city, a complex and expensive project designed to deal with the realities of the Southwest style of living in a high mountain desert prone to periodic drought.

Tom scanned the immense stretches of forests that slid underneath the aircraft. A century of the Forest Service fighting natural low-intensity fires that used to clear out undergrowth had left the country with millions of acres of forests choked with fuel just waiting to explode in a firestorm. All nature needed was a source of ignition. And Kurt Wallerein was determined to be that source.

Skirting the edges of the forest, they watched for ingress and egress routes, vehicles parked or moving in areas they should not be, anything that could be considered suspicious. Twice they circled back to have a re-look at a suspicious sighting, only to decide it was a false alarm. Other aircraft were doing the same thing all over the state. State police, county sheriffs, forest rangers, game wardens, alerted by the BOLO for Wallerein, were scouring approaches into national forests spread all over New Mexico. Tom studied his map in despair—just over fifty per cent of the enormous state was owned by the federal, state, or Pueblo governments, much of it open forest above 7,000 feet. This was an exercise akin to hunting a needle in a haystack, writ large by New Mexico's nearly 122,000 square miles.

Tom pressed his intercom button, "I had forgotten how hard it is to spot somebody in the forest from a moving helicopter."

Tafoya answered. "Yes, sir. Especially if they don't want to be found. The best we can hope for is to flush them out. And these guys aren't likely to panic or run."

They made it almost to Coyote, a small town tucked into a valley in the Santa Fe National Forest northwest of Española when Tafoya called out, "Colonel, you have a message from Colonel Adams." The crew chief leaned over and adjusted Tom's radio to pick up the phone patch from Guard headquarters.

"Tom, this is Brice. Over."

"Go ahead, Brice."

"The governor needs to see you ASAP. There have been two more attacks. He wants you to be here when he talks to the president. Return to base, my friend."

Tom lowered his head, slumped his shoulders and sighed. Damn. "Wilco."

Tafoya banked the Blackhawk into a tight turn, rolled out pointing towards Santa Fe and accelerated. Despite flying hundreds of miles over thousands of acres and millions of trees, they had accomplished exactly nada.

NM State Highway 4

Porter Nelson hit the save button, shut down his laptop computer with a satisfied sigh and settled back into the passenger seat of his rented SUV. "Done."

"What were you doing?" asked Michelle Duregger as she maneuvered the big car along the twisting highway.

"Revising my latest draft for the *Post*."

"Don't you mean our draft?"

"Oops, sorry. Our draft," he said, as his face burned. "I'm not used to working with a partner."

"I can tell." She paused. "So what were you doing while I was collating all the information of the attack on the middle school?"

"I was with Brice Adams. The TAG wanted either Tom or Brice to stay at headquarters as liaison with the White House. Adams chose to

251

stay behind. He knows that Tom is a hands-on type. He needs to get out and do something. Nothing is better for Tom right now than flying. Brice will aid the TAG in the strategizing and mission planning."

"I don't know Tom as well as you do, obviously, but it seems like he's eating himself up with guilt about Colleen's kidnapping and worrying about her condition. Not to mention the baby."

Porter slid the computer into his backpack and carefully placed the pack on the rear floor. "I gave Brice my read on what Wallerein is up to and where he might be."

"Based on?"

"Michelle, I know Wallerein's background. I am almost as German as he is. My grandparents and parents were intellectuals in Germany in the late thirties. They were not just *intelligencia*, they were also smart enough to get the hell out of the country in 1939. I was raised German. When I visited Germany in high school, I passed myself off as a native Berliner."

"Back to the topic, Mister-big-time-investigative-journalist, what did you tell Brice?"

"That I know Wallerein, not just as a German. He murdered a good friend of mine last year. I've studied the bastard. I've read his writings, in the original German and even the Russian translations—which were not all that good, by the way. I even went to the same university in Germany that he did, albeit just for one year. I wanted to get back to UC Santa Clara."

"You mean to the girls at UC Santa Clara."

"Are there girls at Santa Clara? Gee, I must have missed them. Maybe when we're through here, I should go back."

Michelle gave him the finger and they both laughed.

"Don't underestimate this guy, Michelle. Wallerein is smart and ruthless—a psychopath, but a smart one. He isn't just randomly burning things, blowing stuff up, or launching shootings. He's up to something, something bigger. He's too calculating for mere randomness. Like a chess grand master, he prides himself on always being a couple moves ahead of everybody else."

She smiled. "Sounds like somebody else I know."

"I'll take that as one of the very few compliments you've given me," said Porter. "Now tell me, what does New Mexico have in abundance?

"Mountains? Beautiful scenery? Mexican food?"

Porter chuckled. "Yes, that too. More importantly right now, it has highly classified government facilities. Lots of them. For a rural state—and New Mexico is certainly rural—it is one of the most wired places in the country. This is where the first atomic bombs were built! There are several National Laboratories. Phillips, Sandia, Los Alamos, and don't even get me speculating about what stuff goes on at Kirtland Air Force Base at the Air Force Research Lab. Hell, Tom isn't even cleared to that level, and he works for the president!"

"So these labs are connected to why Wallerein is concentrating on the Southwest?"

"Makes sense to me. Hurting Tom Callahan is a bonus."

"And that's why we're heading towards Jemez Springs? It's rural and near Los Alamos? That's all you have?"

"Yep. Just a hunch. I think Los Alamos is a target—maybe *the* target—although I have no idea why. Yet. But it makes sense. Most of the super brainpower in the state is concentrated in Albuquerque or further down south in White Sands, which is desert. No point in lighting fires there. The rest of the high-level secret work is in Los Alamos. Which is, conveniently for Wallerein, surrounded by forest. Jemez Springs is just west of Los Alamos, upwind and also conveniently surrounded by mountainous forest. I'll just bet that either Wallerein is there or has been there… at least some of his guys would pass through there."

"Okay then. Jemez Springs, here we come."

"At the very least we'll get a chance to chat up some of the locals to see if they've seen any suspicious characters lurking about, have a few brewskies, and listen to great music tonight in the Los Lobos Restaurant and Saloon, then go for a soak in the hot springs in the morning before we head off to Los Alamos."

They checked into a lovely B&B by the river. Michelle was amused by the reaction of the hostess who seemed surprised, but pleased, that they booked separate rooms.

Porter whispered as they carried their overnight bags to their adjacent rooms. "This must be a place where those nearby married city folk partake in their *cinq à sept* or wild weekends."

"What does *cinq à sept* mean?

"Five to seven in French. On their way home from work, many French adults stop to dally with their lovers from five to seven o'clock, then head home to the arms of their spouses and families. You've never heard of this quaint custom?"

"I'm from Iowa."

Oops. Porter felt his face go red. "Well, I just told you that I'm more German so this wouldn't apply to me."

She arched an eyebrow. Suppressing a sigh, Porter slipped into his room. Alone.

NM National Guard headquarters

Forty-five minutes after speaking to Brice Adams, Tom entered National Guard Headquarters and was escorted by a young major to the conference room where the governor, the TAG, Colonel Brice Adams, and a handful of brass were already seated around the huge conference table. The governor was a heavy-set man, his thick black hair mussed as was his suit. He had had a bitch of a morning. First the shock of the Ruidoso fire and a long helicopter ride. Now this new attack, whatever it was. He was staring down at the remains of his coffee as if he might find an answer there. When Tom entered, the governor looked up and gave a wan smile and a brief wave. "Thank you for coming so quickly, Colonel."

"Tom," said Brice, motioning him into a chair. "The Guard filmed this from a Blackhawk near the Town of Rio Tercero less than an hour ago." He nodded to a sergeant who inserted a VHS tape into a video player.

The first scenes were of a concrete and earthen dam, water pouring through an ugly gash near the center of the ruined structure. The water level was now significantly lower than the line of grass that outlined the lake.

The camera panned around and pointed downstream, revealing a path of massive destruction. The governor said, "Our engineers say it looks like an explosion sent a wall of water some fifteen to twenty feet high crashing like a freight train down the valley."

Tom visualized the water slamming into anything in its path, ripping away bridges, roads, entire homes, taking out electric and telephone lines. When the millions of tons of water hit the town, it was carrying tremendous amounts of debris. The mass of trees, mud, vehicles, and houses burst into the town and flattened the buildings. What used to be Downtown was covered in a sheath of brown mud, with timbers, upended pickups, branches, and smashed buildings poking through the muck.

The floodwaters had effectively erased the town of Rio Tercero.

The whole valley was now inundated, with only patches of high ground and tops of trees showing above the water. The effect on the land was devastating—hundreds of acres of arable land were washed away and would be unusable for years, farms stripped bare of crops, and the bloated bodies of people and domestic animals were already adrift in the water and scattered on high ground.

Tom said, "This was no accident."

"No chance," said the TAG through clenched teeth. "My guys say explosive residue is plastered all over the crest of the dam." He scowled. "Plus the two rangers who live on the park have disappeared."

"Casualty estimates in the town, sir?"

"Unknown," said the TAG. "The flood hit just before breakfast. Citizens who weren't swept away drowned when the water backed up and flooded the town. Best guess is 600 plus. Almost the entire population."

These were Americans, thought Tom. And American civilians, to boot. Civilians were not supposed to be exposed to this kind of violence. His shoulder and neck muscles started to tighten.

The governor buried his face in his hands. Brice watched the footage for a few seconds more, then looked away. The TAG's face was white, fists clenched.

The governor looked up and said, "Those murdering sons-of-bitches!" His voice was hard, more determined now than angry. "I have to call the president. This flood is going to be on half the television screens in America by lunch."

"Montero, Ruidoso, and now Rio Tercero. Fire and floods," said Tom. "Attacking the Homeland, just like our intel sources predicted."

"Fat lot of good that does us now," said the governor.

Tom shook his head. "Sir, we've got to trust Emergency Management's first and second responders to handle this. We have to focus on what's next and get there first."

Jemez Springs, NM

After breakfast, Porter and Michelle drove the short distance through the town to the hot springs. As they entered the bath house, a friendly middle-aged woman met them and began her rehearsed introduction to the wonders of hot soaks.

As Porter paid for two half hour sessions, he asked, "We were wondering if you have many foreigners passing through."

She nodded, then offered, "We do get foreigners here quite a lot. Especially Europeans."

"I'm looking for a friend of mine from university in Germany who is visiting the States right now. He said he might pass through this area." Porter held up his hand over his head. "A little taller than I am, stocky, blond hair, mid-fifties, really blue eyes, typically sort'a grumpy."

"With a limp?"

"Yes, left leg," said Porter, trying to keep his voice neutral. He pulled a sketch of Wallerein from his backpack. "This is an old sketch."

"Oh yes, that was him. I remember the eyes. Very blue, but not friendly. He stayed for almost an hour. Didn't leave a tip, either."

256

Chapter Thirty-Four

Mission Planning Room,
National Guard Aviation Facility
Santa Fe Municipal Airport

Tom leaned over a chart of New Mexico, engrossed in the north-central portion of the state. Chief Tafoya entered the room. She stood quietly for a moment, hands on hips, then tapped him on the shoulder.

"Excuse me, Colonel."

"Sorry, Beth, I didn't hear you come in."

"Sir, the mechanics found a small hydraulic leak during preflight. They estimate they'll have it fixed in forty-five minutes."

"Thank you." He gestured at the chart. "I've been looking at this map since midnight. Nothing makes sense. I've plotted and dated each fire or incident over the past few weeks. I don't see a pattern for the way they play out."

"Did you sketch in the new fires near Raton and Los Alamos?"

"I was briefed this morning at Headquarters. They look bad. Low humidity, high temperatures, and high winds are forecast today."

"Why Raton, sir? Why would Wallerein pick a relatively insignificant town like Raton?"

Tom ran his finger along the curve of the Sangre de Cristo Mountains. "Here's the current location of the fire. It's marching towards the east. It's a monster already. On a scale of one to ten, it'll be at least a nine."

"And right along Interstate 25 almost to the Colorado border," said Tafoya.

"Yep. Makes for good television footage," said Tom. "Exactly the kind of publicity Wallerein wants. It also puts the people in Colorado on notice."

"Our governor spoke with the Colorado governor about the danger last night."

"Word does get around quickly," said Tom. "That phone call was supposed to be kept quiet."

"Their Guard just got called up, Colonel," she said with pride in her voice. "We Guard types are tight across the country."

"Good to hear. We'll need all the help we can get."

She hesitated. "I also heard that you spoke with the president."

"My, oh my, Chief Tafoya, I am impressed with your networking skills."

"You are kind of a big deal around here, sir," she said with a grin. "The TAG called me personally to make sure I didn't put you in danger."

"We're all in danger here, Beth, if we don't catch this madman. That's the mission. Stop him. Any way and every way we can. Preferably with extreme prejudice."

"Copy that, sir." She hesitated. "Do you think the fire near Los Alamos is because of the national lab or that the forest around the city is part of the watershed for Albuquerque?"

"I think it's more because it's such a famous city. Maybe because Wallerein has now decided to shift to hitting population centers. Maybe because Los Alamos is a genuine, prosperous city, in the middle of nowhere, near a national forest. Who knows? All we know now is that the fires are fast-moving and dangerous."

"You still think we should go up to Chama again, sir?"

"Just a guess, but yes."

A sergeant stuck his head in the door. "Excuse me, Colonel, Chief. We'll be ready to go in about fifteen minutes."

"Thank you, Sergeant," said Tafoya. She reached into her flight bag. Satisfied that all her maps and mission documentation were there, she visibly relaxed, sat at the table and took a drink from a plastic bottle.

Tom joined her at the table. "Beth, what made you want to fly?"

"My uncle was a door gunner on Hueys in Vietnam. He told me flying stories when I was a little girl. When he got back, he wanted to keep flying but injuries and PTSD kept him from it."

"Too bad," said Tom.

"Yes sir. He drank himself to death about ten years ago. But not before he passed on his love of aviation to me." She slid back the sleeve of her flight suit and crosschecked her watch with the large clock on the wall. "It sounds like a cliché, but as a teenager I worked at an airport washing planes and doing odd jobs in exchange for stick time. Then I joined the Ninety-Nines which changed my life. I won one of their scholarships to pay for my commercial and instrument ratings. Now I'm flying helicopters for the Guard and lovin' life. How about you, Colonel? Who turned you on to flying?"

"Both my grandfathers and my father were military pilots."

"What did they fly?"

"My paternal grandfather flew Spads in WW I with Eddie Rickenbacker and later Mustangs in the Army Air Forces in WW II."

"No shit?" Her face went red. "Sorry, Colonel. But that's really cool! Eddie Rickenbacker. Wow! And the other grandfather... Army Air Forces as well?"

"No. He flew Nieuport fighters with the Imperial Russian Air Force, then switched to bombers with the White Russian Air Force in Siberia during the Russian Civil War. After the White Russians lost the war, he escaped with his family to Shanghai, then Italy. He was the one who taught me to fly."

"Your grandfather is Russian?"

"Actually, he was Russian. Now he's deceased. Buried outside Siena. Great big guy with a magnificent handlebar mustache. Looked every bit the Russian general that he was. A wonderful man."

"Do you speak Russian?"

"*Da*. My mother raised us speaking Russian and Italian. My dad was a USAF fighter pilot. Sabre jets and Phantoms were his favorites."

"Does he still fly?"

"I would like to think so, but the chances are really slim. He was shot down over Vietnam in late 1972. Still listed as MIA."

"Sorry to hear that, sir." She started. "72! That's my call sign, Lobo 72!"

"I noticed. A good year for lots of folks. Not so much for my family—and lots of others."

The door opened again, and the crew chief stuck his head in, "Ready to go, Chief."

Tafoya did her walk-around inspection of the Blackhawk while the co-pilot started lighting things up and Bennett and Tom strapped in.

After takeoff, Tafoya pointed the aircraft northwest. "Colonel, can you see that?" The skies were dark along the ridgeline of the Santa Fe National Forest in a long arc from northwest to southwest. Smoke billowed up thousands of feet overhead.

"Holy cow," said Tom. "That fire isn't even twelve hours old and look at it! It's exploding!" The line of fire blazed for miles, just to the west of Los Alamos. Even from this distance they could distinguish tiny flicks of flames.

Mesmerized, Tom watched the colossal fire slide by the aircraft as they motored northward through the lumpy air towards Chama. He folded and re-folded his in-flight chart as he traced their course over the rising terrain, identifying landmarks on the chart and locating them on the ground. Down below, he picked out roadblocks set up by the state police along Highway 84 heading north past the national forest towards Tierra Amarilla and Chama. The cops were under orders to stop and check all SUVs containing exclusively male passengers heading towards the area. Tafoya made several passes over the Chama Wilderness Area, helicopter rocking as they flew through the light turbulence. Wheeled vehicles, even mountain bikes, were prohibited in wilderness areas. Any vehicle detected would, by definition, be suspicious.

Nothing.

Tafoya turned them almost due north and headed deep into Rio Arriba County, named for the highlands where rivers began. To the east was the Kit Carson National Forest; to the west, the Santa Fe National Forest and the Jicarilla Apache Indian Reservation. The air buffeted the aircraft as the late morning sun heated the rocks below. Tafoya flew them farther east over the ridgeline of the Sangres, along Highway 64 deeper into the Carson towards Taos.

"Lobo Seven Two, this is Guard Headquarters," Tom heard on the secondary radio.

"Lobo Seven Two, go," said the copilot.

"Put your passenger on."

The crew chief again leaned over and flipped the switch to activate the rear radios.

Tom adjusted his boom mic. "This is Callahan. Go ahead, Headquarters."

"Tom, this is Brice. Ruhi called. Colleen's in and out of consciousness. She's so weak you won't be able to hear her clearly in the chopper. You need to call us on a landline. Head for the closest airport and call me. I'll patch you through to her hospital room. Move it, brother!"

"Wilco. Land ASAP. Out here."

On intercom, Tafoya called out, "Colonel, I copied that. Taos is the closest airport. I've got us on a direct course to it. ETA..." She scanned her instruments, "Nineteen minutes, sir!"

The aircraft couldn't go fast enough for Tom. An eternity later, he heard the co-pilot's call. "Taos traffic, Lobo Seven Two, five miles northwest, inbound for landing."

"Roger, Lobo. Taos Unicom. Altimeter setting three zero zero one, winds variable. No reported traffic."

"Three zero zero one. Be advised, we have a VIP passenger who needs to make an emergency call to Guard headquarters."

The helicopter ripped into the Taos air space. Tafoya skidded to a hover directly in front of the Fixed Base Operator building and set the machine down with only a slight bump. Tom yanked his harness connections apart and bolted for the building.

A heavy-set man stood behind the wooden counter and pointed at the Pilot's Lounge door. "Use the phone in there, sir. More privacy."

Tom found the phone and punched in the number for the command section. Brice answered on the first ring.

"Tom, Ruhi is with Colleen. They're on the other line. Let me put you through." He hesitated. "Be ready, pal. Colleen's in pain and not entirely coherent."

A long pause. Then a soft voice. "Tommy, Tommy, listen to me. Wallerein is behind all this. He had his men follow me—flew me to Mexico... beat me...." She faded.

"Colleen?" His throat closed and he nearly gagged. "Colleen. Sweetheart, talk to me!"

Her voice again, faint as if she were in a deep hole. He clutched at the phone and plugged a finger into his other ear.

"I knew he was going to kill me. Got him mad...; he screamed his plans to me... he was so smug.... Los Alamos, something important about Los Alamos—I can't remember, but that's where he's going, where he'll be, Tommy."

"Darlin', I have the State Police, the National Guard and the FBI working on this. We'll get him."

"Promise me you'll get him. He needs to die. So many people have died...,our baby died, Tommy.... I'm so sorry.... Promise me," she whispered. Silence.

He closed his eyes and tumbled down an abyss of more pain than he thought possible. He dropped the phone. Hunched over. Clenched his fists, his jaw. He struggled to breathe. How long he sat there, he didn't know.

No time for pain, Tommy boy. Not now. Later.

He forced himself to control his breathing, reached deep into his core for strength. Finally, he unclenched his fists and sat up. Opened his eyes, picked up the phone and called Brice Adams.

"Brice, did you get that?"

"Yeah. Los Alamos."

"Get everybody you can spare over there."

"Way ahead of you, buddy. Word's out. The place will be swarming with cops and Guardsmen in minutes." He hesitated. "How are you holding up, Ace?"

Tom ignored the question. "As soon as I hang up, we'll get airborne and head towards Los Alamos."

"Hold on, Tom. You need an update. Those new fires around Los Alamos you heard about? They're exploding and spreading fast. Nasty. Porter just called in, not fifteen minutes ago from Los Alamos. He found a woman in Jemez Springs who said she saw Wallerein two days ago."

"Where is Porter now?"

"Not sure. I lost him. Comms are out now. Maybe the cell tower went down from the fires. Knowing Porter, he and Michelle are tracking down Wallerein as we speak."

"Damn."

"Hey, Tom. Don't worry about Porter. He spent time with the Spetsnaz. He can take care of himself."

"It's not him I'm worried about. I'm afraid he'll get to Wallerein before I have a chance."

"Be careful, Tom. Porter described the area around Los Alamos. They're evacuating the city. Roads are jammed. It's a mess, like a war zone out there. And you know what that's like. If you get a location on Wallerein, let the cops take him down."

"Stay in touch, Brice. If you get any more updates, call me on the radios."

He hung up and just sat there. Wallerein was in, or, at least, around Los Alamos. That was the place to be.

The crew chief poked his head around the door, took a look at Tom's face. "Is everything okay, Colonel?"

Tom stood, squared his shoulders and started for the flight line. "Let's go fly."

Chapter Thirty-Five

Near Los Alamos, New Mexico

Porter Nelson maneuvered the SUV through the heavy traffic as they entered Los Alamos. An emergency evacuation order had been issued by the governor. People were packing up to leave. Long lines of cars and trucks snaked through the city down the mountain. Police and National Guard troops moved people along efficiently. Everything was so orderly and calm that it looked like a major league sporting event had just let out and people were heading home instead of leaving their homes behind.

Michelle dialed up the local radio station. The announcer was covering the explosive growth of the nearby fires and giving detailed updates on the state of the evacuation. She checked her cell phone. Still no bars. "Good thing you called Brice earlier, Porter. No reception here."

"Probably a tower downed by the fire. Man, look at all the people. I'm going to pull into the mall over there and see what's happening." He sliced through traffic and made his way across the crowded parking lot.

"I'm ambivalent about Los Alamos, Michelle. I've read a lot about it, but this is my first visit."

"Why ambivalent? Looks like a pretty nice, prosperous town to me, except for all the smoke, of course."

"Oh, it's prosperous all right. According to the census bureau, Los Alamos County has the fifth highest family median income in the United States. It is awash in federal dollars. The annual budget of the national lab approaches two billion dollars. Much of the work at the lab is to figure out ways of containing the nuclear waste generated during WW II and the Cold War. There are radioactive dumps all over the mesas here. Undocumented."

"What!"

"Yep. For decades, workers used the canyons and arroyos around the city as dumping grounds for radioactive waste. There's a six-acre dump within the city limits called Technical Area 21 where the lab moved its plutonium processing operation in 1944. It was closed in '48 and nobody knows exactly what's buried there."

"You're kidding, right?"

"Nope. They don't know what's in the surrounding areas, either. There are bunkers all over the outlying plateaux and canyons. The Feds are spending tens of millions of dollars, examining classified documents and interviewing retired workers to locate bunkers and dumps that have fallen through the cracks."

"So, Porter, you're telling me that basically, they don't even know what was buried where. Or worse, they don't even know what they don't know."

"Again, yep. It's all classified. Stuff got lost, or maybe even stolen. Who knows? One thing's for sure, nobody at Los Alamos is saying anything."

"Well, that's disturbing. And now, here we sit with a massive fire bearing down on us."

"This isn't just a fire, lady. It's a fire near a national laboratory. A nuclear laboratory." He laughed as he pounded the steering wheel. "Welcome to the crazy world of investigative journalism! Ain't life grand!"

A pickup backed out of a parking space. Porter worked his way through the people milling around and slipped into the slot. "Let's hit that bagel shop and grab something for the road. As they say, a man's mind is always on his stomach."

Michelle said, "That hasn't been my experience with men."

A long line of people clustered around an ATM at the nearby bank. Porter and Michelle slipped through the crowd. Inside the bagel shop, shelves were nearly bare, and workers were trying to shoo people out.

Porter grabbed the last bag of day old bagels and a tub of cream cheese. Michelle took the last cold drinks from the cooler.

Two televisions mounted over either end of the long counter blared out the news. Aerial photos, video, talking heads, all describing the extent and intensity of the fire, or, more accurately, the chain of fires approaching Los Alamos.

Engrossed in the drama, Porter almost missed a nearby conversation moving towards the door. *German. Where?* His eyes followed the words. Two fit-looking men, dressed in scruffy outdoors clothes and boots. He stiffened. Maybe nothing, maybe everything. He handed the bagels and cream cheese to an annoyed Michelle. "Pay for this. Be right back."

Outside, he watched them get into an SUV. Another man sat in the passenger seat. Too far away to see a face, only a profile. The vehicle turned away, opposite the direction of the cars fleeing the fire, directly up the hill, headed into the distant blaze. Porter trotted after it, dodging through the traffic. The passenger looked right to check traffic.

Son-of-a-bitch! Wallerein!

The vehicle lurched across two lanes of traffic, blaring its horn and turned away from Porter. *Shit! So close!*

He sprinted back to the bagel shop. A teenager was emptying the register. Porter slapped the counter and held out his hand. "Emergency! I need to use your land line phone! My cell isn't working."

"Dude, communications are down. Only things working are the emergency comms."

"This is an emergency!"

The kid shrugged. "Talk to one of the Army guys. They have radios."

"Michelle! Follow me!" He dashed outside, stood searching for the big SUV. Michelle slammed into his back.

Porter pointed up the hill. "See the black SUV heading west into the fire area?"

"Yeah."

"Wallerein's in that car with two other guys. Come on!"

"What the hell is he doing here?"

"No idea… but he's not here on vacation."

266

They raced to their car and jumped in. Porter leaned on the horn as he forced his way through the traffic. He cut across the highway, swung uphill, and mashed the accelerator to roar up the nearly deserted road. Ahead, the winding road slipped around a switchback, and he lost sight of all vehicles. "Try the cell again. Get Brice if you can. Hurry!"

"No bars, Porter," she said, grabbing the seat handhold as Porter wheeled his way up the serpentine road towards the forest. They skidded to a halt around a corner. A National Guard Humvee security roadblock blocked the road. Three uniformed bodies lay askew in pools of blood.

Porter jumped out and checked the bodies. "They're all dead." He glanced around. A map case! He riffled through it. U.S. Geological Service maps. He took pistols from the men. Pulled a radio off the vest of the dead female sergeant. "Let's go!"

As they roared off around the Humvee, he tossed the map case to Michelle. "Inside are USGS maps. The one we need is on top. Know how to read them?"

"Of course I can read a map. I'm a sailor. And we call them charts by the way."

"Find out where we are."

She studied the chart. "Got it. Here, along this highway."

"Do you see any trails marked that branch off to the..." he checked the car compass, "southwest?"

"Yes."

"How far?"

"About, let's see... one, two, almost three miles."

"Any after that?"

"Yes, but much farther." She looked up. Smoke and flames dominated the skyline." Porter, that fire's pretty close. Headed this way."

He nodded. "Yeah, a hundred bucks says he takes that first turn into the national forest... Otherwise he'll end up in the fire."

"Okay, my friend, that trail branches off pretty quickly into three different logging roads... Too many variables."

"We have to try, Michelle. Maybe we'll get lucky."

"And if we do catch him, what then?"

267

"That's what the radio's for, sweetheart. Get on it and start screaming for help. Maybe somebody's out there."

They came upon the trail turnoff a few minutes later. Porter whipped the SUV left and they bounced through the trees. The bumpy trail and the swirling smoke forced him to slow. At the first Y intersection, he braked and looked at Michelle. "I don't see any tracks. Too much ash falling."

She held out the chart. "It gets steep real fast to the right. My guess is that he went left."

"Left it is, navigator." He angled down the left branch of the narrow trail. Blowing embers bounced off the vehicle.

Michelle tried the radio again. The speaker crackled. "Station on emergency frequency, this is Civil Air Patrol Highbird. Go ahead."

"Yes!" she shouted. "Stop here while we have contact!" Porter slammed on the brakes, almost skidding into a tree. Michelle keyed the radio, "Highbird, we are journalists chasing a terrorist named Kurt Wallerein in the Santa Fe National Forest. We are working with the New Mexico National Guard. Do you copy?"

"Highbird copies. Go ahead."

Michelle related their status, location coordinates, and details about Wallerein before requesting the CAP aircraft pass the information to the National Guard and New Mexico authorities. Many questions and replies later, the CAP bird acknowledged her request.

More embers glanced off the roof, flaring into showers of sparks. Tendrils of thick smoke curled around them. Porter gave Michelle a thumbs-up and punched the accelerator. Tires spinning, the SUV slewed, then rocketed down the trail deeper into the forest. To their right, spot fires coalesced into roaring fires. The noise was nearly overpowering. Hot air poured into the vehicle. The trail wound across the face of the mountain, splitting again and again. Intermittent waves of smoke nearly blinded them as they raced to get ahead of the blazes. Michelle tried the radio again and again. No response. She stowed the radio in her shoulder bag. "Porter," she shouted, "I think we need to give up on finding Wallerein."

"I agree. My self-preservation gene just kicked in. Let's head for the barn."

"Did you say barn or bar?"

"Either. Both. Let's get the hell out of here!"

"Good man."

They careened downhill. Fire erupted all around them. Hot air blasted the vehicle. Michelle screamed as a tree torched right next to her window. Another fell across the logging road behind them.

"So much for going back," he bellowed. "We're committed now."

"We should be committed," she said as she wrapped a wet kerchief around her nose and mouth.

Porter downshifted as they banged over the rough and rutted trail. The constant jarring tested the suspension at every turn. They roared around a curve and slammed to a stop behind a Forest Service truck. A group of firefighters stood clustered around the front of the truck, studying charts spread on the hood. A burly man wearing a dirty uniform and hard hat, trotted over to them.

"What the hell are you doing here?"

"We're journalists," said Porter, knowing that sounded really lame. "We were trying to follow the arsonists who started these fires. But we lost them."

"Whatever you think you're doing, you need to get out of the forest. Now!"

"Believe me, sir, that's exactly what we're trying to do."

"You have a chart?"

"Yes." Michelle leaned over and handed it to the ranger.

He pointed. "This is where we are... right at this fork. We—and I mean all of us—need to go here, where there are a couple of meadows. I have another team working that area. This logging road should get us outta here. Follow us. The downhill incline is pretty steep for a mile. Watch what you're doing. Stick tight and for God's sake, be careful!"

The Forest Service truck sped away, Porter tight in behind. Fire spotted all around in the dry underbrush. Dust from the Forest Service truck swirled with the blowing smoke and ash. Flames to the right side of the road raced towards them, steep drop off to the left. Whoever was driving the Forest Service truck either knew the road or was a former Formula One driver. It was difficult—and dangerous—to stay close.

Porter was scared fartless. In his mind, being burned to death ranked right up there with the worst possible ways to die. He skidded around a corner in time to see a boulder in the road. The forest service truck slowed. Porter caught movement off to the right. A figure crouched in the bushes. The man stood and hosed the truck with automatic gunfire. The truck wobbled to the left. The downhill tires drifted over the road edge. The truck toppled over in slow motion, then rolled down the gorge into the trees.

Porter slammed on his brakes and slid to a halt. The shooter jumped into the road and stalked them, weapon at the ready. Porter shifted into reverse but another man banged on his side window with a pistol. The shooter raised his weapon to fire.

"Nein!"

Chapter Thirty-Six

National Guard Blackhawk

Tafoya didn't waste any time. She had the Blackhawk on a line for Los Alamos. Tom knew the max airspeed was supposed to be 160 knots—they were doing every bit of that.

Through the radio chatter, Tom heard a Civil Air Patrol Cessna 182 on VHF with the CAP relay aircraft. "Highbird, this is CAP Four Two Five Three. We are in contact with journalists on the ground who say they are tracking Kurt Wallerein." The aircrew rattled off a brief summary of the information and their coordinates. "We are heading their way to stay in contact. Be advised we are low on fuel."

Tom could hardly believe it. "Chief, that has to be Porter Nelson. Put those coordinates in your GPS!"

"Already done, Colonel. Turning left." The ground filled Tom's window as Tafoya banked the aircraft for the new heading.

He settled back for the ride and tried to think as the earth hurtled by. The fires ahead were colossal. In the space of a few hours, the blaze had grown explosively, expanding like a balloon and moving very fast. Great masses of smoke swirled and swelled as they boiled upwards. Radio chatter filled his ears as air traffic control tried to keep firefighting aircraft away from each other. He felt strangely at ease as the chaos filled his ears. Brice Adams was right, it was like a war zone, something he had trained for all his adult life.

The smoke was closer now. Flames were shooting up hundreds of feet. The helicopter rocked and wallowed in the heated thermals. They were bathed in sweat.

"Highbird, CAP Four Two Five Three. We have the black SUV in sight. There are two other vehicles nearby. None are moving, one is upside down. Very close to the fire." The crew updated their coordinates, then said, "Highbird, CAP Four Two Five Three is bingo fuel."

"Thanks, CAP Four Two Five Three. Head for home. Good work, gentlemen."

Tafoya's voice came on the radio. "Highbird, this is Lobo Seven Two. We copy updated location. We are two zero minutes out. I say again, two zero minutes out. We have law enforcement on board. Keep us in the loop. Over."

***

"*Nein!*"

The shooter in front of the car lowered his weapon but did not relax. Porter forced himself to turn his head to look at the man beside him who had shouted the order.

He chuckled as he rolled down the window. "Well, if it isn't Kurt Wallerein himself," he said in German. "How's the leg, Kurt? Still recovering from that gunshot wound?"

"Herr Nelson, I must admit I am surprised to see you here."

"I'll bet you are."

"Why are you here?"

"We're on to you, Kurt. Our government knows what you are trying to do. Your attacks are doomed. Failed. Kaput."

Wallerein gestured uphill at the apocalyptic wall of fire and sneered. "You call this kaput? I think things are coming along quite nicely." He paused. "We have, however, had a slight accident with our vehicle. We need yours."

Porter looked around. "Where's your other guy? Did he have a 'slight accident,' too, Kurt? Or, did you shoot him because he was injured in the car wreck? Was he going to slow you down?"

Wallerein glowered.

"Not good leadership, Kurt," taunted Porter. "You're getting very careless, old man."

With a wave of his pistol, Wallerein motioned his partner to pull Michelle from the vehicle. "Tie them up. We'll leave them here. Let them see the fire up close."

The terrorist pulled open Michelle's door and grabbed her. She fought back, her bag and papers flying out the door. He dragged her screaming and thrashing to the side of the road. Wallerein jerked open Porter's door and grabbed for his shoulder. Porter switched off the ignition and exploded out of the car. He hurled the keys into the forest. "Good luck finding them, asshole!"

"*Scheißkerl*!" screamed Wallerein, then slashed Porter across the head with his pistol. Porter dropped to his knees like he was sledge-hammered. Woozy from pain, he was dragged over to Michelle's side.

"I should kill you for that, Herr Nelson, but I have a better idea." Wallerein kept his pistol trained on the captives while the shooter trussed them up. "Hurry!"

Wallerein pointed up the hill. "I would love to stay and chat, Herr Nelson. But you can see that the approaching fire will not allow me the pleasure." He smiled a grotesque smile. "You will experience the boiling of your blood and the bursting of your flesh. Pity you will not be able to describe it to me."

The shooter leaned over Michelle and fondled her breasts. She tried to knee him in the groin. "You disgusting animal!"

He punched her in the face. Then again. Blood flowed from her nose.

Porter thrashed in his bonds and cursed him in German, Russian, and Arabic. He dredged up every single filthy word he had ever heard and spit them out like a machine gun. The terrorist kicked him in the head. Porter saw flashes before his eyes. Agony lanced through him. He tasted bile. Another kick. He heard Michelle scream. Or was it him? The terrorist swung his foot again. The pain was instant and incredible. Then blessed blackness.

National Guard Blackhawk

Turbulence from the fire rattled the Blackhawk, forcing Tafoya to slow down. She worked the terrain, flying low for the visibility but high enough to keep out of the worst of the unstable air.

Below them Tom could see bushes, grasses, trees burst into flames as the heat consumed everything in its path, feeding on the fuel, slashing through the forest faster and faster as it created its own windstorm.

The flames flowed up the hills, and leapt across ravines into the treetops on the other side, faster and faster. Irresistible. Implacable. Inevitable. Centuries old, majestic Douglas fir and ponderosas exploded. Spires of flames towered up two hundred feet. Great clouds of smoke spouted into the sky, roiling the air. The helicopter lurched and rolled.

"Lobo Seven Two, Highbird. Stand by for message."

Forty-five long seconds later, "Lobo Seven Two, this is Highbird."

"Go ahead, Highbird."

"There is a civilian female on an emergency radio, claiming that she has a man with her, wounded by Wallerein. Do you copy?"

Tafoya turned in her seat and looked at Tom. He gave her a thumbs-up. "That's gotta be Michelle Duregger, Porter Nelson's partner. She's one of us."

"Lobo, this is Highbird. The female says they are on the edge of a small meadow. She has lat and long. Ready to copy?"

"Go, Highbird." The CAP aircraft rattled off the new coordinates. "I copy, Highbird. Tell her our ETA three minutes." Tafoya paused. "And Highbird, her name is Michelle Duregger. Tell her the air cavalry is on the way!"

Tom scanned the ground, trying to pick out something, anything moving through the haze and the trees. Out in front of the fire, swirling winds tore gaps in the dense waves of smoke.

"There she is! Beth, go left!"

"Tally ho, Colonel." The aircraft swung left and headed directly for the figure on the ground frantically waving her arms.

Tafoya circled once, then let down at the edge of the meadow. Tom ripped at his seat straps, unplugged from the intercom, leapt from the aircraft and sprinted towards Michelle.

Michelle hugged him hard. "Thank you! Thank you! Everything Porter says about you is true."

"Give yourself some credit, Michelle. You vectored us in. Otherwise, we'd still be just boring holes in the sky."

They bent down over Porter. Tom pulled back the bandage Michelle had wrapped around Porter's bloody head and winced at the sight of the gash on his head. He checked Porter's pulse. "His pulse rate's good. He should be okay, I think."

"Wallerein pistol-whipped him." She took a moment to stroke Porter's cheek. "Wallerein has a hurt leg, Tom. He's limping badly. They needed our car, but Porter threw the keys into the woods."

Tom shook his head in admiration. "Nobody intimidates my boy Porter."

Jerry Bennett trotted up. "Where's Wallerein?"

"He and the other man went that way on foot." Michelle pointed downhill ahead of the fire. "Less than twenty minutes ago. He has a pistol. The other guy has a submachine gun."

"Jerry, we need to get Porter on the chopper. Then we'll go after Wallerein."

They carried the inert Porter to the aircraft. The crew chief hopped out and helped load him inside. Michelle clambered aboard and held Porter's hand.

Tom plugged into the helicopter intercom. "Beth, you take Nelson back to Santa Fe. But first, take Jerry and me downhill about two clicks. We're going after Wallerein. The fire's moving that way. He's hurt and on foot. He has to move away from the fire down this canyon. Right into us."

"Colonel, the TAG's orders are to keep you safe. I cannot leave you behind."

"Chief, we've already had this discussion. Our mission is to get Wallerein. He's right here. It has to be us. It has to be now."

A long pause. "Okay, sir. But take a radio."

Tom swung himself into the helicopter bay, the crew chief handed him his radio.

Tafoya lifted off and maneuvered the big chopper into the fingers of the canyon reaching downhill. "There," said Tom, pointing out another meadow. "Drop us off there. Then get on the radios and muster everybody you can to bottle up the lower canyon."

"Wilco, sir."

The two men hunkered down as rotor wash whipped dirt, brush, and pine needles around them as the helicopter departed.

"Jerry, I don't know much about military ambushes but as a hunter, we divide the canyon. We're about in the middle. You go over that way about half the distance to the slope, and I'll do the same to this side. And we wait. They're not expecting us. Let them slide by you, then get the drop on them. Don't forget, one of these guys has a submachine gun."

They looked at each other for a moment, then Bennett extended his hand. "Good hunting, Colonel." They shook, then Bennett turned and disappeared into the smoke.

Tom paced about thirty yards to his right. Cinders crackled under his feet. He slipped through the smoke and settled down behind a fallen tree. In the distance uphill from him, flames raced up trees, ravenous. Embers cascaded from the sky, bounced off his flying helmet, his clear visor protecting his eyes.

Hot air, almost painful, washed over him in waves. Smoke burned his eyes and filled his nostrils. Hot smoke everywhere. Winds thrashed the treetops, louder and louder. The ash fell so thick that it softened the outlines of the undergrowth to look like snowfall at a ski area. The forest was drained of color, everything wore hues of gray.

Tom checked his watch. Then checked it again seconds later. Doubts assailed him. Maybe Wallerein had moved faster than he thought and was already past.

The winds and flames were loud, making it hard to think. The wind was hurling debris downhill, right into his face.

A muffled shot from his left. A pause. Then another shot. Tom prayed it was Bennett doing the shooting. Stay calm, Tommy boy.

The smoke was thick, dark. In the dimness he made out some movement. Animal? Or human? Tom exulted. It's both—that *untermensch!* Dragging a leg through the underbrush.

Tom ordered himself to wait. Wallerein shuffled through the tangled forest floor, stumbling, hunched over. Tom made himself smaller and watched his target move clumsily past.

Ten yards. Enough space. "Halt! Hands in the air, *Schiesskopf!*"

Wallerein froze, raised his hands slowly, still holding a pistol.

Tom closed in, his pistol aimed in the center of Wallerein's back. "Turn around."

Recognition spread on Wallerein's face. "So it's you." He gave a bark of a laugh. "Your German is terrible."

Tom replied in Russian. "How's this then, *mudak*? I said, drop the pistol! Or, if you prefer, go for it, Kurt. Please. Give me an excuse to shoot you."

"You have no idea what's going to happen here," Wallerein sneered in Russian.

"Why don't you tell me about it, Kurt? Like you did my wife before you almost beat her to death. She told me of your little shouting episode in Mexico."

"I should have killed her."

"She told me that you needed to die."

Wallerein stared back in silence, hatred burning in his eyes.

"So, Kurt, whatever you thought would happen here, you'll not be a part of it any longer."

Wallerein lowered his arms. "I would like to live, Herr Oberst."

"All the people you murdered would have liked to live, Kurt. Hands up or I will shoot you."

Wallerein lunged to his left, brought up his pistol. Tom shot him in the chest. Wallerein crashed to the ground.

"That's for the people of New Mexico you've murdered, you *ublyudok.*" Tom kicked the pistol away from Wallerein's groping hand. He stood over Wallerein and watched his face as Wallerein struggled to breathe.

"*Bitte, bitte,*" pleaded the German, holding up one good arm. "*Bitte,*" he gasped.

Tom stood at the ready, waiting.

Wallerein uncoiled, rolled, and whipped out another pistol.

Tom shot him in the face. Blood bloomed from the shattered skull.

"That's for Colleen." He pulled the trigger again. "That's for my son who will never get a chance to live." He pumped in another round. "That's for the children you had murdered yesterday." He glared at the ruined face. Then fired again and again into the body, the recoil kicking back into his wrist and shoulder. Magazine emptied, he threw the weapon away. "Never again, Kurt Wallerein, you *sukin syn*, will you cause pain to anyone, anywhere."

Tom dropped to his knees. He stared at the body. So many innocent people had died because of this angry psycho. So much pain.

Jerry Bennett ran up. "I got the other guy. Then I heard your shots. Are you okay?"

Tom pointed. "That's Wallerein. Was Wallerein."

Jerry nodded. "Good work, sir."

"Is he dead?"

"Shit, Colonel, he's full of holes!"

"The last time I told the president that I thought Wallerein was dead, I was wrong. You're FBI. Check to confirm that he's dead."

Bennett bent down and felt for a pulse. He looked up at Tom. "No pulse, Colonel. He's as dead as he's ever going to be."

"I want you to call Jacob Borenstein at FBI Headquarters and tell him you confirmed that Kurt Wallerein is dead. Understand? Then have Jacob call my wife."

"Yes, sir."

Tom turned and started trotting downhill.

Chapter Thirty-Seven

Christus St. Vincent Regional Medical Center, Santa Fe

Porter Nelson slowly emerged from his drug-induced sleep. He pried open one eye, then the other. Focusing was difficult, but after a few minutes, he could make out a blurry form that resembled a female human sitting nearby.

"Where am I?" he croaked.

"Porter!"

His heart jumped at the sound of her voice. With great effort, he managed to focus on her face. He was rewarded by a radiant smile as Michelle slid nearer. She carefully sat on his bed, leaned close enough for him to catch her scent. "Welcome back! You're in the hospital in Santa Fe."

"Wow, that's some shiner you have there, Michelle."

"Ha!" she said. "You should see yourself, buddy."

He reached up and traced the bandage on his head. "How bad is it?"

"Fifteen staples in your scalp. Mild concussion. Two black eyes. You'll live."

Still woozy, he asked, "How did I get here? Last I remember, we were tied up like cowboys and the fire was closing in. We should be dead."

"Oh, those terrorists," she said dismissively. "Total landlubbers. Nobody ties knots like sailors—which means we can untie them as well. As soon as those bastards ran off, I got myself free. Then you."

"But... you carried me?"

"No problem. In karate class, we often practiced carrying our opponents. Great for the legs. Good thing you're a little guy. And going downhill with a load is easier than going uphill." She reached up with both hands and swept her long hair back in a movement he found enticing. Another radiant smile. "After I got us clear of the fire, I used the radio to scream for help and help arrived." She chuckled. "Just like in the movies."

"Don't tell me. It was Tom Callahan to the rescue."

"Yep. Just like in the movies."

Porter tried to shake his head in amazement, but it hurt too much. "Damn. That's the second time he's saved my life." He paused. "On the positive side, after Tom rescued me the first time, we became good friends. You saved me. Maybe we could become good friends, too."

She reached for his hand and kissed it. "I think we already are, Porter." Face red, she carefully placed his hand back on the bed. Then picked it up again with a smile. "The Los Alamos fire's still raging. So's the one in Ruidoso. We caught a break, though. Temperatures are dropping and the winds have subsided. And no more shootings, bombings, or new fires."

"And Wallerein?"

"Tom nailed him."

"Dead?"

"Really dead." She formed a mock pistol with her right hand and pantomimed eight times with her thumb.

"No kidding?"

"No kidding."

He closed his eyes. "Give me another hour or so to recover, and we'll go from there."

Ninety minutes later, Porter found the remote for his bed and brought himself upright. "Okay, I'm back. Hand me that water, please." Michelle handed him the cup, and he rinsed his mouth, savoring the cool liquid. "That leaves only one more thing for us to do."

As if she read his mind, she picked up her laptop. "This should help. Here's my first draft on our article for the Post—I've had some time on my hands waiting for you to wake up."

He scrolled through the document. Then went back and re-read a few sections. He looked up, startled. "Are you sure about these details? Especially the White House stuff?"

She nodded. "I made a few phone calls. It was amazing how people opened up when I used your name. I'm impressed by the power of your reputation, Mr. Nelson."

Porter asked questions; Michelle answered. They debated some points, agreed on others. Twice they stopped to make calls to settle a disagreement, then spent another forty-five minutes smoothing the text.

"Ready to send?" Porter asked.

"This is going to be great!" she said, eyes shining. "We are going to rock the capital!"

He looked back to the screen and started typing.

She leaned over. "What are you changing now?"

"The byline. It should start with your name. You da man, Michelle!"

Chapter Thirty-Eight

Oval Office
The White House
Washington, D.C.

"And that, Mr. President," said Porter Nelson, "is the whole sordid story."

"Mr. President," began Mark Freiberg, the chief of staff, "I'm sorry. I accept full responsibility—"

The president held up his hand. He took two pencils from his drawer and snapped them into small pieces while he thought. Freiberg, FBI Deputy Director Jacob Borenstein, Porter, and Michelle Duregger sat, unable to meet each other's eyes. After what seemed like an hour to Porter, the president pushed the intercom. "Helen, ask, no, tell Isabella Orsini to come to my office now."

Three minutes later, Orsini was announced and entered, slightly out of breath. *Must have run all the way for more brownie points,* thought Porter. She paused at the door, apparently surprised at the audience, smoothed down a few wayward hairs, and tugged at the bottom of her suit jacket. "Good afternoon, Mr. President." She moved towards an empty chair and started to sit.

"I did not offer you a seat, Isabella."

Startled, she stood.

"You know Mr. Nelson, I'm sure. The lady is Ms. Michelle Duregger, of the *Washington Post.*"

"How do you do?" Orsini said, glancing in Michelle's direction, her face showing no emotion.

"Ms. Duregger has been on assignment with Mr. Nelson, helping Colonel Callahan stop Wallerein depredations in New Mexico. Something I understand was done over your objections."

"Mr. President—"

The president held up his hand to silence her. "Before that, Ms. Duregger wrote the column piece about Colonel Callahan's group meeting at his home."

Orsini looked confused. "Yes, sir?" she said, hesitantly.

The president studied Orsini carefully for a long moment and then asked, "Does the name Edward Harrison the Third ring a bell?

Orsini went pale.

"Well, does it?"

She stood a little straighter. "Yes, sir. I know him."

"I'm a little curious just how Mr. Harrison, a member of the legislative branch staff, obtained such detailed information about the inner workings of the executive branch of our government. Specifically, the White House." He paused. "Which he then leaked to the *Post*."

"I have no idea, sir."

"Really? That's interesting." He paused and stared at her a long moment. "Your good friend Eddie is, by the way, being questioned over at FBI headquarters as we speak. What do you think he might say about his source?"

Suddenly nervous, she said, "Sir... Mr. President, I had no idea that he would do such a thing."

"Well, he did. Besides my personal feelings, most of this information was classified 'need-to-know.' That makes these leaks criminal."

"Sir, I say again, I had no idea."

"Isabella, up to about fifteen minutes ago, I would have believed you. But now, as it happens, you've lied to me twice."

"Sir?"

He looked at Borenstein who handed him a folder. "This is your updated FBI background check. It seems that you lied about your education status. You did not complete an accepted dissertation."

283

Face flushing, Orsini blurted, "Sir, I can explain. I finished my coursework. I was desperate for money and an associate professorship teaching job came open—"

He cut her off. "You falsified your records in order to start your career. You weren't qualified for that first job either. You don't have a doctorate."

"What difference does it make?" she challenged. "I've done this job! And well."

"You used your position to withhold a report that Colonel Callahan had prepared connecting Wallerein and the attack on Kirtland Air Force Base. People died as a result, Orsini. You passed along classified information to your boyfriend. You also falsified a government document, and you lied to me. Those reasons are what make the difference."

"I deserve this job!"

"Not any more. Try the next president. Ms. Orsini, you are fired." He turned to Borenstein. "Jacob?"

Borenstein stood and handed her a document. "Ms. Orsini, this is a court order for you to turn over your passport. You are not to leave the country until the FBI investigates further." He motioned to the president's Secret Service agent. "Please escort her to her residence and obtain her passport. Then have someone send her the contents of her office. Cancel her clearances. You know the drill."

Porter watched as Orsini was marched out of the office.

"That was rather distasteful," said the president. "Porter, this isn't the first time you've come through for me, for our country. I owe you, sir. Thank you."

"Sir, Michelle saved the day, and my butt, there in New Mexico. And she's the one who turned up the information on Orsini."

"Mr. President," Michelle protested, "I could only get the information by using Porter's name and contacts. He deserves all the credit."

The president laughed. "Michelle... sorry, may I call you Michelle?"

Michelle's face turned red, and she stammered out, "Of course, Mr. President."

"Thank you. The articles about the fires in the *Post* were great, especially the one about the slow recovery progress in Montero and Rio Tercero, New Mexico. I called the governor this morning and promised him more assistance. And I appreciate your efforts to set the record straight with the public about the source of the attacks. They deserve to know what really happened and why."

He turned to Mark Freiberg. "Tell the press secretary to issue Michelle a White House press pass. And see to it that she has a good seat at our press conferences."

He turned back to Porter. "By the way, does Tom Callahan know you're here?"

"No, sir. He's busy with Colleen and Mikey."

The president nodded. "Good. How's he doing?"

Porter hesitated. "Sir, he's okay. Colleen is having difficulty dealing with the loss of the baby but is doing better every day. Brice Adams has them all out at his ranch. They're getting the best care possible."

"Please pass along my regards, and let him know I was serious when I told him to take all the time he needs."

***

Outside the White House fence, Porter stopped and turned to face Michelle. He took both her hands in his. "What now?"

"I've been thinking of sailing the Ruby Slipper down the Intracoastal Waterway to the Keys and maybe looping back here via the Bahamas. As far away from forest fires and Washington politics as I can get."

Wow. Disappointment slugged him in the gut. He let go of her hands. "Well, damn. I was sorta hoping we could do something together."

She smiled, moved closer and touched his face. "I could use a crew." She brushed her lips across his. "I think I could whip you into shape pretty quickly."

"What about the press pass?"

"It'll be waiting here when we get back."

Chapter Thirty-Nine

White House,
Washington, D.C.
Three weeks later

Tom Callahan swore to himself, then turned back the page of a technical report outlining Russian nuclear capabilities to read it again. He could not remember a single meaningful idea from what he had read. This was only one of several dozen reports that towered over his in-basket. It was going to be a long morning.

His mind wandered back to Colleen. Today was her first day back at work for the World Bank. He had asked her to stay home another week at least, but she insisted that she had recovered. Colleen, the old Colleen, the pre-kidnapping-and-beating Colleen, had always been feisty and her own woman. So, in some perverse way, insisting on doing what she wanted rather than what Tom thought best was a positive sign of recovery. She had marched out of their house that morning, grim faced but determined. He was doing his best to be supportive, but still he worried.

The intercom buzzed, and his secretary's voice said. "Colonel, the president would like to see you. He says it's important."

Tom entered the spacious Oval Office to see the president in conference with the Secretary of the Department of Energy, the Director of the Los Alamos National Laboratory, and the president's chief of staff. Tom knew the secretary, a distinguished-looking physicist, from several conferences; he knew the corpulent director, also a physicist, only from his post-fire research and after-action report.

The president sat behind his famous Resolute desk, something he rarely did when working with cabinet level officials. He was not smiling. The secretary sat stiffly in his chair with his arms crossed; the director seemed totally engrossed in one of the Oval Office paintings.

"Tom," said the president, "do you remember that there were two Lab security guards missing after the Los Alamos fire?"

"Yes, sir."

"They're not missing any more. Their bodies were found three days ago. They were incinerated by the fire."

"I'm sorry to hear that, sir."

The president shook his head. "It gets worse, Tom. They were not burned to death. They were executed, then burned. The skulls had bullet holes in the back. There is a damaged bunker nearby. Empty."

"Damaged?"

The president said, "The door looked like it had been blown open."

"What was in the bunker, sir?"

The president gestured to the secretary who seemed reluctant to speak. The man licked his lips before replying. "We're not sure."

Tom was sure. Sure he was lying.

"Mr. Secretary," Tom said, "To be clear, you're not sure of what was in the bunker or you're not sure you want to reveal classified information?"

The secretary glanced away and said nothing.

Tom felt his temperature rise. He despised liars, another reason to detest living in Washington where lies were passed around as casually as joints at a rock concert. "Why were the guards there, Mr. Secretary?"

The secretary looked at his colleague then back to Tom. "I'm not sure we should be getting into this with you, Colonel."

"I'm sure," said the president. "Answer the bloody question!"

The secretary shrugged. "The bodies were found in an area we had recently started investigating."

"What do you mean, 'investigating'?" asked Tom.

"As part of our clean-up of Los Alamos, we've been researching our classified archives to see about the location of designated waste dumps and storage bunkers."

The president slammed his desk with his fist. "Stop pussy-footing around and speak up. I don't have time for ass-covering, Mister!"

The secretary's face went red, and his voice rose. "Around last Christmas, this area was identified as a former storage area. We just started excavating it about seven weeks ago."

"Tell us what was stored there," said Tom.

"We're not exactly sure."

"Not exactly sure, but you posted guards," said the president, menace in his voice. "Then give me your best guess."

The secretary hesitated.

"I'll not ask you again."

"Plutonium. It was possibly a plutonium depository. Possibly."

"Plutonium, as in plutonium triggers for nuclear weapons?" asked Tom.

The secretary rubbed the back of his neck and would not meet Tom's eyes. "We engineers call them pits." He hesitated. "But, yes. Possibly."

Tom looked at the DOE officials. "But the bunker was empty. Was it looted?"

"Nobody knows," said the secretary.

"You discovered this site six months ago?" Tom thought out loud. "The Soviets had agents, spies, inside the Manhattan Project at Los Alamos. They must have obtained copies of the same classified documents your people recently located. Which means the Russians now have those documents—"

He stopped abruptly and looked at the president whose face had just gone pale. Tom was sure the president was thinking what he was thinking: The Wallerein organization had a spy inherited from the KGB inside the number one nuclear laboratory in the United States. Somebody inside Los Alamos who knew of the investigations and the location of this bunker. Just as Wallerein did with an Army scientist spy inside Ft. Detrick with the Machupo virus. Jesus! More spies inside our government!

"Sir!" Tom warned. No need for these bureaucrats to know about that other incident with Wallerein. The president nodded his understanding.

Tom and the president fell silent with the realization that the fires were just a ruse, a distraction for Wallerein's real goal—the plutonium. Tom shuddered.

Who had it now?

Tom remembered what Kurt Wallerein had told him, "You have no idea what is going to happen next."

The End

About the Author

    Brinn Colenda is the award-winning author of *Cochabamba Conspiracy* and *Chita Quest*. He is a graduate of the United States Air Force Academy and a retired lieutenant colonel.

    He serves on the Board for the David Westphall Foundation and spent nearly six years as an elected official for his village government.

    He and his wife, Linda, live in northern New Mexico.

Follow Brinn Colenda at:

http://brinncolenda.us/
Facebook - Brinn Colenda Author

www.ingramcontent.com/pod-product-compliance
Lightning Source LLC
Chambersburg PA
CBHW030956260626
47169CB00002B/571